GRACE STARED UP AT THE TALL MASTS

She didn't realize that she was stepping backwards until she tripped over a bucket and landed hard on her bottom, her skirts drenched in dirty water.

Giles hauled himself from the plank that had just pulled him up to the deck, vaulted the rail, and was at Grace's side. "Are you all right?"

She gave him a wry grin. "Well, you see, I *wanted* to get wet one way or another today, and you kept *saving* me. I had to be creative."

He chuckled and lifted her into his arms. "Well, had you but said so . . ." He carried her to the rail and swung his arms back as though to hurl her overboard.

"Nay!" she squealed. She wrapped her arms around his neck and held on for dear life.

God, she smelled sweet, Giles thought. The heady scent of jasmine and the feel of her light but nicely rounded body begged an immediate response from him, and he had to fight the urge to kiss her long and hard.

Grace grinned up at him, pleased to see the lines on his face deepen with laughter rather than worry. Then his eyes left hers, dropping to her mouth, and she could feel the heat of his gaze nearly palpable upon her lips. Something happened inside of her, a peculiar pull that made her pulse quicken. Her smile faded. "You may put me down."

"Of course," Giles said, doing so. He cleared his throat and tried to clear his mind.

Grace didn't know which was more fascinating, the sea or the man . . .

BOOK YOUR PLACE ON OUR WEBSITE AND MAKE THE READING CONNECTION!

We've created a customized website just for our very special readers, where you can get the inside scoop on everything that's going on with Zebra, Pinnacle and Kensington books.

When you come online, you'll have the exciting opportunity to:

- View covers of upcoming books

- Read sample chapters

- Learn about our future publishing schedule (listed by publication month *and author*)

- Find out when your favorite authors will be visiting a city near you

- Search for and order backlist books from our online catalog

- Check out author bios and background information

- Send e-mail to your favorite authors

- Meet the Kensington staff online

- Join us in weekly chats with authors, readers and other guests

- Get writing guidelines

- AND MUCH MORE!

**Visit our website at
http://www.kensingtonbooks.com**

FOR HER
LOVE

Paula Reed

ZEBRA BOOKS
Kensington Publishing Corp.
http://www.kensingtonbooks.com

ZEBRA BOOKS are published by

Kensington Publishing Corp.
850 Third Avenue
New York, NY 10022

All Kensington titles, imprints and distributed lines are available at special quantity discounts for bulk purchases for sales
promotion, premiums, fund-raising, educational or institu-
tional use.

Special book excerpts or customized printings can also be created to fit specific needs. For details, write or phone the office
of the Kensington Special Sales Manager: Kensington Publishing Corp., 850 Third Avenue, New York, NY 10022. Attn.
Special Sales Department. Phone: 1-800-221-2647.

Zebra and the Z logo Reg. U.S. Pat. & TM Off.

First Printing: October 2004
10 9 8 7 6 5 4 3 2 1

Printed in the United States of America

For my mom, Margaret,
and in memory of my dad, Ralph,
with love and gratitude.

Prologue

Mosquitoes whined faintly in the overly warm room, despite the strong odor of incense that Matu always kept burning at night. Grace had told her silent, ebony-skinned nursemaid that it did no good, but the woman had only shaken her nappy head and continued to light it anyway. With elaborate gestures and pantomimes, Matu had explained that mosquitoes could not breathe such perfumed air.

Unfortunately, neither could Grace.

Then again, she could not have taken a comfortable breath, even if the air had been laced with nothing more than the light scent of the Jamaican breeze and the flowers from the garden below her window. If she breathed, she would miss the stealthy sounds of Uncle Jacques's cautious footfalls just outside her bedroom door. If she failed to hear the sound, he would suddenly be in her room and startle her, as he had the first time, five nights past. Hence, Grace set her small lungs to the task of breathing as little as possible. Her arms and legs were held utterly motionless, so as not to rustle the sheets. If only he might think she was asleep and go away.

When Grace was very small, she was afraid of the dark, and Matu had slept by her bed on a little mat. Grace had quailed even at that. "What if the monster under my bed eats Matu because she is closest?" she had asked her father.

"Then it will not be the first sacrifice Matu has made to keep you safe, little one," Edmund Welbourne had replied.

At the age of eight, she declared that she no longer needed Matu's protection; she was a big girl and did not believe in monsters. So Matu had been given a small closet in the hall to sleep in. She was the only servant allowed to sleep in the house. Two years had come and gone since then, and Grace knew that she had been wrong. Now, more than ever, she believed in monsters. But she could not call for Matu. The first thing the monster had told her was that if she ever spoke of his visits, he would kill her beloved nursemaid, and it would be all her fault.

Grace noticed that each night he was getting better. He was learning which floorboards creaked and managed to avoid most of them. However, he carried but a single candle, so it was impossible to see them all. Tonight, he rested his weight on only one, and Grace, barely breathing, heard its protest. The door clicked softly open and he slipped in, the candle casting eerie shadows around the room. Clutching the sheet in her clammy hands, she looked away, while he closed the door as quietly as he had opened it. He set his candle down on the little table next to her bed.

"Were you waiting for me, Grace?" he asked. His French accent made the words fluid, like oil, dripping thickly through his lips.

She dared to look at him, but couldn't answer. Slick,

dark hair fell to his shoulders, and he wore a linen nightshirt. His eyes were in shadow, looking like empty, gaping sockets. Grace wanted to cry out, but only a tiny whimper crawled from her throat.

"I must eat your tongue, *ma petite,* just as you ate your nursie's."

He said that each time that he came to her, and it confused and terrified her. Matu had but half a tongue; that was true. No one before would ever tell her why.

Her uncle had come to visit only a little over a week ago. On the third night, he had slipped into her room and told her that Matu knew a secret about Grace, a secret so terrible, so dirty and vile, that her father had had the woman's tongue cut from her mouth so that she could never tell.

"She lost her tongue because of you, *ma petite,*" he had said, "and you must be punished. You may keep your tongue during the day, but at night, it belongs to me."

He had put his mouth on hers, choking her with his own tongue, devouring her cries. He'd held her hands tightly at her sides and crushed the breath from her ten-year-old body. When she could struggle no more and thought she would faint, he had pulled away.

"If you ever tell anyone that I come to you, Matu will die."

Uncle Jacques was white, and Matu was black. If he wanted Matu dead, then she would be dead. As the daughter of a Jamaican planter and the granddaughter of a Saint-Domingue slave trader, Grace knew well the bitter reality of the situation.

Jacques sat on the bed, his knee pressing against Grace's leg. He sighed regretfully. "It is a shame that the breaking can only be done once," he said, almost conversationally. "I have put it off, savoring the anticipation, but I have never been a patient man."

He drove his hands through the tight, golden brown ringlets that covered her head, pulling cruelly. "I have never broken a girl as fair and pretty as you. Always I have had to content myself with slave children. But you, *ma petite*, you are almost one of us."

In his thick, too silky voice, he told her of places where women submitted to many men, every night, for money. "That is where you should be, *ma chère,* a little girl made of honey, like you." He ran one finger over the golden skin of her arm, making her flesh crawl. "You would fetch the highest price." Taking her hand in his, he placed it under his nightshirt, between his naked legs, holding it fast when she tried to yank away.

Grace had seen little slave boys. Her father had said that they were too small to work and so could not earn clothes. She had seen their little, dark, boy parts. The thing under her uncle's nightshirt was not like those. It was monstrously swollen.

With his free hand, Jacques reached under the covers and violated her with the tip of his finger. "What you hold in your hand, little Grace, this is where it goes." Leaning down, he whispered in her ear, "Alas, this will hurt, hurt terribly, but you must be brave and quiet, *ma chère,* for Matu's sake."

But Grace didn't think that she could ever be that brave. She choked on a sob. Poor Matu!

She screamed when the door flew open, slamming back on its hinges. Her father stood there, holding a candle aloft and further illuminating the scene. Grace cringed in fear and shame. Jacques released her hand, and she pulled it away as though burned.

"Damn you to hell, Jacques Renault! Take your filthy,

child-defiling hands off of my daughter!" Edmund Welbourne shouted. He was fully clothed, his yellow hair still tied back, as if he had known what would happen and, like Grace, had been waiting for Jacques to make his appearance. "Stand up! Stand up and at least pretend you are a man while I kill you!"

Iolanthe, Grace's mother, flew around the doorframe and pulled violently at her husband's shirt. In the candlelight, her pale skin seemed paler still, corpse-like against her long, dark hair. A voluminous nightdress hid her small form.

"You will not harm a hair upon my brother's head!" Iolanthe shrieked.

"Do you not see?" Edmund snapped back. "Do you not see what he is doing?"

Iolanthe swept Grace's huddled form with a contemptuous glance. "What are you saving her for, Edmund? Marriage?" She laughed harshly.

Edmund turned to his wife, his face a mask of horrified revulsion in the candlelight. "She is a *child*, Iolanthe. *My* child."

Jacques stood in a relaxed, liquid movement, obviously certain that Iolanthe would not permit Edmund to hurt him. "Really, Edmund, all this fuss over nothing. My sister has indulged your little fantasy long enough. You are sitting on a gold mine here. Let me train the girl. Then I can take her to Europe or even Asia and sell her for a fortune."

Edmund thrust his candle into Iolanthe's hand, crossed the room, and with his fist, split Jacques's thin, perfect lips. "You disgusting animal! Get out of my house!"

Jacques fell back, his hand to his mouth.

"Stop it, stop it at once!" Iolanthe shouted.

Matu appeared in the doorway, her shift rumpled, her eyes wild. She skirted the trio of white adults and sank down onto Grace's bed, scooping the child into her thin arms and rocking her silently. Grace twisted her head around so that she could see what was happening.

"Get him out of my house, Iolanthe," Edmund growled.

"This is not your house!" Iolanthe hissed back, her accent as heavy as Jacques's. "You would have lost this house and your entire plantation if it had not been for my dowry and my father's slaves."

"The law says it is mine!"

"And my father is the legal owner of nearly every slave you have. Where will you be without slaves, Edmund? Right back where you were! You will be utterly penniless, and I will leave you. *Mon père* might even buy this lovely plantation for me to live on in my older years."

"You are my wife. My subject!"

"Ha! In the end, Edmund, you will do as Father tells you, just as you did when he told you to sell that wretched little beast's mother!"

Iolanthe spewed this last sentence with a violent gesture toward Grace. Matu made a strange, gargling sound in her throat, shaking her head vehemently. Jacques, still wiping blood from his chin, smiled malevolently at Grace through his cracked lips.

"Silence, Iolanthe!" Edmund bellowed.

Grace fought Matu's arms that enfolded her. "What do you mean?" she asked. "*You* are my mother."

"Do not be insulting!" Iolanthe snapped. "I am surrounded by men with a weakness for black whores. First, my father begot a filthy little half-caste bitch with some slave wench. Then he sent his abomination here with ninety-nine other slaves and the gold for my dowry." She turned and sneered at her husband. "One hundred slaves. One hundred! And you chose *her* to rut with and make this-this thing!" She gestured again to Grace.

"If you were not a frigid, barren bitch yourself, you would have given me a child of both our flesh," Edmund retorted.

Matu tried to cover Grace's ears, but Grace fended her off.

"My mother was a slave?" Grace whispered, and Matu made that anguished, guttural sound again. "And you knew," Grace added, looking up at her cherished nurse. She tenderly placed her child's hands on Matu's face. Tears welled in the woman's eyes. "You knew, and that's why they cut out your tongue."

"Your father," Iolanthe interrupted. "Your father had her tongue cut out. That is how shamed he is by your polluted blood!"

Edmund's face went deathly white. "Nay. Nay, Gracie. 'Twasn't shame. I simply could not let anyone know. 'Twould have ruined your life."

Ruined her life? She was black. African. Like Matu. She should be a slave. If she were a slave, no one would have stopped Jacques. Her uncle's words came back, full force.

I have never broken a girl as fair and pretty as you. Always I have had to content myself with slave children. But you, ma petite, you are almost one of us.

Her whole world was spinning brutally out of control.

"Naaay," the little girl wailed softly.

"God damn it! This is the last that will ever be spoken of this!" Edmund shouted, and Grace flinched. Her father beat slaves when they made him angry. He whipped them. He had cut out Matu's tongue! "This is my plantation, and it will pass to my descendants. Grace will marry a White, as will her children. In time, this will all be a meaningless splotch somewhere in family history."

A meaningless splotch, Grace thought. I am a meaningless splotch. A meaningless, *black* splotch.

"Jacques," Edmund said tightly, "you will leave on the morrow or so help me God, I *will* kill you."

Jacques looked at his sister, who rolled her eyes and gestured to the door. "Go for now," she said. "We will talk again when my husband regains his senses."

Grace's uncle shot Edmund a murderous look, but he complied.

No, wait, Grace thought, Jacques was not her uncle after all. Somehow, there was some comfort in that. He was no family of hers. Or was he? Were Iolanthe and her mother sisters if they shared the same father? Could a white woman and a black woman be sisters? Nothing made sense anymore.

Edmund turned to his wife, taking back the candle he had handed to her earlier. "Your brother will go back to Saint-Domingue, and things will return to normal. As far as the rest of the world is concerned, Grace is *our* child. I have never asked you to love or care for her, Iolanthe, and I have never placed her needs or desires before yours. Unless you can tolerate my presence back in your bed long enough to give me another heir, you *will* abide by this."

Iolanthe gave him a haughty look. "I will write to my father on the morrow," she said.

"You do that. He will undoubtedly insist that I sell Grace, but he will just as undoubtedly insist that you resume your wifely duties. He understands the need for heirs as well as I do."

Iolanthe drew her hand back and let it fly with all her

might against Edmund's cheek. He hardly flinched. "That, my darling," he said, his voice laced with irony, "is the only mark you've hit tonight."

The enraged woman stormed out, and Edmund turned to his child. Matu was frantically petting her, as if trying to smooth the tight curls that hinted at the girl's heritage.

"She's so light, isn't she, Matu?" he said, reaching down to pat her rich, golden brown hair himself. "My little golden girl."

A little girl made of honey, like you. You would fetch the highest price.

"If—Iolanthe gave you a baby, would you sell me, Father?" Grace asked, her voice small and fragile.

Edmund smiled at her. "There's little chance of her doing that, poppet. No one's going to sell you."

Poppet. Grace had a poppet. A soft rag doll that Matu had made for her when she was tiny. A plaything.

His face sobered again. "What—what has he done to you? You must tell me all."

Grace hid her face against Matu's nearly flat chest. "I cannot."

Edmund sighed. "Did he put anything between your legs?"

Grace's answer was muffled against her nurse.

"What?" her father pressed. Matu waved her fingers in the air. "His fingers?" Edmund asked. Grace nodded. "Examine her," Edmund commanded Matu. "So help me, if he's breached her, he's a dead man."

Once Edmund left, Matu soothed Grace, calmed her wordlessly. Then she performed the required examination and gave the child a reassuring smile.

"Is it all right?" Grace asked, not entirely sure what she was asking. She didn't know what Matu was looking for. Perhaps to see that she was not torn in some way. Jacques had spoken of "breaking her."

Matu nodded and pulled Grace back into her own small lap, rocking her for an hour or more until Grace could fall asleep. Once again, Matu was there to ward off the monsters, to sacrifice herself, if need be, for Grace's safety.

One

1674

"Well, Giles, she's in perfect order and all yours," Geoffrey Hampton said, clapping his oldest friend on the shoulder.

Giles Courtney grinned at him. "Aye. She's a beauty, Geoff. A fair addition. Do we have a fleet now, d'you think?"

Geoff laughed and turned to his wife, who was holding their son and standing at the rail of the new ship, just purchased by Courtney and Hampton Shipping. "What think you, Faith? Do two ships a fleet make?"

"Well, you've two fleet ships," she conceded. "That's what matters most." The tow-headed boy in her arms struggled to be released. He most resembled his mother, with his pale blond hair, but it might yet darken to his father's sun-streaked brown.

Giles's gray eyes swept the deck of the first ship that would be entirely his to command. Having been Geoff's first mate for nigh onto a decade, he should have felt a greater sense of pride and accomplishment. But he had just reached his thirtieth year, and while 'twas all well and good to be captain of a fine ship like *Reliance*, surely there was more to life. Thirty, and he had yet to make any lasting mark upon this world.

Faith carried little Jonathan over to Giles and handed the boy to his godfather. "Isn't Uncle Giles a fine figure of a commander?" she asked the child. Jonathan responded by reaching behind Giles's neck and tugging upon the neat, dark brown queue of hair that hung there.

Giles laughed. "I don't think he finds me overly imposing."

Faith brushed the shoulders of Giles's deep blue jacket with gold trim. "I daresay your men will quail to displease you."

Quail? Giles doubted it. Men quailed before Geoff. Geoff was the intimidating one, Giles the reliable one. It had always been so. How it had stung when Geoff had rushed into the office and said, "I've found the very ship meant for you, Giles. *Reliance*. Could ever a name be more perfect?"

Well, 'twasn't as though he were still privateering. He and Geoff had left that life behind two years past. He was a merchant captain, and reliability was a fine trait in such a profession. Besides, he'd daresay he could still hold his own in any fight. How many times had he defended Geoff's back when the other man had taken wild risks in battle? And they were both still here to tell the tales!

Geoff's son smiled into Giles's face. The lad smelled of fresh sea air and a hint of cinnamon and sugar. How was it that Geoff's life had settled down so nicely while Giles's life seemed to keep sweeping by, with no one truly at the helm? Mayhap the ship was a start. Mayhap a command was the very thing he needed, if not exactly what he wanted.

"So," Giles said, shaking off his brooding mood, "I'm for Welbourne Plantation on the morrow?"

"Aye," Geoff answered, his own disposition sobering.

Faith stepped in and reclaimed her child. "We're off to do some shopping," she said. "It's been some weeks since we've visited the docks of Port Royal."

Geoff and Faith lived outside of the city now, and Giles was more likely to visit them than they were to come to his apartment in the Caribbean's "wickedest city on earth." Giles thought back to the first time Faith had walked these streets alone. She was closer to him than his own sisters in London, and he had been so proud of her. Now, she strolled off into the throngs of criminals and prostitutes with an air of easy confidence. Nonetheless, Geoff motioned to a crewman to follow her, and the man immediately complied. Never mind that he was Giles's man, not Geoff's. Giles's jaw tensed, but he said nothing. Surely his friend had not intended to usurp Giles's authority; he was simply a natural commander. Besides, Giles was only too glad to have one of his crew see to Faith and Jonathan's safety.

"I received a message from Welbourne this morn," Geoff said, and Giles looked back to his friend. "He's hoping you'll take two dozen or so slaves with you to Virginia when you make the other delivery."

Giles made a small sound of distaste in his throat. "We've told him our policy there," he replied.

"Aye. He thought such a small number might persuade us to bend the rules."

Giles looked at Geoff in disbelief. "Are you asking me to?"

"Nay, not at all. Only, 'tis your ship, Giles. You make the decisions. It seemed only fair to give you the option.

'Tis getting harder and harder to hold to the policy these days. We've lost a fair number of customers for it."

"Aye, well, we formed that policy together, Geoff, and I feel no different now than I did before. I'll not traffic in human flesh. We've sins enough to account for in all our years privateering."

Geoff rolled his eyes. Two years of marriage to a former Puritan had done nothing to soften his cynicism toward the idea of eternal retribution. "Well," he said, "I'll not deny, the idea leaves a sour taste in my mouth. Good, then. You'll get there ere we can send a messenger. Just explain our philosophy regarding slaves. In for a penny, in for a pound."

Giles nodded. "And we'll not be taking a pound of anyone's flesh, color be damned."

The decision was an easy one for Giles. What was becoming increasingly more difficult for him was the inescapable knowledge that merely refusing to transport slaves was not enough. They were certainly willing to ship sugar, rum, tobacco, all products of slave labor, and in that sense, aided the despicable practice. Still, one couldn't live in the Caribbean and escape it.

He spent the night on ship, gazing about him at the captain's cabin. The porthole was large and square, made of heavy glass that let in more light than view. The bunk, covered by a serviceable russet, woolen blanket, was large enough to accommodate a wife, should he ever find one. The furnishings, a desk and several oak cabinets, had been well maintained and glowed with a rich golden hue.

The next morning, he rose at dawn and set his quarters to rights. All charts were neatly stored, the bed crisply made. Geoff had often teased him, said that he would have been a natural in the navy. The thought made Giles grin. He'd no problem following Geoff's commands, for they were given by a friend in mutual respect. But Lord, he'd chafed at orders given by other captains he'd served. Still, when he glanced around the impeccably tidy space, it struck him as somehow empty. There was no sense of the man who occupied the space.

He forced the feeling aside. A place for everything and everything in its place, like keeping his appearance neat and crisp, were not merely military virtues. If one couldn't command respect through intimidation, as Geoff did, one gained it through efficiency and competence. Giles carefully combed his hair back and tied it, tucked in the hem of his loose-fitting shirt, and gave the toes of his boots a cursory buffing. Already, he could hear footfalls on the deck above. The day wasn't waiting for him.

Welbourne Plantation was but a few hours' sailing. The real voyage wouldn't start until they had loaded up Edmund Welbourne's sugar, molasses, rum, almonds, and other goods into *Reliance's* hold and set sail for Virginia, then on to Boston. Once there, he would empty the hold and refill it with lumber and finished goods from New England to be sold upon his return home. The venture should take two months or a bit more.

The day was fair, the breeze warm, and the sea breathtakingly blue. Giles had chosen his own crew and was well pleased. The mood on deck was calm but productive. Above him, a vast expanse of canvas stretched and bowed.

His. He searched for some sense of fulfillment in that thought.

Around him, the men were relaxed, at ease. He had a new lad on board, and one of the older sailors sat with him on a pile of rope, teaching him to make knots. The

helmsman had nothing more taxing to do than follow
the lush, green shore of the island. A man stood in the
crow's nest, keeping an eye out for dangers and obstacles, but they all knew this stretch well, so there was little
chance he would see anything of concern. It was a fine
start for Giles's first command.

Welbourne Plantation had its own small bay, an easy
place to drop anchor and row to shore over smooth,
blue waters. There was a wooden dock, and beyond that
a lawn that stretched to the front of a two-story, Tudor-
style house. The farm was built on the side of a hill so
that, even from the ship, Giles saw the network of buildings behind the main house. There was the kitchen, the
cook's house, a carriage house, and of course, the sugar
mill and sugar house. A glance through the spyglass
showed that the plantation's slaves were very busy operating the huge, heavy sugar press and boiling enormous
vats of crushed cane. Then, thick vegetation took over
the property—banana and almond trees for the Whites,
fields of cassava and corn for the Negroes, all manner
of indigenous plants and trees. The grounds continued
up the hillside to the cane fields, where a wide swath
had been burned and slaves moved in and out, cutting
and gathering sugarcane.

Edmund Welbourne waved from the dock. He was as
Giles remembered him, a short man with a paunch and
yellow-blond hair that shone in the sun. Around him,
twenty or more slaves rose from where they had
sprawled on the ground, preparing to help load the vast
number of crates stacked all around them. Between the
boats *Reliance* carried and two others belonging to Welbourne, it would make for an afternoon of hard work,
but all should go smoothly. Giles and his first mate dis-

embarked from their rowboat and joined the planter and his men.

"Captain Courtney," Edmund said, extending his hand. "Good to see you again."

Captain. He would have to get used to that. Giles took the proffered hand. "The pleasure is mine. You've a goodly number of men here. We should be back underway in no time." He wondered when it would be best to explain that he would not be transporting those men anywhere.

"No rush," Edmund replied. "My daughter is seeing to refreshments. I knew you'd want to oversee this process, but no sense sweating over it ourselves. Your man there can supervise. Did you receive my message?"

Giles opened his mouth to answer, but nothing came out. Over Edmund's shoulder, an exquisite woman of pure gold moved with fluid grace across the manicured lawn. She wore a gown of muted green that offset flawless, honey-colored skin. Her hair was pulled off of her neck, but 'twas a mass of golden ringlets that defied careful styling. As she drew closer, he felt himself pinned by a pair of intelligent, green eyes.

Edmund looked behind him, then back with a smile. "My daughter, Grace Welbourne."

Giles flushed a bit. He had been staring quite openly, and with her father standing right there! He cleared his throat and tried to keep his voice nonchalant. "A lovely girl."

Having had a chance to catch his breath, Giles now noted a small, black woman attending Welbourne's daughter. She carried a basket lined and draped in white linen in one hand, a bottle of wine in the other. A blanket was folded over her arm. Another African woman followed behind them, toting a wide tray loaded with goblets, plates, cheese, meat, and fruit.

"Grace, dear," Edmund called out, "allow me to present Captain Courtney."

Grace stopped a bit farther away than good manners might require and cocked her head. A ship's captain, she thought to herself. This was an unexpected development. It was progress. Much better than the slave trader (what had possessed her father?), the numerous other planters, and the various lower-ranking members of French and English nobility. Of course, she would no more accept this sailor than she had any of the others.

"How do you do, Captain Courtney?" she said, dropping into a graceful curtsey.

"Miss Welbourne," he replied, bowing crisply.

He was handsome. She had to admit that. He looked just what a captain ought, clean and tidy. His face was mature, with deep lines around the eyes, and yet there was something boyish about it. His eyes were gray, kind, and sharply observant. Although he was not overly tall, he was broad of shoulder and had an air of quiet authority. Judging by his gaze, he also thought she was beautiful, that much was evident, but most men did.

"So," Edmund interrupted, his eyes cutting back and forth between the young people with keen interest, "my message?"

Giles shut his eyes lightly for a moment. Apparently he was going to have to have this confrontation in front of Welbourne's beautiful daughter. "About the slaves?"

"Aye. I know you do not count yourselves actual traders. I but need transport for a handful of bucks."

Squaring his shoulders, Giles said, "I'm afraid I cannot help you there, sir."

Edmund blustered a bit. "But you've Blacks of your

own. I can see them on board your ship." He gestured across the bay.

"Aye, well, they're free, sir."

"The devil you say!"

"Quite. They're paid, same as the white crew members."

"Paid?" Grace asked. "You pay your Africans?"

"Aye, Miss Welbourne. They do the same labor, give the same loyalty. Some of the best sailors on the sea are Negro."

"How extraordinary," Grace replied, her face showing her acute interest.

Edmund shook his head, obviously perplexed. "Hardly economical."

Giles only shrugged. He wasn't here to preach to the man, but neither would he apologize for his principles.

The little black woman smiled at him and raised the bottle of wine in invitation. Then she and the other slave spread the blanket in the shade of a sea grape tree. Grace and Edmund sank down next to one another, while Giles took a seat opposite. From there, he could converse while keeping a watchful eye on the bay and the men loading cargo several hundred feet away. The serving women passed around fine porcelain plates, an obvious sign of wealth in a land of wooden trenchers and stoneware. The basket held fragrant, freshly baked bread, and the wine was sweet. Although he remained ever mindful of the business at hand, Giles allowed himself to enjoy the repast, the company, and the breeze that blew in off the water.

While Captain Courtney and Edmund spoke of the weather and other meaningless trivia, Grace's mind churned. In her home and among her neighbors, absolutely no White shared her view of Africans as human beings. In fact, her father had forbidden her to speak of slaves at all whenever they were among other planters. He found her outspokenness an embarrassment. She was truly surprised that he had reacted so mildly to Captain Courtney's statement. There had been subtle censure in the captain's words to her father, a bold move considering that he wanted Edmund's business. But that thought gave her pause.

She looked straight into Giles's face and said, "So, you do not deal in slaves, Captain Courtney, only the crops they sweat and die to produce. And your conscience is assuaged?"

"Grace!" Edmund chastised.

"Nay," Giles protested. "It is a fair observation. Aye, I suppose slavery is a necessary evil. My profession relies upon plantations and the like. As for my personal dealings with Africans, I'd just as soon not be in a position of ownership."

"A necessary evil," Grace repeated, biting thoughtfully into a slice of cheese.

She entirely disagreed with the sentiment, but it was a far cry from the patronizing explanation of slavery that her father and his peers professed. *They're savages, beasts of burden, hardly different from horses or oxen.* If one abused an animal, Grace had reasoned, that animal was ever after hateful and mistrusting. Matu had been doomed to a life of silence for Grace's sake, but she loved her and cared for her like Grace was her own child. Matu was a far better person than Iolanthe and Edmund, those deemed fit to own her. And as for Grace herself, well, she always felt wholly human, if never wholly white.

Nay, she did not agree that slavery was necessary, but

there was something to be said for a man who knew that it was evil.

"Forgive her," Edmund said, casting a cross look at his child. "She is an idealist. I've sheltered her far too much, I must confess."

Again, Giles shrugged and smiled benignly. "Nothing to forgive. 'Twould seem she's far from sheltered. Many a planter's daughter knows nothing of the plight of the people who serve her."

Grace arched a golden brow at him. His subtle barb found its mark. She, too, benefited from slavery. But *she* had no choice. Or did she? She did with that thought what she had done with it for over ten years. She buried it ere she was tempted to let it surface entirely. What sort of choice was it?

She chewed at her lip in consternation. How dare her father bring this man here, a man who, by his own willingness to acknowledge his failings, made her all the more aware of her own? And how dare this man do so with such a charming smile and gentle manner?

"Do you live in Port Royal?" she asked, her voice a little too crisp.

Giles nodded, washing down a bite of bread with his wine. "Aye, when I'm not at sea." He smothered another grin. One could watch her every thought tug at her lips and furrow her brow, and he sensed that this was a young woman whose mind was seldom at rest. He rather imagined that Edmund Welbourne had had his hands full with his daughter.

"I have never been to the city, though I should very much like to," she said. She frowned at Edmund. "My father says it is too rough."

"Well," Giles said, "women of your quality are rare there. Most live outside of the main area of town. There are comings and goings a girl like you would do just as well not to know about."

She gave him a cynical little smile, her eyes suddenly brittle, and Giles wondered what to make of it. He let his gaze wander over the slaves who rowed boats full of crates out to *Reliance* and helped to hoist them up the side of the ship. His first mate directed the operation smoothly. It didn't feel at all right, to be sitting here eating while the others worked, but he had learned much in the last two years about courting customers. It wouldn't do to offend the man after he had already criticized him for holding slaves.

"'Tis a shame your wife couldn't join us," he said, by way of conversation. "I hope that she is not ill."

"Nay," Edmund assured him. "It is only that she is very fair-skinned and burns in the afternoon sun."

"Ah well, at least we are *graced* with your daughter's presence." Ouch! He could see by the look on her face that he was not the first to have made such a pun.

After an initial shake of the head, she smiled again, that enigmatic, almost bitter smile. "Nay, I am not so fair as Mistress Welbourne. What my father will not tell you is that my—mother—never takes her meals with us."

Edmund laughed uncomfortably. "Iolanthe is one of those strange women who does not take regular meals. She prefers to nibble upon this or that throughout the day. Perhaps it is because she is French. Who knows?"

The daughter laughed. "Aye, 'tis a well known fact that formal meals are not the custom in France." And now her expression was one of undeniable disgust.

Giles laughed, too, although weakly. It seemed as if it might have been a joke, an irony, but he felt as though he had missed some crucial detail.

Edmund Welbourne appeared no more successful

than Giles in appreciating the remark. He scowled at Grace and cleared his throat. "Bad form, you know, discussing a lady who is not in our presence."

"We do everything in the best form here," Grace concurred, but her tone was no different than it had been for her last remark, ironic and scornful. And yet in her eyes there was such longing, as though she wanted so much to mean what she said.

The mood had grown intensely strange and uneasy, and Giles rose, unable to sit still in the midst of it. "Well, though I trust my men, I think I'll check on the loading of your goods myself, and then we'll be off."

"So soon?" Edmund said, rising too. "I hope we've not offended you in some way. Grace, entreat our guest to stay."

She looked up at him, and Giles knew not whether he truly saw entreaty in her eyes or only wished that he did. "Can you not linger, Captain?"

Captain. From her lips, the title sounded real, sounded natural.

"I wish that I could," he explained earnestly. "But I can't start a voyage with the crew thinking I shirk my duties. Perhaps, when I return with your father's profits, I could stay a bit longer?"

She regarded him for a moment. He was, in every way, so unlike the other men that her father had brought to call, arrogant men, all so impressed with their own importance. A whole ship's crew entrusted their captain with their lives, obeyed his orders, and yet he asked permission to see her again as though her answer genuinely mattered to him. With a start, she realized that she did very much want him to return and stay longer, but that was a path that she well knew she could never travel down with any man. She had no choice but to send him on his way, like all of the others before. Her shoulders actually ached when she shrugged them carelessly.

"No doubt you've other business to attend to," she said, turning her back to him and helping Matu clear away the dishes.

In the brief time he'd spent with Grace, Giles had seen myriad emotions dance across her expressive face, but the look of bleak despair that she had tried to hide by turning away went straight to his heart. What was going on here that Edmund's daughter should be so scornful one minute, so profoundly sad the next?

Welbourne's slave but deepened the mystery. The small, African woman shooed Grace away with her hands while she sharply jerked her head in Giles's direction. Welbourne's daughter stared at her in obvious shock, but the servant made a strange sound and gestured back to Giles.

Edmund chuckled. "It seems that our Matu approves of you," he said.

"Uh—I'm flattered," Giles replied. *What was a matu?*

"That may be more important than you realize," Edmund explained cryptically.

Grace frowned at the maid and shook her head, but the maid gestured back toward Giles and firmly tugged on a plate in Grace's hands.

"Give me that," Grace snipped.

The maid shook her head and Edmund chuckled. "Your assistance has been refused, Grace. Come, walk our guest to his boat with me."

She turned abruptly to Edmund. "You know very well that this is all perfectly futile. 'Tis cruel, that's what it is."

She spun back to Giles, and for one horrifying moment, he thought that she might cry. God knew, he'd rather face a bloodthirsty pirate with a cutlass in his hand than a comely wench with tears in her eyes.

"Godspeed, Captain Courtney, and a safe journey to you." She released the plate over which she and the maid had been battling, curtsied briefly, then lifted her skirts and ran back toward the house.

The two men watched her retreat: Giles entirely nonplussed, Edmund scowling sourly. Giles broke the tense silence. "'Tis quite all right, sir. I'd not force my attentions upon your daughter. Please, do not fault her too harshly. She is entitled to her preferences."

Edmund crossed his arms. "If ever a man suited my child's preferences, it would be you. I thought that perhaps . . . well, never mind. Even so, I hope you'll plan to spend a few days here when you return. We're actually quite hospitable here at Welbourne. Won't you give me a chance to show you?"

Welbourne's voice was entirely too cheery, his stance too studiously at ease. He was far from ready to let the matter go. Giles murmured something suitably unintelligible and ambiguous and, gathering up his pride, strode back across the lawn to the bay. Upon reflection, he reminded himself that it would be ill advised to court a customer's daughter. Besides, he had been a captain but a few scant days. He'd no time for courting.

On impulse, Grace turned near the front of the house. She watched the captain's strong, fit form move with purpose and grace back to the boats, her father tripping after him. Of course he was fit and graceful. He was clearly a man unopposed to labor, one who asked nothing of others that he would not do himself. She had seen how he chafed at sitting on the lawn throughout the meal. He was a man of action, disinclined to sit idly by.

"Stop this, Grace!" she whispered to herself. "For goodness sake, twenty minutes in his presence, and already you imagine him some paragon. You cannot have him."

Her father caught up to him and stopped him, speaking in a most animated manner, though she couldn't hear what he was saying. Captain Courtney seemed to be trying to make an exit, but then he looked up at the house. 'Twas too far to see his face clearly, but she knew that he was looking at her. She should dismiss him. She should turn her back and go inside, but she could not tear herself away. He must have said something that pleased her father, for they began to move back toward the boats, and Edmund's step was a little lighter.

Despite her best intentions, she could not help but wonder whether Captain Courtney was what she thought him. Then she sighed heavily. If only *she* were what he thought her, but she was not.

An hour later, Grace sat in a straight-backed, upholstered chair in the keeping room of her home, pushing aside her embroidery frame and trying to untangle the knotted mass of threads that sat on her lap. Matu stood by, watching. Iolanthe, seated in a matching chair, carefully pulled a strand from her own neatly organized skeins of thread while studiously ignoring the girl. The only hint that she was aware of Grace's presence was her smug sneer when Grace sighed in frustration.

Many plantation owners lived in homes that were scarcely more than huts, so a house with several bedrooms and such a fine, large keeping room as this was a luxury. The chamber was dominated by a large dining table of polished mahogany surrounded by wooden

chairs, but it also contained several upholstered chairs
for sitting and a small table for tea.

Still, how Grace wished that they had a huge English
manor house with several such rooms! Then she could
entirely escape Iolanthe. Perfect Iolanthe, with her impeccably smooth hair and her flawless embroidery
stitches and her carefully wound skeins of thread. A ten-
dril of unruly curls tickled Grace's cheek, and both her
stitches and her cache of thread were hopelessly tangled. Of course, she thought with satisfaction, Iolanthe
did have one terribly unattractive flaw.

With her rough, dark hands, Matu took up the
threads and carefully began plucking them apart, and
Grace looked up into her smiling face. The older
woman shook her head, her eyebrows raised in such a
manner as to clearly convey the message, "'Tis your own
fault these are such a mess."

"Oh, Matu, 'tis such a waste of time. 'Tisn't even
sewing. I'm not *making* anything, just ornamenting it."

"I should not think you would understand," Iolanthe
interrupted, and as she spoke, she was forced to reveal
her rotting, brown teeth. "Needlework is an art form. Of
course, you lack the refinement—the *breeding*—to appreciate it."

Grace turned to her stepmother, the gleam of battle
in her eyes. "It seems to me that all the fancy stitching
in the world does nothing if the garment itself is infe-
rior. Just as *breeding* means nothing if a person's
character is flawed. Great beauty may hide such decay."

Before Iolanthe could retaliate, Edmund walked
through the front door. Ordinarily, this would not have
stopped her from making some nasty remark in return,
but Edmund's body was tense, and his green eyes
seemed about to burn a hole through his daughter. His

wife swallowed her retort, reaching instead for a bowl of sugared almonds sitting on the tea table and watching with avid interest.

"Is there a storm brewing?" she asked him. Her brown eyes were round and innocent, but there was a catty quality to the gleam in them.

Edmund hardly spared her a glance. Instead, he kept his gaze fixed upon his daughter. "All the man wanted was permission to call upon you. He wasn't asking for your hand."

Edmund's glare turned Grace's insides into jelly, but she kept her voice even and replied, "I thought that was the ultimate goal of calling upon a woman, the idea of asking for her hand."

"Would that be so terrible?" he asked.

Grace looked up at her maid, but Matu only gestured to Edmund and nodded her agreement. Grace rose, knocking her frame and fabric to the floor, where she left them. "You both know very well how futile all this is. And I am especially disappointed in you, Matu."

Iolanthe gave a dramatic sigh and set her own needlework carefully into her sewing basket. "Though it pains me greatly, Edmund, I must agree with Grace." She chuckled as though at some vastly amusing joke she'd only just remembered. "She might well have some explaining to do upon the birth of her firstborn."

"Leave, Iolanthe!" Edmund snapped.

"Do you think that forbidding me to speak of it will change the truth?" she asked. She picked up her basket and rose, moving to ascend the stairs at the rear of the keeping room. "I suppose I will finish this in my chamber," she muttered, though no one cared.

"She's poison, Grace," Edmund said, watching his wife's exit. "Do not listen to her."

"Oh, I am well aware that she wants naught less than my abject despair. But she is right. Refusing to allow her to taunt me with it does not change the truth."

Edmund shook his head, his face reddening slightly. "Look at how fair you are. Add to that a father with looks like this Courtney fellow, and I promise you, Grace, no one would ever guess your child's blood was tainted."

Tainted. Grace sucked in her breath.

He continued, unaware of the insult. "Seven-eighths white. Your grandchildren, fifteen-sixteenths. Who would ever wonder? Damn it, Grace! You owe me!"

It always came down to this. Grace folded her arms and leveled her eyes upon her father's. "And what will you do if I fail to repay your generosity, your *kindness* in acknowledging me as your daughter?"

"I know what you are trying to do. You are trying to get me to say that I would sell you. You are trying to make it seem as if I don't love you, that all I want you for is grandchildren. If that were the case, my dear, rest assured that you would be married by now or else sold into service." His voice lightened, became more gentle. "I want you to be happy, Grace. That Courtney fellow, you heard him. He has no more liking for slavery than you. And Matu likes him, do you not Matu?"

Matu had long since abandoned Grace's embroidery floss. She took Grace's hand and nodded.

"You suddenly think I should marry?" Grace asked.

Matu shook her head. Then, with her hand flat out, she tipped it from one side to the other, then pointed to her head.

"You think I should consider it," Grace translated, and Matu nodded.

Edmund snorted. "God forbid she should listen to

me. I am only her father. Talk some sense into her, would you, Matu?"

"She cannot talk, Father," Grace said, condemnation in every word.

He was unaffected. "Oh aye, she can, louder than any of the rest of us at times. I've work to do. You two need a bit of time alone, I think."

He stalked out of the front door, and Grace turned to her maid. "We have always been in complete accord on this, Matu. 'Tis dangerous for me to marry, both for me and any children I might bear. Would you have me bring more slaves into the world?"

Matu shook her head. With one hand, she held the opposite wrist tightly, like a manacle, then released it, opening both hands and moving them apart, emphasizing the release.

"Freedom?" Grace asked.

Matu moved her hand up and down, like a boat on the waves. She mimed mopping a floor and hoisting with a rope. Then she repeated the gesture that, for her, meant "freedom."

"The Negroes on his boat? The free ones?" Grace clarified, and Matu nodded. "It is a very great step to go from not owning slaves to marrying one."

Matu growled and gave Grace's head a light smack. She pointed to Grace, then pointed to her own head, shaking it emphatically, before repeating the manacle gesture, this time without releasing her wrist.

"I—I know that I'm not a slave, but . . ."

Matu smacked Grace's head again, pointed to her own and shook it.

"I do not know?"

The manacle gesture again.

"I do not know slavery?"

Matu crossed her arms and lifted her chin. Every tense muscle in her body shouted, "So there!" Seeming to feel that her point had been made, Matu marched out the back door and across the rear yard toward the kitchens, leaving behind a very bewildered Grace with her tangled wad of colored threads and her poorly executed needlework.

Two

Giles rose from the sturdy oak table covered with supper dishes and began clearing his place. After a month at sea, it was good to eat a home-cooked meal at the Cooper family's house just outside of Boston. Funny, he hadn't really thought that he'd missed the warmth of hearth and home. After all, he hadn't had a home in any real sense since he was a lad and had gone to sea. But after Geoff and Faith had wed, and even more so after he had been named the godfather of their child, he had come to appreciate every moment he spent among real families. He felt fortunate indeed to have come to know Faith's parents and to be welcomed into their house whenever he was in New England.

"Nay, nay," Naomi Cooper chided, shaking her white-capped head. "You are our guest." She pulled the plate from Giles's hand and gestured with it for him to sit.

Jonathan Cooper, seated next to Giles, chuckled. "She wants you to keep talking. Surely there is some tiny detail about our grandson that you have left out."

"I am just as anxious to hear about Faith and Geoff," Naomi protested.

The Coopers' sons, fourteen-year-old Isaiah and nine-year-old David, took over the table-clearing and dishwashing, squabbling briefly over who would do what. The adults moved from the dining section of the keeping room to the sitting section. A cheery fire burned in the huge fireplace and the trio found seats on the plain but well-built furniture surrounding it.

"I've told you all I can think of," Giles avowed. "Faith and young Jonathan are well. The business is flourishing, so Geoff is having no trouble providing for them."

"Aye," Jonathan agreed, "a second ship. 'Tis a good sign, a prosperous business."

Giles smiled. Faith's father was a Puritan, through and through.

True to form, Jonathan asked for the fifth time that night, "So you really think 'tis the Quaker faith she's settled on?"

"Faith seems to feel that it fits her," Giles assured him.

Jonathan shook his full head of long, graying hair. "Quaker. Think you that we gave the girl too much leeway in her youth, Naomi? Mayhap we should have just chosen a husband for her all along."

Naomi threw up her hands in a gesture of exasperation. "Let it go, Jonathan. You said yourself, her husband's prosperity is a sign of God's grace. And now they've been blessed with a son. Mayhap we could travel back to Jamaica with Giles?"

"No need," Giles assured them.

"He's right, Naomi, they'll be here in a few months' time. We can wait."

Naomi sniffed. "You cannot blame me for wanting to see my grandson."

"You've two others," Jonathan reminded her, speaking of their eldest son's boys.

"Aye, well, they're Noah's, and I see them daily. I long to see Faith's boy, that's all."

Giles cleared his throat, and brought their attention

back to him. "Might I ask you two something about Faith, before she met Geoff?"

They looked at him, their eyebrows raised. Obviously, his request struck them as improper somehow. Lord, how did Geoff ever navigate his relationship with his Puritan in-laws? Still, he knew that the Coopers had done a fine job raising their daughter, and perhaps they had some insight.

"'Tis not so much about her, personally, as it is about daughters in general, and courtship, and well, what makes one suitor more favorable than another," he explained.

Naomi breathed a sigh of relief, and Jonathan nodded knowingly. "You've finally found a likely maid then?" he asked.

"Perhaps you two would prefer to discuss this alone," Naomi suggested.

"Nay!" Giles protested. "I'd like a woman's views, as well. I think it may be a bit complicated."

"More complicated than Geoff and Faith?" Jonathan asked.

"I do not know," Giles began. He explained to the Coopers about his strange visit to Welbourne Plantation, and how the Welbourne girl had seemed to like him, and yet had sent him on his way, although reluctantly. He also mentioned that Edmund had seemed unwilling to let the matter rest and had chased after him, insisting that Giles stay a night or longer when he returned.

Jonathan shrugged lightly. "It seems to me that her father already sees you as an acceptable match. I think there's very little complicating this."

"That is only half the battle," Naomi said. "You said that the girl dismissed you."

"Aye. That is, she seemed to. Her demeanor was most confusing. Mayhap she only meant not to be too forward."

Naomi shook her head. "'Twould not have been too forward to offer further hospitality, especially not when her father had made his approval clear and you had expressed some interest of your own. Tell me, Giles, what is it makes you think that you and this girl would suit?"

"Well, she's . . ." He found himself hard-pressed to put his feelings into words. She was undoubtedly one of the most beautiful women he had ever seen, but even he knew that that was no basis for a marriage. Nay, 'twas more than that.

Giles leaned toward Naomi. "Mistress Cooper, the ocean is a lonely place. 'Tis a fine thing to have a ship of one's own, but I've not even my best friend across the corridor anymore. I am not a man so in love with the sea that I am fulfilled by sailing alone. Of late, I find myself restless."

"And so you seek a wife. 'Tis natural enough," Naomi replied. "But why this one?"

"She is no simple farmer's daughter, that much was clear. She has a sharp mind and a quick wit. And she is unhappy where she is. Something there is hardening her, haunting her, I think. She has no love of slavery, and yet is surrounded by it. I cannot explain it except to say that you would know it, too, could you but see her face."

Jonathan interrupted. "Have you not thought that it may have nothing to do with her home? Mayhap she is merely prone to melancholy. There's naught you can do for her then."

"Nay," Giles said, "she is passionate, cynical, but only at moments, sad."

Naomi shot her husband a look of concern before looking back at Giles. "All this in one brief conversation? Forgive me, Captain, I am sure that you are well-intentioned here, but you have no real knowledge of her."

Giles nodded. "I have said just that to myself time and time again in the last few weeks, and yet I cannot seem to shake free of thinking about her. Something's deeply troubling there. Consider this, she called her mother 'Mistress Welbourne' and mentioned that the woman will not take meals with her family."

"Perhaps she is unwell," Jonathan suggested.

"Nay. I asked after her health. Mister Welbourne says it is because she is French."

Both Jonathan and Naomi raised their brows. "The French do not eat? I've never heard anything more ridiculous," Jonathan said.

Giles nodded. "It struck me false. I tell you, I have a sense that Welbourne is hiding something."

"And what of Grace?" Naomi asked.

"I have just the opposite sense. She seemed ever on the edge of blurting something out."

Jonathan rose and clapped Giles on the shoulder. "You are not my son, but I will advise you as I would Isaiah or David. I would not weave myself into another family's web of deceit by the bonds of marriage. Choose another, Captain."

Naomi stood up, too, and offered more gentle advice. "Mayhap she is all you say, and mayhap a life with you would give her something that she seeks. You are a good man, and a sound judge of character, I think. She is surely a decent woman or you'd not feel drawn to her at all. Now, you say that her father has extended you a few days' hospitality. Accept his invitation. Just remember, tales of old tell of rescuers and fair damsels, but they recount naught of the years that follow, when the heroics are done and the real work begins."

At the Coopers' invitation, Giles stayed the night in the upstairs cubbyhole that had once been Faith's quarters. Jonathan's advice was sound indeed, but he was more inclined to heed Naomi's. What harm could there be in paying the Welbournes a social call? How high could the stakes possibly be?

It did no good to stay inside. Screams of agony pierced the walls of the house, even with the windows shuttered. It was instinctive for Grace to shut her eyes as she heard the whistle of the whip, the sharp crack against flesh, the soul-searing scream. By sheer bent of will, she opened them, kept them open and stared at the pendulum of the wall clock. At the age of fourteen, she had begun to defy Iolanthe's orders and ceased to attend whippings, but by then, she had witnessed over a hundred. She did not need to see the man being tortured in the front yard. When she closed her eyes she saw far too many others, their dark torsos striped and running with blood, jerking spasmodically; women not even permitted the dignity of covering their breasts; children, some younger than she by the time she had found the courage to stand up to Iolanthe.

Even the proudest, most dignified men were finally betrayed by their bodies. Before it was over, they would twist and writhe in their bindings, tearing the flesh on their wrists in an attempt to avoid the relentless lash. And through it all, Iolanthe would stand in front of them. It was not the sight of the blood that she craved. She stood where she could look right into their tortured faces and smile sweetly at them with her rotting teeth while they begged her for mercy.

On and on it went. Grace studied the pendulum and watched the minutes tick by so slowly that they hurt. Traitorously, she thought of how marriage to a man who had no desire to own anyone would mean that she would never have to hear these horrible sounds again. Nine minutes later, the hundredth lash fell. There was no more cracking of leather against flesh, no more pleas for mercy from a man now surely unconscious. Only the ticking of the clock dared to break the silence.

Iolanthe breezed through the front door, her face flushed and her eyes unnaturally shiny. She would often become rather giddy, infused with energy after such an event. She smiled at Grace. "Have you been crying, Grace? Feeling a bit ashamed perhaps, letting your own kind suffer while you live in luxury?"

Grace narrowed her wet eyes. "I have no cause for shame, Iolanthe. The shame is upon your head. That poor man only stopped to take a drink of water. Matu told me that 'twas past noon, and that he had not stopped since morning."

"He left the area where he was working. They all know that is strictly forbidden."

"There was no water near him! It is unconscionable, Iolanthe! I hear that we have lost seven slaves this season to thirst and heat."

Iolanthe shrugged her silk-clad shoulders carelessly. "There are several wenches breeding."

"The babies seldom live."

"Then *mon père* will send more adults. Once you lose discipline, Grace, once they cease to fear you, the profits drop and it becomes quite dangerous. Do not think

for a moment that any of them would hesitate to murder all of us in our beds. Even you."

"Who could blame them?"

Iolanthe shook her head and tsked her tongue. "Do
not let your father hear such words. He might just put
you in the fields, where you belong."

The door swung open again, and Matu stepped into
the room. She held her slight body rigid and kept her
face averted, betraying no hint of emotion.

"Matu knows," Iolanthe continued smoothly. "Best
you all keep to your place." With that, she swept upstairs, where she would spend the remainder of the
afternoon.

It is a shame really, Grace thought, that looks cannot
kill. If they could, the daggers Matu stared at Iolanthe's
back would have ripped the woman right out of both of
their lives. The Negro woman turned back to Grace, her
look of defiance dissolving into despair.

Grace nodded in acknowledgment of Matu's mute
sadness and whispered, "Every time it happens, I feel a
very liar. I stand here safe in my father's shadow."

Matu pointed to Grace and grasped her wrist in the
gesture that meant "slave."

Grace nodded. "I should be. I should be a slave and
suffer as you do."

Matu shook her head emphatically. She pointed to
herself and her lips. "I said . . ." she pointed to Grace,
then to her head, shaking it, "you didn't know . . ." the
manacle gesture, "slavery." Now she came to Grace,
wiped her tears and hugged her close. Pulling away, she
tapped her rough finger to Grace's chest, right over her
heart, then made the manacle gesture again.

Grace sniffed back a sob. "My heart *is* enslaved, Matu.
Mayhap it seems shallow, but truly, I do hurt when one

of them is beaten. I think I would rather it happened to me."

Matu made a harsh sound in the back of her throat and shook her head. Her back bore puckered scars of its own. She knew the feel of the lash. She took Grace's hands and led her to a chair, pushing her gently into it. Then she bobbed her hand up and down like a boat on the waves and followed it with the gesture for freedom.

"No!" Grace shouted, standing right back up again. "I'll not hear another word about that damned ship's captain!"

As though it did any good to keep Matu from mentioning him. Not a night had gone by since she'd met him that her own mind hadn't brought up pictures of his handsome face, with that smile that went all the way to his eyes. He had seemed like such a *nice* man. Mayhap another would have found the word lukewarm, but Grace knew enough to know that it was a rare quality indeed. Still, for her, marriage was complicated, no matter how nice the man.

Her voice softer, she added, "He is but salt to the wound. There's no sense wanting what one cannot have."

But Matu resumed the same argument she had been using lately. She would point to Grace and flex her arm, meaning strength or power. No matter how many times Grace explained to Matu that she was powerless, the other woman would only shake her head. Then she would point to it and open her arms broadly, "think big" or "think of everything." Grace had no idea what she meant by that.

"I do not understand!" she wailed. "All along you have agreed with me that I should never marry, and now you've seen this man for perhaps half an hour and you're set upon betrothing us."

With a shrug and a sigh, Matu tapped her head and then lightly patted her chest.

"How can you know this in your heart?" Grace asked. "You hardly know him at all. You heard him. He deems slavery a 'necessary evil.' He sits upon a fence."

Matu laughed at her. She pointed to Grace and then acted out the process of hiking up her homespun skirt and straddling something.

"All right! All right!" Grace snapped. "Mayhap I sit upon a fence, too."

Matu appeared to climb off of her imaginary fence. She gestured for the boat and for freedom.

"I shall never be free, Matu, not really. My heart will always be with the slaves."

Matu held her own dark arm next to Grace's light golden one. With a look of resolution on her face, she gestured again for freedom, once on each of their arms.

"Freedom for both of us?" Grace asked. She hadn't thought of that. She could not take everyone on the plantation, but she could take Matu with her. They could both sail away from Welbourne Plantation and never see it again. But it would not cease to exist. Perhaps she and Matu would be far beyond this place, but the suffering here would go on. And the screams of the tortured ones would still ring in her ears.

Iolanthe snapped her fingers impatiently. "Hurry! Hurry up and then get out of here," she barked at the young black girl who was loosening the laces of her gown. The bodice was stiff and tight, and Iolanthe needed to breathe. The moment she could draw air

deeply into her lungs, she shoved the servant from the
room, then rushed to the open window to bask in the
sultry, warm air.

Her heart pounded furiously and she had the overwhelming urge to fly. She almost thought she could.
There was a deafening hush all about the plantation.
The slaves dared not speak. Even the birds and insects
in the surrounding jungle had been silenced by the
screams of the kindred beast she'd had tortured in the
front yard. God, she loved the whippings.

In this primitive, uncivilized corner of the world,
Iolanthe might as well not even exist. She had grown up
in Saint-Domingue, the French portion of the island of
Hispaniola. There, her father had worked ceaselessly,
overseeing shipments of Africans; disposing of the many
bodies of those who had not survived the journey, as-
sessing what must be done with those who had in order
to make them healthy enough for sale. Dysentery and
inactivity had taken their toll. Slaves had to be "seasoned," taught submission and respect, without
breaking their spirits entirely. Their spirits would break
eventually, but they often died soon after, so 'twas better
to leave that to their masters. In all, these duties left precious little time for his family.

Her mother had pined for France. She had filled
Iolanthe's mind with tales of handsome men and ban-
quets, of clothes and perfumes. If there was nothing
more to being a woman than to be an ornament, a pos-
session, at least in Europe she could feel that she was
one of great beauty and value. In the Caribbean, *Màman*
had said, a woman was of no value at all, except for
breeding. She had said the word distastefully. Breeding
was for livestock, not for women of culture and refinement.

So Iolanthe had set out to be beautiful, to be the sort of woman a man might treasure and be proud of. But *Màman* was right. There were no grand balls in Jamaica; there wasn't even a decent city. There was no one but Edmund to see her in her European gowns, made according to the highest fashion, and he was unimpressed. Unless she took great measures to be noticed, she was invisible.

But when an African was whipped, she was a goddess. And as with God Himself, one could beg all one liked, but mercy was seldom granted. Hadn't she asked God for happiness? Some measure of satisfaction? She hadn't asked to be deliriously happy. She hadn't asked for rapacious wealth or a husband who was an Adonis. All she had asked for was some pliable, undemanding man who lived anywhere but these barbarous islands.

Moving from Saint-Domingue to Jamaica was no improvement, but when she had realized that her father was making no effort to seek her a husband in Europe, she had chosen Edmund. At the time, he had seemed so mild mannered, so biddable. Men were such liars during courtship. He had been polite, genteel, when he had come to visit her at her home. Once they were married, he was just like her father, always working, as obsessed with his farm as her father had been with his business.

She lifted the cover from a little crystal dish of sugared almonds that she kept by her bed. It had ruined her looks, all the damned sugar, but what else was there? Well, besides the lash? She should know better than this, to allow herself to think too hard about how her life had turned out.

Edmund was a boor. He was an oaf in bed, demanding and rough. So what if he slaked his lust on the slave wenches? She didn't really care about that. She didn't even care that he'd sired a number of children with them. But to ask her to claim one of them as her own, just because the brat was fairer than most! An animal, under her roof, posing as her daughter!

And the wretched thing wasn't even grateful. Neither she nor her nurse. Iolanthe's eyes narrowed, the giddy rush of the beating fading at the thought of the two black vipers nesting in her house. She didn't trust Matu any farther than she could spit her. If Edmund had had the slightest bit of good sense, he would have cut out her heart, not her tongue.

Iolanthe exhaled slowly, closing her eyes and forcing her body to relax against the frame of the window. Someday. Someday Edmund would die. She was only forty-two, thirteen years younger than he. And women often lived longer, so long as they weren't propagating like rabbits. It was God's one kindness to her that she had not conceived in those first few years. Of course, she had done nothing to hide her disgust whenever Edmund had come sniffing to her bedchamber, so he had slowly come less and less often. Iolanthe would never have tolerated Grace at all but that having a daughter had finally ended his conjugal visits entirely. He left his wife alone now and rutted with slaves exclusively.

She snorted in derision. The vile little pretender could marry or not, as she liked. If she married and produced offspring, Iolanthe would reveal the secret the very moment Edmund finally had the decency to die. Grace would be cast off by her husband, the children sold, and Welbourne would be Iolanthe's. It would be hers to sell, and then she would sail across the ocean and never look back. Who needed God? If a woman wanted a scrap of contentment in this world, she had to make it for herself.

She whirled abruptly. It was so bloody hot! She stripped off her heavy gown, shoes and stockings. In nothing but her fine lawn shift she stretched across the soft, comfortable bed. All of these regrets and dreams did her no good right now. Right now, she needed a balm for her rattled nerves. Staring up at the deep blue silk bed hangings, she conjured up the face of the writhing field hand, recalling his screams much as one might recall a passionate opera, a satisfied smile curving her lips. There was something so . . . so . . . *stirring* about it.

That was why she could forgive Jacques. He rutted with slaves, too, but that was only because he couldn't get what he wanted from white girls, and she understood. She knew the need to make others suffer, the need to be the one in complete control. She rather imagined that rape was, to him, like that moment of satisfaction that came when the ultimate lash was struck. When all defiance, all pleading, all hope vanished from a slave's eyes and he was hers. It was as addictive as opium, as sweet as . . .

She popped another almond in her mouth and savored the crystals that coated it.

Three

Sitting across from Geoff at the double-kneehole desk in their Port Royal office, Giles couldn't help but note that his friend's eyes danced with mischief. He had just informed the Hamptons that he would be visiting Welbourne Plantation for a couple of days, once *Reliance's* hold was emptied and its contents sold. Now Faith's face was the reflection of pure joy and Geoff was grinning slyly.

"Now, do not look at me so," Giles protested. "I'm only going to give the man the monies I collected from his goods."

"That's only a day's work," Geoff replied.

"Aye. 'Tis interesting that you would choose to spend so much time with this particular customer," Faith joined in, leaning on her husband's shoulder.

"A customer with a fair daughter," Geoff added.

Faith made a face of mock chagrin. "Oh Geoff, surely you are not accusing Giles of being more interested in the woman than the business relationship with her father."

"I? Never say it. I only mention the girl as an unimportant side note. Just as Giles did."

"I *did* but mention her," Giles said defensively.

"Aye," Geoff said to Faith. "He did but *mention* her golden curls and green eyes."

"*Extraordinary* green eyes," she amended.

"Deeply *mysterious* eyes," Geoff agreed.

"And her enigmatic smile. He did but mention that, as well." Faith could barely suppress a giggle.

"All right!" Giles shouted. "Mayhap I have *blathered* a bit." He said the word as though it were sour to the taste. "But damn me if she's not something unique. And not just for her looks. She's a thinker and speaks what's on her mind. Why, she came right to the point about the way I profit by slavery . . ."

"Aye," Geoff cried, raising his hands to stop the tale ere it could be told for the tenth time. "And took it well when you challenged her, too."

"Is that not what you say pleases you most about Faith, that she gives and takes a challenge well?"

Faith beamed at her husband. "Did you tell him that?"

Geoff scowled. "Do not encourage her, Giles, else I shall never get a moment's rest." The scowl disappeared, replaced by a wide grin. "Aye, though, you've the right of it there. Choose well, Giles. Merely pretty wenches can be bought aplenty, there's no need to wed for that."

Faith frowned, but the men ignored her.

"And no need to tell me that," Giles said. "As Faith's father said, it seems Edmund might favor a match. It occurs to me now that, if his daughter is of an abolitionist bent, mayhap he challenged our policy on purpose. It may be that he wanted her to know my sentiments, as well. It gives us common ground. Still, the time I spend there will be spent getting to know her some, seeing if she is what I first thought of her."

"Have a care," Faith warned. "Try to see her for what she is and not what you want her to be."

"You're much like your mother, you know," Giles said. "Aye, I may know her only a little, but there is depth to this woman."

Geoff chuckled. "One can hardly fault a man for wanting to plumb a woman's depths." He was rewarded with an indignant shove from his wife.

"'Tis a serious thing, Geoff," Giles chided. "It might well be that I can know her for years and never fully know her. I think that I would never find her dull."

He took a deep breath and tried to keep his thoughts clear. Faith was right indeed. He mustn't let his obvious infatuation cloud his judgment. He would spend a bit of time at Welbourne Plantation, but he would proceed slowly, judiciously, *reliably*.

It was stifling hot in the kitchen, but not nearly as hot as it was in the sugar house, from which the sickening sweet scent of boiling sugar permeated everything. The smell was so overwhelming that Grace could hardly detect the spicy scent of pimento, or allspice as it was also called, which Keyah had been grinding. Keyah was the main cook, a wiry black woman with solid muscles despite her thin build. She sweated as she worked at a table on one side of the round, open hearth and cookfire that dominated the center of the room.

Grace groaned in frustration when Matu ran in, tapped her on the shoulder, and began emphatically gesturing about a ship.

"Let it rest!" Grace cried. "Can you not see that I am busy?" She turned back to Keyah. "Aye, Keyah, the fish will be fine for dinner. Oh—and Mistress Welbourne is out of sugared almonds."

Keyah threw a cautious glance over her shoulder before muttering, "As many of dem as her eat, her don't get no sweeta."

Predictably, Grace laughed. "Well, if they do no good for her disposition, we can always hope that she chokes on one." Keyah laughed, too.

Again Matu tapped Grace on the shoulder, and Grace brushed her hand away. "Gwey!" she said, using the slaves' dialect.

Matu gestured for the ship and then pointed to the back of the kitchen, in the direction of the sea. She grabbed Grace's hand, tugging her out the door and toward the front lawn. Finally Grace understood her maid's urgency. *Reliance*, her sails billowing in the breeze, floated sedately into the bay.

"He's returned," Grace breathed.

Matu nodded and gestured to Grace to think on it.

She had been thinking on it. No matter how many times she had told herself that it was a useless fantasy, she would find herself contemplating a life with this quiet man who preferred to own no one. What about a wife, Grace wondered. Would he prefer not to own her, as well? A wife was as good as property by English law. She had never spoken of it, not even to Matu, but there were reasons beyond her birth that she shied away from marriage. Reasons more unspeakable than her mixed blood and that sometimes plagued her dreams in the form of a shadowy wraith in a nightshirt, speaking with a French accent.

Still, she ran her hand over her hair and was dismayed to feel that it was its usual unruly tumble of curls. A glance at her skirts reminded her that she had donned one of her oldest gowns this morning. Unwittingly, she cast a desperate look at Matu, who grinned and tugged her back toward the house. Surely Captain Courtney would have business to discuss with her father. There would be plenty of time to set her looks to right.

Well, then, mayhap she *would* think on it.

Grace sat patiently while Matu massaged in the hairdressing she had concocted of various fruit and seed extracts. It did a fair job of relaxing the curls and certainly made it easier to pull her hair up into one of the more fashionable styles of the day. Matu also chose her gown, a deep rust-colored damask. Grace swallowed hard as she put it on. Well she knew the maid had chosen the dark fabric to make her skin seem paler.

As she had expected, Captain Courtney and her father were sitting in the keeping room discussing the sale of Edmund's goods and when next he might be in need of Courtney and Hampton Shipping's services. Grace paused at the top of the stairs, listening, before descending to meet their guest.

Below, Giles had been hard-pressed, as he sat and chatted with Welbourne, not to crane his neck and look around for the daughter. Edmund had said that Grace was upstairs "primping." That seemed a good sign. A woman did not primp for a man she had no interest in.

When he finally heard soft footfalls on the stairs behind him and he turned to greet her, he found himself masking a vague sense of disappointment. It seemed that she had nearly "primped" all of the charming curls right out of her hair. Then he smiled. It was a small sacrifice. The color of her dress would have left most women looking sallow, but Grace's skin fairly glowed next to it. Her full lips were parted, begging a kiss, and her nose, slightly broader than most, lent her face a soft quality.

Good God, man, he thought to himself, *snap out of it!* He was not here to have his head turned, yet again, by her extraordinary looks. He had come so that he might get to know her better.

Grace stared back, then squelched a little smile. Why were she and Matu worried? So she was darker than some and her hair was wild. These things had yet to do anything but draw men to her all the more. For once in her life, the thought didn't fill her with contempt for either herself or the man. Perhaps it was his boyish face. His admiration seemed more open, less insidious than other men's had appeared. Again the word *nice* drifted through her mind and filled her with a soft, comfortable warmth.

She moved across the room and lifted her hand in greeting. "How good to see you again, Captain," she said, and noted with pleasure that he bowed low over the offered hand, but refrained from kissing it. She detested when they did that.

"Miss Welbourne," he replied, "the pleasure is entirely mine."

"Nay," Edmund interrupted, too cheerfully, "the pleasure is ours indeed. I'm happy that you've decided to accept our hospitality for the week." He looked at Grace as he said this, his gaze heavy with meaning.

"The week?" she asked.

Giles stepped back. "Your father has extended his invitation, and as I told him, I've no pressing business just now."

A week? Suddenly the visit stretched ahead like an eternity. Whatever would she do with this man for a week? She furrowed her brow and silently reminded herself that if she was to consider marrying him, she had better figure that out. She spoke to Matu, who had come down the stairs behind her. The breathless quality of her own voice irritated her. "Well, we shall have to make sure that we extend the very best hospitality. Matu, will you bring us some refreshment?"

The maid nodded and slipped out the back to the kitchen.

"Matu?" Giles asked. "That's your maid's name?"

"Aye," Grace answered.

"Your father mentioned her when last I was here, but I didn't know what it meant. I didn't realize it was a name."

"Matu was kidnapped from Africa—"

"Brought," Edmund corrected. "She was brought here from Africa when she was young. My wife's father owned her first. She was a field hand for him, but she had such a way with the little slave children that we made her Grace's nursemaid. The two are inseparable."

"I see," Giles commented. So this was the source of Grace's aversion to slavery. She had bonded to her nurse and come to love her. One mystery solved.

Later that afternoon, over tea, he came to understand why she had bonded with her nurse rather than her mother.

Mistress Welbourne was also an attractive woman, but in no way did her daughter favor her in looks. The mother's face was chiseled into high cheekbones, a sharp nose, and a small mouth. Her hair was deep brown, sleek and glossy, and her eyes were the color of strong tea. Her skin was porcelain-white and flawless. It was obvious that she took great care to keep it so. But for all her beauty, there was absolutely no warmth. She might have been made of porcelain indeed.

Edmund smiled broadly at his wife, though the expression struck Giles as more of a grimace, and informed her that their guest would be staying for a week or so.

Mistress Welbourne's lips formed a tight smile, and when she spoke, the smile was marred by the mottled teeth behind it. "How delightful. You and Edmund must be hammering out the details for a rather extensive business agreement."

Giles smiled back with genuine warmth. "I must confess, my visit is more social than commerce." He let his gaze fall on Grace.

There was a subtle strangeness to both their reactions, the same mysterious tension he had sensed on his last visit when he had mentioned Mistress Welbourne. Grace lifted her chin in a manner that suggested some slight defiance. Mistress Welbourne's tight smile tightened even more, and though it hardly seemed possible, her eyes became slightly colder.

"I see," Mistress Welbourne said. The brief silence that followed was strained, and Giles thought of the stillness in the air just before hurricane clouds appeared on the horizon.

"Grace," Edmund said, and his voice seemed to shatter the air like glass. "Perhaps Captain Courtney would enjoy a walk along the river." He turned to Giles. "We've some lovely falls, nothing too tall and spectacular, but lovely nonetheless, and a mineral spring the most amazing shade of blue-green."

"Of course," Grace replied, though she wished she could stay close enough to hear her father upbraid Iolanthe. She rose and walked to the back door, gesturing for Captain Courtney to follow. Then she frowned slightly at Matu who was gathering up the tea things. "Are you coming, Matu?"

Matu straightened up and made a huffy squeak. It was a sound Grace knew well. Matu made that sound whenever Grace suggested something absurd, like doing Iolanthe some devilish mischief. The maid set her hands on her hips and shook her head, like Grace was nothing more than a naughty child, then waved the two of them off.

Grace's hand felt like it was glued to the door latch. Walk alone with this man? If they were to see both the falls and the spring, they would be walking for three-quarters of an hour or more. Alone. Together.

"Oh. Well." Her eyes shifted from Giles to her father to Matu and back again. "If it wouldn't be too improper. That is—the two of us walking for so long without a chaperone."

Giles would have preferred to have a bit of time alone with her, but he did his best not to show his disappointment. "I have no objection to having your maid join us," he lied.

Matu shook her head and smiled regretfully, gesturing to the teacups and plates.

"True enough, Matu," Edmund said. "You've your hands more than full here, and Iolanthe and I have a small matter to discuss. I shall have to trust you to be a gentleman with my daughter, Captain."

"How could a man be anything else in the presence of such a lady?" Giles returned, and he was stunned by Mistress Welbourne's snide giggle.

"Such a *lady*, indeed," she said. "I hope you will not be too disappointed to discover that Grace is probably far more suited to plantation life than the sea. Is that not so, Grace?"

Grace's eyes narrowed almost imperceptibly. "I really don't know. I have never been to sea." Sheer spite propelled her hand from the door latch to the crook of Giles's arm. "We have a bit of a walk ahead of us, and I want to hear all about your adventures, Captain. You must have seen so many things."

They paused long enough to shut the door behind them, and Giles looked about him at the outbuildings. At the mill, to the rhythmic, incessant crack of a white guard's whip, four Blacks pushed two stout, crossed, wooden beams in a perpetual circle. Sweat ran freely down their raw backs, and Giles could only imagine the pain as the salt irritated their wounds. Their actions caused three grinding wheels to rotate in the center while three other slaves fed sugarcane through them, pressing out the juices to boil in the sugar house.

"Wouldn't oxen be more efficient?" Giles asked.

"They are expensive and hard to obtain," Grace replied. "And they eat a great deal. Father finds slaves to be more economical. He can buy several Africans for the price of an ox."

"But they cannot be as hardy."

"They're not. A single slave's life is worth about half a ton of sugar, Captain. They are a rather cheap commodity." She watched his face carefully, gratified to see his eyes widen a little in shock, then his brow furrow and his lips turn down in distaste.

A small trail broke through the leaves and trees, and Grace pointed to it. "We'll follow that path. It leads past the slaves' quarters, though there will be only the old ones and very small children about. Those who must still be nursed are carried into the cane fields by their mothers. When they are old enough to wander off, yet not old enough to work, they stay here with the aged and weak."

"I've little experience with children, but I remember my sisters at that age. I cannot imagine the old ones have the energy to keep up with them."

Grace shook her head sadly. "They are not well-fed, happy children, Captain. They do not bounce and frolic. Africans do not breed well in captivity, and over half of those conceived by slaves die before their first birthdays. By the age of six, they are put to work with domestic chores, hauling heavy buckets of water the mile from the river to the house, building up their strength to join their parents in the fields, mill, or sugarhouse in a few years. And the discipline is as harsh for the children as it is for the adults. Mistress Welbourne and the overseer are fond of the lash."

"Mistress Welbourne?"

Grace paused and seemed to search for something in the leafy canopy above them. "My mother and I do not get on well together."

"I gathered that."

"We do not hide it well, I fear."

"And so you have your Matu."

"Matu is not mine," Grace replied harshly. "If she were a White, and her name were Mary, would you call her my Mary?"

Giles's face flushed, and he bristled, but then he thought of how he might feel if his mother had come from such a cruel life. He was sure that 'twas her love of her maid, not any personal animosity toward him that had made Grace snap. He shrugged. "I might. The two of you seem to belong to each other. Much as a mother and daughter should." He was pleased to see Grace's tense shoulders relax.

"Aye. I may have been robbed of my mother, but I love Matu with all my heart, just as she loves me."

As far as Giles could tell, Grace's mother was no great loss. "She doesn't say much, Matu," he said.

"Father had her tongue cut out over twenty years ago," Grace replied, without missing a step, as though it were the most common thing in the world to say.

Giles stopped dead in his tracks. "Good God! Whatever for?"

Grace paused, and for just a heartbeat of time, her green eyes darkened with anguish, seemed to look through him at some ghost in the shadows of the jungle surrounding them. Then she focused on him, and he felt an ache that pierced him through.

"It is a common practice, Captain Courtney. Matu is not the only slave on Welbourne Plantation without a tongue. The penalty may be inflicted for stealing a morsel of food that is intended for the overseer's dogs or for knowing a secret that the master wishes to be kept at all cost."

Giles didn't have to ask which was the case for Matu. "What does she know that would cause your father to silence her forever?"

And again, that cynical, enigmatic smile. "If I told you, he might cut my tongue out." She turned her back and resumed walking, leaving him behind to wonder what in God's name he was getting himself into.

Ahead of him, Grace fought back the niggling sense of regret that plagued her. He had been shocked, of course. She had known he would be. She had forced herself to speak of these realities coldly, when in truth, they still had the power to shock her, too. What might Captain Courtney have done if she had told him these things with all of the sadness they made her feel? Might there be some comfort in sharing her pain with a kindred soul? Mayhap she should have allowed herself to find out.

He ran to catch up, and they came to a pair of neat little cottages among the trees. "We've four white guards who live here," Grace said. "That one over there," she pointed to a smaller cottage with a kennel and five barking dogs in back, "belongs to the overseer. The dogs are let loose at night. They make sure that none of the workers leave their huts after dark. They are also used to track and sometimes kill runaways."

"Why track them only to kill them?"

"It is a rather unforgettable and therefore intimidating spectacle for the rest."

Giles shuddered, and again, Grace found some solace in his reaction.

Several yards deeper into the forest, the foliage gave way to a clearing and the slaves' quarters, tumbledown huts with dirt floors and thatched roofs in need of repair. The doorways and windows were wide open with no means of keeping out insects or rain and providing no privacy for the occupants. The place seemed like a small village, with ten or twelve of the structures. A dozen dark, naked children between two and five years old sat or chased each other unenthusiastically in the dirt. Their limbs were thin and their stomachs distended, the product of a diet comprised entirely of grain and cassava. Some chewed on bits of sugar cane, several were crying. Six older slaves, probably not much older than Giles, but weak and decrepit, and seemingly alive only by the grace of some miracle, sat on the ground with them. One woman, her crippled fingers shaking, mended a tattered garment hardly worth her efforts.

A man with leathery black skin and wiry gray hair looked out of one of the doorways and gestured to Grace. "Missy!" he called. "Missy!" Then he said something else, his words rapid and staccato, almost English and yet not. Grace moved toward him, through the squalor and despair.

"What's he saying?" Giles asked.

"I don't know. They speak a sort of combination of African languages, mixed with a smattering of English."

Giles wondered if she should be entering the hut, but since that did indeed seem to be her intention, he followed her. Instinctively, he placed himself between the black man and Grace. As he would in any situation with the potential for danger, he assumed a stance and demeanor that challenged the other man to cross him. The slave cringed in fear, and Giles found himself ashamed. A frail slave, old before his time, was no threat to Grace.

Grace watched the exchange intently, unsure which touched her more deeply, the captain's desire to protect her or his obvious remorse for having frightened the slave.

The black man moved aside and gestured to a mat on the floor. It was one of ten mats in the crowded space, but while the others were empty, this one held a little girl of perhaps four years. The child was doubled over and whimpering softly. She was so little that it hardly mattered, but it struck Giles that she ought to have some garment to cover her from strangers' eyes.

"Does your father provide these people with nothing?" he asked.

Grace shook her head. "These slaves are too old or too young to be of any real value to him." She knelt next to the girl and placed her hand on her forehead. "She's burning up. What have you given her?" she asked the old man. "Herbs?" she pantomimed brewing something, then pouring and drinking it.

The man hobbled outside and returned with a handful of leaves and bark. Grace nodded. "These are good for fever. What else is wrong with her?"

The man knelt and tried to pull the girl's arm away from where she had it tucked against her swollen stomach.

"Her stomach?" Grace asked. "Is she vomiting?" She acted it out, but the old man shook his head. He pulled again at the girl's arm, and she let out a tortured wail.

"Help me," Grace commanded Giles. "I need to see her hand."

Now, he knelt next to the girl. Gritting his teeth and steeling himself against her cries, he pulled the hand out where Grace could see it. She gasped in horror.

"Oh, God," she whispered.

"What?" Giles asked, loosening his grip and trying to see more clearly.

"No, keep it out. I need to look. . . . Oh, God."

He caught a trace of the scent of something rotting and looked closely. The index finger on the little girl's hand was smashed. It was angry red and oozing greenish pus. The rest of the hand was swollen to twice the proper size and was also bright red under her black skin. The redness traveled all the way up her sticklike arm to her swollen armpit.

Grace and the old man exchanged looks. Woeful, helpless looks.

"What—what do we do?" Giles asked.

"Tell my father that I will be here for the night," Grace replied.

"All right. What can I bring back? Surely you have

some medicine at home, something besides these leaves."

She studied him for a moment. The lines around his gray eyes seemed somehow deeper, and she had to stop herself from reaching out and trying to smooth the lines away.

"How long have you been a sailor, Captain?" she asked softly.

"Just over a score of years."

"Have you ever seen a wound do this?"

He looked back down at the child. Aye, he had. Battle wounds. He nodded gravely, unable to speak. The child would die. There was nothing to be done but try to comfort her to the end. "Because of a smashed finger?" he choked. It was so senseless. If the wound had been treated properly long before, she would have healed by now.

Grace shook her head sadly. "The overseer would never waste his time seeing to the treatment of a useless African child, Captain Courtney. Many of the children may die from easily preventable problems, but they are replaceable, so it is of no consequence. My father would explain that it is a matter of financial expedience. A 'necessary evil,' I believe you once called it."

"I didn't mean this," he said, his voice filled with horror.

She placed a gentle hand on his arm. "I know you didn't. I'm sorry that you had to see this, but I can't leave her now. Can you understand?"

"I'll be back," Giles promised. "I'll let your father know, and then I'll return to sit with you."

"'Tis not a pretty thing, Captain."

The look he gave her was hard and determined. "I've held men down while the surgeon cut off putrefying limbs. I once held a shipmate's hand while his tongue swelled and he turned black in the face and died of lockjaw. 'Twas a flesh wound inflicted by a rusty cutlass. I'm not the sort to leave another human being to die alone and in pain."

What he did not add was that he had never sat and watched a little girl suffer and gasp her last breath, and that the thought made him want to sink to the floor and weep like a woman. Instead, he turned on his heel and headed back to the house.

Grace watched him go. *Another human being.* She looked at the child who was once again cradling her arm against her stomach. The captain would come back. She knew that as surely as she knew that she would not leave this child's side. What manner of man was he? He was brave and compassionate, strong, but willing to bend. He hadn't wanted Matu to come with them on their walk, she had sensed that, but he was willing to let her. He hadn't wanted Grace to come inside the hut. She had been well aware of that, too, but he had merely followed her and sought to protect her.

He could have retreated. No one would have faulted him for staying with Iolanthe and her father at the house. Now, instead of joining her for a lovely walk and perhaps a bit of wooing, he was probably in for one of the worst nights of his life. She hadn't missed the convulsive clenching of the muscle in his jaw or the mist of tears in his eyes. If he had seen all that he had said, it would take a great deal to make the eyes of a man with his experience tear.

The little girl began to keen softly, each thin wail ending with a series of sobs. Unable to hold back, Grace let her own tears fall unimpeded onto her rich, red skirts. She set her hand to slowly stroking the child's burning brow and coarse hair, and through her tight throat she hummed one of Matu's African lullabies. This was not the first time that she had offered what comfort she could to a dying slave. It would, however, be the first time that anyone would be there to comfort her afterward.

"So help me, Iolanthe," Edmund growled as soon as he estimated that Grace and Giles were well beyond hearing, "if you stand in the way of this . . ."

"In the way of what?" she asked Edmund, her voice deceptively sweet.

"She is about to break, I sense it. She will accept this one."

Iolanthe shrugged. "You indulge her too much. My father let me choose for myself, for all the good it did. And what do you think your captain will do when she bears him a child that is dark as dirt? I would be doing you a favor by telling him now."

Edmund laughed harshly. "Then our secret is safe. The last thing you would ever do is a favor for me."

His wife crossed her arms and glared at him. "Why, Edmund, why? I will never, as long as I live, understand what you see in this place. It is not some English estate with a title to pass on. It is a farm!"

"It is *my* farm. You are delusional, Iolanthe. You have these notions of how wonderful life would be in Europe. I have no land there, no source of wealth. Our life would not be a series of voyages back and forth across the Channel. The fine gowns you love so much are paid for by the sugarcane cut from *these* fields."

"But why do you need to pass it on? What has this

poor man done to you that you would deceive him so? Why do you need to call that girl ours?"

"We have had this discussion too many times. I can explain it all again and still you will refuse to understand." Edmund gestured to Matu, who had been silently cleaning. 'Twas unnervingly easy to forget the woman's presence altogether. Not for the first time, he regretted having silenced her. "Fetch me something to drink. Something strong. I care not what."

"Oh yes, Edmund, do have a drink," Iolanthe scoffed. "Have four or five and tell me that *I* am delusional. Have you asked this sailor if he wants to inherit your farm? Do you really believe that Grace will deny her slave blood and become mistress here? Why not leave Welbourne Plantation to one of your many other black children?"

Edmund ran a hand through his blond hair, and his face was flushed pink. "Keep quiet, Iolanthe."

"'Keep quiet, Iolanthe,'" she mimicked, her voice falsely low. "Whenever I speak the truth, it is 'keep quiet, Iolanthe.' One bastard elevated to daughter of the house, the rest left to work the fields. Oh, if your precious Grace only knew!"

"It matters not whether Grace comes back. She'll bear children. White children. One of them will want Welbourne. How could they not?"

"African children," Iolanthe taunted. "Black children who have been taught by their mother that slavery is evil, who will not have anything to do with your *great legacy.*"

"Damn-near-white children who will desire wealth as all men do," Edmund countered.

Matu returned with a glass and a bottle of rum. She appeared to be absorbed in the task of filling his glass and finding just the right place to set the bottle, but when she looked at him, it was with keen interest and uncanny intelligence. She was far smarter than any house servant should be, but by the time he'd realized that, it was too late. Grace would never have forgiven him if he had sent her back to the fields or sold her.

So he looked to use Matu to his advantage. "Matu, I am relying upon you," he said. "Do not leave my wife and our prospective bridegroom alone together, and separate them if ever it seems the mistress may be feeling a bit free with her tongue. You and I, we want the same thing, do we not? We want Grace to be happy?"

Matu nodded solemnly, but he could see something whirring busily behind her dark eyes. *Why* had he made it impossible to ever know exactly what she was thinking?

"Good, then. Why do you not check with Keyah and make sure that dinner is worthy of our guest, perhaps lay out something suitable for Grace to change into." He clenched his jaw a moment and added, "Iolanthe, is it not your custom to take a rest in the afternoon?"

Iolanthe's brown teeth peeped through her lovely lips. "Aye, Matu, let us leave the master alone with his drink and his dreams, shall we?" She glided serenely toward the stairs and drifted upwards while Matu exited through the back door.

Alone at last, Edmund tossed back his glass of rum and refilled it. Were it not the middle of the afternoon and did he not have a guest to impress, he'd have headed to the slaves' quarters to see if one of the younger wenches might be about, but Giles and Grace had gone off that way. He drained the second glass, as well. It was bloody near the happiest day of his life. He was but a hair's breadth from marrying off his daughter, and he was not going to let his malicious wife spoil it.

So, Grace was tainted. So she wasn't lily-white. She was smart and had a quick wit, attributes that he had given to her. Surely they hadn't come from her mulatto mother. His daughter was exotically beautiful and far more refined than his pure, French wife. The bitch was jealous, that was all. She knew damned well that a savage, ignorant African had done better by him than she could ever have done. He poured more rum and smiled malignantly. It only made sense that she was bitter, but she had made her bed.

Oh, aye, she had made her bed—entirely separate from his. She spent inordinate amounts of money on clothes that were completely impractical, not that she would have stooped to do one practical thing on the plantation. Well, except for overseeing discipline, a task that she was disconcertingly good at. Then she pouted because he could not stop the labor that placed that finery upon her back, just to pay homage to her great beauty.

Edmund heaved a heavy sigh. She *had* been a great beauty. Still was, if one overlooked the teeth. She had taunted him with it, wearing deep necklines and swinging her hips, but the moment he had put his hands on her, she had become a block of ice. And now, he doubted that he'd feel the least bit enticed even if she took to wearing nothing at all.

Lately, he had begun to worry that Grace would be as unyielding and as disappointing as his wife, but he had the feeling that all of that was about to change. How could she not take to this fellow? And Grace was a passionate girl, one with fire and grit. She'd not turn her husband away night after night. How many grandchildren, he wondered. Eight? Ten? Among them, one would want Welbourne, expand it, realize its full potential.

He was pouring his third glass of rum when the door at the rear of the room burst open, and Edmund felt his complacent bubble burst at the look on the face of his prospective son-in-law.

Four

Did one man dare call out another man whose daughter he was courting? When Giles burst through the door of the main house and saw Edmund Welbourne casually pouring himself a drink, it had been his first impulse. He had wanted to berate the man for the conditions in which his slaves were forced to live, to haul him back to the cluster of hovels and make *him* tend to the dying child. Instead he took a steadying breath and ran his hand through his hair, pulling some of it from its careful queue.

"There is a situation in the slaves quarters, Mister Welbourne."

Welbourne swore softly under his breath. "What has Grace done now?"

"She's attending to a gravely ill child there," Giles informed him, his face flushing with anger.

Edmund laughed tensely. "She's always had a soft spot for them. Hardly lady-like, I realize, but a tender heart is a forgivable flaw in the fairer sex." He held his hands open in apologetic supplication.

"I am forced to disagree." Giles noted with satisfaction the way Edmund's face fell. 'Twas almost a shame that his next statement flooded that same face with relief. "I have never considered a tender heart a flaw in a woman at all."

"Well, nay, of course not. Still, I fear that Grace will stay all night if she cannot remedy the situation immediately." Edmund lifted the glass of amber liquor to his lips and drained it. "Whatever it is, I'm certain the overseer will take care of it."

"Grace seems to think not. In truth, the overseer or *someone*," he glared at Edmund, "should have taken care of it days ago. There's little enough to be done now. I fear the child cannot be saved."

Welbourne sighed and shrugged, then poured another glass. "And so nature will take her due course. Tell Grace that I insist she return at once."

Giles stared at the man in astonishment. Welbourne truly had no idea what the problem was! Before Giles could say anything irrevocable, Mistress Welbourne interrupted, calling down from above, "Is that you, Captain Courtney? Is something amiss?"

Edmond sneered and called back, "Iolanthe, keep—" he stopped short and set down his glass, "—close your door and get some rest, darling. 'Tis nothing serious."

Mistress Welbourne fairly raced down the stairs. "Keep *what*, darling?" she asked. "I am quite certain that I did not hear you correctly. Oh my, Captain, you look quite upset." She looked at him with great concern but little sincerity. "Has Grace done something to *disgrace* herself?" She giggled at her own pun.

"The problem is not Grace!" Giles snapped. "The problem is that an innocent child is dying in filth and squalor because of a minor injury that was not tended to! I have seen people treat livestock with greater compassion than your slaves receive!" He addressed Edmund directly. "You have the right of it, sir. Grace does intend to stay with the girl, all night, if need be, and I intend to stay with her. I came here to inform you of that fact."

"Well!" Mistress Welbourne exclaimed haughtily. "You dare to accept our hospitality and then chastise us over a matter you know nothing about? What are you? A sailor! What do you know of managing a fine estate and nearly a *hundred and fifty* workers?"

"Iolanthe!" Edmund bellowed. "Be still!"

His wife looked back and forth between the two men, gritting her brown teeth, her perfect porcelain skin turning a mottled red. "I will not tolerate this! You!" she glared at Giles. "You can have that horrid little beast. I wish you the joy of her. You two barbarians should be well suited, after all. But I promise, you will look back upon this day and know yourself for the fool you are." She spun on her heel and marched up the stairs, her hips swaying and skirts rustling with each step.

Giles didn't look at Edmund. If the wife was this venomously angry, he dreaded to see the husband's reaction, and at the moment, he could hardly trust his own response to it.

In the end, he was more stunned by Edmund's composure than Iolanthe's vehemence. "Well, I suppose we've not made the best impression," Welbourne said dryly, picking up his glass and sipping from it.

Giles's natural sense of diplomacy warred with his moral outrage. At last, he said, "A little girl is dying, Mister Welbourne, and Grace has committed no greater sin than to care. Have you no pity?"

Edmund nodded distractedly. "Aye, 'tis unfortunate, the child."

Unfortunate. Giles shook his head grimly. "At any rate, I find *Grace's* response quite admirable."

Edmund gave up on sipping. He swallowed half the glass in a smooth gulp, then said, "I'm sure she'll welcome your company."

"You'll not be coming?" Giles asked, more as a prompt than an actual question, but Welbourne just shook his head and finished his rum. "Well, then, I'll look after her."

"Knew I could count on you, Courtney," Edmund said. The words were mildly slurred, and he sat down in one of the upholstered chairs.

Giles eyed the half-empty rum bottle and wondered if it might not have been full just a short time ago. Sweet Jesus, what a family! He spun and strode to the rear door, then stopped, emotions churning inside of him, gnawing at him. He wanted out of this place. But even more, he wanted to make sure that Grace never again had to attend the bedside of a dying child, or know another person whose tongue had been cut out, or had to listen to her mother insult and belittle her. God knew, if he never saw Edmund Welbourne in his cups again, it would be too soon.

He was a fool. A complete idiot. He thought of Jonathan Cooper's advice about not weaving himself into this family's problems. He reminded himself that he had yet to accomplish his goal of getting to know Grace at all.

Then, he thought of Grace, alone in the slaves' hut. If he were not here now, what would have happened? With whom would she have shared the burden? If he left her here, how many more times would such a scenario as this play itself out, and what terrible toll would it exact from her? He could not bear to think about the answers to any of these questions. Each one led to a future of hopelessness for a woman he was coming to admire more and more with each minute spent in her company.

At last, he threw all caution, all judiciousness aside and said, "One more thing, Mister Welbourne."

Welbourne looked up at Giles with a vaguely befuddled scowl. "What?"

"I'd like permission to marry your daughter."

Edmund's face split in an ear-to-ear grin. "How soon?"

Today wasn't soon enough.

"Three weeks from Sunday?" Giles suggested. Time to cry the banns, no more.

Edmund lifted his glass in a toast. "Three weeks from Sunday," he agreed.

The stench in the slaves' hut was overwhelming, both a heartbreaking sign that the infection was working quickly in the girl's system, and a welcome sign that she would not suffer much longer. Shortly after Captain Courtney had left, the child had begun to vomit and her bowels had emptied themselves forcefully. She had stopped sobbing and had gone to moaning, but her eyes had rolled back and she was completely insensate.

Now, the slaves were beginning to return from their work. Several had gathered in the hut with Grace, helping her to keep the child somewhat clean, for all that there was little water on hand. One of the older children had gone to the river to fetch more.

"Tell me when her mother has returned," Grace said to one of the women on hand. She was a kitchen worker and spoke English well.

"Her already back," the woman explained. "Outside, waiting."

"Waiting?" Grace asked. "She knows...?" It was hard to say.

The woman nodded. Her voice was deep and heavy. "Her know."

Grace stood slowly. Her knees and back ached from kneeling on the hard, earthen floor. "I'll only be a moment," she said to the little group surrounding her. "Call for me if you have a need." She stepped outside and took a deep breath of reasonably fresh air.

Exhausted women who had been cutting cane all day were now spreading cassava dough over large, shallow pans hanging upside-down above open fires and wiping their brows in the combined heat of the late afternoon sun and the cookfires. The air was thick with the smell of callalou, a spinach-like green, and a rare treat for slaves. It was Grace who insisted that they be fed more than starchy cassava. Children tugged at the women's shift-style dresses and clamored for food and attention. Men stood in groups, talking softly, delivering sharp reprimands to children who had become too troublesome to the cooks. A white guard, armed with whip and flintlock, lounged against a tree, watching the proceedings with a bored expression. The mood was somber, but the activities were no different than they might have been on any other evening. The death of a child was sad, but not at all uncommon here.

Grace couldn't help but smile slightly when she saw Captain Courtney stride into the clearing from the path to the main house. His hair was mussed, and he didn't look at all like the unflappable man who had come to stay just a few hours earlier. She had never before had someone stay with her through this kind of vigil, and was amazed at what relief it provided. Whenever she had tended to sick or dying slaves, her efforts were rather suspiciously appreciated. She was ever an out-sider. It was not easy, maintaining her perch on this fence of hers. Despite his disarray, this captain moved with the confidence of a man who shouldered respon-sibility naturally, and it occurred to her that here was someone upon whom she might lean.

He stopped and gave her a stricken, questioning look. She shook her head and silently mouthed, "Soon."

A small, thin, very dark woman with prominent shoul-der blades and very short hair stood alone at the edge of the clearing. She kept her back to the hustle and bustle, staring into the trees surrounding the quarters. Several other Negroes regarded her sympathetically, shaking their heads and speaking softly to one another, but they seemed to think it best to leave her be. Grace approached reluctantly.

"Do you speak English?" she asked. She did not rec-ognize this woman, but there were many field hands, and Grace knew only a few.

The woman turned around and stared at Grace in open hostility, but it did nothing to deter Grace. She was accustomed to their hatred and could hardly fault them. She simply sighed and continued. "I want to help, but I fear that I cannot save her."

The child's mother said nothing. She only continued to stare at Grace.

"It shan't be long," Grace said. "Would you like to come in and see her one last time?" She gestured to-ward the hut.

Still no answer.

"Do you know who the father is?" She indicated the group of men, hoping to convey the idea. "Mayhap I could fetch him for you."

Captain Courtney stepped in next to Grace. "The mother?" he asked, and Grace nodded.

"Would she rather I spoke to the father?" he suggested.

Grace could only shrug. "I do not think she understands us. It may be that she knows not who the father is."

The slave turned her back to them and looked into the trees again. "Me undastan." She crossed her arms and held herself rigid, utterly aloof. "Da maas de fadda. You axe *him* if him kya what happen to her."

Grace swayed next to him, and Giles reached out to steady her. "Grace?"

"Oh, my God," she breathed. She looked up at him, her face pale, her eyes wide in shock. "She said that the master is the father. That little girl is my sister, Captain." She looked over her shoulder at the hut.

His first instinct was to reply that, of course, she wasn't Grace's sister, but he had the good sense to realize that Grace would not take well to that statement. Instead, he said softly, "'Tis not the same, Grace."

He might as well have said the first thing. She pulled back, and for a second, he thought she was going to strike him. "Aye, it is!" she shouted. "It is *exactly* the same thing. Exactly!"

"I didn't mean it that way," he protested.

"Nay? How, then, did you mean it?" she snapped.

"I—" How *did* he mean it? "They aren't married. I mean, 'tis unfair, but the child is illegitimate, and . . . well, a bastard usually shares its mother's life, however harsh."

"Was that her choice? Does being illegitimate affect whether or not you are a human being, deserving of some dignity and respect?"

"Nay! My best friend is a bastard. It just means that life is harder. Different."

"But your friend is white, and this child is black, and what you really meant is that *that* is the real difference! You think that because she is black, she cannot be my sister."

"Nay!" But that *was* what he'd meant, and he knew it. He raised his eyes to the sky and its dimming light. "I'm sorry. Mayhap it was what I meant. I am . . . out of my element here, Grace."

She looked at him. He almost looked ashamed, and her heart softened. Aye, he was far out of his element. But he was trying to help, trying to understand.

"There is much you do not know, Captain," she said.

"Much I have no desire to know," he agreed. He took her hand in both of his. "I do not know how you endure this."

From the two hands that enveloped hers, warmth and strength seemed to suffuse her whole being. They were strong hands, competent hands. For all that his fingers were wide and callused, marked by tiny scars, they held her so gently. She had the strangest impulse to lift them to her cheek, merely to feel the contrast of his rough skin against her soft face. She wanted to lean into him, allow his broad shoulders to shelter her for a moment. The impulse startled her, and she abruptly pulled her hand away.

"Missy!" one of the slaves in the hut called. "Missy, her jerkin' and chokin' now!"

Giles and Grace raced in together. The little girl's back was arched, her muscles convulsing, and the Negroes quickly cleared the hut, overwhelmed by this latest development. The two Whites could hear the excited chatter outside, but it was impossible to understand. Grace knelt and went back to stroking the child's brow.

Giles knew that the girl couldn't feel it, wasn't aware that Grace was even there, but he also knew that it felt better to be doing something intended to soothe and help. He watched powerlessly as the convulsion ended, the girl's body relaxed, then her bulging, chocolate brown eyes became fixed and stopped seeing altogether. He placed his hand on Grace's shoulder.

"She *was* my sister," Grace whispered.

"I'm sorry," he said, the words completely inadequate.

They returned to the main house in deepening twilight and ran into Matu on the path. She carried a hamper of food obviously intended for them, but neither was hungry. Still, she followed them back home, toting the meal. They found Iolanthe and Edmund in the keeping room. The couple had finished their own repast, and now Iolanthe sat in one of the upholstered chairs, plying her needle, while Edmund sat at the table counting the money Giles had brought. A ledger lay on the table next to him, a glass and bottle in front of him, both empty.

Edmund looked up and smiled in greeting. "I'll have to take your word for the amount," he said to Giles. His eyes were glassy and his hands unsteady. "Can't get the same bloody sum twice. You must have talked some sense into her." He nodded to his daughter.

"'Tis over," Giles replied. "The girl didn't last long."

"Ah," Edmund responded, nodding. "Just as well, that."

Giles took in the serene domesticity of his surroundings. It seemed unreal, given all that had just happened less than a mile away. He couldn't keep the bitterness from his voice. "Aye, sir, just as well."

"You look tired, Grace," Edmund said.

She stared at him for a moment, then walked purposefully to his side. "You never told me there were others."

Her father gave her a dazed look, then reached for the bottle, grumbling to find it empty. "Others?"

"She was yours."

Iolanthe snorted indelicately. "Imagine that."

Matu moved swiftly to Grace's side, setting the hamper on the table and tapping Grace on the shoulder. When Grace looked at her, she shook her head urgently.

Edmund rose, swaying slightly. "Now, Grace . . ."

"Do not presume to 'Now, Grace' me . . ."

Matu tugged on Grace's arm, a pleading look in her eyes. Iolanthe stuck her needle into the fabric stretched across her embroidery frame and left it there, listening to the exchange.

Giles shifted uncomfortably. Obviously this was not Grace's first encounter with one of Edmund's offspring sired upon a slave, and he preferred not to be a witness to the coming confrontation. "Grace, mayhap this is not the best time for this. We are both weary, and this afternoon has everyone on edge."

She glared at him, her eyes as cold and hard as green bottle glass. "You have no place in this conversation," she said icily.

Edmund seemed to be sobering rather rapidly, and with a similar look in his own green eyes, the resemblance between father and daughter was clearer than ever. "Mind what you say, young lady. Mind *everything* you say."

Matu abandoned her attempts to silence Grace and turned her attention to Giles. With a placating smile, she gestured to the hamper of food, then pointed above.

"Aye," Edmund agreed, "a good idea, Matu. You can set Captain Courtney up with supper in his room, and we'll send up bath water, as well. This has hardly been the sort of welcome I had in mind when I invited him to stay."

"Nay," Grace interrupted, "I should think it hasn't. I shouldn't be surprised if the good captain finds some pressing business to attend to after all." She turned to Giles, genuinely sorry that she had spoken so harshly to him. "Forgive us, Captain. I'm sure this was not what you had in mind, either."

Giles cleared his throat and glanced uneasily around him. He wondered how her father might react if he suggested that he simply take Grace with him on the morrow with a promise to wed her as quickly as possible in Port Royal.

Edmund's face brightened. "I'm sure you must have some arrangements of your own to make. You'll have friends to invite, business to delay a few weeks . . ."

"What?" Grace asked.

Giles winced. Damn! If there was one thing of which he was certain, this was not the time or the place to discuss marriage with Grace. "Uh—Grace and I've not really had a chance to talk," he told Edmund.

"About what?" Grace demanded.

Matu groaned and dropped her head, but Iolanthe perked up considerably.

"About the wedding, dear child," she chimed in, her voice wickedly amused. "Your father and Captain Courtney have agreed that you are to marry in three weeks."

"What?" Grace fairly shrieked, and Giles's head began to throb.

"I asked your father's permission . . ." he began.

"And it never occurred to you to ask mine?" Grace countered.

"Of course! Of course, I was going to ask you."

"When?"

Enough was enough, Giles thought. God what a mess! "Well, certainly not at a dying child's bedside!"

"When did you find time to discuss it with my father? My God, did you ask him when you arrived? You didn't even know me. You still don't. You know nothing about me."

"I know what I need to know!" Giles barked, but then he stopped, counting silently to ten. He refused to let the situation run away from him. Well, any further than it already had. "Grace, can we speak on this on the morrow? We are both tired, and I think you have something to discuss with your father."

"There is no need to speak on this further, Captain. You have not deigned to ask me for my hand, but I will tell you now that I refuse your suit. If you had planned to stay and woo me, you need not trouble yourself. Given that, it matters not whether you hear what I have to say to Father or not."

"One more word, Grace," Edmund ground out from between his teeth, "and you will regret it."

She glared right back at him. "What will you do, Father?"

"I will wash my hands of you."

Giles gasped in shock. Disown her? "Sir, I cannot marry Grace under duress."

"I am not marrying you," Grace reiterated.

"Not another word," Edmund warned.

"Mister Welbourne . . ." Giles began.

It was Matu who brought the squabbling to a halt. "Aaaah!" she exclaimed, waving her hands in the air. She looked at Edmund, but gestured to herself and Grace, then out a rear window to the kitchen. Edmund nodded brusquely.

Grace gazed at him in disbelief. "I'm being banished to the kitchen with my nurse?"

"Well, you're certainly acting like a child!" Edmund snapped.

Grace gasped in anger, but Matu squawked again and gestured for Grace to follow. Then she let her deep brown eyes dart from Edmund to Iolanthe and back again.

"Iolanthe, you and I are going for a walk," Edmund said.

"That black bitch is not *my* nurse!" Iolanthe retorted. "I will not be dictated to by her."

"Nay, but I am your husband, and I have not yet sent your last order to the dressmaker. Not sure now that I'll send it at all."

With an indignant huff, Iolanthe flounced out the door, leaving Edmund to follow in her wake.

The older man shrugged. "Sorry to leave you on your own. There's food in the basket there." He indicated the hamper on the table. "Matu has always been the only one who holds any sway with Grace. Oh! But I'm sure that you and she—well—that is, I'm sure she'll be altogether different with you. She's just a little upset. My fault. I should have realized that you hadn't been able to ask her yet. Just excited, that's all . . ." His voice drifted off uncertainly. Then he looked at the door that his wife had left open and squared his shoulders. "Have some supper, Captain," he repeated before he followed Iolanthe.

Giles stood in the middle of the deserted keeping room in speechless astonishment. What had just happened here? What was he doing? If he had a lick of sense he would board *Reliance* tonight, sail back to Port Royal, and buy a simple, straightforward night's pleasure with one of the wenches at the Sea Nymph tavern.

Sail away on a ship he was not entirely sure that he had ever wanted, to lie in the arms of a stranger.

Or stay, and salvage a diamond from the shards of splintered glass that seemed to slice into everyone who brushed against Welbourne Plantation. After all that he had seen tonight, both from Grace and her parents, he was more convinced than ever that Grace Welbourne was an extraordinary woman. She had fire and courage and a keen mind, all miraculously intact despite Iolanthe and Edmund's bitter selfishness. He had spent far too much of his life dealing in treasure not to know a true prize when he saw one, and he had to admit that he was still enough of a pirate to seize it.

Giles ran a hand through his already tousled hair and, scratching his head, contemplated the hamper on the table. For the first time, he realized that the succulent smells of seared fish and fresh rum cake emanated from it, and he wondered if he could keep any of it down.

Five

Keyah had just finished cleaning the kitchen and was about to extinguish the last lamp before she picked up her lantern to leave. Dying embers emitted a dim glow from the big, round hearth and added heat to the already warm night air. When Keyah saw Grace and Matu, she stopped.

"Been a long time since me see you two come in de kitchen an' talk." She left the lamp lit, and moved her slight frame reluctantly toward the door, her round face curious.

Ignoring the cook, Matu led Grace into the lamplight. She drew the edge of her hand sharply against her nose, then tapped her finger against her ivory teeth.

Grace sighed. 'Twas rather pathetic, really. She did it so often that Matu actually had a standard sign to communicate when she thought that Grace was cutting off her own nose to spite Iolanthe. "It is not merely Iolanthe," Grace insisted.

Matu snorted and crossed her arms.

"Nothing's changed, Matu. All the old reasons still exist. I will not marry."

Matu held both hands out, side by side, one open, palm side up, the other in a fist. Another standard gesture.

"This is different? How so?" Grace demanded. "Do you really think that your sainted captain looks at you and sees not the color of your skin, just because he owns no slaves? He thinks the less of you for your dark hide, trust me."

Matu gave her head a frustrated shake. She gestured for a potbelly, the sign for Edward, then followed with the gesture for different.

"Father is different?" Grace asked.

Matu pointed to Grace, then mimed putting a ring on her left ring finger. Reversing the gestures, she pointed out of the still open kitchen door.

"What?" Grace asked.

Keyah moved forward, the light from her lantern preceding her. She had not yet left. "Me hear de maas and his 'ooman talkin' ova dem suppa. De maas sey if you don' marry dis mon, him a-go put you in de fields a mont an' see if dat don' clear you head."

Grace's eyes narrowed and glistened with tears that she refused to shed. Her father had promised never to sell her. He had said nothing about not making her a field hand. "Fine!" she shouted. "At least I will finally know where I stand!"

One moment Grace was standing there, full of defiance; the next, her face was on fire and she was seeing stars. Matu choked on a sob and stared at her open hand, obviously just as shocked at having slapped Grace as Grace was at having been slapped. One hand on her cheek, Grace stared at her lifelong nurse. In all the time they had known each other, Matu had never raised a hand to her.

In a small voice, reminiscent of the child she had once been, Grace whispered, "You hurt me."

"You tink dat hurt, Missy?" Keyah said, her voice hard

and unforgiving. "Try de lash on you pretty back. Her don' know nutten, Matu." With a disgusted "humph!" she trudged out the door, slamming it behind her.

Her head swimming, Grace watched her go. "Do you think that she knows?" A bitter laugh slipped through her lips. "Of course she knows. Father and his big secret. He thinks the slaves so stupid, as long as he does not say it outright, they won't figure it out. A planter would not put his white daughter in the fields."

Matu reached out and gently touched Grace's flaming cheek, a sad look in her dark eyes.

"What if I have a baby?" Grace asked. "What if 'tis too dark?"

Matu looked away and shrugged.

"He will kill me."

Matu shook her head. She made the boat on the sea gesture, followed by the sign for different.

"He is no different," Grace repeated, but she knew it was a lie. Captain Courtney had been horrified by the treatment of the Negroes. He had been moved by the suffering of an insignificant slave child. But that did not mean that he would willingly be married to a woman whose blood he knew to be tainted. A tear finally fell over her stinging cheek. "He would not kill me," she conceded, "but he would hate me."

Matu shrugged again. She mimed rocking a baby, then ran a finger over the light skin on Grace's arm.

Grace nodded. "Father says the same. He is sure that my babies will be light." But she put her head in her hands anyway.

She was such a coward! Other women endured it. They endured it over and over again, as evidenced by repeated pregnancies. Surely she could endure it, too. The thought made her shudder. How could she explain

it to Matu? Mayhap Matu knew better than she the pain
of the lash, but as far as Grace knew, Matu had never
had a man's hands on her. She did not know the shame,
the horror of having her body violated in the dark of
night. A whipping could be avoided, or if not, it ended
soon and did not occur again for a long time. Maybe
not at all, if one kept one's head down and did all that
one must.

Then again, had she not just learned that slaves were
not spared this indignity? Of course, her father would
never use her thus. Then again, shared blood had not
stopped her uncle. She sank onto the dirt floor and
wept, but Matu did not come to comfort her. Instead,
Grace heard the kitchen door open and close, and then
she was alone.

The front lawn was dark. Tiny points of light floated
in and out among the foliage of the gardens and drifted
toward the treetops, fireflies competing with stars that
shone above with a quarter moon. Before of Iolanthe
and Edward, the starry heavens descended to the horizon, where they disappeared into a vast void that
whispered seductively with the voice of the sea. Tree
frogs sang in relentless chirps, nearly drowning out the
tense, fervent, hushed tones of the master and mistress,
who stood facing one another on the grass.

"Damn you, Iolanthe," Edmund was saying, his voice
quietly enraged, "I am botching this whole affair badly
enough without your assistance."

"You are evil," Iolanthe hissed back, "evil to ply this
deception!"

"Oh, have you suddenly found a conscience, Iolanthe?"

Anger surged through Iolanthe's veins. How dare he? What had she ever done wrong? He was the one who had elevated the fruit of his sins to an unnatural place! And now, if Edmund had his way, Grace would marry a sea captain. She would travel the world, see places that Iolanthe had only dreamed of. It was so grossly unfair!

"God is working against you on this, Edmund. It is an abomination!"

Edmund shook his head. "Nay, God is on Grace's side here, if only she were not too stubborn to see. The man is already half in love with her."

Bile rose in Iolanthe's throat. "He does not know! If he knew, he would be repulsed."

Grabbing her arm, Edmund spun his wife to face him, though her features were muted in the darkness. "At least a black wench does not lie like a block of wood under a man. At least if *she* can't give a man a good fucking, she'll have the decency to fight and make it interesting!"

"I will *not* allow you to speak this way to me! I will not allow it!" Iolanthe stamped her foot in outrage. "You disgusting pig! You will be hoist by your own petard, Edmund. One way or another, that bitch will be of no use to you except as the laborer God meant her to be, and you will be left with nothing but your stinking little farm!"

His fingers dug even more cruelly into the arm he held. There would surely be marks in the morning, he thought with satisfaction. "If I am left with no heirs, Iolanthe, I swear that I will . . ." he spluttered a moment.

"What?" Iolanthe scoffed. "You may own the land, but my father owns everyone on it. Including you."

Edmund's voice became dangerously soft and smooth. "What a shame it would be if I had to write a sorrowful letter to your father. 'Dear *Monsieur* Renault, I regret to inform you that our dear Iolanthe has succumbed to yellow fever. Alas, it struck so very quickly that we were unable even to call for the doctor.' Of course, no one would fault my seeking a young bride after a year of mourning. Your last gift to me, the freedom to produce a dozen lily-white children with some fresh-faced girl with a bit of real fire in her."

Iolanthe turned to glare at him. "You had better make sure that she has money or slaves, because my father will take back all of his."

"It might very well be worth it."

"She will never marry him, Edmund. Grace will be your undoing, not I."

The food had smelled inviting enough, but Giles had only taken one bite. He thought of the child, of the poverty and despair to which he had been witness, and the perfectly seasoned fish seemed to turn to ashes in his mouth.

Exhaustion hit with a vengeance. He wanted to sleep, and then he wanted to wake and discover that the whole incident had just been a horrible nightmare. For the first time, he understood why Geoff's wife, Faith, could hardly stand the taste of sugar. She had spent months on a sugar plantation, one with a master and mistress far kinder than these two, but slavery was unavoidably brutal. He was coming to understand that as he had never understood it before.

Another glance in the hamper revealed a bottle of wine. Giles uncorked it and poured a glass. Lethe, he hoped, or at least something to take the edge off his pain. He heard the back door open, and Matu slipped inside, skirting the wall and clearly trying to avoid looking at him.

"Is there any hope?" he asked her.

Matu stopped. She stood just outside of the halo of light cast by the candles on the dining and tea tables, so he couldn't read her expression, but he did see her shrug.

"I would treat her well," Giles continued. "This place isn't good for her. I don't think 'tis good for anyone."

The woman shook her head, then continued on her way up the stairs to the second floor.

They would take her with them, Giles thought. Grace would have her maid, and her maid would have a taste of freedom. Maybe, in time, he would learn to communicate with Matu, and she would help him to understand the nature of the woman he had somehow determined to marry.

And why had he? Why was he so hell-bent on such a hastily set course? He shook his head and sipped his wine. Was he in love? Was this what it was like? Well, if it was, it was nothing like it had been between Geoff and Faith. 'Twould be a lie to say that he had not thought of Grace's smooth, golden skin beneath his hands, but neither was his desire to make her his own driven by lust. Conquest was not generally important to him, nor was he particularly drawn by her innocence. He had no doubt of her virtue, but she seemed worldly in a most disturbing way. Not sexually, but mayhap more like she knew better than he the nature of greed and evil.

More like, that was it. She had the face of an angel, but the look in her eyes was piercing, and the smile on her young, beautiful mouth too cynical for a woman of her age and station in life.

She would wed someone, someday. She was a woman,

and such was the natural order. It just seemed to him that she must not stay on a plantation, any plantation. He wanted to take her on the ocean, let it rock her, let the endless blue swallow up her pain as it so often had his. Mayhap he did not love the sea as deeply as many a sailor did, but it soothed one's hurts and put life into perspective. He closed his eyes and imagined her face relaxed, in awe of a fair day at sea, nothing in her eyes or her smile but delight. He envisioned what she might look like if ever she gazed at him as Faith did Geoff. It would be his undoing. At the mere thought, he felt his mouth go dry and form a ridiculous grin.

The rear door clicked softly open again, and he turned to see her as she stepped into the light. There was nothing of his daydream in her. Her dress was rumpled and dirty, her face swollen and tear stained, her eyes haunted, hunted, and there was no smile at all. She only stared at him as though she half-expected him to murder her where she stood.

"Grace? Are—are you all right?"

She shook her head.

Giles set his wine down and swallowed hard. "God, it's been a hell of a day," he said. Damn! That wasn't what he meant to say. He meant to apologize for how the subject of marriage had come up. He should have asked what he could do to help her. He should have said just about anything else.

One side of her mouth quirked in a ghost of her skeptical grin. "Aye," she agreed softly, "it has."

"I am sorry. I am sorry that I didn't have a chance to court you and propose to you properly. I am sorry that you're being placed under so much pressure. And I am sorry about your—sister."

Grace eyed his glass of wine, sitting on the table. It

would feel good, just now, to have its pleasant warmth in her veins, but she was fairly certain that if she were to swallow anything it would come right back up in a matter of seconds. "I am, too," she said.

"Can we start again?" he asked.

Grace regarded him for a moment. He looked like he had been through hell. He was a disheveled mess, and there was little of the confident commander in him. His shoulders were slumped, and there were faint shadows under his eyes. Again, she felt the need to touch him, to ease the lines of stress that creased his face with her fingertips. She actually clasped her hands before her to keep from doing it. How had this poor man been drawn into the vortex of her life? It would be as much for his benefit as hers if she sent him packing. And yet, when might she ever have such an opportunity again? Captain Courtney was a gentle man, one filled with compassion. He didn't lash out and hurt people, although God knew, the Welbourne family had caught him in their crossfire. He would have been within his rights to fire back.

"Are you sure that you want to start over?" she returned.

"How can the woman I saw in the slaves' quarters today possibly be the child of those two out there?" he asked, gesturing to the front door.

"How indeed? Tell me something, Captain, when did you decide that you wanted to marry me?"

Giles scratched his head. Women had a way of asking questions more volatile than a loaded flintlock. "I came here to get acquainted with you, perhaps to court you."

"Why?"

Now he shrugged. He was, after all, just a man. "I thought that you were beautiful."

She raised her eyebrows. "Ah."

"And intelligent and honest."

"Honest?"

"Your comment about delivering goods from plantations; and you laughed at your father."

"What?" Grace asked, shaking her head in confusion.

"Your father and his absurd comment about the French not eating regular meals."

She smiled slightly. "Oh, that. That makes me honest, does it? And that's important to you, honesty?"

Giles cleared his throat. Honesty was not always easy, and often, someone had to lead the way. "I think perhaps you have spent your life guarding what you say, and mayhap you think that means you are not honest, but the whole world is not like this place. At least, there are some people in the world to whom you can speak your mind."

"And I can speak so to you?"

"Aye, you can."

"And yet, you have not truly answered my question. You have told me that you came here to court me because I was beautiful. But you have not told me when you decided that you wanted to marry me, or for that matter, why."

Giles squeezed his eyes shut and pressed his fingers to them. He was so bloody tired. "Let us talk on the morrow."

Grace felt an insistent tug of pity inside her chest. The man looked like he was about to fall over. No one was going anywhere, and the morrow was soon enough. "Might you show me your ship, Captain? After breakfast, perhaps."

He nodded and gave her a brief smile. "I'd like that."

* * *

Matu had stripped down to her shift and now lay on her pallet on Grace's floor, where she had lain every night for twelve years. At first, she had been there to reassure a terrified child, but in time, each had become an indispensable source of comfort to the other. Once, the master had insisted that Matu leave after Grace was asleep, but the first night she had tried it, Grace had had a nightmare and woken up screaming in her empty chamber. She had begged Matu, pleaded with her never to leave her alone again, and Edmund, shaken by the little girl's terror, had nodded silently to the nursemaid.

Sometimes, she still could hardly believe her own luck in having been chosen for this position. The sacrifice that she had made for it had been a small one. It meant better food, better shelter, and oh, how she loved Falala's girl! Matu closed her eyes and remembered her beautiful mulatto friend, Falala, who had been thrilled when her perfect, golden daughter had been taken into the big house to be raised by the master. So thrilled, that she had gladly accepted her own fate. Of course, the mistress was angry. Of course, she had insisted that Falala be sold, but none of that had mattered to Falala. Her child would be free. There was no way that Matu would allow Grace to jeopardize that now.

Through the floorboards, Matu could hear the hushed voices of Grace and the sailor. He was a good man. She had sensed it the moment she had met him, and a slave's instincts had to be good. A Negro who couldn't read a white man was as good as dead.

No, this man was not color-blind, Grace was right about that, but who was? Would she love Grace as she did if the girl were not such a pretty gold, if she were as pasty white as Iolanthe? Matu wasn't sure.

She sat up when Grace slipped quietly into the dark room, but it took the young woman a while to notice.

"Oh, Matu! Did I wake you?"

Matu shook her head, but since she could barely see Grace, she doubted that Grace could see her. She got up and fumbled to help Grace out of her gown. How differently the day had gone than she had planned when she'd dressed Grace with such care earlier. Folding the dress carefully, she decided that it would have to be laundered on the morrow if it was to be saved from the day's dirt.

"Don't bother folding it," Grace murmured. "'Tis ruined. Leave it on the floor for now."

For all that Grace had a much better understanding of a slave's plight than most planters' daughters, the child was still so white. How many slaves wore the same set of rags day after day until they had nearly disintegrated from their bodies? And Grace thought that this gown was ruined. She was so careless with her possessions. Matu folded the gown anyway and set it at the foot of Grace's bed.

Grace sighed. "He's taking me to his ship tomorrow."

Matu smiled, and a little flame of hope lit inside of her. She had been appalled by her own actions when she had struck this child of her heart earlier, in the kitchen, but now it occurred to her that Grace had needed a bit of sense slapped into her. Guilt over a situation that was not of her making was a foolish reason to toss aside this chance at, not just freedom, but happiness. Matu would have sacrificed her tongue a hundred times over for such a chance. Falala, exquisite, cream-and-coffee-colored Falala, would have forfeited her life to give her child this chance. If Matu had to, she would beat the girl senseless to make her marry the sailor.

"Mind you," Grace told her, "I'm not making any promises, but he is kind and strong, and I would be the worst sort of liar if I didn't admit that I would love to leave this place and never come back."

Oh, baby, Matu thought to herself, *someday you gonna come back. You and dat mon, you a-go come back. Me feel it in me belly, an' Matu belly not eva wrong.*

But of course, she didn't say anything. Sometimes silence was a blessing.

Six

From time to time, Grace traveled in one of her father's rowboats. Several strong-shouldered slaves would row her family up the coast to a neighbor's plantation for a visit and then back again, just as they now rowed her and Giles to *Reliance*. But the ride today was different. For the very first time in her life, she was being rowed out to a tall ship, the kind that sailed clear across the ocean, and her heart pounded with the adventure of it.

Sitting next to her on the narrow wooden seat, Captain Courtney smiled and said, "We'll weigh anchor and sail out a ways—not all that far, but probably farther from shore than you've gone before."

Grace laughed, feeling a little foolish about her excitement. "Undoubtedly farther than I have gone before. Your ship looks big from the dock, but from so close, it is truly enormous!"

"Once you sail from the sight of land, it gets much smaller," he quipped.

His jest only confused Grace. "What do you mean?"

"No matter how big your ship is, the ocean is much bigger. When you leave sight of land for months, and then you finally spy a new and distant shore, well, you understand life a little better."

Grace looked up at him, her eyes wide with wonder, serious, but not cynical. "Do you?"

"Aye. Life is like that. Sometimes you sail with nothing to trust but the stars and your sextant and compass, nothing really tangible. You think of all of the miscalculations you might have made, and you wonder if you will die there in all that cold, blue emptiness. Then you see it, pale and indistinct on the horizon, another place, different people, a new experience. It all works out if you plot your course carefully."

"But if you are rash," Grace argued, "if you do miscalculate, then you *may* die out there. Or even if you do everything right, there are storms, and mutinies, and a dozen other things you might not have anticipated."

"Aye, all of that is true. Sometimes, a good sailor must act quickly, rely upon his instincts."

"Have you good instincts, Captain?"

"Call me Giles," he replied.

As he had many times in the past twenty-four hours, he wondered about his instincts. They were usually sound, but Geoff's were often better. What he wouldn't have done to have his friend here to talk to about all of this. Still, sometimes the weather had blown them off course, and Giles was as skilled as Geoff at finding their way again. He studied Grace, who was gazing at *Reliance* with the dancing, eager eyes of a child.

Damn! How very amusing it had all been when he was the one watching Geoff's world being turned upside down by a woman. Grace was blowing his ship off course with all of the unpredictability of a hurricane.

"How shall we get from this boat onto yours?" she asked.

His eyes widened. "My what?"

She pointed. "Your boat."

Giles gave her a look of mock indignation. "Pardon me, madam, but did you just call my *ship* a *boat*?"

She grinned mischievously and fluttered her lashes. "Forgive me, sir. How shall we get from my father's tiny little boat to your great big boat?"

He laughed and shook his head. "I daresay you'll have a bit more respect for my *boat* once we've hauled you up the side of it on a wooden plank tied to rope thrown over a pulley."

He had wondered if Grace would be afraid of being carried up the side of the ship by a rope, but she only sang out, "Really?" An eager grin spread across her face, and she jumped up and leaned forward, craning her neck to see the apparatus by which this would be done.

Unfortunately, her enthusiasm well-nigh capsized the rowboat. With a little shriek and flailing arms, she nearly went backwards into the water, but Giles caught her by the skirt and pulled her onto his lap.

"Careful, or you'll have us all in the drink and we'll not have our little adventure after all." He laughed, even as he admonished her.

Grace leapt from his lap, nearly upsetting the boat again. She didn't know which was the greater cause for her mortification, the fact that she had been on his lap or the fact that she had nearly drowned them all. But embarrassment couldn't hold up under the onslaught of excitement that she felt. She put a little more distance between them and beamed at him.

"It shall be just like a swing, only way up there!" She pointed to the ship's deck. "I had a swing when I was a little girl. 'Twas tied to a poinciana tree. As far as I was concerned, my father could never swing me high enough."

Giles laughed again. "I shouldn't like to swing overmuch in that thing. 'Twill send you right into the side of the ship, and you'll be back to the very fate I saved you from—waterlogged in the Caribbean Sea."

Still, when they reached the ship, and each pull from above carried her higher and higher, Grace squealed in delight. She didn't give an instant's thought to propriety as she climbed over the rail, hiking up her skirts and petticoats to show a shapely calf. Giles took a moment to appreciate the sight from the boat below her and smiled happily. For the first time since he had arrived at Welbourne Plantation, he felt like he was actually courting Grace.

Once she was firmly aboard, Grace stared up at the tall masts. There were two, something Captain Courtney (no, Giles, she corrected herself with a slight blush) had told her was true of Brigantines. He had said that his company owned two such ships, and that this one was new to them. There were also a series of ropes and rolls of canvas that stretched high above her. She watched several men climbing around up there, inspecting ropes and canvas. Her gaze was so intensely locked upon them that she didn't realize that she was stepping backwards until she tripped over a bucket and landed hard on her bottom, her skirts drenched in dirty water.

Giles hauled himself from the plank that had just pulled him up to the deck, vaulted the rail, and was at Grace's side. "Are you all right?" he asked, his eyes full of concern.

She gave him a wry grin. "Well, you see, I *wanted* to get wet one way or another today, and you kept *saving* me. I had to be creative."

He chuckled and lifted her into his arms. "Well, had you but said so . . ." he replied. He carried her to the rail and swung his arms back as though to hurl her overboard.

"Nay!" she squealed, hardly able to get the word past her convulsive laughter. She wrapped her arms around his neck and held on for dear life.

God, she smelled sweet, Giles thought. The heady scent of jasmine and the feel of her light but nicely rounded body begged an immediate response from him, and he had to fight the urge to kiss her long and hard.

Grace grinned up at him, pleased to see the lines on his face deepen with laughter rather than worry. Then his eyes left hers, dropping to her mouth, and she could feel the heat of his gaze nearly palpable upon her lips. Something happened inside of her, a peculiar pull that made her pulse quicken. Her smile faded, and she said primly, "You may put me down."

"Of course," Giles said, doing so. He cleared his throat and tried to clear his mind.

Averting her gaze, she resumed her scrutiny of the deck while she gathered her wits. 'Twas big, and peopled with very few crewmen. Seven, by her count. There was a hatch in the floor, leading to the lower decks, and stairs leading to a higher deck at the rear of the vessel. Up there was the great wheel used to steer the ship.

"May I?" she asked, pointing to the wheel.

"Certainly," Giles replied. He followed her up the steep stairs, both to protect her from taking a tumble and to enjoy the way her hips gently swung her skirts to and fro. He felt lighter, certainly more himself, here on familiar territory. He called out to his men, and the sails were unfurled to the brisk breeze. The canvas filled quickly, and in no time, they were gliding away from Welbourne and all its sorrows.

Grace didn't know which was more fascinating, the sea or the man. He was back to his former self, dark hair back in a tight queue, impeccably smooth shirt and jacket, boots polished. He called out orders, and the men instantly obeyed, but his voice was not harsh. Indeed, it was quite merry. He held no whip, and 'twas obvious that the men felt no fear. He shouted to a particularly young sailor to pick up the bucket and swab the puddle that Grace had left behind, but the lad was so entranced by the sight of Grace that he slipped in the water and went down as hard as she had.

"Poor sot," Giles said with a grin, "dazzled, no doubt, by the sight of you." Then he made a point of gazing at her with a thoroughly smitten air and tripping lightly over an imaginary impediment. She laughed softly and had to admit to herself that she rather liked being outrageously flattered.

She looked back down at the crew. "They all are white," Grace commented.

"Pardon?" Giles asked.

"Your men, they all are white. And there are so few. I saw many more than this when you were loading my father's goods, and he pointed out your Negroes. Where are they?"

Giles shook his head. "This was but a short pleasure trip. I've no need of a full crew. Doubtless the rest are carousing the streets of Port Royal, spending their wages on vice and sin."

"The Blacks, too?"

"Aye, them, too."

"Do they not fear that they will be sold as slaves while you are gone?"

"A free Black is not uncommon in Port Royal. Neither are slaves."

"I cannot imagine it."

"I doubt me you can. One has to see Port Royal to believe it." So it was on to more serious matters. "I've an apartment above my office. If you come back with me, I'll look for a house outside of town. Mayhap I can find something near Geoff and Faith."

Grace looked up at him, and some of the mistrust that seemed ever a part of her clouded her gaze. "Your business partner and his wife?"

"You'll love Faith," he assured her. "I'm sure you'll be fast friends."

All of her life, she had lived as a white woman, but Grace had never had a white friend. She'd had Matu, and Matu was all. She and Iolanthe had socialized with the wives and daughters of other planters, but she had never become close to any of them. Iolanthe had friends in Saint-Domingue to whom she wrote, and she often visited with the wife of their closest neighbor. They compared embroidery stitches and designs for gowns, exchanged beauty secrets, and complained about their husbands and servants. Grace felt a little sick. She did not want to become Iolanthe.

"*If* I go back with you," Grace said. "If I marry you."

"Would you like to take the wheel awhile?" Giles asked.

They had things to talk about, but the prospect of steering the huge ship was too tempting. She smiled at him and said, "Oh, aye! But what if I make some error?"

"We're not far out and the trip is short. At this point, you can't make a mistake of any consequence."

There was substantial wisdom in that statement. She grasped the wheel firmly and followed Giles's instructions, steering the ship this way and that for no reason but the fun of making it go where she wished. He stood close beside her, and she found that she didn't mind it at all. In fact, she found his presence reassuring, and she rather enjoyed the tingle she felt when his arm accidentally brushed against her shoulder or he leaned down to murmur a suggested course in her ear. The sun was warm and the breeze refreshing. Water glided under them in shades of sapphire and turquoise. The sky was a brilliant azure, though dark clouds gathered in the mountains above the plantation. In time, they would sweep to the sea.

After a while, Giles suggested that they let one of the men take the helm while he showed her the rest of the ship. They toured the galley, and he showed her the passengers' quarters. The lower deck was dark and the chambers cramped, every bit of space used with the greatest efficiency.

"Our other ship, *Destiny*, was never meant to take passengers, so it has no cabins but those for the first and second in command. Since we've started our business, we've taken a few travelers, but it means the first mate must give up his quarters to females. *Reliance* has no such problem."

"Then why did you buy it?"

Giles furrowed his brow. "*Reliance?*"

"Nay, *Destiny*. I should think you would want a vessel that was versatile and could be used for goods or passengers."

"Ah—we did not buy *Destiny*. At least, not until after we had commanded her. Back then, she belonged to the whole crew, more or less."

Grace frowned. "The ship had to belong to someone."

"She changed hands a few times. You see, Geoff and

I and our old shipmates—we took her. Then the two of us bought her from the rest."

"Took her? From whom? Why?"

"From another captain and crew. I haven't always been a merchant sailor, Grace. Geoff and I were privateers."

Grace's delicately curved jaw dropped and her eyes widened. "Privateers? Like pirates?"

"Nay! We didn't prey upon ships willy-nilly. We took Spanish ships for the King. And as for *Destiny*, the Spaniards we took her from had stolen her first from an English crew."

"But you didn't return her to her English captain?"

"He was dead, killed by the Spaniards."

"And what became of the Spanish captain?"

"We killed him."

Grace stared at him, thunderstruck. Then, to his astonishment, she burst into laughter. "Oh, Giles! For a moment I actually believed you!"

"And now you don't?"

"Oh please!" she shook her head vigorously. "You could never kill anyone."

A tiny muscle in his jaw ticked. "As you have oft pointed out, Grace, we do not know one another well at all." Turning away from her and retreating down a tight passageway, he called back, "There's not much to see in the hold, for 'tis empty, and 'twould not be proper to show you my quarters. Shall we go above again?"

Grace didn't move. She watched his retreating back and realized that he walked differently on a ship. Though the rocking should have sent him off balance, as it did her, he only moved more gracefully, rolling with the vessel. He paused at the hatch, looking back at her. In the shaft of illumination from the deck above, she

saw him in a different light. Shadows were cast downward over his face, and his gray eyes that had always
struck her as being soft now seemed hard as steel.

Was no one ever what they first appeared, she wondered.

Wordlessly, she joined him at the ladder, and he motioned her up first, following behind her. Once again,
they stood at the deck's rail, this time watching the
shore grow closer and closer. Grace knew that she was
going to have to be the one to patch the strained rift
that had come between them.

"You still have not told me when you decided to
marry me," she prompted.

He scanned the horizon and replied tersely, "Does it
matter?"

"Aye, it does."

He looked down at her, and now she fancied his eyes
more like the sea in a storm.

"Would you even consider marriage to a man with my
past? A 'pirate'?"

She cocked her head coyly. "Nay, not a pirate, but
mayhap a privateer. And I'll tell you something else,
Giles Courtney. I do know you. You may have killed
men, but every one weighs upon your conscience. I can
see it in your face." She set her hand on the deep blue
velvet of his sleeve. "We all do what we must to survive
in this world. We see things and do things that we pay
for a thousand times over."

"The Spanish are no more merciful to the English, I
assure you," he said laconically.

"I believe you."

He breathed deeply and spread his hands to encom-
pass the horizon. "There was so much freedom. I'd
served under captains I'd no love for, for so long. At

least with privateering came wealth. Geoff and I could swagger into Port Royal as men of means with all the liberty that confers."

"And yet you became merchants."

Giles grinned, and Grace breathed a sigh of relief. "Well, that was sort of Geoff's fault. 'Twas one of the conditions of a pardon he obtained when he was captured by the Spanish. Still, I was ready to settle down." He carelessly brushed a wispy ringlet away from her face where the wind had blown it; such a harmless, intimate gesture that Grace forgot to breathe. "You're right. I'm not a man to whom killing comes easily.

"And now, as for when I decided to marry you, 'twas in that hut, with that little girl." Both of their faces sobered at the memory. "That weighs heavily on *your* conscience. You don't see yourself as any different from them, and you suffer when they suffer."

She watched the shore, unwilling to look into his eyes. "And that is what you have always desired in a wife, a woman who thinks herself no better than a slave?"

"Good God, did it sound so to you? Heavens, no. I just feel ready. I've a ship of my own and a prosperous business, but a man wants more. There comes a time for a family."

"For heirs, you mean. Someone to inherit your business."

"Mayhap, if I've sons with any desire for it. But nay, that is not what I mean. I want children, not heirs. I want a wife, not a slave."

Oh, the words were all so right! Grace squeezed her eyes shut, then opened them into the dazzling sunlight. Keep your eyes wide open, you foolish girl, she scolded herself. "And you chose me because I am beautiful, intelligent, and honest."

"And modest," Giles teased. He took her chin in his hand, forcing her to look at him, and her eyes were full of the bitter cynicism he had come to expect. "You *are* all of those. But they were only the reasons I chose to call upon you. I asked your father for your hand because you deserve better than this. How old are you, Grace?"

"Twenty-two."

"Twenty-two. I am thirty. I live in a city of sin and villainy, have served on crews peopled by common criminals, and killed more men than I care to count, and yet I see more pain in your eyes than ever I have seen in my own mirror."

"And so you pity me?"

"We two, Grace, are in need of a balm. What say you? Together, might we make a corner of the world just as we wish it?"

Her heart ached with the beauty of the thought. Children, not heirs, not poppets, not dolls to be dressed prettily and then alternately coddled or abused, never knowing which or why. A wife, not a slave. She thought of her father and stepmother. Had Father ever wooed Iolanthe with such pretty words, or had they snapped and sniped at one another from the very beginning, each maneuvering for power?

And what if he did not say cruel and frightening things to her before he took her? Aye, in truth, Jacques's words were the true source of her terror. Giles was not a man to hurt people. He must hurt her, of course, to make the children that he wanted, but surely he would be as quick as possible and soothe her if she wept. And she was bigger now. She could bear a man's weight without suffocating, and would probably not tear so badly. In her mind, a silky French-accented voice whispered,

"It is a shame that the breaking can only be done once." Only once, and the worst of it would be over.

"Grace? I'm sorry. Have I said something to upset you?"

Giles's face, not Jacques's. Kind concern, not malicious delight. "N-nay. I'm fine. I think that we might make such a corner."

"Then you're saying . . ."

"Nay! I am not saying anything. Not yet. Only that I will think on it."

In all honesty, it was a relief to Giles that she had not said aye. On the deck of his ship, it felt like they were rushing, going too fast. Here, they had all the time in the world to get to know one another and to proceed carefully. But by the time they reached the plantation's bay, the clouds had begun to roll in, and he had to row swiftly to get them to shore and shelter ere the rain was upon them.

Seven

Edmund was mercifully absent from luncheon and, true to form, Iolanthe took her meal in her room. Grace and Giles ate and conversed loudly over the sound of the heavy, soaking cloudburst that hammered the roof of the house. There was little wind, so rain fell straight to the ground and the windows could be left open, letting in soft, gray light and cool air that smelled of wetness and plant life.

Giles told her about his business, and explained how his partner took his wife with him on long journeys so that they were not separated long. She learned that Giles would seldom travel beyond the New World, for voyages to Europe were most profitable if one stopped in Africa for slaves. This route made for a trade triangle that comprised most of the shipping in the region. Grace had to admire Giles and Geoff greatly for their willingness to sacrifice profits for principles.

"I judged you harshly," she admitted. "I condemned you for profiting from slavery, but as you said, it is unavoidable, and you surely do what you can."

Giles pushed away his plate and leaned back in his chair. A young serving girl whisked the plate away, and he watched her go out the back door to the kitchen. "Before I came here, it seemed like enough. I thought of how much my freedom means to me, and I thought that was the greatest suffering to slaves. You know, the idea that they could never be free. Until yesterday, I'd had no idea."

"I'm sure you didn't."

He leaned forward again, resting his elbows on the table and his chin in his hands. "Nay, that is a lie. I knew. Somewhat, I knew. I have seen slave ships unloaded. But I wasn't a slaver, so it had nothing to do with me. And yet, I see now that it has very much to do with me. I have watched and done nothing, and so it has everything to do with me."

"What can you do? What can I do?" Grace closed her eyes and drew in a deep breath of damp, clean air. They *could* make their own corner of the world. "I could sail with you?"

"I could teach you navigation. Faith navigates from time to time."

Faith. The woman she was supposed to make her friend. How would Grace ever fit into Giles Courtney's world? Mayhap she'd not have to. Mayhap they could sail all of the time. She had enjoyed herself on his ship. "I'd like that, I think, learning about the stars and the sea."

"And you might like to visit New England. 'Tis very different from here. I could take you in the fall." She watched his face light with enthusiasm and felt herself getting swept up with him. His voice eager, he continued, "You've never seen such color as the trees of New England in autumn. And we could go again in May, when the lilacs are blooming."

Grace smiled at him, and her heart began to beat a little faster. She thought of the wide, blue sky and the wind in her hair. She tried to imagine the trees he spoke of, then asked, "Might we see snow? I'd love to see snow."

Giles laughed. "Not on a ship, you wouldn't. But mayhap we could spend a little time in New England in winter. I've friends around Boston." He reached across the table and took her hand in his, a natural gesture for a man courting a woman.

Grace felt her carefree elation slip away. His touch was warm and gentle, but the time would come when that grasp would become rough, when he would pin her hands at her sides and press her into a mattress with all of his weight. Her mouth went dry as cotton, and it took tremendous willpower not to pull her hand away from him. Stop being such an infant, she scolded herself. Everything has a price. Everything. She did her best to smile at him and to keep her hand relaxed in his.

He smiled back, lifted that hand to his lips, and kissed her fingertips so softly and gently that she felt the butterfly touch of his breath more than the kiss itself. Hope seemed to spread from that one touch through her whole body. Her own lips tingled at thought of his mouth doing there what it had done to her fingers. He was so different, she thought, so utterly different from Jacques. It would be all right. It had to be. It had to be, because she was about to steer her ship into the open sea and give this man something that she had only ever given to Matu—her trust.

"I have never been on an adventure before, Giles, but I think that it is high time, and I think that there should be no greater adventure than marrying you."

Giles missed his next breath. A strange feeling, some exhilarating combination of elation and panic gripped him. When he had taken her hand, he had been somehow certain that he had offended her, but then she had smiled at him. And then, in an instant, he had become engaged. He looked at her and saw what he had longed to see. Her gaze was open; there was no suspicion, no cynical reserve. This beautiful, amazing creature was going to be his wife.

Oh, God, his *wife*. What if she became seasick? What if she hated sailing and had to stay in Jamaica? What if she never came to love him, and she met some merchant while he was away? What if he never came to love her, and then he met some woman who was better suited to him?

What if he didn't marry her, and she married a planter instead? What if she lived the rest of her life surrounded by a misery she couldn't ignore and that chipped away at her incredibly resilient spirit?

What if waking to her every morning was going to become the most important thing in his life?

"Giles?" she asked. "Are you all right? You still want to marry me, do you not?"

He felt a little hitch in his chest at the look of doubt and uncertainty that had clouded her face. He hadn't meant to do that, make her doubt him. "Aye, Grace, aye, I do."

He stood, pulling her up from her seat at the table and drawing her close. Grace felt a little like she did when she stood at the edge of one of the limestone cliffs that skirted the sea in places along the shore. The water below was clear and beautiful, but that eased not her fear of the height. Awaiting the touch of Giles's lips to hers was very much the same.

But it never came. The front door swung back on its hinges, accompanied by the sound of Edmund's voice cursing a broken gear in the sugar mill. He stopped in the doorway, his clothes and hair dripping rainwater onto the wooden floor, his eyes devouring the sight of his daughter in Giles's arms. "Damn me!" he cried, his mouth splitting into a broad grin. "Three weeks from Sunday, is it?"

Giles looked down at Grace, and before she could give herself a chance to rethink it, she nodded and said, "Three weeks from Sunday."

By the end of those three weeks, Grace was nearly convinced that she had dreamed it all. Giles had stayed that night, but he had left the next morning, and now it was Saturday, the day before her wedding, and he had yet to return. She had received a brief note that he was delayed by business, but he had promised to have it resolved in time.

Meanwhile, she and Matu had been packing her things and sharing their excitement about all of the adventures that awaited them. Grace glanced guiltily at a trunk that Matu had neatly packed an hour before. Now, it had been thoroughly rummaged through in pursuit of the pair of stockings that matched her gown and that had been mistakenly tucked into the trunk. Really, she could have worn the white ones that she had found almost immediately. White went with everything, didn't it? But she was sure that he would be arriving today. He and his friends couldn't arrive tomorrow, could they? Not the day *of* the wedding. Nay, surely not. Where were her shoes? She started to walk over to the second trunk to dig for them there, but tripped on the way, nearly landing on her knees.

She started to mutter a word that would have sent Matu into a flurry of admonishing gestures had she been there, but when Grace looked down and found her errant shoes, she had to laugh at herself. Good heavens, if she was such a bundle of nerves today, in what state would the morrow find her?

While they had packed, Matu had been very clear in

communicating that the one long sea voyage she had
taken in her life, the one that had delivered her into slavery, was the only one she intended to take. When Grace
and Giles journeyed afar, she would stay behind and keep
their home in order. It was a given that she would not be
Grace and Giles's slave, but she wanted to stay with them,
and Grace wanted desperately to have Matu with her.
From this point on, Matu would be the only one in her
life who knew the awful truth, and it wasn't a burden
Grace wanted to bear alone. It gnawed at her insides.
Giles was marrying her for her honesty, and there would
be so many lies of omission between them.

She managed to spill half a bottle of perfume down
her bodice just as her father called up the stairs to tell
her that *Reliance* had returned. This time the forbidden
word did slip through her lips. There was no time to
change. With no remorse for the disarray, she delved
into the second trunk to find a lace-edged handkerchief
and wipe as much of the oil away as she could. Then she
leaned out of her window into the rear courtyard, waving her hand in front of her breast. Matu and Keyah
were standing in the kitchen doorway, and they both
looked up at her with puzzled frowns.

"You a-go faint, Missy?" Keyah called up.

Matu snorted and shook her head. Grace had never
been one to swoon.

"Nay, nay," Grace proclaimed. "Just a little mishap
with some perfume."

Matu started back toward the house, but Grace waved
her back. "I must greet Giles and his friends. There's
nothing for this now. I think I cleaned up most of it."
She took a deep breath and nearly gagged on the overwhelming scent of jasmine, but smiled in spite of it.
"Aye, 'tis fine," she reassured her maid.

Still fanning her breast, Grace walked into the hallway and headed toward the stairs, almost glad for the minor catastrophe that had taken her mind off of her doubts. She would be a good wife. She would be cheerful and a helpmate, everything that Iolanthe was not.

Iolanthe. Grace paused, straightening her back and squaring her shoulders at the thought of her step-mother. The woman had been so incensed at the news of Grace's impending marriage that she had refused to leave her room or speak to anyone but the poor slave who was assigned to be her maid. The unfortunate girl had been slapped and had her ears boxed repeatedly as Iolanthe had given vent to her impotent rage. It was all a mystery to Grace. Of course, she knew that Iolanthe felt that it was wrong to deceive Giles, but 'twas hard to believe that she was so angry on behalf of a near stranger. One would have thought that Iolanthe would be glad to be rid of Grace.

Those thoughts, too, were banished. She had enough to deal with today. Not only was it the eve of her wedding, but she was to meet Giles's friends. One of the reasons that he had been delayed was that he and his partner had been juggling their shipments so that Geoff and Faith could attend the wedding. She knew not exactly why, but she was nearly as anxious about meeting them as she was about getting married.

She had envisioned going to meet them at the dock but, seized by an uncharacteristic bout of cowardice, she had waited in her room, making a shambles of things and peering apprehensively into her mirror. Belatedly she thought that mayhap she should have had Matu use her special hairdressing on her hair. For Giles, she had left it loosely pinned into a cascade of curls, but mayhap this Faith woman would think her an unstylish bumpkin.

Even from the top of the stairs, Grace heard Giles's voice drift through the open windows at the front. He laughed, and his voice was joined by her father's and another man's. Tinkling like a merry undercurrent, a woman laughed with them.

It would be inexcusably rude not to greet them. With a deep, jasmine-suffused breath, she descended the stairs, swept through the keeping room, and opened the front door to meet her fiancé and his entourage. There were but the four of them, and of course she knew Giles and her father, so she needed no introductions to know who was whom. Geoffrey Hampton was a good-looking man, tall and broad, but he lacked Giles's crisp, polished appeal. His hair hung loose about a face that was hard and vaguely intimidating.

She didn't even realize how tense she had been until her eyes met Giles's and her body slowly relaxed. Giles looked far more like a ship's captain. His grooming was, as always, impeccable, his face soft and smiling. He was the kind of man who inspired love and loyalty, not fear. She smiled back at him and told herself for the hundredth time that everything was going to be fine.

Then she set eyes on Faith, and her trepidation returned full force. She had never seen a woman so white in all her life. White. Everything about her was white. Her hair was silvery blonde, her skin alabaster. She very nearly made Iolanthe look African. On one hip, she balanced a baby as pale as she. How could Giles see her and Grace side by side without suddenly realizing that Grace was so very dark? How could he look at Faith's slim, perfect nose and not see that hers was too broad? How could she ever be friends with a woman like this?

And then Faith smiled, and the smile lit her blue-green eyes. "Grace," she said. "I know you must be. I'd know you among a crowd in Port Royal, Giles has painted you so clearly in our minds." She stepped forward as if to embrace Grace, but the little boy got in the way. He threw his arms around his mother's neck and then plugged his nose, gazing distastefully at Grace. *The perfume, drat it all.*

Grace swallowed hard and smiled back, though she knew hers was not so open a greeting. "He's told me much about you, as well. How nice to finally meet you."

Geoff strode forward and swept her hand up in his, gallantly bending over it with a bow. To his credit, he did a fair job of masking his reaction to the smell, merely blinking a few times and softly clearing his throat. "Giles told me he'd found him a wench as fair as my Faith, but I'd not believed it 'til now."

Grace furrowed her brow in confusion. Fair? Oh, pretty. Then she frowned. A wench was an African woman.

Giles gave Geoff a stern look, but the twinkle in his eyes belied the scowl. "You'll keep a civil tongue in your head when you speak of my wife."

Faith shook her head. "Forgive him. For what 'tis worth, he calls me a wench, too."

Grace looked at her father, her eyes wide with confusion, and Edmund explained, "We've naught but ladies and Africans here. I don't think that Grace has ever heard the term wench but that it meant a slave girl." He gave Grace a sharp look. "Heavens, girl, have you been rolling in the gardens?"

Grace flushed with embarrassment. "A small dispute with a bottle of perfume."

Faith shook her head sympathetically. "I know just what you mean. The stopper gets stuck and when it finally comes loose, you've half the bottle on you."

"I'd not meant to insult you earlier," Geoff interrupted. "Faith puts up with too much from me."

Faith laughed and wrapped her free arm around her husband's waist and squeezed. It was a natural, easy gesture, and Grace continued to stare, her eyes like saucers. She had never seen Iolanthe touch her father in any way. She had never seen other planters' wives or even slave women touch men in such a manner. Geoff was huge, nearly a foot taller than Faith and surely a hundred pounds heavier, and yet she embraced him as though it were her right. As though *he* belonged to *her*, and not the other way 'round.

Giles moved into the cloud of Grace's perfume to take both of her hands in his. They were cold, and he had the feeling she had been nervous about his return. Now, she looked at him with green eyes filled with awe and wonder, and it hit him yet again how little he knew her. Whatever was going through her mind just now? Had she been worried that he had changed his mind? Had she been on the verge of changing hers?

"Forgive me for not making it back sooner," he said. "Geoff has to go to Tortuga soon after the wedding, so we had a number of matters to settle first."

Grace turned to Faith. "Will you and your son go with him? Giles told me that the two of you travel together, but do you not worry about a child so young on a ship?"

"Actually," Faith answered, "I'll be staying at home this time."

Giles gave Geoff a puzzled look. "You never mentioned that." Turning to Faith, he added, "Will you be all right alone? Grace and I could stay with you."

She grinned slightly. "That won't be necessary. Besides, I've been a newlywed. You two shall need time alone."

"I'll leave one of my men behind with her. I won't be more than a week," Geoff explained.

Giles still didn't look satisfied. "If you're sure." To Faith, he said, "I'm surprised you're staying behind, though."

"A few hours' journey up the coast, above deck, wasn't so bad, but I don't think I'm up to the usual first few days of seasickness just now."

Comprehension dawned on Giles's face, and he laughed out loud. "Never say it! A bit queasier than usual are you, Faith? Geoff, why didn't you tell me before?"

Geoff laughed, too. "I'd not wanted to overshadow your big day. Still, now the cat's out of the bag, we've more than enough to celebrate."

Edmund beamed and shook Geoff's hand vigorously. "Congratulations! And you've this fine son, too. See what you have to look forward to, my dear?" he addressed this last to Grace.

Grace was still overwhelmed. Not only was Faith strikingly white, she was pregnant. The thought left Grace feeling distinctly uncomfortable.

Faith gestured Grace to one side and said, "Might you have a room I can take little Jonathan to? He had a bit of bread and some banana on the ship, but he hasn't yet nursed."

Grace nodded and said, "Come inside. I'll have my maid show you to my room."

"Oh, nay!" Faith protested. "Come with me. I've so wanted to meet you. We'll leave the men to their crude bragging about beddings and babies and you can tell me all about yourself."

"Weddings," Grace corrected.

"What?"

"Weddings. You said 'beddings.'"

Faith only smiled. "Ah, aye, well I'm sure it is *we* who will talk about the wedding. Come, come. I can't wait to hear the plans."

Grace led the way, but her mind tumbled all over itself. Perhaps there was no distinction at all between men. Mayhap they were all the same when it came to mating. Had she been deluding herself to believe that Giles was any different? Then again, there might well be vast differences. She looked at Faith, this woman who touched her husband easily and smiled about being pregnant, and she wished that she could ask her about these things.

Faith settled herself onto Grace's bed and carelessly unlaced her bodice. She wore a gown of blue cotton. Its style was simple, but the cut was elegant and the fabric of the highest quality. The bodice laced up the front, obviously for convenience, as she pushed one side down and slid her shift down with it. The little boy, perhaps a year or so old, lay himself down in the crook of his mother's arm and latched onto her breast with cuddly contentment.

Grace was hard-pressed to understand her own discomfort. She had certainly seen African women nurse their children. But this was so different, and not just because of their white-blond hair and pale skin. There was a grim, desperate functionality to the feeding of a slave child. Mothers did not bond to their children, because it was so very unlikely that the babes would live long enough to be weaned. The sight of Faith and her son was so intimate that Grace felt herself blush.

Faith sighed and said, "This will be you in no time. You and Giles will be so happy together, I just know it."

Grace wished that she were as confident.

* * *

Iolanthe felt better than she had in days. When Edmund had first informed her that Grace would indeed be marrying Captain Courtney, she had been violently ill. She hadn't even been able to order a whipping, for she knew it would only feed the burning anger inside of her. She had to be able to inflict the pain herself. But each slap delivered to the face of her maid had simply made her crave more.

She had managed to get two letters, written out of sheer desperation, to some neighbors who were traveling to Port Royal, but time was tight. It was entirely possible that no ships were headed for Saint-Domingue soon enough for her missive to Jacques to do any good, and she'd no way of knowing whether the other had found its mark. Her only hope hung by a slender thread.

Then she had come upon her brilliant idea. True, there would be no physical violence involved, but the emotional anguish it was sure to cause would appease her somewhat. Her heart pounded and her cheeks were flushed a fetching shade of pink. She smiled at her own reflection in her vanity mirror, ignoring her besmirched teeth. On top of her delicious plans, she was wearing one of her newest gowns and her hair was perfect, and downstairs was a couple who had traveled the world and would know a woman of culture and refinement when they saw one.

Better still, when Iolanthe made her entrance from the stairs, Grace was nowhere to be seen. There were only Edmund, Captain Courtney, and another man chatting comfortably in the upholstered chairs in the keeping room. Captain Courtney saw her first and hastened to his feet, and Iolanthe's elation was pierced by the wretched, wretched jealousy that had been consuming her for over a fortnight. Even as the other men rose to greet her, she thought of Grace traveling abroad and being showered with treasures from all over the world, and it took careful effort to keep her face serene and to smile politely. The plan, she reminded herself. Grace would not have all of these things without a price.

The new gentleman made her a courtly bow. "Mistress Welbourne, I should have known that so fair a daughter must have sprung from great beauty to begin with."

For a moment, Iolanthe saw everything through a red haze. How dare he? How dare he spoil her grand entrance and render her fabulous gown a waste with such a careless comment? She wanted to scream, "That beast is not my child!" But Edmund would have killed her for that, quite literally, so she curtsied and murmured her thanks.

There was a commotion behind her as Grace led an exquisite woman down the stairs. Introductions were made, and Mistress Hampton said something about Grace's maid remaining upstairs to watch over a baby while he slept in Grace's bed. That wouldn't do at all. Iolanthe needed Matu down here. She must be present when Iolanthe played her trump card.

"Your gown is truly elegant," Mistress Hampton said, distracting her momentarily from her dilemma. "My aunt designs her own gowns, and she would love to see this creation."

Iolanthe eyed her visitor. The woman knew quality, although she had no sense of style or flair. Still, even Iolanthe had to admit that her looks rendered the plainness of her dress immaterial.

"Thank you. My dressmaker is in Paris. He sends fashion dolls to me each season from which to select. Would you take tea? Grace, send for another wench to look after the baby. I want Matu to serve us."

"I'm sure Keyah has someone in the kitchen who can serve tea," Grace replied.

Iolanthe leveled a frosty look at the girl. Nothing, *nothing* could be done without an argument. Suddenly a pungent wave of jasmine filled Iolanthe's nostrils. She smiled archly. "Rather more perfume than usual, Grace. Did you fear that your fiancé would smell something amiss? I want Matu here, now," she repeated, and there was a subtle warning to her tone.

She could tell by the stubborn set of Grace's face and the stiffening in her shoulders that Grace wanted to defy her, but then she glanced at their guests and seemed to decide that it wasn't worth making a scene.

"Very well," Grace said tightly before she stalked out the back door to fetch another servant.

Edmund pulled chairs away from the dining table so that there would be more seats in the sitting area. Iolanthe tried very hard to concentrate on the small-talk that drifted around her, but she felt giddy, nearly drunk, and she hardly dared to speak for fear that she would begin to giggle.

At last, Grace returned and another servant took Matu's place with the babe, sending Matu downstairs to fetch tea. "Matu," Iolanthe called, "do make sure that Keyah uses fresh cake. I know there was some left from yesterday, but we cannot serve day-old delicacies to our guests." She turned to Mistress Hampton and said, "Our Matu is such a faithful servant. I do not know what I would do without her."

"I'm sure you'll miss her terribly," Mistress Hampton returned kindly.

Iolanthe smiled beatifically. "Whatever do you mean? Matu is not going anywhere."

Eight

Grace stood up, her guests forgotten, cold fear clenching at her stomach. "What are you saying? Matu is coming with Giles and me. She is *my* maid."

"My, my," Iolanthe chided softly. "Such possessiveness from one who professes an aversion to slavery."

"Iolanthe . . ." Edmund warned.

"What?" she replied, her brown eyes wide. "I am only trying to set to rights a slight misunderstanding." She gazed around at Giles and his friends, her hands wide in supplication. "You see, Matu is one of many slaves that my father has sent here to work, but they are an indefinite loan. My father retains full ownership. Matu belongs to him, not us. I can hardly send her away without his consent."

Matu stood, frozen, her eyes never leaving Iolanthe, and Grace rushed to her side, firmly clasping her hand.

"You cannot do this," she spat at Iolanthe.

Edmund laughed uncomfortably. "Iolanthe is right about this being a small misunderstanding. I will write to *Monsieur* Renault immediately and gain his consent."

Grace shivered at the malicious smile that curved her stepmother's mouth. There were times that she and her brother looked so alike.

"You may try, but my father has never approved of

people becoming too enamored of their slaves. It breaks down discipline throughout. I cannot imagine that he will allow you to merely give away one of his Africans, especially to people who will only free her."

Giles cleared his throat, gaining everyone's attention. "A simple enough matter to clear up. How much would your father consider fair compensation?"

"Perhaps not so simple. One of the stipulations when my father loans slaves to my husband is that he cannot sell one without my approval. Is this not so, Edmund?"

Edmund had ceased to try to smooth things over with a smile and a false chuckle. He glared at his wife and said, "I am certain that I can persuade you to cooperate."

"She is invaluable, Edmund. I simply cannot run this household without her."

Faith rose, opening her mouth to speak, but Geoff shook his head. "Would you mind terribly if Faith and I took a walk?" he asked.

Giles glanced at his friend in gratitude. This was to be his family. It was his problem. "We'll catch up to you later," he replied.

"I am so sorry," Iolanthe protested. "How rude of us to discuss family business in front of guests. But since there is nothing further to be said, please stay. Matu, the tea."

"Really, we're not hungry just yet," Geoff answered, and he ushered his wife, whose face was flushed and whose eyes blazed, out the front door.

Giles took a deep breath and plunged ahead. "Mistress Welbourne, I must be frank. I realize that there is some animosity between you and Grace, and I suppose it is really none of my business."

"I do not suppose it is," Iolanthe agreed.

"Nonetheless, this ploy is spiteful and malicious . . ."

"And you will not get away with it!" Grace interrupted.

"Nay," Giles continued, "you will not. Your father is a businessman. I will pay five times the acceptable rate for a Negro woman in her prime, although we both know that Matu is far older than most slaves ever become."

"I will not permit the sale," Iolanthe argued.

"You vindictive little . . ." Edmund muttered under his breath.

Iolanthe turned on him. "Perhaps it is wrong to keep Giles out of this. He is, after all, nearly family. Maybe he should know why Grace and I are ever at odds."

Matu pulled her hand from Grace's, shaking her head. Both hands flat, palms down, she pressed her hands downward: "Settle down. Peace."

"I should think it perfectly obvious," Edmund bellowed. "A slave trader's daughter who allowed her child to become too close to her nursemaid. If you had been a more involved mother, Matu would never have come between you." He turned to Giles, a touch of panic in his eyes. "'Tis old history, you see. Matu is the point of contention."

Matu nodded emphatically, pointing to herself and then to Edmund and Iolanthe.

"You will not stay!" Grace cried. "Nay, you will not!" She reached for Matu, who stepped away, shaking her head and putting up her hands to ward Grace off. Grace faced her stepmother and recognized all too well the euphoric smile, the breathlessness, the unabashed joy taken in another's pain. Though she'd have given anything to withhold the satisfaction it would give Iolanthe, Grace's eyes filled with angry tears. "You bitch! You horrible, spiteful bitch! I'll not marry him! There, are you happy now? But so help me, you will pay! I will make your life a living hell."

"Grace," Giles interjected, "don't be rash. We'll mend this, we will. Mister Welbourne, surely your father-in-law will overlook the technicality if the price is right."

"He may, but I will not," Iolanthe insisted. She and her husband exchanged hard looks, glaring into each other's eyes. In the end, 'twas Edmund who looked away first.

Matu's shoulders dropped and her face tightened in defeat as she gestured that she would go and get tea.

"Nay!" Grace screamed, and Iolanthe quivered at the sound.

It struck Giles that the pleasure on the woman's face was almost sexual, and nausea rippled through him. The entire exchange did nothing but reinforce his belief that Welbourne Plantation was a sick place, and that he was absolutely right in taking Grace far away from it.

Grace grabbed Matu's arm. "I'll not leave you. I'll not marry him. I'll stay with you, Matu."

Matu wrenched herself free, then took Grace's arm in her fierce grip, causing the girl to wince. Never mind that Matu was a small woman; she had hauled buckets of water and heavily laden serving trays nearly her entire life, and there was tremendous power in her hands. She towed Grace through the back door, into the rear courtyard, and spun her around. The glaring afternoon sun shone full on her face as she opened her mouth wide and waggled the stump that remained of her tongue. Then she shoved Grace hard against the side of the house, pointing first into her open mouth, then to Grace. She untied the gathered neck of her simple garment, pulling it to her waist and turning her back. It was mangled by thick, twisted, discolored keloids, severe scarring that was common to African skin and made all the worse by brutal whippings. Clutching the fabric to her breasts, she spun back to Grace, pointing again to herself, then the girl before slipping her dress back up.

The message was crystal clear: "For you. All of this I have suffered for you." Then she pointed back to the house, gestured for the boat on the ocean, and finally grabbed Grace's hand and pointed to her ring finger.

Grace stared at her, shaking her head. "I cannot."

But she would. She had to. Because next Matu did something that Grace had never seen her do before. Giant tears welled up in Matu's dark eyes, spilling over her leathery face. Her lips pulled into a wide, anguished line. She patted Grace's chest and then her own, shrugging. A question.

"Of course I love you, Matu. With all my heart."

Boat. Ring finger. "Marry him."

"But . . ."

Matu placed her fingers to Grace's lips. Boat. Ring finger.

"Oh, God," Grace moaned.

The two women wrapped their arms around each other and wept until they were spent and there was nothing left to do but for Matu to fetch tea and for Grace to return to the keeping room. Once there, she was surprised to see that Giles was alone.

"Your parents are upstairs, and I thought it would be better if I left you two alone for a while," he said. His face was drawn and haggard, like it had been the day he had tended to the sick child with her.

She wiped the back of her hand across her eyes, dashing away the last of the tears. "Thank you."

"I'll not let this happen," he assured her. "There has

to be a way around it. We'll steal her if we have to. It shouldn't be that difficult."

Grace drew a deep breath. "Let us think on it. She's not going anywhere. We will come back for her when we figure out what to do."

"Come back? Then, you've decided to—" he hardly dared say it. She might very well say nay.

"Aye, Giles. I decided to marry you three weeks ago. Naught has changed that. It was my grief talking." Her voice was flat, her eyes dull.

He pulled her to him and wrapped his arms around her. "I'll not let you suffer long, Grace. I swear, you will have your maid."

Fresh tears welled in Grace's eyes, and she held still, letting his strength and warmth infuse her. The comfort that he offered went right through to her bones. "It is not my suffering that matters. And she is not my maid. She is simply Matu."

He nodded. "And Matu will be free. Someday. I swear it."

But how, he wondered, even as he held her close. When had he begun to make promises he'd no idea how to keep? Probably when he had become the sort of man who sailed headlong into a marriage when he'd been given every sign that these were turbulent waters.

The wedding was a simple one, the guests few. The Church of England had arrived at the island of Jamaica when the British had seized it from the Spanish decades before, but plantations were spread far and wide. A single church, not much larger than a chapel, served several families and whatever white workers cared to keep up their religion. Right after the morning service, a handful of neighbors stayed to attend the marriage of Edmund Welbourne's daughter, and Giles's witnesses numbered but two.

Standing at the altar in her best gown of saffron damask, Grace promised to honor and obey the stranger next to her, placing all her trust in the compassion that she had seen him display in their short time together. Giles, resplendent in a velvet jacket and lace cravat, swore to keep her in sickness and in health, wondering if any amount of time could heal her wounded heart.

An inauspicious beginning, but considering how often near-strangers wed, 'twas more than many had when they exchanged these vows. The priest pronounced them man and wife, and Giles brushed her lips with his, so fast that she had no time to react. The contact was minimal, innocuous, chaste. The contract was sealed. As inconspicuously as possible, both bride and groom wiped their palms against their wedding finery.

Slaves with hampers full of food set up trestle tables in the churchyard for an early supper in celebration of the newlyweds. The air was rich with the smells of roast chicken, pumpkin soup, and sweet rum raisin cake. Giles stood in a circle of men, taking a healthy dose of good-natured back pounding and jokes filled with innuendo. Planters' wives who had crossed the ocean from England filled Grace's ears with an abundance of advice for sea travel. Matu worked silently with the other slaves, avoiding the Whites.

Iolanthe stood apart from her family. One of the planters' wives broke away from the group surrounding Grace and smiled as she walked in Iolanthe's direction.

"Mistress Welbourne," the woman said, "how pleased

you and your husband must be. Grace looks beautiful,
radiant, of course. Did your dressmaker design the
gown?"

Iolanthe sneered unpleasantly. "The design is English, not French. For myself, I do not think that yellow
becomes her. I suppose the marriage itself is a blessing.
The girl will be at sea or in Port Royal, too far away to
make a nuisance of herself."

The woman tried to laugh lightly, as though Iolanthe's words had been spoken in jest, but with an uneasy
curtsey, she drifted back toward the group surrounding
Grace.

Edmund was as jovial and elated as any bride's father
might be. But as conventional as his tipsy hospitality was,
against the hostility between bride and mother and the
apprehension between bride and groom, he seemed
out of place. The guests departed for their own farms
well in advance of twilight. In fact, there was yet light remaining when the wedding party returned to the
plantation, and Giles helped his bride alight from the
carriage.

"I thought," he said to her, "if it suits you, that we
might spend the night on board *Reliance*, in my cabin."

Grace's knees buckled slightly under her damask
skirts. On the one hand, she wanted Matu close, on the
other, she could hardly call out to her in the night. She
was a woman now, a married woman, not a child. And if
she did disgrace herself, did cry out, she did not want
Iolanthe to bear witness to her shame. She nodded
mutely, unable to trust her voice.

Giles explained the arrangement to Edmund, who
hesitated a moment, but then squeezed his daughter's
hand reassuringly and bade her good night at the dock.
Reliance had sent one of her own rowboats to fetch

them, and Geoff, Faith, and little Jonathan came too, so they all simply stayed in the tiny craft while it was hauled up to the main deck. Where Grace had once climbed eagerly over the rail to see the ship, she now required Giles's strength to help her over.

Her mouth was dry and tasted of stale wine, drunk too long ago to lend her any courage. *I must be brave and quiet, brave and quiet.* Her uncle's past words were a litany, chanted in her mind by the voice of a ten-year-old girl.

Giles held a lantern aloft as he led her down the ladder below deck, then through the narrow passage with the Hamptons close behind. The group paused between two doors, one on each side of the corridor, and each man set his hand to the latch of one of the portals, though Geoff had the other hand full supporting his sleeping son on his shoulder. Geoff winked at Giles, who took a deep, shaky breath, and it suddenly occurred to Grace that he looked nervous, too. It helped to think that perhaps he was no more eager for this than she.

A small hand slipped inside hers and Grace caught the scent of lavender. Faith gave her hand a gentle squeeze. "'Twill be all right," she whispered. "Giles is a good man, and kind. You've naught to fear."

But it felt like Grace's mouth was glued shut, it was so dry. She only nodded, then followed her husband into his cabin.

It was such a small space, and there seemed to be no real signs that anyone lived there. The bed was neatly made, without so much as a wrinkle to suggest that it had ever been sat upon or occupied. There was a sturdy trunk at the foot of it, but no other personal effects in the room, not even an inkwell on the desk or a jacket draped over the chair. There were a number of cupboards, but their contents were a mystery.

She thought of her own room, its vanity usually scattered with combs and trinkets. Matu tidied up behind her, but Grace was ever tripping over her own shoes, and more often than not she forgot to close her wardrobe, leaving her skirts and petticoats spilling out. She and Giles had so much to learn about each other.

"Would you rather I left you alone to ready yourself for bed?" he asked softly.

She started to say aye, but to her dismay, she realized that her gown laced up the back and Matu was not there to help her. "I can't . . ." she choked. Unable to finish, she simply turned her back to him. Attempting speech again she mumbled, "Matu usually . . ." but it was futile.

"Ah," Giles said, and she could almost hear a little smile in his voice.

She felt his hands tug gently, deftly at the lacing that bound her bodice. They were quick and unerring, as though they had performed just such a task countless other times.

"Did I tell you how beautiful you are today?"

She nodded. He had. Three times, but this made four.

I will be brave and quiet, brave and quiet.

He pushed the thick damask aside and her shoulders and back felt suddenly cool, covered by nothing more than her fine linen shift. Soft as rose petals, his warm breath tickled the nape of her neck, then he pressed his lips just where her neck curved to her shoulder. The shiver that danced down her spine was not entirely unpleasant, not entirely fear.

Giles inhaled the sweet aroma of his bride, lingered over her silken skin. He felt her quiver, heard her breath hitch. An intoxicating mix of desire and reverence reeled in his head. This woman was his. She had never been touched so by another and would not be gone upon the morrow. The seeds they sowed tonight would provide the harvest for the rest of their lives, and so he proceeded slowly, savoring every moment.

His hands skimmed her ribs beneath her bodice and set to work as efficiently on the fastening of her skirts as he had the laces of her bodice. She stepped away from him, not quite willing to let him tug the gown from her body entirely. Tactfully, he turned away and shrugged out of his jacket, folding it neatly and opening his sea chest, giving her a semblance of privacy. As he placed the garment carefully into the chest, Grace let the bodice of her gown fall to the floor. Giles pulled off his cravat and laid it smoothly atop the jacket, and Grace's skirts formed a puddle of costly fabric at her feet. Grace's shoes and stockings topped the mound. Giles's boots were set neatly to the side of the chest. She was unwilling to part with her shift or petticoat; he left his shirt and breeches on in deference to her innocence.

Grace's hands clutched convulsively in her petticoat, balling and rumpling the soft cloth.

"'Tis all right," Giles said, his voice tender and soothing. "We have all night, Grace. There's no need to rush. Matu cared for your hair as well?" At Grace's nod, he crossed to a cupboard and opened it, withdrawing a brush from the shadowy interior. He gestured to the bed. "Sit down."

She sank onto the mattress, but kept her back rigidly straight. He was as skilled at pulling the pins from a woman's hair as he was at unlacing her gown, and Grace could no longer deny what her mind had been trying to tell her. He had done this before, and not just once or twice. With whom? Why? Had he hurt that woman?

But there was no pain now. If anything, he was gentler

than Matu as he spread her mantle of curls over her shoulders and slowly worked the brush through it.

"I have never seen a woman with hair such as yours," he whispered, threading a lock through his fingers.

She raised a hand self-consciously to the mass of ringlets. "'Tis impossible."

"'Tis beautiful."

A smile tugged at the corners of her lips. If he stayed this mild and sweet, she might yet endure the night.

"Near to five hours' wed," he murmured in her ear, "and I've yet to kiss you properly."

She pivoted in place, facing him. There was nothing ugly or cruel in his gaze, only sweet longing, and she found that she actually welcomed the touching of their lips. As she knew he would be, he was cautious, hesitant, giving her time to relax. His lips were soft and undemanding. She sighed, breathing in his vaguely spicy scent and leaning toward him. The sensation that flowed through her was like warm honey, sweet and delicious. His arms enveloped her in a loose embrace, and she felt safe and protected.

Then he changed. His arms pulled her closer, drawing firmly around her. He tilted his head and his lips laid full claim to hers, his tongue brushing against her. She went stiff and tried not to cry out.

Be brave and quiet, brave and quiet, a child's voice admonished.

His hands drifted from her back, clasping her shoulders for a moment before moving downward over her arms. Her wrists! He was going to grab her wrists, hold her down! She parted her lips to protest, but he slipped his tongue inside. Unable to help herself, she began to struggle in earnest, and he released her instantly.

"Grace?"

"I-I'm sorry. I just—"

"Nay," he argued, "the fault is mine. I went too fast."

"I'm sorry. I wasn't entirely expecting you to-to kiss me like that."

His brow furrowed slightly. "I didn't even think to ask if you knew what to expect. I mean, your mother, she did tell you what would happen, didn't she?"

Grace almost gave a hysterical little laugh. Iolanthe? Talk to her about the marriage act? Nay, her education had come from Jacques, and he had told her everything a man might do to a woman. She had just foolishly thought her husband would be different.

"I know what is to be done," she answered. "Perhaps, if you wouldn't mind, just please don't hold me down. I promise, I'll lie still. And mayhap you might not cover my mouth so. I'll be very quiet. I'll not cry out."

"What?" His voice was incredulous.

"I'll not struggle or make any noise, but when you hold me down and do that, kiss me like that, I panic. I cannot breathe." She blinked back the tears that stung her eyes and tried to keep her voice steady. "I'm sorry. I'll learn to bear it, surely. I am just a little frightened."

He reached out to touch her, then pulled his hand back. "My God, Grace, what did that woman tell you? What do you think I'm going to do to you?"

"It hurts, I know."

"Aye, at first, but I'll be gentle with you. I promise. I wasn't going to hold you down. I only wanted to touch you. And I didn't kiss you like that to keep you quiet. I want this to be good for both of us."

She stared at him in obvious confusion, and Giles sighed in frustration. "I do not know what Mistress Welbourne told you, but I think 'twas warped by whatever it is that makes her so angry all of the time. Mayhap she and your father do not suit, in more ways than just their constant fighting, but I assure you, many women enjoy this."

Grace nodded at him, but he could see in her eyes that she didn't believe him.

"I can give you pleasure, Grace, but you must trust me."

"You've done this before," she said. It was a statement, not a question.

He shrugged a little sheepishly. "The rules are somewhat different for men." He expected her to protest the unfairness of it, but that didn't seem to concern her.

Instead she asked, "And she liked it, the woman you did this with?"

"Ah—" he shifted uncomfortably on the bed. *The woman*—singular. If he did not correct the assumption, it was a mere white lie of omission. What was the harm? "Aye."

She didn't miss his discomfort. She, of all people, knew when someone was skirting the truth. "Who was she? And did she—did she come to you willingly?"

"Of course!" he exclaimed. What sort of a monster did she take him for? Then he remembered the little girl in the hut and the slave who was the child's mother. He ran his hands over his face as he worked to master his expression. "I am not your father. I do not force women to do things they don't want to do."

"Women?" She rose from her seat on the bed. "More than one?"

He had swabbed himself right into a corner with that one. "A man has certain needs, Grace."

"That he cannot control?"

"Well, of course, he can. He just doesn't always choose to."

She regarded him through narrow eyes. "And women do not have these needs."

"They do! Most do. But 'tis different. They wait for the right man."

"But men do not wait for the right woman."

Had he told Geoff that he liked the fact that she challenged him? "Well . . ."

"And you were the right man for all of these women, but you are not right for any of them anymore?"

"You make it sound as though I left them in the lurch."

"Didn't you?"

"They were paid!" he snapped, bewilderment getting the better of him. "I was far from the only man in their lives. I don't take innocent women and cast them aside, you know. Mayhap 'tis not a sterling thing, buying an occasional night's pleasure, but 'tis no great crime! And 'twill be different for me now. I'll be a faithful husband to you, Grace. I vowed that today."

But Grace heard none of his last objections. She took in nothing but the fact that he had gone to the places that Jacques had told her of. The ones he had wanted to sell her to. She envisioned frightened girls not yet at the cusp of womanhood, cowering beneath sheets that they held clutched to their flat chests in terror. In her mind's eye, one man after another ripped the sheets aside and violated these girls, and among those men were Giles and Jacques.

Giles took in Grace's pale face and wide, fixed eyes and felt a wash of alarm shoot through him. "Grace?"

She snapped back from whatever dark void had swallowed her. "Do it!" she snarled. "Do it and be done with it. I cannot bear to think of it anymore!"

Giles felt his heart begin to pound and his palms sweat. He felt like he often had ere he and Geoff had sailed into battle against a heavily armed Spanish vessel. While Geoff had smiled and laughed, Giles had tamped down the hidden fear that this would be the battle they finally lost.

"This isn't normal, Grace. Some nerves, mayhap, but not this. Did something happen? You can tell me."

But her eyes had gone back to being unfocused, stark with terror. "Nothing happened. Nothing happened. Please, simply be done with it. You need not even be gentle. I no longer care if it hurts; I don't care anymore. Just do it." He put his hand on her shoulder, but she jerked sharply away. "Do not touch me like that. Do not try to make it better. I just want it to be over."

"I'm not going to ravage you," he protested. "You are my wife. This should be special, more than a mere joining of bodies."

"Was it not a mere joining of bodies with those others? The ones you did ravage? Were they black?"

For the first time during the course of the whole fiasco, Giles felt a surge of raw anger. "I do not rape slaves! I would never rape any woman! I cannot believe that you could have spent any time at all in my presence and believe such a thing of me." He rose and turned his back to her. "One thing is certain. We rushed headlong into this marriage knowing next to nothing of one another. This, at least, can wait."

Unwilling to have his character assassinated further and impotent to quell her fear, Giles did the only other thing he could think of. He left her in his cabin and stormed up to the deck above.

Nine

The sun had set entirely, leaving the sky smeared by stars. Giles was grateful for the cool air that caressed his hot face when he climbed the ladder to the deck. He had been so angry, so frustrated, he doubted not that his face had been nearly purple. He avoided the gaze of the night watchman who glanced curiously in the captain's direction. Then a shadow detached itself from one of the masts and approached him.

"I thought you'd be below with your wife," Giles said, immediately recognizing his friend's silhouette.

"She's asleep. And anyway, I thought the same of you," Geoff returned. "Unless I miss my mark, you've not done your wedding night justice."

Giles didn't answer. He tilted his head back and looked up through the rigging, studying the lights that twinkled overhead.

"Bit skittish, is she?" Geoff prompted.

Skittish. Aye, and a hurricane tended to be a bit blustery, Port Royal a trifle boisterous.

"Was Faith?" Giles asked.

"Aye. Maidens worry some 'til passion gets the better of them."

"Was she just nervous or truly frightened?"

"Frightened of burning in hell. All that talk of sin and retribution she'd been raised on."

"But of the act?"

Geoff sighed. "She knew me better, Giles. We'd been sharing a room and a bunk, spending hours on end together. Mayhap your wench but needs a little more time."

"She's not merely nervous, Geoff. She's bloody terrified."

With a shrug, Geoff said, "I cannot fathom it. You're not a fearsome man except in battle."

Giles crossed his arms and leaned against the mast. "I thought to be her knight in shining armor. I was going to slay the dragon and take her off to live happily ever after. Now, I wonder just how many dragons there are and whether I have what it takes to slay even one."

"You know, Giles, in all the battles that you and I have fought together, I have never once been afraid."

"Nay, you never have. You are the bold one, the one to sally forth and never err. For once in my life I have plunged into the fray without thought, and look what a mess I've made."

"I was never afraid because I knew without a doubt that the finest man ever to sail these waters had my back. I erred. I erred many times, but you were ever there to set those mistakes to right. Mayhap there is a dragon or two that you cannot slay for your maiden. Mayhap she must face them down herself. But one thing is sure, she is safe in your hands. She only needs time to trust in that. For pity's sake, Giles, look at how her own mother treats her. You cannot fault her for her caution. Stay there for her, my friend. Be steady for her, patient and reliable. Faith swears that God brought us together, for each of us was just what the other needed. Mayhap 'tis so for you and Grace, as well."

Giles couldn't help but smile. "Faith needed an unrepentant rogue?"

"Aye," Geoff said with a chuckle. "'Twas exactly what she needed. And Grace needs you. She'll see that soon."

They spoke a while longer ere Giles returned to his quarters. The talk and cool sea air left him feeling calmer, ready to face his wife again. Inside the cabin, Grace was still awake, sniffling and breathing in broken gasps as though she had only just stopped sobbing. He sat down next to her huddled form.

"There now, sweet, there's no need for all this."

Grace drew a ragged breath. "You will hate me. 'Tis not too late. You can have this marriage annulled."

He stretched out next to her, and she pulled away, but he wrapped his arm around her waist. "Stop. Don't fight. I swear to you, Grace, I only want to hold you, no more."

She had had time to think while he was away. He wasn't a brute. He could have ravaged her. She had given him leave to, but he hadn't. And while he was gone, she had become acutely aware of how alone she was in this strange room on a strange vessel, its rocking completely foreign to her. "I'm so sorry, Giles," she whispered.

"Shh. Nothing to be sorry for. Go to sleep, now. One should be well-rested ere one takes on Port Royal for the first time."

"But Giles, I know not when . . ."

He tugged her to him, pressing himself to her like a spoon, but made no further move to caress or kiss her. "When the time is right."

For the longest time she waited for his hands to wander, his lips to return to her neck. Instead, he but kept one arm loosely draped over her hip while the warmth from his body seeped through their clothes and into her cold flesh. The linens on the bed smelled of soap and the distinct, earthy scent of the man behind her, and she felt her body begin to relax. After a while, she decided that he must have fallen asleep and tried to ease herself from under his arm.

"Too warm?" he murmured.

"I thought you were sleeping."

"Nay. Just enjoying the feel of you, the smell. You smell of jasmine." He chuckled softly. "Though not so much as you did yesterday."

She laughed, too. "'Tis the same perfume. I hardly needed any more. You smell of spice and something rather musky."

"The spice is soap from the Orient. The other is probably just sweat."

Whatever it was, it made her feel somehow safe and dreamy. "I'm glad you came back," she whispered.

"And I."

"I haven't slept alone since I was ten. Matu slept with me."

"Since you were ten?"

"I was afraid."

"Of dragons?"

She stopped breathing for a second. "A monster."

He softly nuzzled his face in her hair. "You need fear no monsters now. I have your back, Grace."

He did. Somehow he had managed to wrap his big body all about her, but instead of feeling fearful, she felt sheltered. Oh, if only it would never go beyond this. If only she could spend the rest of his life lying beside him in his arms, and never underneath him.

They rose early, and Grace donned her yellow wedding gown for lack of anything else. Early though it was, when she went up on deck and looked back toward home, she saw that her two trunks awaited her at the dock, along with two muscular slaves to help load them onto the ship. She accompanied the rowboat when it was sent to get them, then went into the house one last time. She mounted the stairs to check her room, just in case she'd left something behind. Matu was sitting on Grace's bed, her posture, her face, everything about her filled with hopeless despair. When Grace walked through the door, the maid looked up, her eyes anxiously scanning the younger woman, seeming to seek signs of harsh use.

"I am fine," Grace assured her, and Matu smiled. "He is very kind and patient."

Matu nodded.

"We will come back for you."

The woman nodded again, but less confidently.

Grace cast her eyes about the chamber. It was as neat and tidy as Giles's cabin, now that all of her things had been packed away. It seemed like it belonged to someone else. "I guess we have everything."

The maid spread her arms, encompassing the room, and shrugged. She guessed so, too.

"How touching." Iolanthe's voice, dripping with sarcasm, came from the hallway beyond.

Grace turned to look at her stepmother, who stood just outside the door. Iolanthe was smirking, having had her victory, but for the first time, it seemed, Grace could really see the bitter disappointment and desperate unhappiness in her eyes.

"Well," Grace said, "you are rid of me at last."

"Not for long," Iolanthe returned. "He will find out."

Grace only sighed. She and Iolanthe could never say a single word to each other without argument. Now could hardly be any different. She turned her back on the woman. "Will you walk to the dock with me, Matu?"

Matu shook her head, blinking suspiciously.

"You never cry," Grace said.

Matu shrugged. They hugged one last time, so tightly neither could breathe, and kissed each other's cheeks.

"I'll be back," Grace whispered fiercely in Matu's ear.

Matu patted her arm, then used her thumbs to pull the corners of Grace's mouth upward into a smile— the message, "be happy."

The smile lingered on Grace's face. "I will. Try not to be too sad until I come for you."

They heard Iolanthe laugh outside the chamber door, but neither deigned to look in her direction. Grace's throat constricted painfully. "How can I do this, Matu? How can I just leave you here?"

Matu made the boat gesture. She pointed to herself and then to the ground with both hands: "I'll wait here."

They hugged again, each reluctant to let go, then Matu pulled away and gave Grace a little shove toward the door. She gestured for the girl to "shoo," and turned away to wipe an imaginary streak from the dressing table with her skirt, averting her face.

"I love you, Matu."

Matu nodded and gestured to her heart and then to Grace, but she still didn't look at her.

Blinking back hot tears, Grace swept into the hall, relieved to see that Iolanthe had gone elsewhere, then down the steps and out the front door. As she walked toward the dock, she wiped the moisture from her eyes and forced herself to focus upon the broad, confident form of her husband, who was overseeing the loading of her things into the rowboat.

Edmund had been missing from the house, but he

had somehow managed to make his way to the dock by the time she returned. He was effusive in his well wishing, but sharper than usual with the slaves, barking at them for being too slow, too careless, anything he could think of. He pulled Grace to the side, away from Giles and the men.

"Are you all right?" he asked fretfully.

"I'm fine."

"Truly? Last night went well for you?"

She blushed. This was not a subject that she and her father ever discussed. "He is everything I could have hoped for."

Edmund's face relaxed in obvious relief. "I was a little worried. I thought, perhaps, the incident with Jacques . . ."

Grace flushed deeper. This topic was strictly taboo. Her parentage her father might speak of from time to time, but from the morning after he had expelled Jacques from their home until now, that event was treated as though it had never happened. Not even Matu ever brought it up. Grace had not been breached. No damage had been done.

"Forgive me," Edmund said. "I shouldn't have broached the subject. Doubtless you'd forgotten all about it."

Oh, aye, forgotten all about it. Grace laughed, but the sound was strained and harsh. Suddenly nothing in the world was more important to Grace than boarding *Reliance* and sailing into her future. She had just one loose end to tie up.

"Promise me something, Father. Keep Iolanthe away from Matu."

"Matu will be fine, dear. You're too attached to her anyway. 'Tis just as well that you separate."

The taste in her mouth was literally bitter as Grace contemplated his words. "I cannot possibly give this marriage my full attention if I must worry about Matu. Whatever you may think of our relationship, it is what it is. I must be absolutely certain that Matu is safe."

Edmund nodded tersely. "I'll send her back to the slaves' quarters. She can tend to the children again. That should keep her out of Iolanthe's sight and mind."

She wasn't entirely comforted, but it would have to do. It wouldn't be for long. "But make sure Keyah knows that she is to be fed well. She must have meat and vegetables, not just cassava and corn. And you must swear to me that she will never be put in the fields or have anything to do with sugar production."

"She'll be well cared for. I swear it," Edmund promised.

That settled, Grace returned to the rowboat and her husband.

"Are you all right?" Giles asked.

She gave an exasperated gasp. "Fine! I'm fine! Shall we go?"

She didn't look back, not even to see if Matu might be watching from one of the windows.

Indeed, nothing could have prepared Grace for Port Royal. Several times a year, a tall ship would stop at Welbourne to take on sugar and rum, and such an event was always met with some fanfare. Now, *Reliance* sailed into a harbor packed with vessels, and each was crawling with men. People sporting clothes of every hue milled about in a tightly packed throng that swelled and receded like waves on the shore.

Stalls lined the docks, filled with cloth, spices, perfume, lumber, exotic pets—from bright and noisy parrots to clever little monkeys—dishes, wine, and trinkets of every kind. People called out greetings, haggled loudly over prices, shouted insults, and called out instructions from the docks to sailors on ships. Mixed in with the stalls were pens, some filled with livestock, others with frightened Africans fresh from the terrifying journey across the ocean.

In strange juxtaposition, still other Blacks swaggered past them, wearing velvet jackets, coins jingling in their pockets. There was little camaraderie between these free Blacks and the many Whites, but no great animosity either. They chiefly seemed to ignore one another.

Leaving Grace's trunks to be sent after them, the group disembarked and made their way through the crowd. Faith walked next to Grace, chatting airily into her ear. "There's a wonderful bakery just up the hill from Giles's home. He has no proper kitchen. Geoff and I lived in the apartment at first, but 'tis much better suited to a bachelor than a couple. I do believe there's a parcel of land close to us, and you can build a house there. Still, the apartment will do for a while. There's a cheese shop and a butcher on that street . . ."

Baby Jonathan sat atop his father's broad shoulders, pointing and squealing at the myriad things going on about them. Giles and Geoff laughed at his antics and teased the boy playfully.

Grace paid scant attention. Her nostrils filled with the odor of sewage and unwashed people, along with spices and perfumes in the stalls and food cooking in the inns and taverns lining High Street. She clung to Giles's hand and tried to keep track of her own thoughts amid all of the confusion.

"This way," he said, pulling her with him up the street, past ruffians and drunks.

Women leaned casually against tavern doorways or out of the upper windows of buildings on either side of the road. Their bodices were laced tightly at the waist, but left to gape open at the neck, spilling out mounds of generous flesh. These women beckoned to men with smiles and jaded taunts.

"Pay no attention," Faith said. "They are most shocking, but you will see fewer of them as we reach the outskirts of town."

"Who are they?" Grace asked.

"Oh!" Faith exclaimed. "Uh—"

Giles shot her a quizzical look. "I thought you had heard of such women."

Grace shook her head. Then, she saw one allow herself to be swept up into the arms of a disreputable-looking man in a tattered jacket. He put his mouth on hers and seemed to devour her, but the woman didn't pull back. Instead, she twined her fingers in his filthy hair. His hand plunged into her bodice, and she slapped it away playfully.

"Where's your coin?" she demanded with a lecherous grin.

The man withdrew a fistful of coppers from his pocket and dropped it down her neckline. The woman pulled it open farther, examining the coins that had fallen in and giving the whole street an ample eyeful of what lay beneath.

"I don't see no silver in there," she chided.

The man extracted a few more coins from his pocket and dropped them in one at a time. The woman smiled and said, "That's more like it." She rubbed her nearly naked bosom against him, then led him inside the building behind them.

"That's what they look like?" Grace gasped. This was a far cry from her image of terrified children.

Giles blushed. What must she think of him? He had openly admitted to employing the occasional prostitute, but he'd never been with women like that one. He had always prided himself on spending a bit extra for women who were more discreet and less hardened. Now, it seemed a pitifully minor virtue. He could hardly save his wife's opinion of him by telling her that.

Grace struggled to make sense of it all. That woman had not been afraid. She had been crass and immodest, but she was not even slightly afraid. Grace turned to Faith, her need for answers overriding her awe of Geoff's fair wife.

"Do you think that she knew that man? Might he employ her often, so she knew what he was like?"

Faith shrugged. "It may be, but 'tis just as likely that the first time she e'er encountered him was when he kissed her there in the street."

"Why was she not afraid of him?"

"Well, you or I would be terrified, of course, but she is accustomed to such a thing."

"Do you think she likes it?"

"I doubt it," Faith replied. "But who's to say?"

Do you like it? Grace wanted to ask. Does your husband kiss you like that, and do you pull him to you like that woman, or do you hold still and will it to be over? But she had already asked too much. Giles was looking at her strangely. He seemed embarrassed. He was probably mortified that she had asked Faith such improper questions.

She had to smile when they finally reached the office

and stepped inside. A huge, double-kneehole desk, sitting in front of a plate-glass window, dominated the room. Down the center, an imaginary line separated one half that was clear of everything except an inkwell and blotter from another half that was scattered with odds and ends. It wasn't a disorganized disaster, but there were stacks of parchment and a dismantled sextant. A child's wooden boat sat on the corner.

"Bo!" Jonathan shouted, reaching toward the desk. "Bo!"

"There it is!" Geoff called. "See Faith, I didn't lose it."

Faith huffed indignantly. "By the grace of God, you didn't. My father made it," she explained to Grace as she went to fetch the plaything. "'Tis part of a whole set with little wooden naval officers and all. I told Geoff that if he'd lost it, I'd be quite put out with him."

"Well, we'd best be on our way and let you two settle in. I've paid some of the more pressing bills, but you might want to look through the rest," Geoff said.

"Right," Giles replied. He perused the stacks of paper on Geoff's desk. "Have you filed anything? By the saints, Geoff, I spend more time sorting through your piles than drumming up clients, or possibly even sailing!"

Faith took Grace's hand. "Come for dinner tomorrow night. Geoff sails the day after."

Grace and Giles agreed to dinner the next day, and the Hamptons headed out to seek passage across the harbor to Kingston. The journey to the other side of the long, narrow bay was much too far by land.

When they left, it seemed eerily quiet. With the door closed, the street noise had faded. Grace could have sworn that she could hear her heart beating.

"Come upstairs," Giles said. "I'll show you the apartment."

The apartment, such as it was, consisted of one very cramped room with windows opening to the front and rear of the building. Unlike the window downstairs, these had no glass, only wooden shutters. A modest fireplace and hearth stood in one corner, neatly swept, with a small pot hanging on a hook inside and a pail of water in front. There was a cupboard containing four each of cups, plates, and essential flatware. There seemed to be no sign of flour, salt, or cooking staples of any kind. In the same general area were a table and four chairs. On the opposite side of the room stood a chest of drawers and a wardrobe. As in the ship's cabin, there was also a broad bed, immaculately made.

One room. Iolanthe and Edmund had separate chambers. Separate beds.

"'Tis a bit small, I know," Giles said, "and the furnishings are naught to admire. I'm not without means, though it might look it at first. You see, I've never spent all that much time here, so I never gave it much thought. But we'll have a house built, and you can furnish it as you like."

Grace looked around her and suppressed a sigh. "'Tis fine. Cozy."

"Not what you'd hoped."

She had two trunks that were easily large enough to store a half ton of sugar each. Even if Giles's clothes didn't take up much space in the wardrobe, it would never hold her voluminous gowns. There was no vanity, only the chest of drawers.

And there was only one room. One bed.

She smiled uncertainly. "I hope you shan't feel I've taken over the place entirely once my things arrive."

Giles's heart sank. She hated it. One more reason he

should have waited. He should have had a real home for her to come to.

"Your trunks should be here soon. I saw my first mate speaking to a man with a wagon as we left the docks. My men will load them, and someone will drive up here as soon as possible."

"There is no rush." She cast another glance at the bed.

Giles came up behind her and put his hands on her shoulders. "No rush."

The trunks came, but they left them packed while they dined in the common room of a nearby inn. It was one located farther up the street, farther away from the less savory sections of Port Royal, but still well within earshot of the drunken revelry down the hill. To Grace's relief, all of the women present looked much like her, fully clothed and quite respectable. The beef stew was passable, the ale warm, but she was ever so grateful to be in a public place. She dreaded a night alone with her husband in their tiny abode.

But she also felt a little disappointed when they walked back and Giles suggested that she go inside and get settled in without him. As much as she had no desire to consummate her marriage, neither did she wish to sleep all alone. She wanted him to hold her again, mayhap brush her hair. But he told her that he must check in with his first mate and then look in on things with *Destiny*. Doubtless, he explained, Geoff had everything under control for the upcoming jaunt, but he would feel better if he double-checked. It was hard to relinquish the position of Geoff's first mate.

After looking over the roster of men hired for *Destiny* and insuring that all watches were covered on board *Reliance*, Giles walked back through the city. Lights shining

from the windows and doors of taverns and brothels il-
luminated the way. Both types of establishments were
doing brisk business, and laughter poured out into the
street. He kept his hand resting lightly on the hilt of
his cutlass, staring down more than one miscreant with
both murderous and larcenous intentions. The trick in
Port Royal was to look sober and determined. Drunks
and nervous newcomers were plentiful and far easier
marks, so Giles made a poor target for criminals.

He was eager to get back, but he had been gone for
over an hour, and he was sure that Grace would be
asleep, or at least pretending. After the previous night's
difficulty, he had thought it best to give her some time
alone. Once back at the office, he saw the light of a
lamp glowing from the stairs above, but he didn't hear
a sound. He tiptoed quietly up, thinking to gaze on
Grace's slumbering face, but when he got there, his eyes
were utterly riveted to the scene surrounding him.

The top of the chest was littered with things, do-dads
and whatnots, bottles and jars, hair ornaments and ribbons, a brush and hand mirror. Next to it, no part of the
wardrobe was shut properly, its drawers and cabinet
spewing frothy lace and fine fabrics. Both of Grace's
trunks sat on the floor, lids open, more clothes spilling
over the edges. A cup had gone from the cupboard to
the table, but somehow had not found its way back
again. Instead, it sat forlornly next to an embroidery
frame and sewing basket. One glance at the needlework
suggested that disarray was not an uncommon state of
things where Grace was concerned.

Finally, he looked toward the bed. Damn him if she
wasn't well and truly asleep, the utter chaos around her
having no ill effect on her complete repose.

With a mental groan, he undressed and dug through

layers of feminine fripperies in his wardrobe drawers to find his only nightshirt. It had been a gift from Geoff. Apparently Faith had made two for her husband, but Geoff couldn't fathom when he'd use even one, so he'd pawned the other off on Giles. He folded his clothes, only to discover that he'd nowhere left to put them. Gritting his teeth, he set the stack on the seat of a chair and climbed into bed.

One reward almost made it all worthwhile. When he gingerly snuggled up to Grace, she sighed in her sleep and melted against him. It was a start.

Ten

The next morning, Giles concentrated on the bacon and eggs on his plate, keeping his eyes glued to the food rather than the ruins of his once pristine quarters. Behind him, he was painfully aware that broken eggshells, a dirty bowl, the paper wrapping from the bacon, and an open crock of butter cluttered the top of his small sideboard.

"Breakfast is delicious," he said. It seemed judicious to compliment her first, then broach the subject of order and organization, and the food really was very good.

"I spent a good bit of time in the kitchen with Matu and Keyah, our cook," Grace explained. "Once we have a bigger kitchen, I'll be able to do more."

"I'm looking forward to that. I must admit that the food at Welbourne was outstanding."

"Keyah's predecessor was a cook sent by Iolanthe's father, and she trained Keyah. As the Renaults are French, a skilled cook was a priority. I'm sure that, even with your little hearth, I can make you very happy to have married me."

He smiled at her. "I'd have been happy even if you didn't know how to boil water."

Grace looked away uncertainly.

"We'll leave for Geoff and Faith's in the early afternoon," Giles continued. "Mayhap you could use the time before that to," he cleared his throat, "finish what you've started in here."

Grace shrugged. "There's not much left to do. Might I help you in the office? My father taught me to keep accounts. I could help with that."

Giles choked on a bit of bacon. "Are you quite certain you wouldn't like to spend a bit more time getting organized up here? How will you find anything?"

"Oh, I've a fair idea where everything is. What I cannot find, I'll simply root through my trunks for." Not for the first time, she thought of Matu. If only she were here. She could help Grace with cooking and organizing. 'Twas embarrassing to realize just how much of a nursemaid Matu had remained to her all these years.

"Grace, I'm afraid it will be weeks ere we'll have a proper house."

"Aye, but we'll manage until then. I promise, the moment I have a room of my own, you'll never again be troubled with all my trappings."

"Excuse me?"

"I'll keep all my disarray in there." She shrugged lightly. "I know I've made a bit of a mess."

A *bit* of a mess? Aye, and she was a *bit* skittish about sex, too. He closed his eyes and counted to ten. "Do you mean a sewing room or some such thing?"

"Nay. A bedchamber."

"You will not have a bedchamber of your own. A wardrobe of your own, aye, a chest of drawers, a vanity, but no chamber." He stabbed at his eggs.

"But . . ."

"I'm patient, darling, but I am no monk."

She blushed deeply. "I was not suggesting that you'd

not be welcome there. Of course you would be free to visit."

"I am not going to visit my wife."

"But, my parents . . ."

"Have one of the most unnatural marriages that ever I have seen."

"'Tis a common practice!"

"Not in our home."

"I'm not a tidy person, Giles."

"You'll learn to be."

She stared at him for a moment. His face was mild, his voice calm, but there was no mistake that on these points he was not prepared to budge. She narrowed her eyes at him. "Have you never thought that this need you have for perfect order borders upon an obsession?"

"Aye."

"Aye? And that worries you not?"

"Nay. It serves me."

Did the man always have to be so damned unflappable? She leaned back in her chair. "Well, it doesn't serve me!"

"I cannot live like this." He finally let his gaze scan the room.

"I have proposed a solution."

"As have I. I'll see to it that you have a place for everything."

"You cannot simply order me about, Giles. I am not a member of your crew."

"As evidenced by the fact that we have conversed on this topic easily twice as long as ever I would converse with a crew member on it. I told you before that I've no wish for a servant, but neither can I abide this!" He gestured broadly.

"There has to be some compromise. I cannot live like

you, either. There is not a personal touch anywhere that you occupy. A body might walk into your cabin or your apartment and wonder whether anyone lived there at all."

"Unwashed dishes are a personal touch?"

"A cup," she replied tartly. "God forbid."

"I have nowhere to put my clothes."

"I'll take a few things out of the wardrobe."

"And put them where?"

"A trunk. There's room."

"And how is it that everything fit into your trunks yesterday, but now that they are half empty, they no longer shut?"

"My gowns. They'll be utterly ruined if they stay crushed like that. I needed to hang out the wrinkles, or at least spread out the skirts, and they don't all fit in the wardrobe."

Giles heaved a sigh. He hadn't thought about the sheer volume of women's skirts. And he had to admit that she did look awfully fetching in the pale green dress she had put on while he had been out purchasing the ingredients for their breakfast. "Green suits you," he said at last, taking another bite of food.

Had she won? She felt a little twinge of guilt. Mayhap he was compulsive, but she was, after all, the one invading his home.

Then the corners of her lips twitched. He liked her gown. "Iolanthe always said that I wore too much green."

"Iolanthe?"

Grace winced. He had caught her off guard.

"Do you never call her Mother? And did the woman ever open her mouth to you without insulting you?"

"No, on both accounts," she admitted. "I called her

Mother when I was a child, but after a while, well . . ." What could she say?

It nagged at him, the coldness between Grace and her mother. "Was that when Matu came between you? She thought it was your maid's fault that you were so distant?"

She nodded, but refused to look at him. All she could think of was the lifetime of lying ahead of her. "I suppose she was right that Matu spoiled me. I'll see what I can do about straightening the mess."

"You had a point. I may be overly concerned with order. Do what you can. We'll muddle through until we can get a larger room and more furniture."

No bedchamber.

"I'll give it my best effort," she promised.

"I should like to have you look at the accounts later. I'm accurate, but too slow."

"Just imagine."

"What?" Giles asked.

She leaned toward him and grinned, resting one hand lightly on his arm. "Fathom that, my Giles being so methodical that his ciphering takes him hours."

The phrase caught his attention. Her Giles?

Giles washed dishes while Grace made another attempt to get her things to fit neatly into the drawers and wardrobe. To her husband's credit, he didn't own an excessive amount of clothing, and some of it was permanently stored on board *Reliance*, but that didn't mean that he had enough room to store both of their belongings.

Finally he came over to her and said, "I think this will be easier if we just sort out what you have in groups.

Then we'll know how much room each kind of clothing requires and we can decide the best place to put them."

Grace's smile was deceptively sweet. Excessively organized Giles. How very certain he was that everything could be made to work if it was just approached methodically enough. He seemed to think that of every aspect of life. She knew better. "Let's begin with my gowns, shall we?" she asked.

He smiled back, aglow with the confidence of a captain in charge of his crew on a glass-smooth sea. "Perfect."

She pulled several from the wardrobe, then more from one trunk and even more from the other, laying them out on the bed and fluffing them. "Wrinkles," she reminded him, then smothered another grin at the daunted look in his eyes.

The skirts created a pile of silk, damask, linen and cotton nearly a yard high, in rich shades of yellow, green, orange, blue and many others. He looked from the bed to the relatively small wardrobe and conceded, "So be it. They'll not all fit in there. Surely these two trunks will hold them. If we divide them between the two, they shouldn't wrinkle too badly and I'm sure that we can still shut the lids."

Grace shook her head. "Why didn't I think of that? But there are a few things still in each of the trunks. I'll just take those out, too, so that we can decide where they'll best fit and be neatly tucked away."

Out from the bottoms of the trunks came layers of petticoats, all edged in flounces of lace, all in colors complementing the skirts piled high on the bed.

"Of course, we want to be organized," Grace continued. "Underthings should all be stored together, do you not think?" From wardrobe drawers that wouldn't close completely, she pulled cotton, linen, and silk shifts and a goodly mound of stockings, again in a wealth of colors. "And what about shoes?" she asked, pulling a half-dozen pairs from the wardrobe cupboard. "And, of course, there are nightdresses in the chest of drawers." She opened a drawer to reveal a frothy mass of still more lace and fine, white silk and linen.

Giles stared at it all. Spread out as it was now, it consumed the entire sleeping and dressing portion of the room. "It cannot be," he muttered.

"What cannot be?" Grace asked, eyes wide, lashes fluttering.

"That a man who has bested some of Spain's finest sailors is about to be defeated by a fortress of frills!"

Grace pursed her lips, and looked simultaneously thoughtful and mischievous. "It certainly doesn't speak well for Spain!"

He walked over to the chest of drawers and delicately lifted out a nightdress. It was sleeveless and made of sheer lawn, trimmed in pink ribbons and lace. "I like this."

Grace blushed. Last night she had slept in her rather substantial linen shift.

He continued to eye the garment, then said, "'Tis badly wrinkled, though." He dug through the drawer. "They all are. Don't tell me. Matu always folded your clothes."

Grace marched over and snatched the nightdress from him. "Matu could defeat the whole Spanish navy," she quipped.

"I don't doubt it," Giles replied.

He carefully folded the garments that remained in the drawer, and when Grace finished folding hers and added it to the pile, she discovered that they took up only half as much space. She looked at it in surprise. "I always thought that 'twas a waste of time to fold these, because they always wrinkled so anyway when I slept in them."

"If we fold the stockings," Giles remarked, "they could probably fit in here, too."

"Fold stockings?" she said. She gazed at him from under raised eyebrows with a look that clearly said she thought he was being methodical in the extreme.

But her skepticism had no effect, and soon her stockings were neatly matched and folded next to her nightdresses.

Without another word, she went to the bed and began to fold her shifts. They were bulkier than the nightclothes and still required two drawers, but when she was finished, both drawers closed all of the way. Knowing that they both needed room in the wardrobe, she lined her shoes up neatly underneath it. Giles frowned at them, but seemed willing to leave them there.

Together they surveyed the intimidating mound of dresses remaining. "They'll have to go in my trunks," Grace said. "And you'll never get them to close."

But Giles had an answer for that, as well. The silks were hung, for they would wrinkle the worst if they weren't. With Grace's help, he inserted each petticoat into its coordinating gown so that it would keep the skirt from being completely crushed. Then he lay the gowns carefully in the trunks, alternating the placement of gathered waists so that the skirts would lie relatively flat. True, neither trunk would close, but skirts no longer spilled haphazardly over the sides.

"Have you always been like this?" Grace asked.

"I've lived in ships' cabins since I was nine. You learn to use space wisely there."

"I suppose you would," Grace agreed. "Since you were nine?"

"That's when my father died. My mother had four children to feed, and though my father had saved money, 'twas not enough. He was a shipbuilder, and I signed on with one of his friends as a cabin boy."

While Grace did her best to tidy the top of the chest of drawers, organizing hair ribbons, tying them together in a big bow, and neatly arranging bottles and jars, Giles told her about his childhood and his three sisters.

"Even when I was very young, I was very protective of them," he said. "And they knew that I could not abide a girl's tears. Whatever was wrong, I would fall all over myself to fix it if they cried. They even picked fights with other children, for I was sure to intervene ere they reaped the just results of their mischief. I haven't seen them much since I left home, for I'm seldom in London, but they're all married now and have children."

"But," Grace said, "you lived with them long enough to become a rescuer of unhappy women."

"I? I've certainly never thought myself such. After all, 'twas Geoff who ultimately rescued Faith."

She urged him to tell the story, and he did. Grace commented that, indeed, it was Giles who had rescued Faith, for he'd tempered his friend during their courtship. Then she coaxed more tales from him, stories about life at sea, descriptions of faraway ports, running narratives of battles with the Spanish.

When all was said and done, they were nearly late to dinner.

Compared to Welbourne, the Hampton residence was quite modest. It was a small cottage with a cozy keeping room, a bedchamber and a nursery. Behind it was a small kitchen surrounded by a neat herb garden. All of the furnishings were very plain, yet wrought with exceptional care.

"My father," Faith had explained, caressing a polished trestle table. "He made all of little Jonathan's furniture, as well."

At the sound of his name, the little boy tossed aside the wooden toy he'd been chewing on as he sat on the floor. He grinned with his few teeth and toddled to his mama, tugging on her skirts when he reached her. Faith picked him up. "Would you like to hold him?"

Before Grace could answer, she found her arms filled with a wriggling boy who went instantly from happy smiles to a fretful scowl. A stab of panic went through her. She'd no idea what to do with a fussy baby. Fortunately, Giles came to the rescue. He took the child from her, tossed him into the air and caught him, eliciting a cheerful grin along with musical giggles.

Grace turned back to Faith. "Does it pain your father, that you are so far and your children will not learn his trade?"

"He's sons enough to help in the shop," Geoff interjected. "The only thing that pains Jonathan Cooper is the fear that I've led his little girl astray." He stepped in back of his wife, wrapped his muscular arms about her waist, and pulled her to him.

Geoff loomed behind her, could have crushed her in an instant, but Faith only reached up behind her and gave the man's solid, square jaw a playful tap. "Not so! He misses both little Jonathan and me fiercely. And he worries more for your soul than mine. You are a wicked, wicked man, you know."

"Aye," Geoff agreed with a grin. "But you've more of the devil in you than e'er you'll admit."

He leered at his wife in a way that would have made Grace's blood run cold, but Faith only smiled and blushed in return. "Behave," she chided lightly.

Eager to distract them, hoping to move into safer territory, Grace asked, "Will your Jonathan be a sailor, then?"

Geoff and Faith answered simultaneously.

"He's but a babe . . ." Faith began.

"Aye, the finest," Geoff boasted.

Grace winced. She hadn't meant to cause a row. Now the evening would surely be spoiled as the two of them stewed and waited for an opportunity to argue away from their guests. But they only astonished her again by laughing.

"Tell her, Giles," Geoff pleaded, stepping away from his wife. "Growing up a stone's throw from the wickedest city on earth, and sailing since ere he could walk. He'll sail for King and country. Outdo his father's most daring exploits."

"Oh, nay," Faith protested. "He'll return to New England and live among the savages, converting their heathen souls and thereby succeeding with them where I failed with you!"

Geoff's jaw dropped, and his golden eyes lit with a dangerous spark. Grace sucked in her breath at Faith's nerve. Even Iolanthe would have known better than to stir up such an intimidating man as this.

Giles laughed boisterously. "She has you!" he called. "Oh 'tis good to know that you can still keep him on his toes," he praised Faith.

Geoff's indignation turned quickly to sheepish confusion. "You *are* jesting, nay?" he asked.

Faith looked at him with guileless blue-green eyes. "Jesting? Think you not that a fine and fitting profession for our son?"

He reached for her, spinning her about and pulling her close. "A *privateer* with a taste for wenching," he replied, dipping his head toward hers.

Grace turned bright red and looked away, though a part of her wanted to watch, to see what happened.

There was naught to see. Faith braced her hand against Geoff's broad chest. "You embarrass our guests," she chided.

Grace spared a glance for Giles, but he was smiling, obviously at complete ease with the playful, lusty teasing between his friends. She was on the outside, again. Married and yet a virgin, just as she had always been neither white nor black, a daughter in her home and yet not.

Giles looked at her, as well, and she did not miss the subtle yearning in his eyes. This was what he wanted, and aye, it seemed a fine life, but the whole experience was so alien to her. She did not know how to laugh and tease like this.

She joined Faith in the kitchen to help with dinner, fish stew and fresh bread, still warm. The air was moist and hot and smelled of fish and onion. The center of the room was taken up by a cookfire and hearth, the surrounding walls lined by cupboards and a table.

"You and Giles are settling in well?" Faith inquired, as she transferred the stew into a serving tureen.

Grace hesitated. She found a shallow basket on the table, next to the bread, and she placed one of the loaves in it. "Aye. Well enough."

"He's a good man. I've long hoped he'd find a bride, for he's sure to be a fine husband."

"Aye," Grace replied.

"Though I do hope you'll teach him that a thing or two out of place is no mortal sin. Or has he met his match there? Do not tell me there is another in this world as orderly as our Giles. Even I, who grew up with the adage that cleanliness is next to godliness, am slovenly by his standards."

Grace had to grin a little. "Nothing in my home was next to godliness. And I fear that Giles may well believe that disorder of the magnitude that I can create is indeed a mortal sin."

Faith beamed her approval. "Good!" She set the tureen down next to the bread and sprinkled a bit of nutmeg into a pitcher of bumboo, a mild rum concoction. "I think a good marriage requires some difference of opinion. Besides, there's little nicer than making up after passionate debate." She flashed Grace a glowing smile, handing her the bread and drink before she picked up the tureen herself. "Come, we'll take the food in."

Giles and Geoff were sitting at the table, discussing business, as the women brought in the food. When they were all seated, Jonathan on Geoff's lap, Faith gave thanks to God for the meal. Throughout, Geoff did not so much as bow his head, but he and Faith smiled at one another after, and in that one shared glance there seemed to be something more sacred than the spoken blessing. Giles had mentioned to Grace a substantial difference of faith between them, but it seemed to cause no tension. Yet another puzzle to ponder.

Giles took a healthy bite of savory stew, made with thick cream and seasoned with pepper, and watched Grace. Her brows were, more often than not, drawn into tiny furrows, as though she could not fathom what she saw. He had hoped that this time spent with a happily married couple might help her to trust him more, to trust that marriage did not have to be what she had seen in her own home. He couldn't have asked for an evening better suited to his purpose. He could tell that Grace was intimidated by Geoff, but soon even she had to laugh as the man attempted to eat with a tot on his lap. The child repeatedly grabbed for his papa's spoon just as Geoff had nearly reached his mouth.

"Jon!" the boy would cry, and Geoff would feed him a spoonful.

"Me now?" Geoff would ask.

"Papa!" Jonathan would answer, but he would grab for the spoon all the same. The scenario played itself out over and over until Faith, her own meal hastily finished, took the child into her lap and fed him a bit of stew remaining in her bowl.

"A small concession to marital harmony, and my first piece of official advice to you," Geoff said to Giles. "Once you have a babe, let your wife eat supper first when you know you'll be sailing without her. 'Twill be the last hot meal she gets ere you return."

"I'll try to remember that," Giles promised.

Grace shook her head in wonder. Concessions made for the sake of marital harmony? She could just imagine the snorts of derision such a comment would be met with by her father and his wife. This was a new life indeed.

Eleven

Once they had returned home, Giles sat at his side of the desk, listening to his new wife's footfalls on the floor above him, hearing the occasional opening and closing of drawers and trunk lids. Though it cost him dearly, he resisted the urge to go and see how well she was keeping up her newly organized trunks and drawers. She had been unusually quiet on the trip home, clearly deep in thought. It had seemed best to give her some time to herself.

While he waited, Giles opened a letter from atop the pile of that afternoon's post. Part way through it, he scowled. The letter was addressed to him, but it was clearly a follow up to some previous missive, one that Geoff had intercepted. Correspondence sent to the office was opened by whoever was handy, so Geoff must have received the first letter, one that had apparently asked Giles to come to Tortuga. Tortuga was a small island, just off the northwest coast of Saint-Domingue, and as popular a pirate lair as Port Royal.

What circumstances were drawing Geoff there? Clearly it wasn't a mere sugar delivery, as Geoff had claimed, although sugar could not be grown on the island made of nearly solid rock, and did have to be delivered. The letter cryptically mentioned that the "situation was getting hotter," and urged Giles to make haste. The name at the bottom was Captain Henri Beauchamp, a French privateer and mere passing acquaintance. He was also quite illiterate. Giles turned the letter over, but could find no indication of the identity of the scribe to whom Beauchamp must have dictated. Neither was there a date. There was no telling how long it had taken for the letter to be delivered. The fact that it was still in very good shape suggested that it had not changed hands very often.

What was the "situation"? Giles rifled through Geoff's side of the desk in hopes of finding the first letter, but he found nothing but bills to pay and haphazardly scrawled notations of monies placed into their account. There was nothing indicating the nature of Geoff's trip.

Well, there was naught to be done tonight. On the morrow he would rise early and catch Geoff ere he set sail. Giles folded the letter and placed it in one of his drawers, then picked up his lamp and made his way up to the apartment.

Grace had only just finished washing and had donned a clean, substantial shift. She wasn't yet ready to appear before him in a thin silk nightdress. Truthfully, she had hoped to hide under the excuse of sleep ere he came upstairs, but she had tarried too long over her evening toilet. From the corner of her eye, she watched him in the lamplight. Casually, he shrugged out of his jacket, then hesitated only a moment before he doffed his cravat and pulled his shirt over his head. He hung the jacket up, folded and put away the shirt and neck cloth, and plucked his nightshirt from a drawer.

Grace had noted before the broad shoulders underneath his clothes, but now she could see the muscles that flexed and bunched in his back and arms, and his skin glowed in the dim light. She was almost disappointed when he donned the nightshirt. But when he shed his breeches as well, she gritted her teeth. She remembered another man in another nightshirt. Spinning away from Giles, she lifted the bedcovers and moved to climb into bed.

"Wait," Giles said. He had a remarkable knack for making a softly spoken word a command. "'Tis warm in here yet. Lie atop the covers."

Grace swallowed hard, but obeyed. 'Twas much better this way, she told herself. The longer they waited, the harder it would become. She stretched out resolutely, staring up at the ceiling.

"Roll over onto your stomach."

She could feel panic begin to boil up inside of her, but again, she complied. She knew not what she expected him to do to her like this, but it certainly wasn't what he did. He knelt next to her on the mattress and slowly began to knead the muscles in her neck and along her shoulders. Like divining rods seeking water, his fingers found every knot and kink and worked it loose, and she felt herself slowly turning to butter underneath his attentions. He hit a particularly tight spot in her back, sending a stab of pain through the sinew. Seconds later, 'twas but a memory.

"Sorry if I hurt you," he said.

"Only for a moment. Now 'tis heavenly," she murmured. She was feeling so relaxed that 'twas an effort to speak.

"Some things are like that," he said, "an instant of pain, a goodly span of pleasure."

She squeezed her eyes shut, bracing herself.

But he just kept massaging, moving down her back with methodical care. His hands lightly skimmed her bottom, raising gooseflesh in their wake, then set to work on her legs.

"I'm afraid that I may have to accompany Geoff to Tortuga," he said conversationally. "'Tis a situation that he might need to know of."

It was hard to concentrate. His hands moved gracefully and firmly up and down her calves, slipping in under the hem of her shift, the skin of his palms warming her legs. "Mmmm," she sighed.

Farther down, his thumbs coaxed all traces of stress and tension from the soles of her feet. "Much as I hate to leave you, 'tis not the best trip to make your maiden voyage, and I wouldn't be gone long. Would it trouble you overmuch if I had to leave so soon?"

All she could think was that she didn't at all want him to leave and stop this divine thing that he was doing. No, wait, he'd said later this week. Not right now. She buried her smile in the pillow. "How long?" she mumbled.

"What's that? On your back again," he instructed, giving her a nudge.

In languid cooperation, she rolled over. What had she wanted to know? The conversation was becoming too hard to track, and her mind was feeling muzzy and fuddled. No, that wasn't quite right. His hands were traveling up her leg again, still under her shift, bare skin to bare skin. Something was happening, a peculiar tingling in a most peculiar place. He brushed his fingers over the flesh of her inner thigh.

Her eyes flew open, and she saw him leaning over her, towering in the semi-darkness.

"Giles!" she gasped, bolting upright.

"'Tis all right," he urged, pulling his hands away. "Had enough?"

"I think so." She was beginning to tremble, but she

wasn't sure why. For an instant she had been startled, but she wasn't really afraid.

"May I ask a small thing in return?"

She eyed him suspiciously. "What?"

Now it was he who lay down on the mattress, locking his hands behind his head. "A kiss."

Small enough. She smiled shyly. "Aye. You may ask that."

"Not just a peck. A real kiss."

"Oh, well, I—"

"'Tis nothing so complicated," he explained. "Just press your lips to mine. Keep them relaxed and soft. Move slowly."

She gave him a dubious look. "You'll stay just like that?"

He nodded, and she thought it wouldn't be that hard a thing to accomplish. She leaned toward him, but he wasn't finished.

"Then I'll open my lips for you. Taste me, Grace. Use your tongue and explore. I am yours tonight."

Her breath caught in her throat.

"It will be all right," he coaxed. "I won't move. I won't touch you in any way. Kiss me for as long as you like, then we'll go to sleep."

She moved closer to him. It felt odd to be above him, the one in control, but 'twas a little exhilarating, as well. The tingling sensation at the juncture of her thighs grew more insistent.

She lowered her mouth to his, following his instructions, moving her lips softly against him. He parted his lips slightly, and with the tip of her tongue, she traced the swell of the lower one before delving inside. He tasted of rum and nutmeg from the bumboo he had imbibed at supper. His tongue moved with hers, executing an intricate dance, but never venturing into her mouth, and he made no attempt to touch her in any other way. To her surprise, she was reluctant to stop. She tilted her head and pressed their lips together harder, thrusting her tongue deeply into the moist cavity of his mouth, suddenly hungry for more. Her hands found their way to his expansive chest, moving curiously over soft cotton and hard flesh.

He groaned softly, the sound vibrating within her mouth, and she pulled abruptly away. "Good night," she whispered, then pulled back the covers and slid between them.

It took a moment before Giles could move. He was so hard it hurt, and though he wanted very much to stay and share her warmth, he knew that he needed a few moments of privacy or he'd never be able to bear the contact of the sheets against him.

"I'll be right back," he told her.

"You're all right?"

"Fine. I just remembered something down in the office."

"Come back soon?"

He sat up, sucking his breath between his teeth. "Shouldn't take more than five seconds." Then he stumbled down the stairs toward blessed relief.

If Matu had known what had just taken place, Grace thought, she would have given Grace one of her typical, light-handed smacks on the side of the head. Grace did it to herself in Matu's place. Why had she stopped? He was liking it. *She* was liking it. Then he had moaned, and suddenly she had feared that it would go too far. But they were married. There *was* no too far! Now, the heat of the moment was cooling, and it was taking her nerve with it.

She wished Matu had been able to come with them. She would have known just what to say. Grace fixed her eyes on the flame flickering in the lamp. Where was Matu now? Was she sleeping on the dirt floor of one of the huts? Would her father keep his promise? There were so many uncertainties.

Such as how much longer could she expect her husband to wait?

Twelve

The morning was off to a dismal start. Giles had arrived at the dock just at dawn, only to learn that Geoff had already left. Next, he inquired after any captains who had lately been to Tortuga to see what news they brought. Beauchamp was well known. If there were some trouble involving him, 'twould be common knowledge. Though he found no fewer than four such captains, all reported essentially the same thing. Beauchamp had been off the island for over a month, presumably prowling the Spanish Main. If there had been trouble, it was a well-kept secret. Soon Giles realized that there was nothing for it. He would simply have to journey to Tortuga himself. He wasn't about to allow his best friend to sail into a situation that was "getting hotter" without being there to guard his back.

In the course of arranging for the trip, he managed to gain a shipment of sugar to take with him, and he felt a little better at the thought that he would at least manage to pay for the trip with the proceeds.

Thus, Giles spent the day rounding up his crew and preparing for a voyage he'd no desire to make. He had never cared for unknown elements of danger, having always preferred to know what he would face so that he might plan a sound strategy to deal with it. Most of all, he wondered why Beauchamp had called upon him. Granted, they both had plundered Spanish ships, but for two different countries. They hardly knew one another. Lord, would he and Geoff never be entirely free of the old days?

In a general cloud of brooding irritability, he arrived at the dock to oversee the loading of the sugar, only to be informed that his first mate had discovered a sizable leak in the hold.

"What happened?" Giles demanded.

"The planking there's no good," his carpenter explained. "'Tis rotted away."

"We careened her last week," Giles snapped, referring to the process of tilting a ship onto its side to clean off barnacles and inspect for other damage. "How could we have missed it?"

"You'll have to ask Freddie Robbins that. He was assigned to that section."

It took fifteen minutes to track down the responsible crewmember, by which time Giles had begun a slow burn. If there was one thing he could not abide, 'twas delays due to incompetence. And in this particular venture, time might well be of the essence.

He found Freddie sulking below decks. For a moment, he considered simply firing him on the spot, but the sailor was young, perhaps seventeen, and Giles took pity on him.

"You cannot shirk your responsibilities, lad," he admonished. "You'll never make a good sailor if you cannot perform basic duties conscientiously."

The young man stared at him with blank, blue eyes. Not merely shiftless, Giles thought, but dull, as well. "Conscientiously. You know, attentively, carefully."

"I did my job, Cap'n. Not my fault the wood rotted. 'Tis the water, you know."

Why had he hired this fellow? "Aye, Freddie, 'tis the water. Water rots wood. It does it all the time. That's why we have to stay on top of it. What if this had rotted through while we were at sea? Our very lives depend upon every man's diligence." Another blank stare. "Watchfulness."

"But we found it."

"The first mate found it. He found it after *you* had been appointed to clean off that section. Finding and reporting problems in an area where you've been assigned is *your* responsibility. Now get down below and man the pump. We'll empty her out and careen her again so the carpenter can do *his* job properly."

Giles rounded up the better part of the crew, pulling them from less urgent tasks of routine maintenance and setting them about securing the goods that were waiting on the dock to be loaded. To his infinite frustration, he found Freddie back up on deck, tapping one of the Negro sailors on the shoulder.

"Quashee," Freddie said, "Cap'n wants the bilge pumped. Go on down and give an 'and. I'll finish splicing that rope."

Giles strode briskly across the deck. "I told you to do that, Freddie."

"Don't matter 'oo does it, Cap'n. Quashee there don't mind."

"His name is Jawara," Giles snapped. "And I didn't order *him* to do it, I ordered *you*. You missed the damage; you can bloody well do the work to help fix it."

Freddie gave him a sullen glare. "Them Blacks is better suited to 'ard labor, and what's the difference what I call 'im? 'E's the only African on deck, and there's no Englishman anywhere answers to Quashee."

Giles had always called each man on his ship by name, but he had never thought much of it when white crewmembers referred to every Black as 'Quashee.' It was a common African name, and was often used to address Blacks of all walks of life in the Caribbean. For the first time, it occurred to Giles that just such generalizations were the foundation upon which slavery was built. It reduced individual men to indistinct members of a servant caste. It stripped them of the fundamental dignity of having their own names.

"Jawara," Giles corrected through his teeth. "And I'll tell you this now. You'll obey my orders or I'll put you off this ship. I don't give a damn if I have to set you on a desert island; I'll not have my men weaseling out of their duties. As for who must perform hard labor, that would be every man on board. If you're too delicate, mister, best you find other employment."

Freddie grumbled, but he made his way below and got to work. Giles checked on him and the repairs, reviewed their supplies one last time, then dispatched a message to Faith that he was leaving on the morrow. Granted, he had promised Geoff he would look after her, but doubtless his friend had left her a guard or two, and Giles hoped to return in less than a fortnight. That reminded him that he'd his own wife's safety to see to. He chose a man for the job, excusing him from his duties on the ship and telling him to report to Grace at the office, on the morrow, where he would stay until Giles returned.

The sun was nearly gone ere the ship was again seaworthy. He stayed and saw to it that she was back in the water without any further problems. It had been a long, exhausting day and, as if the leak and the confrontation hadn't been enough, it began to drizzle as he walked home.

Giles had sent a message that, while he hadn't yet sailed, neither would he be home until dark, so Grace went downstairs to the office, hoping to occupy the hours. It took a bit of self-conscious digging through Geoff's half of the double desk, but she discovered several stacks of unrecorded receipts and unfiled records. She sat at her husband's place, carefully calculating monies received and bills paid. Once the amounts were noted in the correct ledgers, she filed the records in the set of shallow boxes she'd found stacked on a bookshelf. As the day waned, a light rain began to fall, and the light faded.

She had just lit a lamp and begun to worry about her husband when he walked through the office door, looking damp and very testy. When he saw her, he frowned in confusion. "What have we here?"

"You said that you had some need of help with your accounts. I do not doubt it, now that I've seen how far behind you were, but I think I have you nearly caught up."

He closed the door quietly behind him. "I did say that, didn't I? I meant later, when I might show you what to do."

"I found everything I needed on Geoff's desk."

The corner of his eye ticked almost imperceptibly. "Geoff has his own filing system, as it were. I know his desk is a shambles, really, but there *is* a method to it. A mystifying one, but some rhyme and reason, nonetheless."

"Aye. 'Twas not overly complicated. Is there a problem?"

He already had his hands full contending with his partner's accounting. No amount of counsel had ever convinced Geoff that his system was too haphazard. How would Giles ever set their records to right if she had jumbled what little organization there was? He closed his eyes, breathing deeply. *One, two, three* . . . he thought silently, exhaling and pausing slightly with each number.

"Are you counting?" she huffed.

His eyes flew open, gray and somber, like the weather. "What?"

"You count, do you not? You start to feel your temper boil and you count in your head. What?—to ten?"

"It keeps me from saying things I'll regret."

She rose from her seat and glowered at him. "And what were you about to say?"

"Nothing."

"Ha!"

"I just wish that you had waited. There's a structure to all of this." He looked at the desk, his mouth a grim line.

Grace marched over to the bookshelf and pulled off the stack of boxes. Then she stomped back over and set them hard atop the desk. "This," she began, resting her hand on the first box, "is for *Destiny*. It contains shipment records such as inventories and settlements paid to customers, placed chronologically. Receipts for settlement are filed on top of the inventories they correlate with. The next box contains expenses exclusive to Geoff's ship—supplies ordered, repairs made. You'll see that I've added a bill for canvas and another for a recent purchase of lumber. The amounts are also recorded in this ledger." She laid her finger on the spine of a leather-bound register in a stack of books where she had been sitting.

She set *Destiny's* records aside and continued. "The next two boxes appear to have been designated for *Reliance*, since one contained her bill of sale and the other had but the inventory of my father's cargo. You did say that you had only just purchased her. I found the receipt from my father for the money you paid him on Geoff's desk with other records pertinent to your ship. They have all been recorded and filed.

"That big box over there," now she pointed to one on the bottom shelf, "is for documents that relate to your overall expenditures—ink and parchment, pay for sailors, and the like. I noticed that you really haven't two separate, permanent crews. You simply hire sailors ere you leave on each voyage, but many sail with you over and over again. I saw a number of names repeated from one voyage to the next. Incidentally, you have missed a payment to Basil Hale's widow, and there needs be three more such payments ere you have made good on her pension. I found the agreement tucked under a map on Geoff's desk and scoured your books for the records."

"She hasn't received payment this month?"

"Nay, she has not. I will need access to funds while you are gone if you wish me to continue running the office in your place." She regarded him through narrowed eyes. "That is, unless you feel I have bungled the job hopelessly."

Giles cleared his throat sheepishly. "I wasn't aware that we were behind on Mistress Hale's pension. I'd been sailing for your father and then courting you. Geoff is usually adequate at handling accounts, but he has been known to lose track if there's no actual invoice."

"So I noticed."

Giles opened his mouth, then closed it again.

"I believe you were going to say 'thank you.' No need to stop and count. You won't regret it."

"Actually, I wasn't sure which to say first, thank you or I'm sorry."

"I'm not partial. Any order will be fine."

"'Tis just that, after the apartment, knowing what you consider to be organized . . ."

"This is business, Giles, not trinkets and finery. I am well aware that without careful record keeping, your company is sunk—if you'll pardon the pun. I told you, I helped my father quite frequently. I've a decent brain for business."

"I see that now, but you can scarcely fault my mistrust of your father's training. If you'll forgive my bluntness, your father does his accounting drunk."

Grace blinked at him. "Excuse me?"

"That night we came back from the slave quarters. He couldn't even count the money I brought him, he was so besotted."

"'Twas not habit. Father drinks when he is under pressure. Doubtless he was certain that I'd ruined his last chance at more heirs."

Giles paused a moment before asking, "Did your mother never conceive any others besides you?"

"She may have," Grace answered, avoiding his gaze. "I know not. If she did, I never saw any signs of it." Mayhap 'twas not a lie outright, but being purposely obscure did nothing to ease her conscience.

Giles regarded her gravely. "I wish I knew what it is that you will not tell me."

"I know not what you mean," Grace replied, but there was a small catch in her voice.

"Aye, you do. You can hardly speak of your mother without choking, like there are words caught in your throat. *Were* there other babies? Ones with defects?" he prompted. "Idiots? What terrible secret do you hide? What does Matu know that she may never speak of?"

"I think that you have secrets of your own," she returned, fighting panic. "That is why you see them in others where they do not exist."

Well, mayhap he had not been entirely forthright about his upcoming voyage, but that was for her protection. He dismissed the tweak his conscience gave him and replied, "What information about myself have I ever held back from you?"

"You know far more about me than I about you." She picked up the record boxes and placed them back on the shelves with careful precision, glad for the excuse to avoid looking at him.

"What do you wish to know?"

"What of *your* family? I know that you've three sisters and a mother living in London, but you seldom see them. What drove *you* apart? What are your family's secrets?"

Giles sighed. Would he ever be able to scale the walls this woman had built, continued to build around her? Well, he could answer her questions, at least.

"I was nine when I signed on as cabin boy. I just didn't see the rest of my family much after that."

"You could ne'er find time to tarry in London now and again? Is your love for the sea so strong, then?"

"Nay. It's been a matter of convenience mostly." He dropped his body into his desk chair. "I like sailing fine, but 'tis no passion."

At the resignation in his voice, Grace paused from her

labor of straightening up ledgers and bills. "Nay? I had always heard that the sea was every sailor's mistress."

"A romantic notion," Giles conceded, "but not entirely accurate. For many, 'tis but a living."

"Then how came you to choose it?"

"Sometimes, I wonder if I really made a choice. My father was a shipbuilder, so when I needed a job so young, cabin boy was the likeliest chance. I met Geoff when we were still but lads. He had a sense of adventure and ever plunged forward, never stuck, as I often was, trying to decide. When he came by a position on a privateer ship and asked me to join him, it had seemed like a grand enterprise."

"Wasn't it?" Grace asked, genuinely intrigued and having forgotten all about her attempt to divert him from herself.

"In many ways. But there is always a price. There are things I've done that I'm not proud of." Connections made that, however tenuous, were hard to sever. What cared he and Geoff what ill befell Henri Beauchamp? And yet, Geoff had gone to aid him, and Giles would follow.

"But now that's over, and you are an honest merchant captain."

"Because Geoff decided to be one." He gave her a rueful grin. "You thought that you had married a leader of men, did you not? You'd no idea that he was more of an aimless follower."

Grace moved to stand before him. With her fingertips she traced the jawline that he had so meticulously shaved that morning, now rough with stubble. "You are a natural leader, you know. I wonder where *Geoff* would be without *you*. Think you that he would be this successful without you to bring some sense of order and

Take A Trip Into A Timeless World of Passion and Adventure with Kensington Choice Historical Romances!
—Absolutely FREE!

Enjoy the passion and adventure of another time with Kensington Choice Historical Romances. They are the finest novels of their kind, written by today's best-selling romance authors. Each Kensington Choice Historical Romance transports you to distant lands in a bygone age. Experience the adventure and share the delight as proud men and spirited women discover the wonder and passion of true love.

Get 4 FREE Books!

We created our convenient Home Subscription Service so you'll be sure to have the hottest new romances delivered each month right to your doorstep—usually before they are available in book stores. Just to show you how convenient the Zebra Home Subscription Service is, we would like to send you 4 FREE Kensington Choice Historical Romances. The books are worth up to $24.96, but you only pay $1.99 for shipping and handling. There's no obligation to buy additional books—ever!

Save Up To 30% With Home Delivery!

Accept your FREE books and each month we'll deliver 4 brand new titles as soon as they are published. They'll be yours to examine FREE for 10 days. Then if you decide to keep the books, you'll pay the preferred subscriber's price (up to 30% off the cover price!), plus shipping and handling. Remember, you are under no obligation to buy any of these books at any time! If you are not delighted with them, simply return them and owe nothing. But if you enjoy Kensington Choice Historical Romances as much as we think you will, pay the special preferred subscriber rate and save over $8.00 off the cover price!

We have **4 FREE BOOKS** for you as your introduction to
KENSINGTON CHOICE!
To get your FREE BOOKS, worth up to $24.96, mail the card below or call TOLL-FREE 1-800-770-1963.
Visit our website at www.kensingtonbooks.com.

Get 4 FREE Kensington Choice Historical Romances!

💛 **YES!** Please send me my 4 FREE KENSINGTON CHOICE HISTORICAL ROMANCES (without obligation to purchase other books). I only pay $1.99 for shipping and handling. Unless you hear from me after I receive my 4 FREE BOOKS, you may send me 4 new novels—as soon as they are published—to preview each month FREE for 10 days. If I am not satisfied, I may return them and owe nothing. Otherwise, I will pay the money-saving preferred subscriber's price (over $8.00 off the cover price), plus shipping and handling. I may return any shipment within 10 days and owe nothing, and I may cancel any time I wish. In any case the 4 FREE books will be mine to keep.

Name_____

Address_____ Apt._____

City_____ State_____ Zip_____

Telephone (___)_____

Signature_____

(If under 18, parent or guardian must sign)

Offer limited to one per household and not to current subscribers. Terms, offer and prices subject to change. Orders subject to acceptance by Kensington Choice Book Club.
Offer Valid in the U.S. only.

KN104A

4 FREE

Kensington
Choice
Historical
Romances
(*worth up to
$24.96*)
*are waiting
for you to
claim them!*

*See details
inside...*

‖‖..ι..Ɩ.....‖.ι.ι.ι.ι.ι.ι.ιι.ι.ι.ιƖ.ι.ι.ιι.ι.ιƖι.ιƖ

KENSINGTON CHOICE

Zebra Home Subscription Service, Inc.

P.O. Box 5214

Clifton NJ 07015-5214

reason into his life? And none of us entirely chooses our path. I hated Welbourne Plantation, but were it not for you, I would be there yet."

"'Twas not your wish to be born a planter's daughter," Giles said, rising and enveloping her in his damp coat sleeves. "The suffering of the slaves there is none of your doing. 'Tis not as though you chose to be white in a world where Blacks must suffer."

Suddenly the musty, wet smell of the fabric was suffocating, and Grace pulled away. "Nay, 'tis not as though I had a choice."

"Besides, were you African, you would not be here with me now."

"Were I African . . ."

"May we thank God neither of us is, those poor souls." He shrugged. "We are what we are. Is there food in the apartment, or shall we go to the tavern down the street?"

There was no room for food in a stomach where guilt sat like a lump of cold lead, but she acquiesced anyway. "I'll get my cloak."

The common room of the inn was a busy place where serving-wenches bustled from table to table, refilling rum for men who'd already imbibed too much and setting trenchers filled to overflowing before hungry patrons. Giles gave a heated account of the day's problems, and although Grace nodded at all the right times, she paid scant attention and picked at her food. She caught something about an errant crewman, and Giles mentioned something about sending her a guard in the morning. Even the commotion of the crowd dining and conversing around her failed to penetrate her turbulent thoughts very deeply.

Giles thought that she'd had no choice regarding her race and therefore her life, but he was so wrong. Matu was right, Grace had straddled the fence of her heritage long enough. It was time to get down and live life on the side that she *had* chosen. She would give Giles children, children so fair that they would never know that they, too, had a choice. She would begin by trying to conceive one tonight. *Oh please, God,* she prayed, *give me a child soon, in as few couplings as possible. And let it be white.*

By the time they left the tavern, the drizzle had turned to a downpour, and a brisk breeze buffeted her skirts. They raced home down a street lit only by lights in windows. She had left an upstairs window open, and sure enough, the floor in front of it was soaked. Giles closed the shutters and offered to clean up the mess, his thorough occupation with the task giving her a modicum of privacy in which to wash and dress for bed. She changed into her lightest, sheerest, silk nightdress and steeled herself against her rising doubts.

The gesture was not lost on Giles. Thus far, she had been retiring in garments of thick linen. He grinned a little. Until now, each night had been an exercise in frustration, but last night he had stumbled upon what he was sure would be the answer. He would put Grace in control, happily allowing his wary bride to have her way with him at her own pace.

After washing away the day's sweat and donning his nightshirt, Giles fell into bed. "By all that's holy," he complained, "it's been a trying day."

Again, she tamped down a shiver of dread. If he was still angry at the lazy sailor, would he take it out on her? But he made no move to touch her.

"Well, 'tis over and done," she said. "All's well now, is it not?"

"Aye, all's well, but I'm still in knots."

"Oh."

"You might ease that for me."

She couldn't speak. She could only give him a sideways, cautious look.

"The same way I did for you last night."

She wrinkled her brow, puzzled, until he rolled over onto his stomach. Oh, that was all! She breathed a sigh of relief. Tentatively, she knelt next to him and brushed her fingers over his shoulders.

"You'll need to use more strength than that. I'm a fair-sized man, Grace, you'll not hurt me, I assure you."

She brushed his hair to one side, taking just a second to feel of its silky texture. He had loosed it from its tight queue and it lay dark against the white cotton of his shirt. Then, recalling his ministrations to her, she used her thumbs and fingers to apply firm but careful pressure to each knot imbedded in the muscles of his neck and back. The flesh beneath the fabric was warm and firm, and even in repose, it exuded strength. But each sinew was under her dominion, giving up its resistance to her kneading fingers.

She worked across his back, down to his waist, then stopped. The nightshirt fell to mid-thigh, and from that point on there was nothing but powerful legs dusted with hair.

"Better?" she asked.

Giles shifted onto his back, once again folding his hands under his head. "Much."

He let his gaze fall upon her lips, the message clear, and Grace leaned down to kiss him. They were becoming familiar now, his warm, soft lips and moist, silky tongue. This time, he kissed her back, possessing her mouth, tasting and exploring her, leaving liquid heat in his wake.

She pulled away to catch her breath, but she wanted more. This part of mating she could endure all night, she thought. Perhaps it would even be worth what followed.

"'Tis even better if we're touching more," Giles whispered. "If our bodies are pressed together."

She wanted to cry out that she wasn't finished. She wasn't ready to have him on top of her, crushing her, spoiling everything. Still, she lay down next to him and awaited his pleasure.

"Nay," he said, tugging her hand. "You lie here, atop me."

She sat up and looked at him. "I, on top?"

He chuckled softly. "I do not think you'll crush me."

She didn't think so either, but neither did she lie down entirely upon him. Pressed close against him, she lay on her side. Her upper leg rested lightly atop his thick thigh, partly covered by his shirt. With her arms free to twine about his neck, she pulled his head down to hers and kissed him again. He was right. It was better. The heat from his body radiated to the very center of her. In this position, she could brace herself on one arm and let the other hand roam freely, touching him at will.

He tangled one hand gently in her hair, pulling her mouth closer still, but without force. Then he drew free of her curls and brushed his fingertips softly over her arm, down her back to where it curved and sloped outward to her bottom. She shivered, though not with cold, and pressed her pelvis to the side of his leg, seeking something, wanting to slake some need inside of her.

The storm outside gathered in intensity, wind whipping around the building, raindrops splattering against the shutters. The room filled with the scents of rain and desire, a potent mixture, and Grace felt as though time had slowed down. It seemed the whole world was moving languidly through sweet, thick nectar. Giles's hand curved itself around her breast, his fingers gently squeezing her nipple and causing it to tighten in response and send a jolt of desire coursing through her. Then he moved on, skimming her hip, sliding up under her shift.

And Grace's quest grew bolder, too. Her own fingers traced, through his shirt, the faint ripples that creased the muscles in his stomach. Her caress glided over his lean hip, trespassed beyond the boundary of his shirt-tail to feel of the bare flesh of his thigh. He took her hand in his and guided her back up, under the shirt, to touch the rigid evidence of his passion.

Grace's first impulse was to pull away, but she forced herself to prevail. He had taken his hand away, so the decision was entirely hers. She wrapped her hand around him, caressed him, blindly gauging the length and thickness. She had expected him to be hideously swollen, so immense that he would rip into her and leave her bleeding and mutilated. But he wasn't so enormous, and she had to wonder if perhaps her child's memory of a man's sex was somehow distorted. It was a bit intimidating, to be sure, and Grace had no doubt that it would not be comfortable to yield herself to him, but 'twasn't nearly as hopeless as she had expected.

Giles continued to stroke Grace's skin, pushing aside her shift, his hand insinuating itself between their bodies. As he drew closer to his objective, she felt herself grow damp, and a throbbing ache suffused her nether regions. She kept him in her grasp, even as he slipped his finger between the folds of her flesh, stimulating a tiny, sensitive spot and drawing a gasp from her throat. Then, he slid his finger inside of her.

A gust of wind hit the shutter with brutal force, sending it open to hit against the outer wall with a resounding crack, and Grace screamed. Giles leapt from the bed to pull the window shut, and she screamed again. It was like a dam had burst. She was screaming, drawing tight, gasping breaths, then screaming again, unable to stop.

Giles pulled the bolt more securely into place with shaking fingers and ran back to the bed. "'Tis all right, Grace. 'Tis all right." He went to wrap his arms around her and comfort her, but she rolled out of his reach and off of the bed. "Grace?"

She was scooting backwards, her eyes wide, green pools of sheer terror, looking at him but somehow seeming not to see him. "Nay, nay, nay!" she screamed.

He froze. Fear wrapped icy fingers around his heart and squeezed. He knew that he couldn't touch her, but neither could he leave her there, cowering on the floor. "Come back, Grace. I'll not touch you, I promise. Only come back up here."

"Nay, nay, nay," she chanted, and her teeth began to chatter. "This is how it happens! This is how it happens!"

"How what happens? *What happened?*"

"You make me touch you, and then you—you do that to me, and then Father comes. He throws the door open and it hits the wall, and then he yells. He yells, and then the world comes apart. It comes apart! You think that you're something, and then you're not. You think that you are someone, but you are a splotch. A meaningless, black splotch!"

"Oh, God," Giles croaked. He crossed his arms, gripping himself helplessly to keep from reaching for her and terrifying her further. "Grace, 'tis all right. No one's going to hurt you. I swear to God, no one will ever hurt you again."

"Nay!" she shrieked. "It always hurts! It always hurts! It hurts me; it hurts Matu! Oh Matu, Matu," she keened. She pulled her knees up to her chest and wrapped her arms around them. "Matu," she sobbed, rocking back and forth. "I'm so sorry."

Giles watched her rock. His pulse raced, and he felt like he had in battles, when his best friend's life had been his responsibility. But he knew how to protect Geoff. All he had to do was keep the enemy from sneaking up behind him. Geoff could take care of the rest. Not so with Grace. She was huddled on the floor, surrounded by dragons he couldn't see, a monster he couldn't vanquish.

Thirteen

Rain, Grace thought. I smell rain. But she remembered incense. She lifted her head from her knees, exhaustion having finally calmed her hysterical sobbing. The man who sat above her on the edge of the bed was not Jacques. He had his head in his hands, but still, she knew he wasn't her uncle.

Giles. Her husband. She didn't even remember what she had said to him while she had babbled in terror. Had she told him everything? Would he look at her in horrified revulsion?

He raised his head, every line of his face etched with worry and fear. No disgust. It nearly tore her heart from her chest. She had lied to him, disappointed him, behaved like a complete lunatic, and still he was concerned for her. She was so utterly unworthy.

"You must get an annulment," she muttered, her throat raw.

He shook his head. "We shall set this right."

She made a sound that was half laugh, half sob. "We cannot. You deserve better, Giles."

"I can think of no one better than you. You have tried so hard. Had I but known . . ."

"How could I have told you? I am so ashamed."

"Grace, 'twasn't your fault. It matters not to me but

that I would kill the man if I could. Not because he took first what was mine, but because he hurt you. And Matu, did he rape her, too?"

Grace dropped her head back to her knees. "He did not rape me."

"He . . . ?"

"My father stopped him ere he could finish the deed."

"But he did enough. He did enough to scar you."

"What he did to me was worse than rape. He took my whole life from me."

"Nay, he did not," Giles protested. "You have a new life, with me."

"I am not what you think me."

"You are brave, and beautiful, the strongest person that e'er I have met. That is what I think you."

"And you think me honest. You forgot that."

"I understand why you did not tell me."

"God damn you!" she shouted, rising unsteadily from the floor. "Stop it! Stop understanding! You do not know the half of what I have not told you. You do not know me, Giles Courtney, and you never will! Do you think that I could ever tell you everything? Do you think that I will ever place myself in a position where I must see all your understanding, all your kindness turn to disgust and hatred?"

"And do you hold me in such low esteem that you believe I would turn my back upon you?" he demanded. "Who did this to you, Grace? How did he manage to make you feel such self-loathing? What can I do? How can I make you whole again?"

"You cannot make me whole! How can you make me whole if there is a part of myself I can never share with you? This was a mistake from the beginning, and as God is my witness, I am so sorry. What I have done to you is so grossly unfair."

"What was done to you was a heinous sin."

"It is deeper than that. The thing that will ever lie between us has been there since I was born. It has little to do with him, the man who drew it all into the light. Go. Go find your friend, deliver your shipment. I'll be gone ere you return."

He couldn't leave her; that much was clear. But neither could he leave Geoff when everything he knew about Geoff's voyage seemed so suspicious.

"Give me time to think," he said. "There must be some way of taking you with me."

"I do not want to go. I cannot be with you, Giles. Can you not see that?"

Giles's breath hissed through his teeth. "Then promise me one thing. Promise you will give it a few days; you'll stay here, in our home, for three or four days ere you seek passage back to Welbourne. I will be at sea for over a week. You can still be gone long before I am back if that is what you choose."

"What difference can it possibly . . ."

"Promise. Promise, or I'll not leave at all. I'll follow you to Welbourne, speak to your father . . ."

"Nay! You cannot speak to my father of any of this!"

"Then give me your word."

She hesitated. "Three days?"

"Your word."

"Upon my word."

"Will you come to bed?"

She shook her head.

Well, he wasn't going to get a wink of sleep this night. Giles rose and pulled his shirt and breeches from the wardrobe.

"I don't mean to put you out," Grace said.

"You're not. I have to leave early, and there's something I must do first."

"I'll not be here when you return."

The cold fingers that had been squeezing his heart throughout the entire episode convulsed. "We'll see," he replied.

"I'll be gone. But I want you to know what a fine man you are. I am sorry, please believe that."

He clenched his teeth in anger at her pathetic words. What a fine man! A fine man who was leaving his own wife just when she needed him most. And for what? For all he knew Geoff had everything in hand. He was, in essence, a follower. Skilled he was at guarding men's backs, but of what use was he when the enemy was at the forefront?

So be it. He was no Geoffrey Hampton who charged into the fray and relied mostly upon his impulse. He was Giles Courtney who weighed every variable and knew well how to delegate. Aye, Giles Courtney recognized when another knew better than he the best course of action.

"I'll see you when I return," he said. "Remember, you promised. You gave me your word. You'll stay here three days. God willing, you'll never leave."

"Giles, you have lost your mind."

"Mayhap I have lost my mind, but I have something better. I have Faith." He smiled at her, a hopeful smile.

"I wish I did, too," she replied, missing his meaning.

In the morning, Grace packed nearly all of her things away in her trunks. Matu would have a fit when she saw what a rumpled mess all her skirts were, but Grace couldn't muster the slightest concern. This sense of scatteredness and disconnection reminded her of the weeks after her uncle had left. 'Twas just so bloody hard to concentrate on anything. She felt restless, like getting up and running as far and as fast as she could. She sensed that she was unraveling, and that soon, there would be nothing left of her.

The wardrobe still held enough clothes to see her through the next three days. She had been sorely tempted to renege on her promise. Then at dawn, one of Giles's men had tapped on the office door and informed her that he had been sent to see to her safety. Dimly she recalled Giles saying that he would send someone. He was a pleasant looking fellow, and not overly large, but he wore a cutlass and flintlock too comfortably. Having the strange man in the office below did not make her feel safer. It only added to her anxiety.

Now, outside her window, a clock chimed ten. She had not gone to sleep all night, and the hours had passed strangely, marked by periods of oppressive weight and bouts of nervous jitters, all bound together by a cord of burning anger. She would think that she hated Giles, then realize 'twas Jacques she despised, then wonder if it were not her father, really, who had earned her ire. Sometimes it seemed that she was entirely to blame for her own misery.

If only she could focus, understand what she felt. Then maybe she could manage it better.

A sharp rapping on the office door nearly sent her skittering right out of her skin. Fear bolted through her, hot and irrational. A customer, she told herself, vainly trying to steady her breathing. Someone who knew not that both Giles and Geoff were at sea. Suddenly she was glad to have Giles's man with her.

She heard the door open and a woman's voice asking her protector, "Is Grace upstairs?"

Faith Hampton. Could the woman not wait for an invitation?

Then realization dawned. Oh, aye, 'twas Giles she was furious with after all.

"Aye," the sailor replied, "she's up there."

"May I go up?" Faith asked.

"Aye, come up," Grace called down. *Damn*, she thought. *Damn, damn, damn!*

Faith approached the stairs, her pale brows furrowed with worry. Her tow-headed son sat at his accustomed place on her hip, and she used her free hand to raise her skirts so that she could carefully ascend the steps.

"I hope that I am not intruding."

Ha! Grace was no fool. Giles had sent her to intrude. He had Faith, indeed! "I am a trifle busy," Grace said. "Is there something that you need?"

"I simply came to visit," Faith replied, still climbing. Over her shoulder she said to the guard, "You may wait outside. She's perfectly safe with me. My husband's man is out there already."

The sailor smiled and nodded, apparently eager to escape.

Faith swept past her and plopped the baby on the bed. Now, Grace could see that the boy had been obscuring a cloth satchel hanging over his mother's shoulder. Faith pulled from it the wooden boat that had been on Geoff's desk and handed it to the child. Little Jonathan stuck the stern into his mouth and began to drool contentedly.

"Giles would have a fit if he saw that," Faith commented merrily, dropping the satchel next to her son. "Baby spit all over his immaculate bedding. Do you know, I've not been up here since Geoff and I lived here." She looked around, inspecting Grace's haphazard packing but saying nothing about it. "He kept the old furniture, I see, but added a few pieces."

"He said that he spent little time here," Grace replied. Nervous restlessness set in again. She could *not* sit here and make small-talk.

Faith leaned on the table, testing its strength. "'Tis holding up. These things were falling apart until I fixed them," she said with not a little pride. "They seemed hopeless, but when all you have is less than perfect, you do what you must to set it to rights."

"And so that is why he sent you? To set me to rights like a table or a chair?"

Faith sighed. "Have you met Mister Abrams, the carpenter down the street?" Grace shook her head, and Faith continued. "Thank goodness he was there. He was the one who had the tools and lent them to me. I did all the work, but I couldn't have done it without his tools."

"I don't think you have the tools I need."

"I may not. I cannot pretend that I know what you're feeling . . ."

"Nay, you cannot." Grace's voice was glacial, but it did nothing to deter her guest.

"It must have been terrifying."

"To be entirely frank, Mistress Hampton, I have never discussed this with anyone. Not even my nurse. I am hardly going to discuss it with you."

Again, her protest fell on deaf ears.

"Giles thought that you might wish to speak with another woman."

"The mere fact that you are female does not mean that you can help. You cannot possibly understand what it is like to have everything you ever believed about yourself crushed into dust by another's cruelty."

"I have never been the victim of such an attack, that is true. But for what it is worth, I do know what it is to lose my greatest refuge. You see, I was raised a Puritan, one of God's Holy Elect. My home was supposed to be a New Jerusalem. My family, my neighbors, my church told me exactly what I must be and what I must think. I was taught that to be anything else was to incur God's everlasting hatred. It is not the same, I will grant you, but when I was faced with the hypocrisy and corruption within our church, it shook the very foundation of my life."

"So are you no longer one of God's Holy Elect?" There was no trace of sympathy in Grace's tone.

"Aye, I am. So are you. So are Geoff and Giles and your imperfect parents and the African maid you love so much. But that realization was a long time coming. The point is you need not be destroyed by what happened. What you do from here on is up to you. Giles is not the man who hurt you. You can have faith in him to protect you."

"Well, there you have it." Grace smirked. "Had I but known the answer was so simple! Giles is a good man and I can trust him, and that wipes away all the rest. There is little comparison between you and me, Faith. At no point was I ever under the slightest impression that my home was any New Jerusalem."

"Then help me to understand. This goes beyond the rape?"

"As I told Giles, I was not raped."

A bit of color stained Faith's pale cheeks. "I will admit, I am unaccustomed to prying so personally, but I cannot stand by and do nothing while two good people who

belong together are torn asunder. Therefore, you must
forgive my bluntness. When Giles came to me in the
middle of the night last night, he told me that you had
been forced into some intimacy with someone. Perhaps
you could clarify it."

Anger bubbled up again inside of Grace. She was
tired of it all. Tired of talking about it. Tired of thinking
about it. Mayhap Mistress Lily White, God's Holy Elect,
should get exactly what she asked for! The thought of
shocking Faith into silence yielded a vicious satisfaction.

Grace's mouth contorted into a bitter sneer, and her
voice was sharp with anger. "Very well, since you insist.
When I was ten years old, my uncle molested me, not
once, but repeatedly. He stuck his tongue down my
throat and his fingers in my womb ere it had even bled
its first cycle. He told me the ways of a man and a
woman, of how increasing her suffering heightens his
pleasure, how he must hurt her if he is to spill his seed.
He elucidated in minute detail."

"Sweet Jesus," Faith whispered. "You poor child."

"Nay, Mistress! My childhood was torn from me long
ago. My father may have stopped Jacques from raping
me, but he could not stop what followed. Do you know
why my uncle believed that he could use me so with im-
punity? Would you like to hear about that, as well?"

Grace stopped. She felt as though she stood upon a
precipice that plunged a hundred feet into jagged rocks
and churning water. If she let any more of the anger
out, she would be unable to halt it. It would come spewing from that place inside of her where it had festered
and oozed for over a decade, sending her over the edge
to plummet to her destruction. And the despair. The
despair that waited at the bottom. It would close over

her head like water, leave her desperate to breathe but without having the courtesy to kill her.

If she spoke the words that quivered in her mouth like living things, she would forever undo the scant equilibrium that had kept her from falling long ago. Matu's sacrifice would have been for naught.

"Tell me," Faith urged. "Let it out. I can see that it torments you."

Unwilling to leap, unable to retreat, she walked the cliff's edge. "I learned that I am a bastard. My father's wife was barren, or, what was that other word?" She searched her memory for the biting phrase that her father had used that night. "Frigid. I don't even know what it means. I only know that he went to—to another woman. A kind of woman no one respects. A kind of woman whose daughter would never marry a fine sea captain. He rutted with her to make me, like an animal."

"He told you that?"

"His wife did."

"Oh, Grace." Faith's eyes shimmered with tears. "Words are so utterly inadequate."

The sympathetic grief was Grace's undoing. Her defenses crumbled, and her anger no longer had enough force to sustain her bravado. Softly, she confessed, "So much happened that night. 'Tis all mixed up together, the defilement, losing my place within my family, knowing that my nurse, whom I loved, suffered because of me. She was the keeper of the secret; that's why father silenced her. There was no part of me or my life left unsullied. How can I take what Giles has offered when I am so unworthy?"

"Unworthy? What have you done? You did not hurt your nurse. That deed is upon your father's head. And what does it matter who your mother was or by what act you were created? Geoff's mother was a prostitute, too." When Grace opened her mouth to protest, Faith held up her hand to stop her. "That had nothing to do with you. You are here, Grace, and that fact alone makes you worthy. You have lived your life bestowing compassion upon others when you'd had little enough of it yourself. By that, whatever sins you have taken upon yourself are redeemed. If you cannot think yourself deserving enough, then think of Giles. I wish that you could hear him speak of you. He admires you so, and certainly not for your fine parents!" The last two words dripped with sarcasm.

"But . . ."

"There are no 'buts.' Your mother could have been a murderess, she could have been the lowest woman on earth, and it would mean nothing to him, for it would change nothing about you. As for what you suffered at your uncle's hands, Giles has some idea of the nature of what happened. He does not think you any less virtuous or pure. All he wants is to heal you, to love you as God meant you to be loved."

"I've tried to let him," Grace protested. "And I cannot."

Faith sat down at the table and motioned Grace to the seat across from her. "'Tis not just the physical coupling. He wants your happiness. He wants you to care for him as he cares for you."

"I do care for him!" Grace protested as she sank into the chair. "You are right, he is a good man, and I have seen that in him from the start. I just don't think I'll ever be able to let him . . . let him . . ."

"The mechanics are similar, I admit," Faith replied, "but lovemaking and rape are not the same."

"I told you. I was not raped."

"Think you that it mattered to a ten-year-old? You were ravaged. What cared you whether it was with his sex or his hand?"

Grace stared at Faith across the table, feeling as though a window had somehow opened inside of her soul. Something musty and stale filtered out, even as something fresh and clean replaced it. How easily this woman dismissed the notion that she had not been truly hurt, merely because she had not been breached. In a single sentence, Faith had acknowledged what everyone else had ignored, and for some reason, that acknowledgment seemed to rob the incident of some of its terrible power.

Grace's throat tightened with emotion. "It was never—never spoken of," she choked. "It was a shameful thing to be swept under the rug and forgotten." Her eyes fell on the bed, where Faith's son had dug several wooden sailors out of the satchel to man his ship, and she envied him the simplicity of his life.

"But not by you," Faith said. "You remember. You remember the shame and the fear. You remember every word he said, do you not?"

Grace squeezed her wet eyes shut and nodded.

"You cannot forget his words, but you can know them for what they are. They are lies, Grace, bitter, sick, perverted lies."

"I'm not ignorant," Grace protested. "I am well aware that to make a baby the man *must* violate the woman."

"There, you see, that is part of the problem. Even the words you use, 'violate' and 'rut' are frightening and base. To begin with, he does not violate her. He enters her, but she is made for him. I cannot believe that Giles made no attempt to please you, to make you ready for him."

Grace rose and went to the hearth, where she busily struck flint to steel. This was not a conversation that she could have looking into the other woman's face. "Would you like some tea?"

With a sigh of resignation, Faith said, "If you'd rather not talk about it, we won't."

"When I saw you with your husband," Grace admitted reluctantly, her eyes fixed upon her task, "and saw how you were with him, so contented and unafraid, I-I wanted to ask you about it, but . . . well, you simply don't ask about things like that."

"Well," Faith said defiantly, "today we will take tea and speak on all of the things that men brag of to each other over ale and rum. We women are too prone to silence."

"Silence makes a thing seem shameful," Grace remarked.

"So it does, but there is no shame. 'Tis quite natural." Despite her bold façade, Faith smoothed her skirts self-consciously, then folded her hands primly in her lap. "Now, I assume that Giles has touched you? In—intimate places?"

Grace nodded.

"But surely he didn't hurt you."

"Nay. It did not hurt."

"This touching, it is meant to—to stir you—to make your body prepare itself for him. You see, your womb naturally produces something to ease the way. In spite of what you were told, beyond the first time, pain is not an inherent part of joining."

"The first time? The breaking? The breaking that can only be done once."

"Aye, but again, the word you use to describe it is too

harsh. There is a barrier that must be broken, but the pain is brief and the pleasure overrides it."

Her face in flames, Grace recalled the dampness that had sprung at the touch of Giles's hand. He had ignited something, just as now a spark flew from the flint to the char in the fireplace. "But eventually he must seek his own pleasure," she argued, "else there is no seed. My uncle said that the woman must be made to hurt."

"Your uncle is a liar, and that is probably the best that may be said of him. A real man is aroused by his wife's desire. Her release as important as his."

"Her release?"

"It is . . ." Faith searched for the word, "a *completion* that he brings you to."

Grace gave a perplexed frown. "I do not think that that has happened between us."

Faith laughed softly. "You would know it if it had. Mayhap if you understood about that . . . . Oh, I cannot believe that I am about to say this!"

The char had caught the tinder, and Grace added more fuel, blowing gently on it before turning to cast an expectant look at Faith.

Faith cleared her throat. "I had been told that this was a frightful sin, of course, that even the urge to do it was a sure sign that God had not chosen you for salvation. But Geoff showed me how. He helped me to see that it is no sin, for it eases a woman's loneliness when she cannot accompany her husband to sea. It helps her to be a faithful wife. Mayhap it could help to ease your fear."

"What?" Grace demanded, frustrated by her own mortifying ignorance. Surely Faith was not implying that she should . . . should . . .

Faith fanned her hand in front of her furiously red face. "Well, if you, um, touch yourself, as Giles touches you, you'll feel it begin to happen. Then just—just follow where it leads and you'll see what I mean. *That* is what a man seeks from his lover. Not pain."

Grace coaxed the little fire she had started, carefully mulling Faith's words over in her mind. Touch herself? *There?* But it had been good at first, when Giles had done it, before the shutter had blown open and the past had swallowed her up. "You are sure 'tis not a sin?"

Faith smiled sheepishly. "I hope not. If I cannot go to Boston with Geoff, he will be gone two months or more."

The two rosy-cheeked women glanced sideways at one another then looked away. "I am sorry I spoke so harshly to you," Grace apologized.

With a little shrug, Faith replied, "I know how hard this must have been for you, but with all my heart, I believe that you and Giles can work this through."

Grace held her breath. Did she dare to hope?

Fourteen

The coast of Cayonne, the only port in Tortuga deep enough to accommodate a ship the size of *Reliance*, was all too familiar to Giles. It had been a frequent haunt of his in another life. The island itself was made of hills of solid rock; but the unyielding earth had not deterred hearty trees from dominating the land, stretching out their roots above ground, so it was densely forested. Giles knew that wild boar roamed those woods, sustenance for true buccaneers. *Boucanier* was a French word meaning hunters of wild pigs. Buccaneers on Tortuga alternated hunting boars and selling their salted meat with sailing on pirate ships along the Spanish Main.

The French word had, in its bastardized form, sneaked into the English language through criminal alliances. Tortuga had switched hands violently between the Spanish and the French several times throughout the century, but with the help of the English, the French had finally prevailed. Spain claimed official ownership of the island, but its governor, D'Ogeron, was a French citizen employed by the King of France. Privateers and pirates from both England and France were Tortuga's main defense against Spain, and D'Ogeron welcomed them all with open arms.

With England's flag flapping briskly on her mast, *Re-*

liance sailed smoothly into the harbor, only a few ships away from *Destiny*. Through a combination of speech and signs, Jawara had the other Africans working in perfect order, so that Giles hardly had to watch them handle the sails, much less give them any direction. He smiled, pleased with his crewman's initiative. Turning his attention to the harbor, he saw Geoff and his crew making sure that the ship was ready to set sail. He shouted to him, but the breeze carried away the sound, so he had to wait until they docked and he could actually board Geoff's ship.

"Giles!" Geoff greeted him from the top of the gangplank, obviously surprised. "What brings you here? Where are Faith and Grace?"

Climbing quickly, Giles replied, "At home. I left one of my men with Grace, and I spoke with your man when I saw Faith before I left. All's well. With Faith, that is. What I want to know is what brought you here."

"I told you," Geoff protested, "a sugar shipment."

"Not so," Giles countered. He pulled the letter from his jacket and handed it to Geoff.

"Damn me!" Geoff muttered, reading it. "'Tis a mystery to me, Giles." He handed Giles another letter, written on the same parchment, in the same, spidery hand. "This came a few days after you returned from Welbourne, engaged to Grace."

Dear Captain Courtney,

I find myself in a rather tight bind here in Tortuga. I've need of sanctuary, preferably on a merchant vessel, something above suspicion. I beseech you, as one of your brethren of the sea, to grant me aid. Come quickly.

En Fraternité,
Capitaine Henri Beauchamp

"Why did you not show me this?" Giles asked, after he read it.

"You were getting married. Besides, *Destiny* fit the description he gave. 'Tis a merchant vessel. Although why he asked us for help, instead of someone French, I've no idea."

"Why does he need help at all?"

"Well, that's the damnedest thing. I've asked all over, but no one knows anything. I cannot find Beauchamp, and everyone I've asked says he's not been around in a month or more."

"And as you said, Geoff, why us?" He looked at the letter again. "Why *me*? You'd think he would have written this to you, if either of us. You were the captain back when we frequented Tortuga."

"I thought that might be exactly why he chose you. He wanted someone above suspicion, and I was a bit more notorious."

Giles scratched his head and studied the bustling port. It was less developed than Port Royal. Wares went directly from one ship to another. This was a place where stolen wealth was quickly redistributed, not openly sold in a major center of Caribbean trade. The crowd consisted predominately of men. Governor D'Ogeron had imported over a hundred French prostitutes, but they had been for the citizens of Tortuga to marry. As he had hoped, the marriages had helped to settle down the rowdy men who lived there. They had set up traditional housekeeping inland, away from the sailors who made temporary use of the island for commercial reasons.

For a situation that was "getting hotter," it seemed unlikely that no one in the busy port knew anything of it.

"Does it not strike you odd that there are no scribe's

initials on either of these?" Giles asked. "Beauchamp cannot write. Nor is his English this good. And I still cannot fathom why he did not contact another Frenchman."

"He could have a literate Englishman on board. 'Tis not unheard of. Mayhap one of our old men."

"Mayhap," Giles conceded, "but the whole thing smells off. What possessed you to come without me?"

"As I said, you were to be newly wed. You'd no need of this just then. But I could hardly leave a fellow privateer in the lurch. A near stranger saved my life once. Anyway, whatever 'twas about, 'tis a moot point now. We were about to leave," Geoff said.

"I'll not be long after," Giles replied. "I picked up a shipment of sugar and some rum. Once I sell it, I'll be on my way."

They parted, and Giles was able to locate a local merchant who would take his shipment. When he returned to the ship, he was surprised to see his first mate in conversation with a stranger. The man looked to be in his late forties, dressed in French clothes, a *justaucorps* made of indigo silk with breeches that matched the jacket. Under it, he wore a lace cravat and an elaborately embroidered gold vest. Even more lace spilled from the wide cuffs of the *justaucorps*. Dark hair fell smoothly down his back, and there was something about his face that struck Giles as familiar in some way.

"Ah! *Bonjour!* You are the *capitaine* of this vessel?" the man asked in a heavy French accent.

"Aye. Giles Courtney," he said, extending his hand.

The man shook it delicately. "I understand that you are bound for Port Royal. Is this not true?"

"Aye. On the morrow."

"Oui! This is very good. I need to buy passage there. I wish to visit family in Jamaica."

Giles smiled at him. A little money on the way back was a good thing. "I can get you there," he assured the man.

"Merci. Permit me to introduce myself. I am Jacques Renault of Port de Paix. My father is a slave trader in Saint-Domingue, and I came here to do a bit of business for him. Then I think to myself, as long as I am packed and making this journey, it has been too long since I have seen my sister in Jamaica."

"Is she in Port Royal?" Giles asked. He didn't think this man would have a sister who was a prostitute, but 'twas a sure bet she wasn't a laundress either. A merchant's wife, possibly.

"Non. She lives on a plantation quite far from there."

"What plantation? Mayhap I can drop you there and save you the trouble of finding another ride."

"You are very kind, but I thought I would like to stay in Port Royal, first. There is more entertainment there than in Saint-Domingue, *n'est pas?*" He gave Giles an unscrupulous grin.

Giles chuckled. "Aye, there's plenty of entertainment in Port Royal."

"C'est bon! After a few days there, I will travel on to Welbourne."

"Welbourne! Your sister is Iolanthe Welbourne?"

"Oui! You know her?"

Giles's smile broadened. "We are in-laws, you and I. I only just wed your niece, Grace."

"Quelle coïncidence! Iolanthe wrote that Grace had married a merchant captain, but I do not recall whether she mentioned your name. Giles Courtney! *Félicitations!* Our

Grace, such a beautiful girl, *oui?* But so sad, *non?* Perhaps you will finally make her happy.

"And now, I will arrange to have my trunks sent here, and I will join you on the morrow. *Au revoir, Capitaine!*"

Giles stared after him. Grace's uncle. Of all people to land in his lap, just now. What might he know of Grace's past, and how might Giles ask of it, without seeming to question Grace's virtue?

Morning dawned, soft and gray, and Giles hadn't slept well. He was on deck at first light, longing to order his men into the rigging to unfurl the sails. He would have preferred that Jacques Renault had stayed on board ship the previous night, for he didn't want to have to wait for him. He wanted to get back to Port Royal and see whether or not Grace was still there. And what if she wasn't? He had told her that she could leave after three days, but he wasn't at all prepared to let her walk out of his life. Especially not to return to Welbourne forever. Besides, if this Jacques fellow could give him any insight, then he would surely feel compelled to use that information to try again.

He watched the dock come slowly to life. Geoff had sailed the previous afternoon, and a number of other ships had slipped away at first light. Two new vessels were seeking safe harbor and a group of men watched them from the dock through a spyglass. Ere the sky could change from gray to rose, Jacques strolled from a dockside inn and waved. Giles smiled and waved back. Renault was prompt. That reflected well upon a man, where Giles was concerned.

After brief greetings were exchanged, Giles had a crewman show their passenger to his quarters where his

trunks awaited his arrival. Again with Jawara's competent assistance, the rigging was crawling with men, who
unleashed billowing clouds of canvas that caught the
wind and snapped taut and round. The sun broke over
the horizon, gilding the first blush of daybreak, but the
golden hue didn't last long either. The sky changed
quickly to azure and would stay that way unless an afternoon rain swept in.

In these waters, any man on watch was charged with a
serious duty and had to be vigilant. The first part of the
journey would keep them between Hispaniola and
Cuba, and although *Reliance* was only a merchant vessel,
things would be tense between any Spanish and English
crafts that might meet on the Caribbean Sea. If possible,
Reliance would avoid Spanish ships, in general.

Giles had the helm. By mid-morning he had given up
his jacket, but he kept his shirt and boots on, unlike
most of the other sailors. Jawara and another Negro
hung carelessly in the rigging above deck, ebony torsos
and lower legs bare, chatting and signing with their
hands, their elbows crooked around hemp ropes. Most
of these gestures were viewed from the corners of their
eyes. Chiefly, they watched the water, extra eyes to help
a third Black in the crow's nest. They were not all from
the same tribe and did not speak the same language,
but they had managed to come up with this combination of speech and gesture and were able to
communicate. They made little attempt to talk to the
Whites on the crew, nor did the Whites speak much to
them, unless it was to communicate an order. The
Africans quickly learned the English words they needed
to know to do their jobs, and they did those jobs well.
The grim possibility of slavery made them some of the
hardest-working men on any ship. Giles shook his head.

Yet another advantage he had gained from the institution, whether he had asked for it or not.

"How do you do it?" Jacques's liquid voice interrupted Giles's thoughts.

"Do what?" Giles asked, glancing over at his fashionable passenger.

"Keep your slaves so obedient without appearing to break them? Most have to be kept under constant threat of the lash or they are useless."

Giles's gaze turned icy gray, but Jacques's eyes were fixed on the rigging above.

"I find that a little respect goes a long way toward obtaining any man's loyalty. That, along with the fact that they are not slaves, seems to be sufficient."

"Ah," Jacques said, his eyes alight. "No wonder Grace chose you. I am sure that I do not need to tell you how Grace feels about slavery."

"Nay. I am well aware of it."

"Remarkable, *n'est pas?*"

"Not really. One has only to look at how very much she loves her maid to see where her aversion to slavery comes from."

"Oui," Jacques agreed. "Of course, I always thought that Iolanthe should have separated the two when Grace was old enough to do without a nurse. Especially considering . . ." He trailed off with a guilty look, as though he had said more than he intended.

"Considering what?" Giles demanded.

"Nothing. She is a planter's daughter, that is all." He gave Giles a quick sideways glance.

Giles's heart began to beat a little faster. Jacques knew something, something he was being cautious not to tell. He seemed much like Edmund in that regard, only even less adroit at covering it. Giles looked back out to sea and kept his demeanor casual.

"Aye, she is a planter's daughter. But what of Matu? Why did you think that they should be separated?"

"Personally, I never thought that she could be trusted."

"Why not?"

Jacques's eyes followed Giles's out to the horizon. "It is hard to say. A feeling."

"There must be something," Giles coaxed.

"There was an incident," Jacques replied reluctantly.

"The attack?"

The look on Jacques's face was one of genuine shock. "She told you about it?" He stepped backward, and his eyes narrowed warily, then he frowned in perplexity. "I think she has not told you everything."

"I have some understanding of what happened," Giles said. "She did mention something about Matu being involved, but wouldn't explain."

Now the corners of Jacques's mouth turned up into a smile, and Giles realized how very much he and his sister resembled each other. "She will protect that woman at all costs. What has Grace told you?"

"May I speak frankly, *Monsieur* Renault?"

"Bien sûr. Of course."

"You are quite right. I do not know the whole story. I know that she was attacked, but Grace insists that the attack was stopped before . . . before . . ."

"You are her husband, surely by now you would have confirmed her honesty."

Giles actually blushed. It felt awkward, wrong somehow, to be discussing his wife so frankly with another man. But this was her uncle, he told himself. This was a man who might know the whole story and be able to help him help Grace.

"We haven't known one another very long, and Grace has been understandably reluctant—" He stopped and shrugged.

Jacques gave him a sympathetic look. "I understand completely. It is good to know that she has married such a patient man. We French know love. We also know wine, and the two are similar, *non*? Worth the wait. I can assure you, *Capitaine*, unless something has happened that Iolanthe has not told me, and my sister tells me everything, your bride is a virgin. There was a rather close call many years ago, but Grace has told you the truth. It was stopped short of rape."

"How many years ago?"

"Over a decade, I think."

Giles's face went white. "Dear God. Tell me what happened."

Jacques shook his head. "Perhaps I should not have said this much."

"*Monsieur*, you may be our only hope. You do want to help, do you not?"

With a heavy sigh, Jacques nodded. "Very well. She has told you nothing more than you have said?"

"Something about Matu being hurt, and something about her father coming in and the world coming apart. She mentioned thinking that she was one thing and finding out that she was something else. I could make no sense of it."

Jacques crossed his arms tightly across his chest and turned his back to Giles. "She was emotional when she spoke of it?"

"Terrified," Giles confirmed.

"Terrified," Jacques echoed softly. "After all these years. She has nightmares, I suppose."

"There is no doubt that the event left her deeply scarred." Giles waited while Jacques, his back still turned, seemed to struggle with overwhelming emotion. "Forgive me. I do not mean to add salt to family wounds."

At last, Jacques turned back around. He didn't seem overly distressed after all. "The wounds are more Grace's, I imagine. She was attacked in her bed at night by a slave. He went crazy. Surely he must have known that he would be put to death, and of course, he was. Matu claimed that he threatened her in order to get into Grace's room, but I have always wondered if she had not let him in and shown him the way. They're very spiteful, those Africans."

Giles ignored the editorial comment in favor of gaining information. "I don't think that Matu would ever be a part of that. She adores Grace."

Jacques waved his hand in dismissal. "Perhaps. Who knows?"

"What about the world coming apart, thinking that she something other than what she was?"

"She could not imagine a Black assaulting a white child. For a while, she thought she must have been black for him to do such a thing. A child's reasoning." Jacques shrugged.

"That's why she feels so close to them, the slaves on her father's plantation?"

"Perhaps. If you ask me, Matu uses her."

"You share Iolanthe's dislike for Matu."

Jacques smiled, and again, Giles thought of Iolanthe. "Iolanthe and I share many things in common. *Capitaine*, Grace and I were very close when she was a child.

In fact, I was there the night that she was attacked. Perhaps you could direct me to your home, and I could speak with her alone before you return from your ship. If I can, I would like to help."

Giles's mouth drew into a grim line. "If she is there."

Jacques's eyes opened wide in alarm. "She may not be?"

"She spoke of going home, but my friend, Faith, is trying to stop her."

"Your friend is staying with her?"

"Nay. She lives across the bay."

"So if she has convinced Grace to stay, Grace will be alone?"

"I suppose so. You're welcome to attempt to talk to her. At this point, I will try anything."

Jacques gave him a brotherly pat on the shoulder. "Let me take care of her, *Capitaine*. I have always had a special touch when it comes to my niece."

Fifteen

Grace surveyed the results of several hours' work. It had taken the better part of a week to decide, but decide she had. She was staying. She had tried to recreate the perfect organization that Giles had contrived, but in the end, she could only be grateful that she didn't have the same compulsion about it that he did. Her things were reasonably well arranged, and most of the drawers could be closed if she'd had any mind to close them.

Exhausted, she lay across the bed. It was rumpled, but it was made. She thought about her few brief attempts to heed Faith's advice, but ultimately the intensity of the sensation and the knowledge that a man slept in the office below had restrained her. She still did not fully understand what Faith had been talking about, but it had left her more willing to try again with her husband. Just thinking about what she had done brought a guilty blush to her cheeks, and she jumped when a knock sounded on the office door. 'Twas almost like being caught in the act itself.

"We're docked," a man's voice bellowed. "Cap'n wants you at the harbor."

"'Allelujah," Grace's guard replied. "Bloody dull 'ere." He called up the stairs, "Cap'n'll be 'ere soon, Mistress Courtney."

"Aye, I heard." She started to go down, thinking to join the men at the harbor, but one look at the disheveled state of the apartment gave her pause. At the very least, she could close the drawers and straighten the bed. "Tell him that I await his return," she called back. "Make certain that you tell him that."

"Aye, Mistress!"

She was more than a little relieved to have a bit of time alone to prepare herself for Giles's return. As she smoothed the bedclothes and tidied the apartment, she kept repeating to herself that all would be well. Giles wanted her. She wanted him.

Her heart fluttered and lurched in her chest when she heard the office door open. She would have thought that he would stay and oversee his men a while longer. "Giles?" she called out.

When no one answered, a strange uneasiness coiled itself around her insides. "If you seek my husband," she said, moving to the top of the stairs, "he will return at any moment." She looked below and felt her throat constrict. A wave of shock nearly impelled her straight down the stairs, but the man who had entered was blocking the door. She was trapped!

"Well, well," Jacques Renault remarked, and his voice was every bit as thick and slimy as she remembered. "You have grown, *ma chère.*"

His brown hair was pulled back tightly away from his pale face, skimming the shape of his skull. His eyes were dark and sunken, shining with malice. He smiled at her, his thin lips pressed tightly together. Fear bubbled inside of Grace, but it churned with a goodly measure of anger, as well. Here before her, the man who still wielded far too much power in her life.

She lifted her chin. "My husband is on his way home,"

she warned. "I have told him all. I need only speak your name and he will split you upon his cutlass. And I warn you, he was first mate to the notorious Geoffrey Hampton!"

Jacques chuckled. "Aye, so I am told. But you lie, *ma petite*. You have told him so little. He has no idea who has caused his bride to hold so fast to her virginity."

Grace gasped. "How . . ."

Moving with all the predatory grace of a cat, Jacques glided to the foot of the stairs. "He brought me here. Brought to you your worst nightmare. You still have them, he says, nightmares, memories."

She shook her head in mute denial.

"Mais oui. You see, Grace, it is I who know everything. Imagine your *capitaine's* relief to meet a member of your family who did not hide your past."

A whimper escaped her tight throat. "You told him . . ."

"About your near rape at the hands of a crazed slave? *Oui.* And I told him about us. About how close we always were. He is, even now, delaying his return so that I may allay your fear of the marriage bed." Jacques chuckled as though at some clever irony.

"But he will return. You only delay the inevitable. When he comes, I will tell him who you are. What you have done."

The door opened again behind Jacques, admitting two sullen-looking men in filthy rags. They held flint-locks in their hands, and cutlasses hung in scabbards at their hips. "The others is on the ship," one muttered. "They're makin' it damn 'ard for 'im to put 'em off, but 'is patience won't 'old long. That 'er?" He nodded up the stairs toward Grace.

"She is the one," Jacques answered. He looked at her. "We are in a bit of a hurry, *ma petite.* I have two more gentlemen in my employ who are with your husband right now. They will delay him for a time, then follow him home. Unless they receive the proper signal from me, he will not make it back here alive."

"He is very strong, and was once a pirate," Grace protested, but fear for Giles began to churn in her stomach. "He will defeat your hired killers."

Jacques shrugged carelessly. "I wonder which of us is more certain of the outcome? I will tell you what, Grace. We will wait and see, together. I will stay here, and if my men fail, I will take the consequences. I imagine you are right about one thing, if he returns and you tell him what I did, he will kill me." He propped one foot upon the bottom stair and leaned forward. "I am staking my life that your captain will die ere he can dispatch me."

The fear had wormed its way from her stomach into her throat. "What do you want?"

"I have booked passage to Havana for the two of us. I want you to board that ship like *une bonne jeune fille.*"

"I am no longer a little girl," she retorted.

His eyes swept over her with a look of pure disdain. *"Quelle dommage.* A pity. You are a beautiful woman, but you were much more appealing as a child. Nonetheless, I want you to accompany me."

"Why? Why Havana?"

He shrugged again. "Why not?"

Why not, indeed, she thought. It seemed to her that Cuba was better than Saint-Domingue. He would have many friends in French Hispaniola, but Cuba was surely more neutral territory. And 'twasn't too far from Jamaica. Granted, it was Spanish, and perhaps that was why Jacques had chosen it. He thought that a Spanish port would keep Giles at bay. But Grace was no longer a terrified child. She was a woman fully grown. She had been given life and had been raised by women who had survived the worst that life could deal them. She had a future worth living for. Jacques had stolen her past; he would not have her future.

She set her mouth in a grim line and squared her shoulders. "Very well. I will accompany you to your ship. But I tell you this now, somehow I will come back here, and if you have not kept your word, if anything happens to my husband, I will go straight to his best friend, and you will rue the day that you were born. Ere he has finished with you, you will beg for death."

Jacques stepped to the side and made a sweeping gesture to indicate that she should pass him. "No doubt. This way, *Madame* Courtney. You have been kind enough to warn me, so I will return the courtesy. I will walk behind you with my hand upon my flintlock. Do not make a scene."

Flanked by Jacques's hirelings, surrounded by the stench of stale rum and sweat, intensely aware of her uncle's sinister presence at her back, Grace walked briskly out the door and down High Street. Her rough-looking escorts seemed to deter the usual crude comments of men passing her on the road, though for once, she would have gladly welcomed their attentions. She looked all about her, hoping to see some face in the crowd that she recognized, but she had seldom ventured beyond the office of Courtney and Hampton Shipping. She knew no one here. Faith, her newfound friend, was clear across the bay, and Geoff with her, Grace could only assume.

How could this be? How could whores smile at sailors and men laughingly swill rum in the taverns that lined the busy street? How could she cast such desperate looks at the people crowding High Street, only to be ignored?

But Port Royal was filled with desperate people, and the last thing that any of them wanted was to encounter the likes of her entourage.

Tantalizingly, frustratingly, so much so that she could have torn the hair from her head, she saw *Destiny* at the far end of the dock, but ere they came close to it, Jacques and his minions turned sharply and they all mounted the gangplank of a decrepit looking vessel. Once on deck, she looked over and saw Geoffrey, his broad back to her. She looked even more frantically and saw *Reliance*, her sails furled and quiet, no sign of Giles on deck.

"Oh please," she whispered. "Please, Captain Hampton, look behind you. Turn around and see me."

But he didn't, and a shifty-eyed swab with but five teeth, had he any, led her and Jacques to the hatch that would take them below the deck. Another brief look around revealed that sailors were quickly climbing about the rigging. They would be setting sail within minutes. Then Jacques gave her a little push toward the ladder and they descended into darkness. The sailor took Jacques and Grace to a dim, stifling cabin with a narrow bunk covered in stained linens that smelled of mildew. Grace thought longingly of Giles's immaculate bed. There was also a trunk bound in highly polished leather. She assumed it to be Jacques's, as it didn't seem to fit in with the rest of the surroundings.

"Giles will notice that my things have been left behind," Grace informed him. "He will never believe that I left without packing so much as a change of clothing."

Jacques crossed to the one tiny porthole in the wall and gazed out. "Again, I have no doubt that you are right. Of course, now that we are under way, the realization will be of little use to him."

The knowledge that they were heading out to sea made Grace's heart begin to race, and she was finding it hard to breathe. Still, she forced herself to stay calm. "Giles would never trust you. He knows what kind of person Iolanthe is. How could he trust her brother? He came home by another route. I saw his ship ere we left, and he was not on it. He'll search for me and learn that I have been taken here. You think yourself so clever, but you marched me straight up High Street, in front of God and everyone. It will take him no time at all—"

Jacques turned away from the window and back to Grace, no trace of worry or concern on his face. "Who knows where he was? But he was not on his way home. He left you to me, *ma chère*, whether you wish to think so or not."

"Nay. Not with the brother of Iolanthe Welbourne."

Jacques shoved her hard, and she fell onto the narrow bunk behind her. Then he stood so close to her that she could not rise without being far closer to him than ever she intended to be again in her life.

"I acknowledged my sister's faults. God knows, she despises you so, I could hardly hope that she had hidden it. I told him that, in my sister's mind, Edmund spoiled you. She was jealous. It does not take a genius to see that Iolanthe is vain and selfish."

"Ha! But that was not the explanation my father gave! Giles would have seen right through you. You, who claimed to know me so well!"

"*Oui.* He said that your father had cited Matu as the cause of the rift. I explained that it was but one of many such problems. I told him that Iolanthe had wanted you and Matu separated when you had grown too old for a nurse, and that Edmund's indulgence in allowing you to keep her, despite her failure to protect you from other Africans, had incensed his wife."

That would have made perfect sense, but Grace refused to admit that. Instead, she smirked and said, "I *have* told someone though, told her all. How long do you think it will be ere my husband seeks his friend's counsel over my disappearance? How long ere that man's wife reveals my attacker to be none other than my uncle. He will seek you out. He will find me."

"If it is I whom he seeks, then he will never find you."

"What—what do you plan to do?"

Jacques ran his fingers lightly over the side of her face. "Are you afraid of me, Grace? Was it rape you thought I had on my mind?"

She swallowed hard. Aye, 'twas exactly what she thought, but she'd not say as much to him. She gave him a mutinous glare.

"Save your defiance, *chèri*. You are no longer to my taste. Too hairy, too plump in all the wrong places, on the whole, too big. But my tastes are somewhat— unique. In fact, many men prefer women just like you. The money I make from a Havana brothel for your voluptuous body and untouched maidenhead will buy a dozen flat-chested, slender mulatto girls, with coin to spare."

Grace's brave front began to crumble. Nonetheless, she whispered, "He will find me."

Jacques moved away again, back toward the window. "By the time he does, will he want you? You will be sold for what you are. Not an innocent white woman, but as an African slave. 'What?' witnesses will ask your *capitaine*. 'That mulatto wench? She is your wife?' Is he so noble, Grace, your fine husband, that he will claim before the world that he bound himself to a Negro whore?"

"I am not purely Negro," she snapped back. "You forget; my pure African blood is tainted by my white father's—and yours! I am your sister's child."

"So you would have the world believe . . ."

"So I am! I remember much of that awful night. I remember the tale Iolanthe told. My mother was conceived of a union between your father and one of his slaves. I am the daughter of your black half-sister!"

Jacques's face went purple. "You dare to place yourself on the same level as . . ."

Grace rose to her feet. "Oh aye, I dare! I will not cower before you, Jacques Renault. I believe myself to be your equal or better. I believe that I am worthy of the freedom I have known all my life—freedom to which my mother was entitled as well! And aye, I believe Giles will want me, because I am a woman worth having. Nay— not worth having, worth loving. Can you say the same of yourself, *mon oncle*? Whom have you ever loved? Who has ever loved you?"

Jacques sneered at her, but there was something in his dark eyes, something almost intimidated, when he looked at her. "A few days in a Havana *bordel* will teach you your place."

"I already know my place, and by God, I will not lose it to you again."

Giles had been relieved to finally be rid of the two men who had come on board his ship seeking work. He had sent them on their way, but now that he was striding up High Street to the office, they were back, a few yards behind him. His hand resting lightly upon the hilt of his cutlass, he paused once to take a long, hard look at them. 'Twas better they should know that he was aware of them. But they seemed unperturbed. Then a man, an acquaintance of some sort, beckoned to them from a tavern across the street, and they went inside.

For days, Giles had been steadfastly refusing to consider the possibility that Grace had done as she had vowed and gone back to Welbourne. Now, although his man had confirmed that Grace had not left, doubts assailed him. His palms were sweating as he opened the office door and paused to listen for the voices of Grace and Jacques. When he heard nothing, he went to the foot of the stairs and called up softly. "Grace? *Monsieur* Renault?"

Silence. On the other side of the office door, the street was filled with the usual sounds, shouts and laughter, all softly muted. He stood at the bottom of the stairs, half wondering if she had convinced her uncle to take her away.

"*Monsieur* Renault!" Giles called, mounting the steps. "Is anyone here?"

He reached the top and smiled. The bed didn't look like he had made it, but it was presentable. Combs, jars, trinkets littered the dresser top. To reassure himself, he opened the wardrobe and saw tiny bits of lace trapped at the edges of drawers. He glanced at the kitchen table and spied an unwashed cup and plate. There was no fire, but when he walked over to the hearth, some warmth radiated from it, and a pot of hot water hung over coals that had not long been cold. He used a bit of the water to wash the dishes and put them away.

They should have left a note, Giles thought, feeling a little irritated and more than a little uneasy. Port Royal was not exactly a city suited to pleasant strolls. Restless, he walked swiftly down the street to the inn where he and Grace often supped, but the proprietress said she'd not seen Grace since the day before. Shopping, he wondered, taking a meal elsewhere? Suddenly this city that boasted but two main streets seemed impossibly large. How was Renault with a weapon? Could he defend Grace if called upon to do so?

He headed back to the docks on the off chance they might have thought to go looking for him. Mayhap he had merely passed them on the street. He arrived at the harbor and spotted Geoff just leaving *Destiny*.

"Geoff!" he called.

"Giles! I'd have thought you'd be back home with your bride."

"'Twas my intent, but I seem to have lost her." He tried to smile and make the comment lightly, but his throat was tight and his voice sounded unnatural, even to his own ear.

"Y'ought to be more careful with your wenches," Geoff chided. Then he grew serious as well. "I'd have stopped by, but after talking to Faith last night, I thought to leave you two alone awhile. Are you sure that Grace knows you're back?"

"Aye, I'm sure. She was there when I sent for my man, and he returned with a message that she awaited me."

"Aye, Faith said Grace was staying, but that there was much between you."

"She has the right of that. You don't know what it meant to me, having Faith to help me. It seems that between her and Grace's uncle, we might have a fighting chance. 'Course, I'll have to find her yet."

Geoff frowned. "Her uncle?"

"Aye," Giles replied. "'Twas a stroke of luck, that. I picked up a passenger in Tortuga, and who should it be but Mistress Welbourne's brother?"

Geoff took hold of Giles's shoulder in a crushing grip. "Iolanthe's brother?"

At the look on Geoff's face, alarm surged through Giles's blood, and his scalp began to tingle as it often had just before a battle. "Aye, him. He told me everything that happened to her. It was terrible, and she was but a child."

"He told you everything? Did he tell you that the terrible thing that happened, happened at his hands?"

Now Giles was cold, ice cold. The man had looked so damned much like Iolanthe. But Giles had shaken that off. He had ignored his instincts. He told himself that physical resemblance didn't mean that the similarities went any deeper. But there had been something in the eyes, the same coldness.

"He said a slave . . ." he protested.

Geoff uttered a sharp expletive under his breath. "Grace told Faith. She said that her uncle had hurt her, done terrible things. Where is he now, Giles?"

"He went ahead of me to see her." It was, indeed, very like sailing into battle. There were those moments of doubt, the edge of panic, the icy touch of fear, but when the fight was upon them, all of that vanished. Hot anger poured through his veins, banishing the cold. The usual noise and confusion of the docks began to sort itself out into neat pieces. "Ask about the taverns," Giles said, his tone the same clipped voice of command he used on board his ship. "See if anyone remembers seeing either of them. I'll look here."

His gray eyes scanned the harbor and he searched through his memory for every ship he had passed or sighted during the day. Which had since sailed? He never spared a thought for the fact that he had just given an order to a man he had ever considered his captain.

By the time Geoff met up with Giles on board *Reliance*, they had both heard the same story. A beautiful woman fitting Grace's description had been seen walking down High Street with what appeared to be two pirates and a dark-haired Frenchman, given his style of dress. They had been headed toward the docks. From what Giles could glean, she had last been seen somewhere around *La Dame de la Mer*, a French pirate vessel that had set sail an hour or two earlier. No one seemed to know where it was bound. Pirate ships seldom had a specific destination.

"I've twelve men of my own," Giles told Geoff. "I need more to chase the likes of D'Olivier and his cutthroat crew. How many on your ship right now?"

"Not many more."

"Two dozen should do it."

"Not if we have to engage D'Olivier on the high seas."

Giles smirked. "You've not taken the measure of his ship lately. Bloody miracle *La Dame de la Mer* hasn't sunk of her own accord. Get your men. We leave tonight."

"Wait a minute, Giles. You're the level-headed one, remember? 'Twill be well past dark ere we can take on supplies and set sail, and we've no idea where to go. The Caribbean Sea is a big place, y'know."

Giles turned to his friend, his mind well set. "I can sail out of this bloody harbor in my sleep, and I know just where we're headed. Welbourne Plantation."

"Welbourne? From what Faith told me, Welbourne would kill Renault. He'll know nothing."

Giles shook his head. "God, I'm an idiot. Two urgent missives directing me, specifically, to come to the aid of a *French* privateer I barely know, one who can't even write. And then, by pure chance, I happen upon Jacques Renault."

"Your engagement was less than three weeks long. Renault couldn't have learned about the wedding and then sent for you so fast."

"Nay, but someone else could. Someone who learned of our engagement immediately. Someone who could summon Renault and me simultaneously. Someone who hates Grace and would stop at nothing to see her unhappy."

"Iolanthe Welbourne," Geoff confirmed.

"Mayhap no one here knows where D'Olivier is sailing *La Dame de la Mer*, but I'd wager my ship that Iolanthe knows where Renault is taking Grace."

Sixteen

Aside from architecture that was decidedly more Spanish, with the buildings covered in pale adobe, Havana was not unlike Port Royal. Spanish was the predominant language, but the din in the streets and taverns was heavily laced with Portuguese, Italian, Dutch, even a good deal of English and French, for Havana knew no enemies. Spain and its rivals were an ocean away. Here, anyone with gold in his pockets was counted a friend. In fact, Havana was even more permissive than Port Royal, and so it was popular not only with pirates and the like, but it was the capitol city for European spies. One could buy anything in Havana, whores, slaves, traitorous secrets, along with goods from the world over.

The glistening buildings made the street seem sunnier, in contrast to Port Royal's Tudor-style structures, but the brightness did nothing to soothe Grace's horror. It seemed impossible that she was about to be auctioned off at a block right in the middle of a sun-drenched square in the center of town. Such an unconscionable act was best suited to dark alleys or decrepit buildings in the dark of night. Her hands were bound so tightly behind her back that she could feel the hemp biting into her flesh. Jacques led the way while one of the pirates

from the ship shoved her along from behind. He wore
a sheathed cutlass hanging at his side by a sash, and she
could hear it rattle softly and dangerously with each
step.

The auction block was surrounded by pens, each one
rented by an individual slaver. She scrutinized all of
them, trying to ascertain whether or not the Whites in
charge might speak English. Most of them spoke in
rapid Spanish among themselves, so it seemed useless
to try to enlist their aid.

Toward the rear of the auction block, Jacques stopped
and beckoned another man over with his hand. Grace's
captor stopped her several feet away and whispered in
her ear, "Listen wench, 'old still and don't say nothin'."

While Jacques and the slaver spoke, Grace perused
the enclosure next to her. To her complete revulsion,
she saw that it was filled with women. There were a number of dark Africans, as Grace would have expected, but
there were also lighter ones, some appeared Arabian,
others East Indian and Oriental. There were even white
women in tattered garments. Some wept, some stared
blankly, some simply looked bored until a particularly
handsome or well-dressed man strolled by. Then their
faces lit with hard smiles and they beckoned to the men
in languages Grace didn't understand.

It would have been easy to allow the sight to overwhelm her, easy to become one of the women who wept
or whose faces were masks of hollow-eyed shock. She
gave her head a shake and strained to catch Jacques's
conversation. It was in French, a language she could
speak, thanks to her father. His commerce with Saint-
Domingue had left him quite fluent, and he had
insisted that she learn it, as well.

Jacques and the slaver walked casually over to her,

and the pirate, seeming to know the custom, forced her to turn for inspection. The slaver, a squat man whose sun-dried face defied any guess at his age, actually pulled back her lips to peer at her teeth. Grace jerked her head away and exclaimed, *"Mon père est trés riche! Il payera le rançon pour moi."*

Both men laughed, and Jacques replied, "He knows that your father is rich. Of course, I have also explained that your mother was his mulatto slave. It is unlikely that he believes your offer of ransom."

"Vous avez dit elle parle Anglais," said the slaver.

"Oui. Elle parle Français et Anglais. Je n'ai su pas."

The slaver smiled and Jacques turned to Grace. "I did not know that you spoke French. It makes you more valuable, to be able to understand men's commands in two languages. I suppose Spanish is too much to hope for?"

She glared at him through narrow eyes. *"Cochon!"* It seemed an insult to pigs, but she didn't know any of the words she would have rather called him.

"Quel marmot!" the slaver said with a chuckle.

"Did he just call me a woodchuck?" Grace demanded.

"Brat," Jacques corrected with a sneer.

"Une vierge avec beaucoup d'esprit," the slaver said. *"C'est bon. Les bordels payeront beaucoup d'argent pour la."*

Perfect, Grace thought wryly. Apparently insulting her uncle and showing some spirit had also only increased her value, along with the fact that Jacques had apparently told this man about her virginity.

The slaver looked her over one last time and barked, *"Viens."* Come. He opened a gate and shoved her into the wooden pen with the other women before moving on to talk to someone else. She and Jacques both looked quickly around them. The gate and perimeter of the pen were guarded by three enormous African men with gleaming ebony skin. They possessed neither firearms nor swords, but each held a whip coiled loosely in his hand, as though poised to unfurl it upon the back of anyone who dared to cross him.

Jacques looked back at Grace, triumph in his eyes. "I think that I can leave you in their capable hands. *Monsieur* LaMont will handle your sale. Even after he has taken his generous commission, I am quite sure that I will have a sizable purse to ensure my enjoyment of this little excursion."

"And when my father finds out?"

"He will be furious with me, but he will not touch me. My father tolerates yours only for Iolanthe's sake. He will not allow Edmund Welbourne anywhere near me."

"Iolanthe," Grace gasped. She hadn't even thought of it before, but now, she was certain of the answer even as she demanded, "Is she behind all of this? She told you of my marriage and where to find me, didn't she?"

"Not that Edmund can prove."

Grace leaned against the wooden side of the enclosure, only to be shoved back by a large, black hand. She looked over at the guard who gazed impassively back at her.

"You see, Grace," Jacques crooned, "your kind turn so easily upon each other. All those years you wasted feeling sorry for these Africans, and now, they will deliver you into bondage."

She ignored the taunt. "My father may not be able to get to you, but Giles can. And you had better have a care for your sister. The moment Giles tells Father what became of me, her life will take a turn for the worse."

"She despises your provincial father. With just cause, she can leave him, come home where she belongs. He is the one who had better have a care. If she leaves, she will take our father's slaves with her. Are you so certain that you mean that much to Welbourne, or will he endure the loss of his African brat in exchange for his plantation's labor force?"

She had no answer for that, and he seemed to read it on her face, for as she faltered, he laughed. "Accustom yourself to being scrutinized and purchased, *ma chère*, for it is to be your lot in life."

He backed away to be swallowed by the throngs of people who passed, and his cruel face was quickly replaced by scores of men ogling the occupants of the corral. Grace was not to be undone. She knew that Giles was partly responsible for the fearsome reputation that *Destiny* had obtained in the Spanish Caribbean in her privateer days, but his name would not inspire the same fear as that of the captain of that vessel.

In a loud, ringing voice, she proclaimed, *"Mon frère est Capitaine Geoffrey Hampton. Il se battra pour moi. Si vous m'achetez, il vous touera!* Captain Geoffrey Hampton is my brother. He will fight for me. If you buy me, he will kill you. Do you hear me? I must be released, or the man who buys me will incur the wrath of my brother! *Combien des Espagnols ont se batté avec Capitaine Hampton? Combien des les Espagnols ont survivu? Il payera le rançon pour moi!* He will pay my ransom! How many Spaniards have fought against my brother and lived? Very few, I assure you!"

Most of the men passing by the enclosure gave her curious looks. A few simply laughed. A guard, the same one who had pushed her away from the side of the pen earlier, snapped his whip at her, tearing her sleeve and biting into the flesh on her arm. Burning pain shot through, silencing her. Then he went back to staring apathetically into the crowd.

Grace's head sank to her chest, even as her heart sank into her stomach. She had expected her threats to create a stir of fear, but either no one understood her or no one cared. She jerked her head back up again when a soft voice with a slight Spanish accent cut through the din.

"*Señorita,* you say that Geoffrey Hampton is your brother?"

"Aye!" she exclaimed softly, keeping her own voice low so as not to attract the attention of her guards. Subtly, she moved closer to the man who had spoken. His thin face was framed by long dark hair, and he was leaning casually against the side of the pen, looking as if he were merely shopping for a female slave.

The man shook his head. "You will save yourself no trouble by lying. Geoffrey Hampton is an only child."

Grace looked around self-consciously. Was this a trick? Was Geoff an only child? Faith had said his mother was a prostitute. How could a prostitute have only one child? Still, she decided to play the game a bit differently.

"Actually, he is my brother-in-law. Faith, my sister, is married to him."

This time the man smiled at her, but it was not unkind. "Faith Cooper has only brothers."

Grace's eyes widened. Whoever this man was, he had more than a passing acquaintance with Geoff and Faith. He didn't seem hateful or bitter, so it seemed unlikely that their relationship was entirely adversarial, despite the fact that the man was obviously a Spaniard.

"You know them well?" she asked.

"Well enough to know that you are a liar."

"Please, sir, I'll tell you the truth. Do you know Geoff's first mate, Giles Courtney?" The man didn't react; he simply waited for her to continue. *"He* is my husband. I lied because no one's ever heard of Giles Courtney, and they'd not be afraid of him." She started to say that they should fear Giles, for he'd killed as many Spaniards as Geoff, but then she realized that such a statement would hardly endear her to this man.

"Then what are you doing here?" the man asked.

"I was kidnapped. Please sir, I am a gentlewoman. I should not be here!" She looked around her and felt the same flush of guilt she had felt at home during a slave's whipping. These other women belonged here no more than she. Still, staying would not serve them, and it would destroy her with them. "Geoff and Giles will pay you! They are successful merchants, now. You have only to buy me yourself, then send word." Dear God, she prayed silently, let me be telling the truth about that.

By now, the slaver caught sight of the two of them in conversation and hurried over. *"Parlez-vous Français?"* he asked. The Spaniard shook his head, and the slaver motioned another man over. Apparently he was a translator, and soon the French and Spanish were flying so rapidly that Grace could only catch a few words.

The Spaniard regarded her narrowly. "They say you are a Mulatto."

She wanted to deny it, denounce the men as liars, but it stuck in her throat. She said the only thing that she knew she would be able to say without choking on her own words. "My mother was a Mulatto. Giles doesn't know. But he hates slavery. He will pay you back to keep me free, I'm sure of it."

The Spaniard said something to the translator who

passed it on, then he disappeared back into the crowd, taking Grace's last shred of hope with him.

A short while later, *Capitán* Diego Montoya Fernandez de Madrid y Delgado Cortes sat at a table in *El Paraíso*. A man of many tastes and moods, he was certainly capable of leading his men into a local *taberno* for a night of hard drinking. But this afternoon, he preferred the relatively quiet atmosphere of this spacious and pricey *posada*. He had rented a room here earlier in the day, with every intention of discretely entertaining a lovely young widow of his acquaintance that evening. Now, he found himself sipping from a goblet of wine and contemplating the auction block, visible through the window of the dining room. The slaver had said that the women would go up for sale in an hour.

He was a merchant sea captain by trade, and spent most of his days on the high seas between Spain, Africa, and the Caribbean, but he stood on solid ground in Havana more often than anywhere else on the globe. With long, slim fingers, he lifted the heavy glass goblet to his lips. Like his hands, his face was narrow and aristocratic. His mahogany hair curled at the ends and fell across the shoulders of his black jacket. He was a handsome man with a fetching *amiga* in each of the cities where he most often made port. Nothing serious with any of them, but satisfying enough friendships that he had no need to purchase a woman from the block or anywhere else. He wouldn't have noticed the one he had spoken with except that she had called out the name of a man he had known all too well.

Diego took a more liberal swallow of wine, relishing the sweetness that lingered in its wake. The flavor brought to mind the mouth of a particular woman. Not one of his casual lovers, of whom he expected nothing permanent and who expected nothing of him but a lovely bauble or two. He closed his eyes and could still recall this particular woman in perfect detail, exquisitely fair, infinitely ingenuous, utterly Protestant.

He opened his eyes again on that thought. So Faith Cooper had chosen Geoffrey Hampton over him; it was all for the better. Diego had even managed to stop thinking of her so much. Only on those nights when Magdalena, his patron saint, neglected her watch over his dreams. Then Faith would slip in and lie willingly in Diego's arms for a while.

He searched his memory for what he knew of Hampton's first mate. He had not seen much of him. He did, however, recall the man's kindness to Diego's cabin boy, Galeno. The lad had rushed the pirate in the heat of a battle, and . . . what had the woman said her husband's name was? Courtney? Courtney had scooped the boy up, rendering him powerless, but not hurting the lad. Later, when the boy was under control, he had even patted his head and smiled at him.

Diego set his goblet down on the table and pursed his lips thoughtfully. He owed Hampton and his friend nothing. Less than nothing. In fact, they owed him. Were it not for Diego, Hampton would have hanged in Cartagena over two years ago. Merchant captains now, Hampton and his friend. Merchant captains because of the deal Diego had struck to spare Faith's lover from the Spanish courts. He shook his head at the memory. 'Twas water under the bridge now, and he'd never truly regretted the choice he'd made.

And anyway, none of the things that had transpired in Cartagena were the responsibility of the poor woman he'd met outside. Her clothes, her carriage, her accent, all spoke of a woman gently reared. And she was so fair. Likely as not, she had lived her whole life as a White. He thought of his own dear sisters at home. How devastated they would be if they suddenly found themselves for sale! Even his eldest sister, who could hold her own against anyone, would rather die than be in that young woman's position.

He rubbed his hands over his eyes. *Magdalena*, he prayed silently to his patron saint, *I cannot allow a gentlewoman to face such a terrible fate. But would it be so much to ask that you stop sending me Englishwomen in distress? A Spanish maiden would be most welcome.*

He paid his bill and sauntered back out to the auction block.

To her horror, Grace was to be first at the block. She was grateful to have eaten almost nothing since her last meal in Port Royal, for otherwise, anything in her stomach would have been instantly expelled as she made the humiliating journey up the steps to the raised platform. She stood with the auctioneer and a translator, surrounded by a crowd mostly of men. Many wore the plain clothes of common laborers and farmers, and they eyed her wistfully for a moment before turning back to scrutinize some of the other women in the pen. This one was too rich for their blood. No hope that an honest man might purchase her to be his wife. If one had, she might have convinced him to return her to Giles for a reward.

The men, and even a handful of women, who jostled forward to bid were well dressed, if a bit garish. They looked her over as if she were a prize heifer and regarded one another with competitive gleams in their eyes. Grace felt like she couldn't catch her breath, and the harder she fought to breathe, the less air she seemed to take in. The fear she had experienced with Jacques paled in comparison to the stark terror that pumped furiously through her veins. Her hands, still bound behind her, were numb, blood roared in her ears, and black spots began to dance in front of her eyes.

The auctioneer growled something threatening at her in Spanish. The translator snapped, "Do not faint, *estúpida.* Breathe slowly."

Actually, it occurred to Grace that unconsciousness would be the best way to endure this whole process, but the abhorrent idea of waking in a strange place, with no knowledge of what had happened, helped her gain control over her breathing. Slowly the spots faded, but the nausea held fast to her insides.

In Spanish, Dutch, Portuguese, French, and English, her finer points were highlighted by the auctioneer. "A beautiful face, a body made for pleasure, a fiery spirit shown earlier, but obviously able to submit, as you can see by her current, subdued demeanor. Fluent in French and English. Best of all, ladies and gentlemen, a virgin!"

At this final announcement, a collective gasp of approval went up, and the crowd pressed closer, though a few of them fell back, shaking their heads. Her value had just risen dramatically.

There was a commotion to Grace's left, and the Spaniard she had met earlier waded through the mass of potential bidders. He spoke to the auctioneer in rapid, challenging Spanish, and the crowd began to mumble discontentedly. The auctioneer responded defensively, shouting at the man.

"Qu'est-ce que c'est?" drawled a detestably familiar voice from the edge of the circle.

The Spaniard turned and addressed Jacques, first in Spanish, then English. "I speak no French. Do you speak Spanish or English?"

"Aye, English," Jacques answered.

"I spoke with this woman earlier. She told me that she had been married. How can it be that she is a virgin?"

One of the women in the group shouted back in a heavy Spanish accent. "If I am to sell this *puta's* maidenhead tonight, she had better damned well have one!"

Bile rose and scalded the back of Grace's throat. These people were *all* procurers! Even the women!

Jacques, his usual confident self, shrugged carelessly. "She lies, of course." He glared venomously at Grace, although he addressed his next words to the auctioneer. "If you wish, *monsieur*, examine her for yourself right now. I assure you, she is intact."

Grace shook her head violently. "Nay, nay! Do not touch me! I swear he speaks the truth!" She turned back to the Spaniard, desperation making her voice shrill. "But I did not lie to you, *Señor*. I am married to Giles Courtney, just as I said. Surely in Spain a gentleman is patient with a new wife if they were not well acquainted when they married."

He gave her a doubtful look. "Your stories do not hold together well, *Señora.*"

"Please!" She sounded hysterical now, but she couldn't help herself. "Please, you must believe me!"

Jacques laughed harshly. "You see, a consummate liar and a brilliant actress. Think of how she will delight your customers with such a cry. Please! Please!" he imitated her in a falsetto voice, but he made it sound carnal, and the company around him laughed in appreciation.

She might have fallen apart completely but for the pure, strong hatred of her uncle that filled her. Shamelessly she fell to her knees and looked straight into the Spaniard's deep brown eyes. "I swear upon my soul, upon my body that I am telling you the truth. If I am not, if you send for Giles and he disavows our union or refuses to ransom me, I will do anything you wish. You may auction me yourself and make the money back."

The man looked at the people around him and the block before him with undisguised revulsion.

The auctioneer yanked her to her feet and began speaking again. Once more, in a variety of languages, Grace listened to him hawk her more valuable assets, including now her skill at performance. The bidding came fast and furious at first, then slowly dwindled to three men in loud silks and lace. The Spaniard shrugged apologetically at Grace, lifting his purse and shaking his head. Her price had outstripped his means.

The one word that was now being repeated in several languages by the auctioneer and translator washed over Grace until the translator reached English. "Sold!"

She looked back at the trio that had been competing for her, and one of them, a stout man with thick, dirty blond hair, mounted the steps to claim her. He spoke to the translator who obligingly repeated the message in his many tongues.

"The wench's virginity will go up for auction tonight at *El Jardín de Placer*. Bidding begins at ten o'clock. *Don* Ramon promises to have her biddable and eager to please by that time."

"Don't mark 'er, though! Leave all that pretty golden

skin fer me!" called a man from the back. He wore an expensive jacket and fine linen shirt, but the shirt was stained and unfastened, the jacket crusty. He had with him a motley assortment of men—a pirate captain and his crew, no doubt. He leered at her and actually wiped his mouth with the back of his hand as though he were salivating in anticipation.

After receiving a translation, the procurer smiled and said, "¡No, no! No cardenal. No bruise. Perfect for you, Señor."

He took her by the arm, and Grace acted purely from instinct. She brought her heel down hard on his foot and bolted for the stairs. Once there, a half dozen pairs of hands pushed her back up where the auctioneer and translator grabbed her and held fast until the procurer stopped hopping around. She didn't know any Spanish curse words, but she was fairly certain that she was being regaled with quite an assortment from her purchaser. Nonetheless, he doled out the gold that he had agreed to pay.

"On second thought, mate," called the pirate, "leave 'er as she is! I likes a wench with some fight in 'er!" His men laughed.

The procurer grabbed her arm again, but he raised his hand, clearly intending to strike her if she tried to escape again. Grace refused to cringe, but neither did she resist. Any attempt to escape here would be futile. She had to wait until she was no longer surrounded. Unable to resist, she looked once more in her uncle's direction. He smiled at her and rubbed his fingertips lightly together. She had just made him a small fortune.

The man who had bought her shoved her down the stairs and through the streets. Periodically, he would force her to stop while he called out to men that he apparently knew and said something about a *subasta*. The men would nod, and the procurer would rattle the purse that hung at his waist and laugh.

After the seventh or eighth such stop, he pulled her into an airy inn, through a shaded foyer, and into a courtyard that must surely have rivaled a Spanish palace. The décor was Moorish, with a mosaic floor of brilliant blues, purples, and golds. A marble fountain, splashing water down three tiers, dominated the center of the yard. Large cushions of rich silk littered the tile floor. Gleaming white benches lined walls covered by trellises of flowering vines. The flowers lent an odor of overpowering sweetness to the air, and Grace didn't know how much more she could take before she would lose her battle with her stomach.

On the other side of the courtyard, he stopped, unlocked a door, and shoved her through it. The chamber appeared to be a huge dressing room with an assortment of vanities and wardrobes from which a profusion of colorful silks spilled out. There was one small, barred window that threw a patch of striped brightness on the floor. As in the courtyard, the floor was scattered with cushions, but beautiful women draped in caftans or scanty, silk shifts occupied many of them. Like the women in the pen, they came in varying shades of brown, and they looked up at Grace with expressions of vague interest. The man muttered something in Spanish to them, pointing to Grace. Then he left, locking the door behind him.

A woman with deep caramel skin offset by a dusky rose shift glided over to her and removed the bonds from her wrists. She took Grace's chin in her hand and moved her face from side to side, inspecting her. "You Mulatto, like me," the woman said. "You gotta pretty color. De maas sey you a virgin. Him a-go sell you tonight an' we tell you what a do."

Grace felt like she was in a dream. No, more removed even than that. Someone else's dream. She wanted to beg for help, but she couldn't seem to open her mouth and get the words out.

"No worries. Fight a little, den give up, an' when him stick it in you, moan *'Oh muy grande Señor, muy grande.'* It don' matta how tiny it be. Dem like dat, an' it ova in no time." She snapped her fingers for emphasis. "It hurt a little dis time, but it betta dan a beatin'. You get use' to it."

Grace stared blankly at her for a moment before politely asking, "Have you a chamber pot in here?"

The woman jerked her head toward a screen in the corner, and Grace rushed behind it where she knelt and vomited bitter, yellow acid until she thought her stomach was going to turn inside out.

Seventeen

Iolanthe paced the length of the keeping room, blood thrumming excitedly through her veins. How long should she wait ere she could be certain that Edmund was truly on his way to their neighbor's farm and would not turn back for some forgotten item? Once well away, he would be gone for twenty-four glorious hours, and she would have freedom. It was not enough that he had ruined her life. He had to take away even her smallest pleasures.

Perhaps she *had* been a little overzealous with the last whipping. Now the slaves were being much more cautious. They would rather drop dead where they stood than step out of line and be punished. Several actually had. And of course, Edmund demanded that there be an actual reason before she could bring another to the post. But with him gone, how was he to know what had taken place? She could bribe the overseer into backing any story.

With a sigh, she picked up a pillow that she had embroidered for her bedroom and had just finished stuffing. She had to admit that she hadn't realized how very entertaining Grace had been. Needlework had been more satisfying when she had been able to take as many jabs at Grace as she had at her embroidery. Even that stinking little maid of hers was never around any-more. She had demanded the return of the woman, but Edmund had insisted that he didn't like having Matu about the house, and Iolanthe wasn't about to dirty the hem of one of her gowns by traipsing out to the slaves' quarters to look for her. "Oh!" she said aloud, a sullied smile marking her lovely face. Perhaps she would have *that one* brought 'round! Aye! Matu would slake her crav-ing!

She had just decided that she could wait no longer when a slave knocked hesitantly at the back door, then opened it timidly. He was one of the mill workers, and he was drenched in sweat. Iolanthe wrinkled her dainty nose.

"What are you doing in the house?" she demanded. He wasn't actually *in* the house, but he was close enough.

He shook his head, a mix of fear and loathing in his eyes, but no comprehension. He mumbled something in an African tongue, then pointed toward the front of the house and said, "Ship."

"Ship?" Iolanthe repeated impatiently, her hands on her hips. She would have this one beaten, too. Who did he think he was, stinking up her home with his sweaty, black skin?

He pointed to the sugar house. "Bakra—sey—ship."

Oh. Bakra was their word for overseer. The overseer had sent him to tell her there was a ship. Why did he al-ways send one of these ignorant savages with his messages? For God's sake, they didn't speak any English, even as barbarous as that language was. Nothing like French, melodious and civilized. Her upper lip curled. She looked the man over one last time before shutting the door in his face. With Edmund gone, it would be her duty to find out who was on the ship and what they wanted. The plantation had nothing to transport, so she would send the captain and crew on their way.

She took a step outside the front door and then smiled at the sight of the ship entering the bay. *Reliance.* Iolanthe's mind began to spin with the possibilities. The most delicious, of course, was the prospect that Grace was gone. If her letters had done the trick, she had lured Captain Courtney to Tortuga, and Jacques had slipped into Port Royal. Iolanthe laughed out loud and hugged herself. Grace would be in Havana by now, auctioned off and spreading her legs in a *bordel.* Someplace filthy and teeming with the worst kind of men. Worse than Edmund. Iolanthe, of course, would be entirely unable to help the good captain with his search. Alas, since Grace had not returned home, there would be no telling where his bride had gone.

Of course, it was also possible that her letters had not reached their intended recipients in time. In that case, it might well be that Captain Courtney had learned of Grace and Edmund's deception. Perhaps he was here to drag Grace home, beaten and finally humbled, so that he could throw her at her father's feet. If that was so, it was a shame Edmund was not here. Iolanthe would explain that she had been against it all along. She would appease Captain Courtney by having Grace tied to the post where she would pay dearly for both her father and herself. The captain would finally see that Africans were not anything like Whites. They were deceitful and barbaric. He would be so apologetic for how he had spoken to her in her home.

She was so happy that she fairly skipped down to the dock and danced impatiently there while he and his friend rowed out to meet her.

* * *

"I don't know," Geoff commented from his seat across from Giles. They rowed together toward the dock, Geoff facing the house, Giles the ship. "She looks happy to see us. Thrilled even. Not the countenance of a woman who has sent a man's wife to some terrible fate and now has to face the husband. Were she guilty, would she not be cowering in fear?"

Giles looked briefly over his shoulder. "Mark my words, she lusts for suffering, that one. She thinks to celebrate Grace's plight."

Geoff shook his head. "Has she no care for her own neck, or think you that she is as fond of receiving pain as giving it?"

"Mayhap she thinks Welbourne can protect her."

"Is she in need of protection? You have not spoken of it once, Giles. What do you intend to do to her?"

"If she gives me the information I seek, and we find Grace unharmed, then I will leave her to her husband's justice. He is far from perfect, but he cares for his daughter. If she is not forthcoming, or Grace has been—" he paused. "Well, then I shall delight in wringing her scrawny neck."

Geoff grinned humorlessly. "You'd never lay hands upon a woman in anger."

Giles hissed in frustration. Geoff might well have the right of it. He didn't think that he could do actual harm to a woman, but Iolanthe did not know that. By the time he was finished with her, she would be well convinced that he was within an inch of murder.

As they rowed up to the landing, Iolanthe called down, "Captain Courtney, Captain Hampton, what a pleasant surprise. But where are your wives?"

Geoff tied the boat and Giles leapt out. He reached her in three strides and grabbed Iolanthe's shoulders in both of his hands, squeezing like a vise. "Where is she?" he growled into the startled woman's face. "What have you and that filthy, disgusting bilge rat of a brother done with my wife?"

"I-I have no idea what you are speaking of. What has my brother to do with anything? What has become of Grace?"

Giles shoved her away from him, but then began immediately to advance upon her again. Iolanthe tripped and fell over the back of her skirt as she tried to retreat.

"If you place any value on your wretched life, you will not lie to me," Giles warned. "Your brother has stolen my wife, and he has done so at your bidding! So help me God, if any ill befalls her . . ."

Iolanthe looked desperately over to Geoff, who stood behind Giles, his arms folded across his broad chest. "Please, Captain," she begged. "Your friend is quite mad. Why would I allow any ill to befall my own child?"

Geoff, famed across the Caribbean for his ability to slay a man without a trace of emotion, gave her a look of bored indifference. "Since we left Port Royal, he's spoke of naught else but carving you into pieces with his cutlass and feeding you to the fish. The same for your brother, though he'll feed his balls to them first before his living eyes. I would not continue to lie to him just now."

She turned her attention back to Giles, and there was unrestrained terror in her brown eyes. "Please, tell me what has happened. What has Jacques to do with it?"

Giles took another step forward, purposely planting both feet on the edge of her skirt and forcing her to remain sprawled before him on the ground. "First, I get two strange missives from a French privateer whom I barely know. An *illiterate* French privateer who bids me come to his aid in Tortuga. I do not find that Frenchman there, but I find another, a man by the name of Jacques Renault."

Genuine confusion warred with fear on Iolanthe's face. "Jacques went to Tortuga?"

"As well you knew he would!" Giles shouted. "He deceived me, betrayed my trust. When we arrived at Port Royal, he took my wife. I am no fool, madam. You are at the root of this! This plan was of your own invention. Tell me what your whoreson brother has done with Grace!"

"Think for a moment," Iolanthe pleaded. "Grace is my own flesh and blood . . ."

"That she is not!" Giles yelled. "I know not the particulars, nor do I care. What I do know is that, thanks be to God, Grace is no child of yours."

By now, the overseer and a guard were running down the hill from the sugar house, flintlocks drawn. "Hold there!" one of them shouted.

At their arrival, evil calculation slowly crept into Iolanthe's expression. "You know not the particulars, Captain? Then mayhap I *can* help you."

"You will tell me what I wish to know or pay dearly."

The woman seemed to grow calmer with each passing second. Her breathing slowed and her cheeks regained a bit of their color. "I will answer your questions. But first you will get your filthy boots off of my gown."

"Back away!" the overseer shouted, as he and the guard drew near. "Back away or I shall shoot!"

Geoff laced his hands atop his head to show that he was unarmed, though the gesture seemed more like a comfortable stretch than surrender. He strolled over to the two armed men with an air of easy confidence. "D'you see that ship across the bay, mates?" he asked with a grin. The guard nodded, and Geoff lowered his hands before adding, "She has two dozen armed sailors and cannons." The men traded worried glances.

During the exchange, Giles had stepped off of Iolanthe's skirt, but he made no move to assist her as she struggled to her feet.

"Where is Edmund?" Giles demanded.

"At our neighbor's. He has business there," Iolanthe snipped.

Giles shrugged stiffly. "No matter. My business is with you."

"Quite to the contrary, Captain. Your business is very much with Edmund. I did naught but set to right *his* crime against you."

"What in the hell are you talking about?"

Iolanthe turned to the guard. "Fetch Matu." At his blank look, she barked, "Grace's dumb maid! Bring her to me this instant!"

She muttered under her breath in heated French as the man stumbled off to obey, then looked back at Giles. "I will concede that I wrote the letters. I will even concede that I wrote to my brother and bid him remove that lying baggage from your life."

Giles saw red, and for just an instant, he thought he might actually kill her after all. He took another step toward her, and she put up her hand in an imperious gesture of halt.

"I must warn you," the overseer said nervously, pointing his flintlock at Giles while glancing uneasily toward the ship.

"Silence!" Iolanthe snapped. The overseer glared at her. To Giles she said, "You will thank me for it, when you know the whole story. I cannot imagine what possessed Jacques to seek you out in Tortuga. He was to go to Port Royal while you were gone. It was never my intent that you should know of my involvement. It was to be an anonymous good deed."

Giles stared at her incredulously. "You are out of your bloody mind."

"Do not speak that way to me!" Iolanthe shrieked. "I will not stand for it! I must tolerate it from my husband. I even had to take his vile little brat's insolence. From you I demand respect! You owe it to me! You have no idea what I have saved you from!"

"Saved me? Do you honestly think I care that Grace's mother was a prostitute?"

Iolanthe laughed wildly, doubling over in demented mirth. "A prostitute? Is that what she told you? Her mother was never paid for her services to my husband. The woman was a slave. She cut sugar by day and spread her black legs for Edmund at night."

"What are you saying? You cannot expect me to believe that. A woman so fair as Grace could not possibly be half black."

"Nay, but she could be one-quarter. The bitch who whelped her was Mulatto!"

"That is a lie!"

"Is it? Where did she get her coloring, Captain? From her blond father? What about her flat nose, those grotesque lips?"

Nay, he thought to himself. They were beautiful, her nose and her lips. And her skin, it was golden and perfect.

"And that hair," Iolanthe continued. "Dear God, what white woman has hair like that? Birds could nest in it."

He stared at her, his eyes wide in disbelief. The guard

rushed back up, Matu in tow, and Iolanthe pointed to her. "Tell him, Matu! No need to say anything. Just nod. Is Grace's blood not as black as yours?"

Matu's face crumbled in horror. She began to gesticulate frantically, falling on her knees before Giles and folding her hands in supplication.

"Matu—" he began, but his throat constricted.

In desperation, Matu tried to talk, her words garbled, indistinct, impossible to understand.

"You see, Captain?" Iolanthe said. "Black. African. Negro. Half-caste. Mulatto. It does not matter what you call her. She is an animal."

He stood there, trying to wrap his mind around what she was telling him. Grace was African. Part African. Did it matter? *Should* it matter?

"Giles," Geoff said, but his voice sounded like it had come from miles away. "Giles, are you all right?"

Giles looked back at his friend, whose face was no longer a mask of indifference. Pity. Sympathy. Dismay.

"Do not dare to look at me like that, Geoffrey Hampton," he cried. "Do not dare!" He turned back to Iolanthe. "Nay, mistress, it does not matter what you call her. She is my wife. *Now where is she?*"

Iolanthe glared at him with molten hatred. "She is exceeding even her mother's accomplishment. She is being used by not one, but countless white men in Havana, Cuba. One after another after another after another . . ." She began to laugh again, a maniacal, hysterical laugh.

"Sweet Jesus," the overseer muttered.

Matu continued to try to talk, her hands moving wildly in motions Giles couldn't grasp. It seemed like everything around him was moving through some thick, clinging medium. He was torn between the desire to slap Iolanthe until she finally shut up and the urge to board his ship and set sail for God knew where. He looked down into Matu's pleading face. He wouldn't abandon Grace to Jacques, he knew that much, but he knew nothing beyond it.

"'Tis all right," he said to her. "I'll go and get her." But she kept staring up at him, weeping quietly now, with yet another question in her eyes. "I cannot say any more than that just now," he said. "I-I have to think."

He pivoted toward the deranged Iolanthe, his hand lighting upon the hilt of his cutlass, but Geoff grabbed him. "You cannot kill her, Giles."

"'Twould be a death more richly deserved than any other I've ever caused."

Geoff nodded in her direction. She was pausing to gasp for breath and then beginning to laugh again. "She's mad, poor bitch. A raving lunatic."

Giles stood, fighting emotions more primitive than any he had ever before experienced. Never had he hated anyone the way he hated Iolanthe Welbourne. "But Grace . . ." he whispered.

"Killing Iolanthe would be a kindness," Geoff coaxed. "Forcing her to live is your revenge, old friend."

"Aye," Giles said, at last. "Aye, it is." He eased his hand away from his sword, clenching it into a tight fist at his side. If only he could believe that what she had told him was but a symptom of her madness.

"What now?" Geoff asked.

"Cuba," Giles replied.

Eighteen

Grace and Encantadora, the Mulatto, stood alone in the large dressing room. The night was dark outside of the barred window, and candles cast a flickering, golden glow. Encantadora wore a thin, purple caftan that skimmed her lithe form. Grace's own body was barely concealed by her sheer, white, sleeveless gown. It was cut like a shift and belted at the waist, leaving little to the imagination. From the courtyard just outside the door, voices and laughter drifted in.

It was nearly ten, the time advertised for the auctioning of Grace's maidenhead, and while they waited, Encantadora tried to distract Grace by telling her her own story. *Don* Ramon had purchased her at an auction in Jamaica, where she had lived as a child. At the age of twelve, she had come to the attention of her master at the plantation, and he had realized that she was pretty enough to sell to a procurer. She had once had an African name, Ciatta, and though *Don* Ramon had changed it after he had bought her, and she had learned to speak Spanish, she still thought of Jamaica as home.

"How old are you now?" Grace asked.

"Me tink maybe sixteen. Nobody here donkya 'bout how old me be."

"Sixteen!" Grace gasped. She had thought Encantadora to be much older. Her skin was still smooth and young, but her eyes seemed a thousand years old. "I would have rather died," Grace added.

Which was the crux of why Encantadora had been left in the room with Grace. She was there to prevent another incident like the one earlier that evening. Grace had discovered a razor used by one of the women to remove body hair, and she had picked it up, eyeing her wrists. Two quick slices, deep and wide, she had thought to herself.

Encantadora had snatched it from her fingers. "Da maas come in an' fine you inna puddla blood, him a-go skin us all for lettin' you," she had scolded fiercely. "Whey you so worried for, eh? Dis place not so bad. It not de cribs where you gotta take twenty men a night. Dese men, dem gotta lotta money. A lot of 'em's clean an' dem get it ova quick."

Grace had clapped her hand over her mouth and stared at the other woman in horror.

Encantadora had frowned back at her. "Whey you from girl wit' you fancy talk? Whey you tink you life a-go be? You tink you a-go marry some fine, free African wit' big shouldas an' jinglin' pockets? Maybe when dese white men be tru wit you. For now, you betta spread you legs and ac' like you like it." She stopped a moment and cocked her head at Grace. "You eva be on a plantation?" Grace nodded and Encantadora continued, "Den you seen how it be. Me—me lay down for a tousand men 'fore me go back to one of dem places, dat for sure. Me tellin' you, it not so bad here."

"But isn't it far worse than a plantation? I mean, I suppose it is worse to be whipped . . ."

"Ev'ryting 'bout de plantation worse. Aye, de lash be

de wors' of all, but sweatin' in de sun wit no watta, standin' ova de shugga vats in de steam, draggin' youself to de huts an' cookin' for ev'rybody else. All you tink about be dyin'. Me not seyin' dis where me wanna spen' me whole life. Me jus' seyin' deh be worse tings."

"Encantadora," Grace asked, her face flushed. "Have you ever lain with a man you wanted?"

The other woman laughed. "Me? Me firs' time happen jus' like you, right here. Dat mon, him want a girl him can teach. Him like watchin' me be shocked at what he sey an' do. Him not mean, but me pretty scared. Since den, dem all de same, pretty much. Some be a little rough, but it get too bad, you call *Don* Ramon. But aye, me tink about it sometime, what it be like wit' a good man dat you love. A lotta dese men, dem want you to like it, an' me preten' me do, but someday, me wanna really feel it, you know?"

A key turned in the lock of the door, and *Don* Ramon stuck his head in. He rattled something off to Encantadora, and she responded, then spoke to Grace. "Him sey it time. Him axe me if you gonna be a problem, an' me tell him no, you don' want no trouble. Whateva foolish dreams you got, you betta get rid of dem now. Dreams don' give you nutten but heartache."

Grace backed away from the door, shaking her head. "I cannot do this."

Encantadora gave her a shove. "You do what de maas sey. One of us make trouble, we all pay."

Grace didn't want to think about what that might mean. Somehow, she managed to put one foot in front of the other and follow *Don* Ramon out into the torch-lit courtyard, Encantadora behind them. Grace wore sandals that moved quietly across the colorful tile, and her skirt rippled softly around her ankles. The pirate captain in his grime-encrusted velvet leered at her. "Been dreamin' o' me since ye left the block, love?" he called out, and Grace shuddered. *Please, God, not that one,* she prayed.

Judging from the murmurs she heard and the style of dress sported by most, the majority of the men were Spanish. Their eyes roved freely over her body, ill-concealed by her clinging gown. One by one, she looked into their lasciviously smirking faces and thought to herself, *and not that one, nor that one, nor that one . . .*

There was no way out. On the morrow, or someday soon after, she might yet find another razor, but for now, there was naught that she could do. She thought of how she had gone to bed with Giles feeling this way, and she knew not whether to laugh or cry at her own stupidity. Now, she would have given anything to see him again. Anything to have given herself to a chance to be loved and cared for. Now she would never understand the mysteries that Faith had spoken of.

Don Ramon stopped, and she stopped with him. Unlike the first time she had been sold, this auction was conducted entirely in Spanish. She didn't have to listen to anyone's cold, calculated description of her in multiple languages, and yet, she would have welcomed anything that might have delayed the inevitable but a few more moments. This sale was similar in that bidding began quickly and finally dwindled. The English pirate tossed a heavy purse back and forth between his two hands merrily, keeping pace with the bids of a corpulent Spaniard with a pock-marked face and a rail-thin man with teeth as bad as Iolanthe's and an accent that Grace couldn't quite place.

At last, the fat Spaniard dropped out of the race. "Leave 'er to me," the pirate shouted. "I speaks 'er language. I'll teach 'er all she needs to know for the rest o' you swabs tomorrow night!"

The gaunt man bid again, and the Englishman's confidence dimmed a bit. Grace knew herself to be between the devil and the deep blue sea. Bear the weight of the pirate's filthy body or the taste of the other man's rotting mouth.

"*Cincuenta doblóns,*" a new voice called from the back of the room. The bid was met by exclamations of surprise from most, gasps of indignation from the two remaining bidders. Grace's heart skipped a beat and her breath caught in her throat. It was the Spaniard who had spoken to her in the pen and challenged the auctioneer at the block! His arms were crossed and his expression sour. He looked like he would rather be anywhere on earth than *El Jardín de Placer.* Their eyes locked, and he almost looked a little angry with her.

"My arse!" the Englishman exclaimed. "Nobody pays fifty gold doubloons for a wench! Not for just one night!"

The Spaniard gave *Don* Ramon a tight smile and said something else, something that seemed to account for the outrageous sum, for a number of men nodded in understanding, and his strange, foreign competitor bared his black teeth in a sneer of revulsion. Standing behind Grace and *Don* Ramon, Encantadora gasped.

"What?" the pirate protested. "What's that? She won't what? Talk slower."

The Spaniard's dark eyes swept over the pirate's filthy finery with contempt. In English, he replied, "When I have finished with her, she will not be able to work for several days. Naturally, I am willing to compensate *Don* Ramon for her incapacitation."

Grace's knees buckled, but Encantadora was there to

catch her and help her to stand more steadily. She had thought that perhaps this man was a friend of some kind, but now she had to face the fact that he was from an enemy country. Who knew what might have transpired between this Spaniard and her once privateer husband and his friend? What revenge might he enact against her for her association with them?

Don Ramon and the Spaniard were now in serious conversation, and the rest of the men in the courtyard spoke in whispers, their eyes darting back and forth from the newcomer to her.

Grace met his eyes again, and what had once seemed the man's distaste for the auction now seemed contempt for her. She turned away from him and looked to Encantadora for a translation. The pity in the younger woman's eyes did nothing to ease her mind.

"Him promise him a-go leave no scar," Encantadora offered weakly. "If de mon do dis a lot, den him prob'ly good at it. *Don* Ramon got skill, never leave no mark wit' de lash dat don' fade."

The lash? Grace wanted to flee in terror, but her feet seemed to have taken root beneath her. Finally satisfied with whatever the other Spaniard had to say, *Don* Ramon took the money and then spoke to Encantadora. She took Grace by the hand and pulled her through the courtyard with the Spaniard close behind.

"Deh be a cottage out bak. It where him send you when him know deh a-go be a lotta noise. Now listen good, an' remember whey me tell you. Only fight a little, den give in. Scream an' beg mercy even 'fore him hit you, an' den louder evr'y time de lash fall. It more 'bout makin' you beg dan really hurtin' you." The three of them walked out of the back gate, past two African guards. Sure enough, a tiny cottage sat just across the back alley. Encantadora continued in a soft voice. "When him take you, go ahead an' cry. Act like him got de biggest *pene* in de whole Caribbean an' ev'ryting be jus' fine." She gave Grace what was surely meant to be a reassuring smile. "Dis be de worst it get, me promise, an' you see, it not so bad if you cry an' beg a lot. You make it tru dis night, an' de rest be so easy. Me soon come an' see how you be."

A four-poster bed nearly swallowed the one-room cottage that Grace and the Spaniard entered. It was swathed in linen and littered with silk pillows, but the bedposts were reinforced with leather to keep the chains and manacles from biting into the wood. Encantadora lit candles in wall sconces and on a small table, next to a whip made of a cluster of knotted strands that looked like a mass of black snakes. She spoke to the Spaniard, but he shook his head and gestured her to the door.

The prostitute shut the door softly behind her, but to Grace, it sounded as loud and definitive as the clang of a prison door shutting her away for life.

Diego moved swiftly from one window to the next, until he had assessed all three in the tiny space. All were barred. The only way in or out faced directly toward the back of the *burdel* and the two guards flanking the rear gate.

"This is not going to be easy," he said over his shoulder as he tested the bars and found them absolutely secure.

"P-please—don't—"

At the sound of the terrified woman's voice, he turned and took a good look at her. Her arms were wrapped tightly over her breasts and her teeth appeared to be chattering. He couldn't decide whether he pitied her her fear or was annoyed that she thought him the sort of man who beat women for pleasure. In the end, pity won, and he handed her his jacket to cover her scandalous gown. At the same time, he picked up the whip from the table, and Grace cried out.

"I am not disrobing, *Señora* Courtney," he assured her. "I thought you might prefer to wear something more substantial than that flimsy silk. As for the whip, we are going to have to make this convincing."

"You-you mean that you are not going to rape me, only-only use the whip?"

Diego laughed at the absurdity of such a notion, but stopped as soon as he realized the depth of her terror. "Were you whipped before?"

She shook her head. "N-nay. But I have seen it done more times than I can count."

"Well, this time when you watch a whip being plied, no one will be hurt." He glanced around the room. "The pillows will not work. We will need something to make a more persuasive sound."

Comprehension finally dawned on her face, and she accepted the jacket with a shaky smile. "Something leather," she suggested. They both looked all around the room. The leather reinforcements on the bed didn't seem a feasible solution. Everything else was soft, more likely to produce a mild thud rather than a sharp crack. Then Grace's face lit up. "Your boots!"

Diego looked down at his feet. His boots, with their wide tops lying side by side on the bed, should be perfect. He pulled them from his feet, tugged self-consciously at a hole in his stocking, and set them on the mattress. He lifted the whip and looked at Grace. "I will take care of this part. The real performance must come from you."

She closed her eyes and took a deep breath, and when the first lash hit the leather, she let out a blood-curdling scream. He let the whip fall twenty times, and her cries and tearful pleading were so hauntingly convincing that he felt sick to his stomach. It took several minutes after he had stopped for her to begin to calm down again.

"Obviously you told me the truth about witnessing more than your share of whippings."

She opened her eyes and took a gulp of air into her lungs. "You have no reason to believe me, but I don't generally lie, Señor—"

"Capitán," he corrected, "Diego Montoya Fernandez de Madrid y Delgado Cortes. I do not generally have much patience with liars."

"Then why did you come back? And what possessed you to sacrifice that kind of money?" Her eyes fell down to his threadbare stockings.

Diego sighed. For all that he preferred the full truth, in this case, it was hardly credible. He had gone back to his ship, fully satisfied that he had done his duty as a gentleman. He had tried to purchase the woman at the block, but the bidding had gone far beyond the funds that he'd had with him. He had felt terrible for her, of course. He wasn't heartless. He just didn't see what else he could have done for her.

But Diego's patron saint knew him all too well. *She* knew that he had been saving most of his money to buy his ship, *Magdalena*, a ship named in her honor. Maria Magdalena was well aware that he was hoping to open his own shipping company here in Havana, and that he kept the majority of his savings here. After all, it was her protection that had made his every voyage so successful and had allowed him to amass those savings.

Sometimes, she came to him in visions; other times, it just seemed to him that he knew what she expected of him. The truth was, he had sat in his cabin most of the evening trying to talk himself out of coming to *El Jardín de Placer* with such a sizable portion of the funds that he had hoarded to buy his ship. But all along, he had known that Magdalena would never forgive him if he did not make one more attempt to save the Englishwoman from the life that Magdalena herself had escaped by the grace of her Lord and Savior.

It was far simpler to reply, "It helped that you should have mentioned Geoffrey Hampton. Now, unlike *you,*" he gave her a reproachful look, "I can honestly say that I am related to his wife, Faith. We are cousins."

"Never say it! *That's* how you knew 'twas a lie when I claimed that Geoffrey was my brother!"

"And still a lie when you changed your tune and claimed Faith to be your sister."

"But Faith is English."

"And so is her aunt, who is married to my uncle, who is Spanish."

Grace narrowed her eyes, but they glittered with mischief rather than malice. "So 'twas not a blind bet you made with your money. You knew that Faith would likely intervene if Giles were to balk at paying you."

Diego waggled a finger at her. "It was nearly blind. How was I to know that you were telling the truth? And even now, how do I know that your husband can repay me? I, of all people, know that he is no longer robbing Spanish ships of their gold."

"He and Geoff are doing well. He will repay you, I'm

sure." Her face took on a faraway look. "He is a good man."

Diego gave her a reassuring grin. "We will get you back to him. Is it possible that he is here, looking for you?"

Grace shook her head. "I do not imagine that he will look anywhere that is held by the Spanish. It may be that he has gone to Saint Domingue. He will know only that my uncle has taken me."

"Then we must get you out of Havana. The woman who brought us here, she seemed concerned for you."

"I hardly know her, but she has done her best to help me."

"Do you think that she will do a little more? Can she convince *Don* Ramon to leave you in her care while you 'recover' from tonight? If she will, I have bought us a little time, and I will come up with a plan."

Grace chewed her bottom lip thoughtfully. "Possibly." She started to remove his coat.

"Keep the jacket. Whatever you do, do not let *Don* Ramon see your back. If you can, try to stay out here. In the pocket of that coat, you will find a few silver pieces. Perhaps they will help to buy your friend's silence and her help."

"You'll get your money back, Captain, every penny."

He heaved another sigh. He certainly hoped so.

Giles stood at the helm of the ship and stared at the stars. It was after ten. Where was Grace now? What was happening to her? Whatever it was, she would never recover. Every time he thought about it, he wanted to go back to Welbourne and beat Iolanthe as he would any man who was guilty of the same crime. His hands tightened on the ship's wheel as if he had them around Iolanthe's neck.

And he tried so hard not to think about the rest. But the more he forbade himself to contemplate it, the more it snaked its way into his thoughts. *How could she not have told him? Why did it matter?* He looked down onto the deck below where one of his men stood, smoking a pipe and gazing out to sea. It took him several minutes to summon the courage, but finally he called out to him. "Jawara!"

The man looked up. "Aye, Cap'n?"

"'Tis quiet on deck tonight. Come and pass a while with me while you smoke your pipe."

Jawara stayed where he was for a moment and looked around him. "Me?" Between the darkness of night and the deep ebony of Jawara's skin, 'twas impossible to see the expression on his face from this distance.

"Aye," Giles said.

Reluctantly, Jawara climbed up the stairs, but he didn't approach the wheel. He leaned his shirtless, dark, muscular frame uneasily against the rail behind him and waited.

"A fair night," Giles commented, and Jawara nodded somberly, lifting his pipe to his lips. "Fair night indeed. We'll make excellent time, do you not think?"

Jawara nodded.

Giles searched for something to say. He cleared his throat and finally asked, "Do you like it here, on board *Reliance?*" he asked.

Another nod.

"Are you truly content, or is it simply better than being a slave?"

"You gotta problem wit' sinting me done, Cap'n?"

"Nay! Nay! I was—just making conversation."

"Makin' convahsation?" This time Giles nodded, taken aback by the heaviness in Jawara's deep voice. "We neva make no convahsation b'fore, Cap'n. You tink me not pullin' me weight?"

"Nay, Jawara, you pull more than your weight. I know that. I appreciate it. You're a good man."

Jawara nodded. "Dat all?"

Giles scratched his head. This wasn't the first time he had ever spoken to Jawara. He spoke to him all of the time. Why was this so damned hard? He never thought twice about saying, "Jawara, climb up there and give me more sail" or "Jawara, take this barrel of water down to the galley." Why was a simple conversation so difficult?

"We only converse," Giles protested. "This isn't business." The comment, meant to set the crewman at ease, only seemed to increase the strain between them.

Jawara took a deep draw on his pipe and then frowned at it. "It a-go out," he explained. He knocked it against the rail and let the ashes fall into the sea. "Me tink you gotta be worryin' for you wife."

"You have no idea," Giles said.

There was another long, uncomfortable silence before Jawara replied, "Me tink me gotta idea."

"Are-are you married?" Giles asked. 'Twasn't a question that had ever occurred to him to ask. Jawara was a more or less permanent fixture on board either *Reliance* or *Destiny*. Giles had never seen him leave for any kind of home in Port Royal.

"Me don' tink so. Me wife an' me, we got separated when we got here. One mon buy her, smaddy else buy me. Me got away an' a-go look for her, but me don' know where a look. Dat be tree or four year ago. Her prob'ly dead now. Her carrying me firs' chil', but me tink her lose it on de ship." Jawara's voice was hollow, the voice of a man who had emptied himself of emotion. "You know, me never been a slave. A lotta slaves here be slaves in Africa, but me be a free mon me whole life."

Giles had never felt more ashamed in his life. How could he have worked with this man for so long and not known this? "I'm so sorry."

Jawara shrugged. "You not a bad mon. You pay me, treat me wit some respec'. But what me wanna know, me wanna know dis—how can white men do dis? How can dem take a free mon's wife an' sell her away from him?"

It was hard to speak, but Giles replied, "I have no idea."

"It drive me crazy sintime. Sintime, me lie in me hammock an' wonder 'bout her. Me wonder, dat mon who buy her, did he rape her? Did he beat her? Did her jus' drop dead in de field and dem trow her body in some hole in de groun'? Me love dat 'ooman, you know?"

"I'm sure you did." God help him, he thought, struggling with his own emotions.

"Sorry, Cap'n. Me not de best person a talk to 'bout dis. It not helpin', me talkin' like dis."

"Nay! 'Tis good. I thought no one could possibly understand. It helped to be able to talk to you."

"We get her bak. You see," Jawara assured him. "Her a white 'ooman. Nobody a-go hurt her."

Giles winced. "Tell me about your home, your family, back in Africa."

Jawara smiled wistfully. "Me got me a madda, a wife, an' tree sistas. Me use' to tink dat be too many 'oomans. Dem keep me fadda an' me jumpin' alla time."

Giles smiled back. "I have three sisters, too. All younger."

"Mine be two younga, one olda. You gotta olda sista,

you might as well got two maddas. Dem always bossin'
an' complainin', but dem lookin' out for you, too, you
know?"

"Were your mother and sisters taken into slavery?"

"Don' know. Me not see dem on de slave ship, so me
tink maybe dem got away. Me hope so."

"So do I."

"Can me axe you sinting Cap'n, sinting business?"

"Certainly."

"You like de work me do?"

"Aye, Jawara. I meant what I said. You pull more than
your weight."

"If me be white, an' me work as hard as me do now,
what den?"

"What then?"

"Aye."

Giles thought for a moment, and then realized with a
fresh surge of shame exactly what would have happened. Jawara might well have been first mate by now.
But would white sailors follow the orders of an African?
Giles couldn't see it. "I don't know what to say."

"You don' gotta sey nutten. Jus', me hopin' you might
tink 'bout it some. Not now. You got plenty a tink 'bout.
Jus' maybe later."

"Thank you, Jawara. I appreciate your work and
your—your friendship."

Jawara replied with a wordless sound. The two men
went back to their quiet contemplation of the sea, and
while they may not have been completely at ease, Jawara
made no move to go back to the deck below.

Once again, Iolanthe found herself pacing the length
of the keeping room and brooding about her husband.

God, what a disaster this whole affair had turned out to be! She grabbed the embroidered pillow that she had left in the keeping room that morning and used it to muffle a scream of frustration.

It was getting late, past ten at night, but she couldn't even sit, much less sleep. That dreadful Captain Courtney should have fallen to his knees in gratitude, and what had he done? He had glared at her as though he wished her dead! It was not her fault, what had been done to him. She was only the messenger.

She searched for a comforting thought and found it. Mayhap the man felt some misguided obligation to go and rescue Grace, but Iolanthe had seen the look on his face when she had told him. He had been shocked. Devastated. He might retrieve Grace, but he would not keep her. As delicious as that thought was, it always carried fast on its heels the concern that was likely going to prevent her from sleeping at all tonight. One way or another, Edmund was going to find out what she had done. Courtney would return to bring Grace home and demand an annulment, and the truth would be out.

Edmund would kill her. There was absolutely no doubt in Iolanthe's mind that the very second he had a chance, he would murder her. That knowledge should make what she had to do easy, but it didn't. She was terrified. However there was no way around it. It was self-defense. She had to think. She had to have a plan. Nothing complex. It was not as though she hadn't thought of it before. She had.

Looking back now, she thought it all seemed rather silly. She and Edmund and Grace had gone together to visit one of Edmund's business acquaintances on the way to Port Royal. Grace had been particularly awful. The wretched thing had put on a show of disgusting affection, linking arms with Iolanthe, even kissing her cheek, all because she had known how it made Iolanthe's flesh crawl. And Edmund's friend had gone on and on about how refreshing it was to see a mother and daughter get on so well in an age where children had so little respect for their parents. Edmund had been thrilled with Grace, believing her charade to be for his benefit, to impress his business associate. He had insisted that Iolanthe go along with it.

By the time they had left and continued their journey to the city, Iolanthe had been murderously angry. When they'd arrived in Port Royal, she had gone shopping on her own, and she had stopped at an apothecary shop in the very worst part of town. The two little glass vials that she had purchased were still under the false bottom of her jewelry box. By the time they had returned home from that repugnant trip, Iolanthe had thought better of her plan; she was angry, but it was not worth hanging for.

Now, she had nothing to lose. If she did not kill Edmund, he would surely kill her.

Nineteen

Encantadora stared at the silver coins in her palm. The morning sun shone through the cottage's barred windows and glinted off of the money. "Me gotta good place a hide dese," she whispered. "But you neva keep a secret 'round de ottas. Dem know in two seconds you got no stripes on you bak. You got sinting for dem, too?"

"That's all," Grace explained. "Can't I just stay out here until I can pretend I've recovered?"

Both women jumped at the sound of the bolt sliding outside the cottage door. *Don* Ramon called to them, and Grace dove under the covers on the bed, Captain Montoya's jacket still over her shoulders.

Encantadora stood, blocking the door, and engaged the procurer in earnest conversation. The sun through the windows was warming the room, and Grace felt her skin break out in sweat as she huddled under the covers in the sea captain's heavy coat. *Please, please, please,* she chanted to whatever power might be listening.

In time, her new friend closed the door quietly, her finger to her lips. She plopped down on the bed next to Grace and whispered, "Moan an' cry a little."

Grace whimpered dutifully, throwing in a few sobs for good measure, and Encantadora went back, pressed her ear to the door, then made a slicing motion in the air

with her hand. The gesture made Grace think of Matu.
It was exactly the gesture she would have used to tell her
that she had made enough noise. What she wouldn't
have given for Matu's comforting presence.

Encantadora returned to the bed and lay down next
to Grace. "Him wanna see you bak, see how bad de damage be. Me tell him you bak not so bad, jus' welts, but
you cryin' an' maybe a little crazy. Me tell him, no mon
for two, maybe tree day, not even him. Me swear me a-
go have you ready a work, but me gotta spen' some time
alone wit' you 'cause you first time so rough."

"Oh Encantadora, I don't know how to thank you."

"You jokin'? Dis almos' like a room of me own. Don't
gotta be wit' dem otta 'oomans when dem all nasty an'
spiteful. We get bored an' we go afta each otta. It be a
bad ting."

"You hurt one another?"

"Sey nasty tings. We don' touch each otta. We all *Don*
Ramon's property. You mon pay big for de damage him
sey him do. We do damage, we pay too, only we don' got
no money."

"But if he doesn't want his property damaged, what
can he do to you?"

Encantadora went a little pale under her dark skin.
"De 'ooman dat work on her bak don' need de soles of
her feet." At Grace's skeptical frown, she continued,
"You tink him can't do nutten so bad to two little places
like dat? You don' wanna find out."

Once they arrived in Havana, Giles instructed Geoff
to begin searching brothels while he made inquiries at
the market. The docks and main streets of the town
were bustling, and the market place even busier still. A

large shipment of slaves had just arrived, and it was nearly impossible to approach any of the auctioneers. He waded through people, inspecting the contents of various pens, looking for one that might be more inclined to cater to the local whorehouses, but most seemed to be hawking sugar workers.

He was ready to give up and seek Geoff when he spotted a familiar form at one of the pens several yards off. Jacques Renault was apparently concluding a transaction and had begun to haul a screaming African girl with him through the crowd. She was small, only a little higher than his waist, and she was no match for him. Giles tried to run after them, but he collided with one man after another and found himself cursed in a variety of languages. He lost sight of the pair, then picked them up again well up the street.

By the time he had shoved his way through to where they had been standing, sweat drenched the front of his shirt and dripped unpleasantly down his face. Jacques and the child had vanished. Giles grabbed a passing man by the jacket.

"A Frenchman," he gasped. "Did you see a dark-haired Frenchman and an African child here? Just a minute ago?"

The man jerked his arm free and muttered something about *"el loco."*

"Damn it!" Giles spat.

He started to grab for someone else when he heard voices through an open window above him. First a terrified, high-pitched wailing, followed by a sharp slap and an unmistakable voice shouting, *"Fermé la bouche, marmot!"* The wailing settled down into a whimper. *"Et maintenant, ouvert la bouche pour moi."*

Giles spun and burst through the door of the inn that

he'd been standing in front of, then hurled himself up the stairs, past a shouting innkeeper. The upstairs hall had three doors on each side, and Giles scrutinized the ones whose rooms would face the street. Behind the middle door came a series of muffled thumps and then a child's voice pleading in a strange language.

Giles launched a booted foot against the door with all his strength, splintering the wood surrounding the lock and sending the door flying open into the room. Jacques, his breeches around his ankles, had the girl pinned, naked, to the bed. He spun around in alarm that turned to terror when he saw Giles.

"Ce n'est pas votre affaire!" he squealed.

Giles pulled him away from the girl before he threw his fist full force into Jacques's jaw and sent the bastard flying bare-assed onto the wooden floor. He was dimly aware that his knuckles hurt and that the girl was screaming, but he hauled Jacques to his feet by his hair and then struck him twice in the stomach. This time, he let the man sink to the floor, gasping for air.

"Where is she?"

"Je—ne—sais—pas," Jacques wheezed.

A kick to the ribs had Jacques writhing on the floor, his shirt bunched around his waist, his breeches tangled around his feet.

"Where is she?"

"She is an African!" Jacques whined. "She lied to you!"

The kick to his back hit his kidneys, and the Frenchman screamed.

"Where is she?"

"S-sold," Jacques whimpered. "Spaniard p-paid a fortune."

"Who was he?" Giles demanded.

"D-do not know." Giles drew his foot back and Jacques screamed, *"Je ne sais pas! C'est vrai!* A very rich procurer. That is all I know! I swear it!"

"Tell me the name of your connection. Who auctioned her for you?"

"Claude LaMont. Do not hurt me again!"

It would have been honorable to allow Renault to put his clothes to rights and defend himself, but Giles found that, where Grace's vile, despicable uncle was concerned, he hadn't a trace of honor to spare. If he lived, how many other children would suffer at his hands? He drew his cutlass, knelt, grabbed a handful of dark, oily hair, and ran him through the heart. The cur gasped and then went limp. Even under these circumstances, Giles felt a deep weight inside of him. No matter how many battles he had been through, he had never acquired Geoff's ease with death.

A commotion was stirring up in the hall. Spanish voices chattered excitedly, then Geoff's ringing voice interrupted. "Out of my way. Out!"

Giles looked back over to the bed. The little girl sat in a tightly curled ball, her coffee-colored knees tucked under her chin and her arms wrapped fast about her legs. She stared at him with wide, brown eyes. Here, terrified and alone, was someone's daughter. Someone's cherished little girl. Giles stepped forward to comfort her, but she shrank back, her eyes darting over to Jacques's undignified corpse.

"Get back!" Geoff said, somewhere behind Giles and the girl.

There was a heated spate of Spanish, then the sound of coins clinking. It was the rich, thick chink-chink-chink of gold doubloons rather than the merry jingle of silver. The Spanish protests died. Through it all,

Jacques's blood pooled on the wooden floor and soaked his fine, white, linen shirt.

Finally, Giles faced his friend.

"Do you feel better?" Geoff asked with a little smile.

Giles didn't answer. He opened a leather trunk at the end of the bed and pulled out one of Jacques' shirts, tossing it to the little girl. Better? He didn't know. Gradually, a feeling of calm began to infuse him. He didn't feel exactly good about killing Renault, but neither did he regret it. He dreaded the moment when he must face Grace, having failed so completely to protect her. But he was going to find her, of that he was certain.

"What should I do with this?" Geoff asked, indicating the child.

"Goddammit, Geoff, she's not a thing!"

Geoff looked away. "I'm sorry. I didn't mean it that way."

"Take her back to the ship. I'll be along with Grace."

"What are you going to do with her?"

"I don't know. It depends upon how she is when I find her. I cannot think about the future just now."

"Not Grace. The girl."

Giles studied the silent, frightened child. "I don't know about her either, but we're not leaving her here."

Geoff reached for her, and the move seemed to galvanize her. She scampered out of reach and objected in a barrage of African words.

Giles left Geoff to deal with dressing and transporting the resistant girl. On the street below he heard the girl's protests and then Geoff's grunt of pain. She has spirit, Giles thought, just like Grace. With grim purpose, he headed back to the marketplace to find Claude LaMont.

* * *

Diego was anxious to leave the seedier section of Havana behind him. A crowd had gathered outside of one of the inns. As he skirted it, he heard men speak with great relish of some Frenchman's murder in the rooms above the street. This was a side of the city he had conscientiously avoided in the past, and it was quickly tarnishing his view of the place.

A few streets away, the front of *El Jardín de Placer* was deserted. It was a quiet place in the light of day. Outside of the back gate, however, two Africans sat on guard. They were substantially less vigilant than the previous night's pair, as they leaned their backs against the plastered wall that blocked off the *burdel* courtyard from the alley. They chatted quietly, sparing an occasional glance for the little cottage where Diego had last seen Grace. He would have to cross an open stretch of alleyway in order to reach the barred window at the rear of the cottage and to see whether or not she was still there.

A guard reached into his pocket and withdrew a small pouch. From it, he extracted several dice, and soon the two men were tossing them onto the hard-packed dirt between them. Diego used the opportunity to make a dash for the back of the cottage. Through the barred window, he could see a female form reclining on the bed.

"*Señora* Courtney!" he whispered urgently.

"Captain!" she whispered back, but she rose from the other side of the bed, where she had been hidden from view.

The other woman sat up and looked sleepily around her. "Work already?" she murmured drowsily. When she spied Diego at the window, she came instantly awake. "*Buenas tardes, señor,*" she said.

He smiled. In the light of day, with her face still soft

from sleep, the prostitute looked very young. *"Buenas tardes."*

"This is Encantadora," Grace supplied. "She, too, is from Jamaica. She has kept *Don* Ramon at bay for me."

"Usted es muy amable."

Encantadora shrugged, as though reluctant to admit herself capable of an act of kindness. "It a break for me, too."

"So, what would you recommend as the best way to get Mistress Courtney out of here?" Diego asked.

She shrugged again. "It betta be when me not 'round. Me not takin' de blame."

"Surely you'll have to go back inside to get ready for tonight's customers," Grace suggested.

With a glance at the sky, where the sun had already passed its zenith, Encantadora said, *"Don* Ramon soon come. You betta tink of sinting. When de men get here, de new guards show, an' dey *serious* 'bout dey work."

"Bueno," Diego said. "We will wait until you are inside, but act before the new guard is posted. Encantadora, can you distract the two men on guard now? Perhaps call them inside for a moment, once you are in there?"

Encantadora gave him a wary look. "Den her get outta here an' me left holdin' de bag. *Don* Ramon not stupid. Me call dem men in, an' him a-go know me got sinting to do wit' it."

Suddenly both women spun toward the cottage door with startled cries. Diego dropped quickly to the dirt. He hadn't seen who had caused their distress, and he prayed silently that whoever it was had not seen him either.

"What is this?" *Don* Ramon demanded in Spanish. "What are you doing?"

Encantadora's Spanish was thickly accented, and in

many ways as hard to follow as her English, but she efficiently conveyed that the room had been stuffy and that she had thought the fresh air would be good for Grace.

At the mention of Grace's name, *Don* Ramon demanded, "Turn around. Let me see your back." Diego heard Grace's cry of protest and Encantadora's hasty explanation that Grace needed more time, then there was a brief scuffle and the room was silent. Diego could hear his own blood pounding in his ears. Between his teeth, he felt the grit of the dirt he'd stirred up when he'd dropped out of sight.

A string of curses ripped through the silence. Diego was sure that they were nothing new or shocking for the prostitute, but he was glad that Grace understood no Spanish. "There is not one mark!" Don Ramon shouted. "Not one damned mark. What in the hell is going on here?"

"Me explain—" Encantadora began, but her words were cut off with a cry of pain.

"No, don't!" Grace implored in English. "Please! It was my fault. *Ma faute! Parlez-vous Français?* Damn it! I do not speak Spanish! Tell him, Encantadora! Tell him that 'tis all my fault!"

But Encantadora was busy with a litany in nearly perfect Spanish, words she had obviously spoken countless times before. "Please, Master, do not hurt me! I am sorry! I am very, very sorry. Please, please, mercy! I will do anything, *anything*! I will . . ." she recited a list of such degrading sexual acts that Diego ground his teeth in indignation. The girl was so young to know of such things.

But inside the cottage was another young woman. An innocent who would also learn the depths of human depravity if he did not get her out of there soon. He heard the door slam shut, and he stood up. Grace was pounding on the portal and weeping. From the alleyway, he could still hear Encantadora's pleas for mercy.

"*Señora* Courtney," he said.

She spun back around. "We have to stop this! Captain Montoya, we have to help her."

"*Señora,* I am truly sorry . . ."

"Nay! Do not tell me that there is nothing that we can do. I will *not* accept that!"

There was no time to reason with her. Diego glanced around the corner of the cottage. One of the guards was now helping *Don* Ramon pull the struggling Encantadora through the back gate. The second guard was glancing warily around him, and Diego pressed himself tightly against the cottage wall.

From the side window, Grace called out to him. "Captain Montoya, are you still there?"

"Be quiet! If they find me here, I will be of no use to either of you."

He closed his eyes and felt sweat trickle down his sides as he stood in the heat of the sun bouncing off of the plastered wall. *Magdalena,* he prayed fervently, *what am I supposed to do?* From behind the courtyard wall, the first crack of rod to flesh and a scream of agony rent the air. Diego's eyes flew open, but he forced them shut again. *Magdalena! I need your help!*

Inside the cottage, Grace began pounding on the door again. "Someone please get *Don* Ramon. This must stop! Captain, please, I cannot stand this!"

The remaining guard left his post and wandered toward the cottage door. "*¿Qué es lo que pasa?*"

It was now or never. The guard leaned toward the door and pressed his ear to it, his broad, ebony back turned to the side of the cottage where Diego was hiding. Silently, Diego drew his sword from the sheath at his side. He stepped quickly to the front of the cabin and drove the blade forcefully between the guard's shoulder blades until he felt it hit the breastbone just beyond the man's heart. The dying man's cry was lost in another of Encantadora's screams.

The door had been bolted from the outside, and Diego slid the bolt back and opened it. Instantly Grace tumbled through it, but she stopped short and stifled a cry at the sight of the guard.

"Is he—?"

"Come," Diego ordered.

"Captain, surely you didn't have to kill him!"

If there had been time, he might have given her a sound shaking. "There is no time! Ramon will come for you next, *Señora* Courtney!"

"Nay!"

"Nay?"

"We are not leaving her here!"

"I told you, there is no time."

"Captain, I don't want you to suffer on my account, as well. Thank you. Thank you from the bottom of my heart! You can leave now, and know that you have done everything that honor might require of you. But I have to at least try to get her away from here."

"*¡Caramba!*" he cried in frustration. "We will return to my ship, and if it is at all possible, I will come back to get your friend."

"Nay, you do not understand. I am not leaving Havana without her." Encantadora screamed again and again, and the look in Grace's green eyes turned hard as glass. "We both leave or we both stay. I will not abandon her."

Diego sighed. "Follow me."

They could hear Encantadora's horrible cries all the

way around the building until he and Grace reached the deserted front of the brothel. Though it was dangerous for them both to linger, he had to admit that Grace was right, they could not leave the other girl here. She had risked much to help Grace, and deserved to be aided herself. He motioned to Grace to stay at the edge of the street while he cautiously approached the open front door and peered inside.

The door led into the shadowy, covered foyer and the sunny courtyard beyond, and he saw immediately how it had come to be left wide open. A man, dirty and disheveled, strode purposefully from the shadows into the light. His back was turned, so Diego could not see his face, but the moment the man reached the yard, Diego caught the glint of sunlight on an unsheathed, bloodstained cutlass. The scene unraveling did not bode well. He quickly ducked back out and joined Grace in the street.

"We cannot do this now, but I am fairly certain that *Don* Ramon is about to become too busy to do your friend further harm."

Grace looked at him with apprehension. "What do you mean?"

"Come, there is nothing we can do right now. You will simply have to take my word that he will probably leave the woman alone a while. We will go to my ship, but I promise, *señora*, we will come for your friend tonight."

Giles felt sick. Sick to his stomach, sick in his heart. A wildly sobbing Mulatto was lying on her stomach on the beautifully tiled floor of the brothel's courtyard, an African man sitting on her back and holding her feet up by the ankles. Standing before them, a white man in a sweat-stained shirt held a crop in his hand, poised to strike another blow to the already raw soles of the woman's feet. Giles raised his cutlass in response.

"Hold! *¡Pare!*" Like Geoff, he knew the handful of Spanish words required to board and take a Spanish ship.

The Spaniard dropped his hand to his side and gave him a contemptuous look, responding in his own tongue. Giles swore softly. "Does anybody in this bloody place speak English?"

The Spaniard gestured the African man aside, and as soon as the man lifted himself from the Mulatto, he yanked her off the ground by her arm. The woman cried out in pain, sinking cross-legged to the ground and cradling her injured feet. When the man moved to strike her, she cringed and wailed, "Me speak English! Me tell him whey you sey!"

Giles took a threatening step forward. "First, tell him that if he raises his hand to you again, I will kill him where he stands."

"Nay, nay! Me already got big trouble!"

"Tell him that he has purchased my wife, and that I have come to retrieve her." He twisted his wrist slightly, making sure that his bloodstained blade caught the sun.

The woman pulled herself to her knees. "Take me wit' you, maas! Take me wit' you, an' I show you where her be! Please, maas. Grace tell you me a good girl! Me help her."

His heart lurched in his chest. "You've seen her?"

The Spaniard shouted at the woman, and she cringed again, hands up, responding in Spanish. Then she turned to Giles. "Please help me, maas!"

"Tell him I want both of you."

"Him no a-go sell us!"

Giles took another step toward the procurer. "I'm not offering to pay."

The African man shouted in alarm, glancing time and again at the rear gate. Giles braced himself for another opponent, stepping smartly behind the procurer and holding his blade to the man's throat. To his surprise, the second opponent never emerged.

He turned his attention back to the woman. "Tell him that if he wants to live, he will keep his man back and give me my wife and you."

The procurer responded with a furious burst of Spanish, but he had clearly ordered his man to keep his distance, because the guard made no move toward them.

"Him sey him kill you 'fore you get us. But me know, maas! Me know where Grace be. Only you gotta promise a take me, too!"

"You have my word. Where is she?"

She pointed to the rear gate. "De cottage out bak. Dey anotta mon wit' her."

It took every ounce of willpower he possessed not to draw his blade against the throat of the man he held. The mere thought that the bastard had sold Grace to someone, someone who was, even now, using her, sent him into a blind rage.

"Show me," he ordered the woman.

She rose reluctantly, cried out when she put her weight on her ravaged feet, and limped slowly to the gate. Giles nodded to the guard and, with a jerk of his head, indicated that he should go next. Then he dragged his stiffly compliant hostage with him to bring up the rear.

The door to the cottage stood wide open, blocked by the crumpled body of a black man. The second guard ran forward to inspect the fallen man, and a sound of anguish slipped through his throat.

The woman fell to her knees again. "Her gone. Dat otta mon take her. Please maas. Don't leave me! Me help you find dem! Me seen de mon."

Giles roared in frustration. He shoved the procurer away from him with all the force of his pent up rage, then brandished his sword. "Get in the house!" he shouted at both the Spaniard and the African and pointing them in the right direction. "Get in the god-damned house, now!"

The two men stumbled over the third man's body, but they retreated quickly into the cottage. Giles pulled the door shut and slid the bolt home. He turned to the woman, still kneeling in the alleyway, and ground his teeth. He still needed her, but with those feet, she was going to slow him down.

"Where do you think they've gone?" he asked.

She looked up at him, her face set, her chin lifted in defiance. "You gotta take me."

He swept the woman up into his arms. She was surprisingly light, and up close, very young. "Which way?"

"Me tink de harbor. Her call him Cap'n."

Grace wanted to climb the walls of Captain Montoya's cabin. Instead, she paced, pausing to sit at his desk a while, then moving to his bunk to study the crucifix on the wall above it, before she resumed her pacing again. She wore a set of clothes borrowed from Diego's cabin boy, Galeno, even though it would be hours before she would need them. As soon as the sun set, she would return to *El Jardín de Placer* with Captain Montoya and one of his crewmen. The crewman would be able to investigate inside of the brothel as a patron, without arousing suspicion. Outside, she and Diego would dispatch the guards and help to get Encantadora out. She could hardly wear her shift in public, and although the boy's clothes were snug, they made a good disguise when paired with a large jacket. The plan was dicey, but there had been little time to plot their course.

She was standing at the cabin window, fretting over the amount of daylight yet remaining, when Diego joined her. His long face looked even longer with the corners of his mouth turned down into a grim frown.

"What is it?" she asked.

Diego sank into his captain's chair and rubbed his lean jaw distractedly. "We are setting sail."

"What? Nay! You promised!"

"We are too late."

Grace froze. Oh God, had *Don* Ramon killed Encantadora? "Too late for what?"

"I had my man go to the *burdel.* I thought that there might be some side entrance that we had missed, a better way in or out. He found that *El Jardín de Placer* will not open tonight. *Don* Ramon had gathered a group of men in front, and my man blended in with them. Ramon was ranting about having lost two of his women. Then he said something about a man with a sword stealing one of them. He is coming after us."

"Two women? Then, Encantadora has already escaped. But that's good news!" Diego forced a brief smile, and her heart sank. "You don't think she did."

"It is possible."

He didn't sound convinced, and her heart sank a

little further. "You think he killed her. You think that when he found that I was gone, he killed her." Then a hopeful thought slipped in. "But maybe the man you saw when you went back inside . . ."

Diego shrugged heavily. "I do not know. I think that if Ramon would beat her so for lying to protect you, he would be very angry if he believed that she had helped you to escape. She told you that he whipped their feet to punish them. How could she have run away? Now, he searches for us."

"We don't know that! He never saw you, and you said that there was another man—a man with a sword!"

Diego leapt to his feet. "He did not have to see me! All he needed to see was the man I killed with my sword outside your door. He is looking for a man with a sword and the woman that he stole. Who else could that be? One way or another, whether she was killed or escaped, your friend is beyond our reach, and we are in grave danger!"

Grace turned back to the window. "He will know to look for you."

Diego nodded sternly. "He knows that I bought you last night and that I did not do to you what I claimed to do. If he has any sense, it will not take him long to figure it out."

"Does he know your name?"

"I am well known in Havana. A few questions in the right places and . . ."

"And he will know just who it is that he seeks." At Diego's nod, she said, "Then you must sail. Just give me time to get off of the ship."

Diego blocked the door, feet spread wide, fists on his hips. "We will not sail without you. If you insist upon placing yourself in harm's way, then I must insist upon being there with you."

She thought of Encantadora just a few hours earlier, stretching out upon the bed, thrilled to have a few moments of relative privacy. She remembered the shrill screams coming from behind the courtyard wall. But she could not ignore all that Diego had risked, both his safety and his savings. She owed him much. They might very well be too late to save Encantadora, in which case, she would be placing Diego at greater peril for naught. Grace closed her eyes and whispered, "Then we sail."

What had become of Encantadora after they had abandoned her that afternoon? And if Diego was wrong, and she was still alive, what would become of her now that they were abandoning her again?

It had been a long and arduous journey to the harbor with the woman called Encantadora, since she could barely walk. And it had taken Giles longer still to sort out her story and learn that whoever had taken Grace seemed to be trying to protect her. But the woman had not known the identity of the man who had befriended Grace, so he had to keep her with him as he went from ship to ship, and their progress was maddeningly slow.

They had paused a moment while Encantadora nursed her sore feet, and Giles looked out to sea. A small merchant ship was gliding gently from the dock, and it struck him that he had seen it somewhere before, a long time ago. Of course, he'd seen more than his share of Spanish merchant vessels in his years as a privateer. After a while, they all looked the same. The only thing that mattered was the sure and certain knowledge that the captain of so small a ship could not have paid fifty gold doubloons for a night with a prostitute. He need not worry that his wife was sailing out of his reach on board that vessel.

Twenty

The kitchen was suffocatingly hot, as always, but it was the best place to find out the state of things at the big house, so Matu endured it. She helped Keyah cook by chopping vegetables at a small table that sat under a window facing the house.

"Dat 'ooman drunk, me tell you, Matu," Keyah commented. "Her lookin' kinda antsy ova breakfas'. Den, her come out here an' get a bottla rum. At lunch, her giddy as de maas when him got a gut fulla rum."

Matu nodded, but Keyah's gossip had set her to thinking. The master was the drinker, not the mistress. When Iolanthe needed something to settle her nerves, someone else, someone black, paid the price. But it was late afternoon, and the master would be home any minute. If Iolanthe were going to order a whipping, she'd have done it by now.

Keyah glanced out of the window overlooking the sugar house and mill. "Him here! De maas! Him at de mill!"

Matu looked out the window with Keyah. Edmund dismounted from his horse and the overseer came over to speak with him. The conversation became quickly animated, rising in volume until Matu could clearly make out every vulgar word out of Edmund's mouth. She turned to Keyah, pointed to her eyes and then the house.

"Nay, Matu!" Keyah protested. "Dem catch you spyin' on dem an' dem a-go beat you dead!"

Matu didn't care. She had to know what was to become of Grace. She was still holding out hope that the Captain would come to his senses, but if he didn't, she had to make sure that Grace's father would do right by her. This whole situation was no fault of Grace's. She waved Keyah's protests away and watched avidly from the window. Edmund thrust the reins of his horse at a slave, grabbed his satchel of clothing from the saddle, and stalked into the house. Matu was not far behind. A quick glance in the direction of the sugar production confirmed that no one was watching. She raced silently to the far side of the house, stooped under one of the open windows, then raised herself so that her eyes were barely above the windowsill.

Edmund pitched the satchel onto the floor. Sinking into one of the upholstered chairs, he picked up Iolanthe's embroidered pillow and stared at it with a look of disgust and despair. "Stupid woman," he muttered, tossing it aside. It slid across the wooden floor and came to rest near the back door.

Iolanthe had quietly descended the stairs behind him. She wore one of her best gowns, sapphire silk that offset her ivory skin to perfection. "Edmund?" she said softly. "Thank God you are home. A horrible thing has happened."

Edmund didn't rise. He didn't even bother to turn and face her. In a tense voice, he replied, "I've heard it all, already. Roger told me."

"He told you that Grace's husband came here? Oh, Edmund, the man was crazed."

Finally he rose and leveled her with a look of pure contempt. "Crazed because you couldn't keep your bloody mouth shut! What the hell have you done, Iolanthe?"

"Sooner or later he would have found out. It was unrealistic to believe that you could hide it forever."

He gave a disheartened half laugh. "It was unrealistic given that I have *you* for a wife."

Iolanthe made a poor attempt to conceal her smug smirk. "And so it is all my fault, of course. What are you going to do about it?"

"I don't know," he answered, but his hands fell to the back of the chair and tightened convulsively.

Under the windowsill, Matu swallowed hard. It was almost as if the mistress were goading him. As though she didn't realize that this was the one area in which no one played games with the master. Matu knew better than anyone how dear this secret had been to him. She was relieved to see Iolanthe sigh and soften her demeanor.

"You think that I took the first opportunity to destroy your life, but it was not like that. Have a drink, Edmund. Have a drink and hear me out. What is the harm in that?" She picked up a bottle of rum from the table and held it out like a peace offering.

Edmund snatched the bottle from her hand. "I have the feeling I'm going to need something strong to wash down whatever lies you've dreamed up since yesterday."

"If you have already made up your mind," she retorted, "I do not know why I should waste my breath."

He took a long draught and settled back into his chair, eyeing the bottle with distaste. "Bad batch," he muttered, then returned his skeptical gaze to his wife. "Never let it be said I'm not a fair man, Iolanthe. I'll hear you out. Hopefully your tale is more palatable than this rum."

Matu eyed the bottle of rum in Edmund's hand. Obviously Iolanthe had not gotten drunk on it.

"Take another sip," Iolanthe urged. "I daresay what you tasted was your own bitterness. Perhaps, for a moment, you should consider the possibility that you do not have all of the facts. Personally, I think that Grace must have run away."

Edmund laughed sharply and took another hard swallow. "Surely you can do better than that, my darling."

She sat down in the other chair, leaning on the tea table that separated them. "Who knows what had happened between them? She had obviously already told him something of her past. Captain Courtney had some wild idea that I had sent my brother to abduct Grace. How could he have learned of Jacques save from Grace's own lips? And who is to say how he reacted when she told him? He was insane when he got here. I had to go along with his ranting. I feared for my life!"

Edmund took another long pull at the bottle, frowning thoughtfully. "Foolish girl! She should never have told him about that. What purpose could it have served?"

Iolanthe watched him drink, her eyes lit with an unnatural fire. "It obviously drove him mad. He was insanely furious. And let me tell you something else. He knew that Grace was not mine, that we had lied to him. What was I to say? I was truly afraid that he would kill me if I did not try to appease him. He was violent. He shoved me, stood on my dress!"

"God forbid, one of your bloody dresses!" Another gulp of rum.

"The pink one with the satin ribbons!"

"Never say it!" Edmund snapped derisively. "So Grace *may* have told him, and you took it upon yourself to make absolutely *certain* that he knew everything!" Yet again, he raised the rapidly draining bottle to his mouth. "Jesus! I've never had such rot-gut rum!"

"You do not look well," Iolanthe agreed sweetly.

Matu's heart began to pound. She was watching Iolanthe murder her husband! She knew that she should stop it somehow, but everything was happening so quickly, and she didn't know what to do.

Edmund tried to stand, but he couldn't seem to straighten and clutched his hand to his middle.

"What is wrong, Edmund?" his wife taunted. "Is it too painful to accept that perhaps you do not have as much control over your women as you thought?"

He tried to set the bottle onto the tea table, but it slipped from his hands and fell on its side. Golden-brown liquid trickled over the edge.

Iolanthe laughed. "And now, you discover that it is I who have all of the power." She stood and faced her husband, who rocked unsteadily on his feet. With her pretty, white hands she caressed his face, letting them glide down to his chest.

Edmund grabbed her wrists, panic in his eyes, and Matu immediately recognized the expression of sublime ecstasy that slowly transformed the mistress's face.

Sinking to his knees, Edmund stared up at his wife. His face was turning a mottled shade of red, and he began to wheeze, sucking for air. "Iol—"

"Be quiet, Edmund," she snapped. She pulled her wrists from his grasp, then took his head in her hands and kissed him full on the mouth.

Matu clapped both of her hands over her own mouth to keep from crying out. Captain Courtney's friend had been right. Iolanthe Welbourne was utterly insane. Murderously, dangerously insane.

When Edmund fell to the floor, Iolanthe knelt next to him, heedless of the dust and her expensive gown. He lay gasping for air, and her breath matched his, gasp for gasp. A tiny whimper of excitement slipped through her lips. *"Oui, oui,"* she urged feverishly as she watched his body writhe.

Matu felt sick. She had no love for the master, honestly didn't care whether he lived or died, but what she was watching was sick beyond reason. And what would become of them all once Iolanthe, indeed, held all of the power? There would be no one to temper her, no one to stop her. Welbourne Plantation had seemed like hell on earth, but it had only been a taste of the hell to come.

Now, the only sound of breathing that came from the room was Iolanthe's as she lay next to her husband, her eyes closed, her face rapturous. And Matu knew that she had no choice.

Without a sound she rose and slipped back around to the rear door. Still, no one in the sugar structures was looking toward the big house. She slipped quietly through the door and her bare feet raced lightly across the room. Iolanthe turned her head and opened her eyes just as Matu stooped and swept up the pillow that Edmund had so carelessly tossed aside. Before the mistress could rise, Matu was on top of her, pressing the pillow into her face with all of her might.

Iolanthe's hands formed claws, and she tried to pry Matu from her, but Matu mashed her chest into the pillow atop Iolanthe's face and grabbed Iolanthe's hands in her own. She held them over Iolanthe's head, pressing her palms flat against her mistress's, their fingers interlaced. She knew that she had to restrain Iolanthe while leaving as little bruising as possible. She lay with her full weight against the struggling woman, not daring to move, even after Iolanthe went slack and still.

Finally when her own heart had slowed down and she was absolutely certain that Iolanthe's heart was no longer beating at all, she pulled the pillow aside. Brown eyes, wide but sightless, stared up at her, and Matu shuddered. She took the pillow and ran upstairs to put it in Iolanthe's room. There, on Iolanthe's small bedside table, next to her favored sugared almonds, sat two small, glass vials with traces of white powder.

Matu picked them up and glanced out the window into the rear courtyard. Empty. Then she ran back downstairs and pressed the vials into one of Edmund's still warm hands. She took Iolanthe under the arms and dragged her to the sitting area of the keeping room. Another covered crystal dish of almonds sat on the tea table. Matu removed the cover and knocked the dish to the ground where the almonds scattered. She picked up two of them and, with her face set in grim determination, forced them tightly into Iolanthe's throat. Finally, she pulled Iolanthe's hands up to her neck and carefully turned the body over to hold the position.

All that remained was to inform the overseer of her grisly discovery.

Diego stood at the helm of his small merchant ship, *Magdalena*, and tried not to think about his aching back. Since she had come on board, Señora Courtney had been so touchingly grateful, so insistent that she not inconvenience him any further, so utterly willing to sleep in whatever small space that he might afford her. What else could he possibly do but give her his cabin and sleep in a hammock with his men? Well, try to sleep. He had missed his comfortable bunk. The next time they had a female on board, the first mate's cabin would house her.

Movement at the top of the hatch caught the attention of several of his crew, which in turn caught Diego's. His guest was awake. She had been left with little choice but to wear Galeno's clothes, but the breeches were hardly appropriate in front of the crew, so she had kept Diego's jacket. It reached well past her knees and was sufficient for hiding most of her form, but it left most of her shapely calves exposed, and it was this feature that drew the eye of every man on board. Her hands were lost somewhere inside the embellished cuffs of the sleeves. She had done her best to braid her hair, but it was too curly to be contained so easily. Diego grinned at the picture. Mulatto or not, *Capitán* Courtney had done well for himself in his marriage.

"*¡Buenos días, Señora!*" he called down to her.

She looked up with a smile and waved to him. "*¡Buenos días, Capitán!*"

He watched her cross the deck, looking studiously ahead of her, ignoring the appreciative stares of the crew, and moving with as much dignity as she could muster in the oversized jacket.

"I trust you had a good night's sleep."

Señora Courtney ducked her head self-consciously. "Wonderful. I feel terrible for putting you out of your bed, but I am truly grateful. I really cannot thank you enough . . ."

"You have thanked me, many times. *No importa.*"

"*No importa?*"

"It is of no importance."

"You have saved my life, *Capitán!*"

"You exaggerate," Diego protested, but he stood a little straighter.

"Nay! What would a Spanish maiden have done in my place? I fully intended to take my own life at the first opportunity."

"That is a mortal sin, *Señora!*"

"Then you saved my life *and* my soul!"

Diego felt his cheeks grow warm. He had done all of that, hadn't he? "It was an honor," he replied.

And while that was true, it had been an honor, it didn't hurt that he had decided that it would be fair to ask a tidy little sum over and above the reimbursement he was owed. A finder's fee, passage for the woman from Cuba to Jamaica. . . . He was not a greedy man, but he expected reasonable compensation.

Unfortunately, he had met with a number of obstacles to collecting it. They had already attempted to approach Port Royal and had been greeted with warning shots fired across their bow by no fewer than seven English ships, *Magdalena's* white flag of truce having been summarily ignored. They had sailed on, heading toward Welbourne, but had been forced to turn away by an English naval vessel patrolling the coast. Now, they were sailing toward the western end of the island, in hopes of finding refuge at Winston Hall, the home of Diego's uncle and his English aunt.

Suddenly, Diego felt overly warm, and the morning sunlight became too bright for his eyes to bear. It was a familiar feeling, one that had come to him many times before. Of their own accord, his eyelids lowered, and a voice echoed inside of his head.

Diego. It was a woman's voice, speaking in strange and lyrically accented Spanish. *The ship just on the horizon, the one that flies a French flag, they are privateers, and you are far from Spanish waters.*

He didn't have to open his eyes to know that the ship she spoke of must surely be there. In the two years that she had been coming to him, Magdalena had never led him astray.

Although he knew the answer, he could not resist thinking, *Can you not send them in another direction?*

She didn't dignify the question with a response.

Shall we fight? he asked.

Flee, she answered.

Damn! *How am I supposed to get this woman home? You are the one who insisted that I rescue her. I felt that as clearly as I hear your voice now. Surely you can offer some help!*

The wind on his face felt like the sigh of a woman's breath. *Now is not the time, Diego.*

She was gone. The breeze cooled him, and he opened his eyes again into sunlight that dazzled, but did not overwhelm him. Grace was frowning at him in concern.

"Are you quite all right, Captain?"

"Sí," he answered distractedly. Under his breath, he mumbled, "Now is never the time. Now is not the time to play the hero. Now is not the time to get what you want. Now is not the time to take this woman home." It was a litany of things that, in the past two years, Magdalena had relegated to some distant, indefinite future.

"Excuse me?" Grace asked.

"Nothing," he said. She was looking at him as if he were crazy. How could he fault her? He often wondered himself. To his crew, he shouted, "Evade that ship!"

The crew knew better than to argue. Their captain's ability to sense danger was acute, and his judgment in knowing when to fight and when to flee was uncanny. If he said that the ship they could barely see was a threat, a threat it was. *Magdalena* swung away from the coast of Jamaica, out toward the Spanish Main and friendlier seas.

Her home receding before her very eyes, Grace held herself rigid. Captain Montoya had good reasons for doing what he did, she told herself. Too many English ships had already fired upon them. But he hadn't even let that last ship get close enough to see if it was a threat! What if it had been another Spanish vessel, or one from some other friendly country?

Tears burned her eyes and a lump formed in her throat. She didn't know where Giles was, but one thing was certain, he wasn't going to look for her near the Spanish Main! Damn her uncle! If he had taken her to Saint Domingue, Giles might have found her.

If he had taken her to Saint Domingue, Diego might not have found her. She might have, at this very moment, been on her way toward becoming a well-seasoned prostitute. Still, Jamaica had been so close!

"Captain Montoya, are you quite certain that the ship you saw was . . ."

He glared at her, and she closed her mouth. The whole episode had been so strange. One minute she had been thanking him for all that he had done for her, the next he had gone as pale as the sails billowing above them. He had closed his eyes and looked like he might even pass out. When he opened them again, they'd had a glazed quality, and he had begun to mutter something, obviously angry. The next thing she knew, they were avoiding some unidentified ship and sailing away from home. Away from Giles.

But in all honesty, was she ready to face him?

"I am sorry, *Señora,*" Diego said. "Believe me, I am as frustrated as you are by this turn of events. Forces beyond our control seem to be conspiring against us on this voyage."

She smiled weakly at him, and he excused himself to confer with his first mate.

Was the delay so terrible, really? Grace shuffled over to a giant coil of rope and plopped down, wrapping Diego's jacket more snugly around her, as though it might be Giles's arms keeping her safe and warm. But the jacket still smelled of citrus and Captain Montoya. It didn't envelop her in the spicy, musky scent of her husband.

She had to tell him. Everything. And she had to tell him before they consummated their vows. In all fairness, she had to give him a way out, once he knew the truth. Giles was such a good man. She wouldn't be at all surprised if he felt honor bound to stay with her, but she couldn't bear the thought. Once, she had dreaded sharing his bed; now, she dreaded that he would leave her to sleep alone. Once, she had feared a real marriage; now, it seemed she might well be left with naught but a sham. Aye, Giles was a good man, a compassionate man, but was he the kind of man who would not care that his children's blood was mixed? Even her own father had always seen her as tainted.

How could she tell him? She looked back out to sea. Her island was gone. Maybe 'twas better that way. Maybe she needed just a little more time to build up the courage she needed to show herself to him fully, though she risked losing him forever in the process.

Twenty-one

Giles watched bleakly as Welbourne's dock drew nearer. His hair hung limp and unbound down the back of the rumpled shirt that he'd slept in for two nights. Geoff stood at his side with a hand on his friend's shoulder. Jawara positioned himself at the other side, his thick arms crossed over his bare chest, intervening whenever a crewmember was fool enough to approach the captain with some trivial concern. If the first mate or any other man balked at Jawara's self-appointed position, one look at the captain's haggard face kept them from bothering him with their complaint. Encantadora and the little girl from Havana sat together atop an empty crate on the opposite side of the deck. The older girl patted the younger one's shoulder comfortingly, but she eyed with hostility the plantation in the distance. From time to time, her gaze would wander to Jawara's broad back, and her face would soften, almost imperceptibly.

"You could take *Reliance* and plunder the Spanish Main for the next ten years and not find her," Geoff said to Giles. "She'd not want you to go back to that life for her."

"I'll be damned if I'll leave her to be some Spaniard's whore!"

"Whoever he was, he wanted to help her. He may very well have brought her home."

"Were she here, she'd be at the dock with that man." Giles nodded to the overseer, who stood at the landing watching the ship.

"Unless she is in Port Royal," Geoff suggested.

Giles snorted skeptically. "A Spanish ship, docking in Port Royal. Why can I not fathom such a thing?"

"Sintime you gotta jus' go on," Jawara advised. "It don' do no good a kill youself tinkin' of it. You kill de mon dat stole her from you. Dat more dan me got."

Giles brought his fists down on the ship's rail. "I want the man who stole her from the brothel! I cannot believe that we combed the entire dock and every tavern, and no one knew who he was!"

"Giles, upon my word, if I thought we'd any chance of finding her, I'd sail right by your side until we did. He could be on his way back to Spain for all we know."

"What am I supposed to do, Geoff? Am I to just go on as though I had never met her? Just pretend that none of this ever happened? What am I to tell her father?" He looked back to the dock, annoyed that he saw no sign of Edmund. "And where the hell is he?"

"We'll tell her father that his bloody wife is the one responsible for this."

"Grace is my wife! I was supposed to protect her! For the love of Jesus, Geoff, *I* delivered her uncle to Port Royal. I gave him time alone with her! God help me. How am I to live with this?"

"You didn't know!"

"Were it Faith, would you accept that as an excuse from yourself?" When Geoff didn't answer, Giles nodded. "I thought not."

"You a-go drive youself mad tinkin' like dat," Jawara interjected. "Sintime deh jus' nutten you can do."

Giles finally tore his eyes away from the shore, and he looked at Jawara. "Is that what 'tis like to be black? You become accustomed to being powerless?"

Jawara's eyes flashed with anger. "Nay, dat not what it be like! Not in Africa! In Africa, we not black. Dem otta men dat steal us, dem *white*. We jus' people. Sum be slaves, an' sum be free. *Me* be a freemon. Even in de white mon's world, me *not* powerless. Do me be anybody slave? Me jus' know whey a hold on an' whey a let go."

Giles clenched his teeth in frustrated rage. He would not just let go of Grace! In the past few days he had gone back through every memory he had of his wife, searching for something that made her one thing and him another, and he had yet to find it. She had a quick wit, a sharp mind, an infectious laugh. And what of Jawara, his newfound friend? Mayhap he looked different, but he had sisters with whom he quarreled and whom he loved nonetheless. He grieved the loss of his wife and their unborn child. And he had ambition, wanting things from this life. If these things did not make a man, what did?

When he reviewed all of these things together, he came to one inescapable conclusion. Grace was a woman, like any other woman, no matter what color her parents. But there was something that *did* set Grace apart. She was the woman he loved. He could not bear the thought of returning to his empty apartment. He wanted to have to dig through untidy mounds of lace to find his cravats. He wanted the top of his chest of drawers to be scattered with pots of mysterious creams. The thought of sitting at his immaculate desk all alone and adding up numbers slowly in the night filled his chest with a sharp pain. When he said something arrogant or was too certain that he had everything in hand, he wanted someone to narrow her discerning, green eyes at him and put him in his place with a cynical grin.

He wanted Grace.

Aye, he wanted Grace! He wanted to hold her in his arms and erase every evil thing that had been done to her at the hands of men who had not seen her for what she was. He wanted to turn her cries of fear into cries of delight. And he needed her to hold him back, to let him know that he was important to someone, that his life meant something. He thought with painful longing about the children they might have had. Bright children with their mother's penetrating refusal to take anything at face value and his loyalty and competence.

How could he possibly live with himself if he left her alone with some faceless Spaniard, never knowing what had become of her? The only answer was that he couldn't. Nor would he return to the relative civility of privateering.

"I'll turn pirate, if I must," he said to Geoff.

Geoff pondered for a moment and replied, "Then we'll sail together again."

Giles's brows shot up in surprise. "You cannot do that, Geoff. 'Twould mean your very life! Montoya could not save you from Spain again."

Geoff gave him a steady look. "Would you do any less for Faith?"

Giles swallowed hard, humbled by a profound sense of gratitude. Still, he shook his head. "You have a wife to think of, and two children."

"Her family would take care of them. Besides," Geoff added with an excellent imitation of his old, wicked grin, "we are a formidable team. That Spaniard caught me off guard! It won't happen again."

Giles sighed. He would stay at Welbourne no longer than a night. Then he would get back to sea and find Grace ere she had sailed forever beyond his reach.

Despite his impatience, when they dropped anchor and lowered a rowboat into the water, Giles found himself wishing that he could delay the moment when he must confess to Edmund his utter failure in Havana. If Grace had indeed been awaiting him on the dock, Giles could have rowed there effortlessly. As it was, the strain of the last several days and the weight in his heart made every pull of the oars a Herculean task.

"Cap'n Courtney!" the overseer shouted. "Thank God you're here. I've only just sent word to your office, and I feared you were at sea!"

Giles looked into the man's distraught face. He was clearly nervous, the front of his shirt soaked in sweat, his dark-circled eyes constantly moving. Whatever it was that he spoke of, 'twas ill news indeed.

"I've only just returned," Giles said. "What word?"

The overseer took a deep breath and rattled off words that smacked of too much practice. "'Twould seem Mistress Welbourne choked to death on those almonds she's always so fond of. When Edmund found her body, he must have been beside himself with grief. He swallowed poison."

Giles pinned him with a penetrating gaze. "Beside himself with grief? Over Iolanthe? I can hardly credit such a thing. Were there witnesses?"

"Nay, none. Your wife's maid found the bodies and reported it to me. I, myself, found the almonds lodged in Mistress Welbourne's throat and vials with traces of powder in Edmund's hand."

"A very neat scenario, but most unlikely given their stormy relationship. I should think that Edmund would have danced upon her grave."

The overseer scowled darkly. "The mistress's death was an obvious accident. If Edmund did not kill himself, then the next likeliest suspect is your wife's maid. You can accuse her if you like, but we've far bigger problems to face, and they'll be all the worse if you cross Matu."

"What problems? And what has Matu to with them?"

The questions made the overseer markedly more anxious. "We've been three days with no master or mistress. The slaves are growing hostile, harder to control. We have better weapons, Captain, but we Whites are outnumbered here. That dumb witch has too much power. I told Welbourne that he should have sold her soon as his girl married you. 'Tis an ill thing, the way the other slaves look at her. Think she has some kind of magic protection because she's lived so long."

He leaned closer and lowered his voice, although there was no one else close enough to overhear him. "Welbourne went into the house that day mad enough to throttle his wife. It may be Welbourne thought himself well rid of her when she choked. But what if he *was* murdered? The last thing any of us needs to do just now is to stir up the rest of the Blacks by confronting the one person who most likely killed him. Were I you, my first act as the new master would be to sell her."

The new master? Giles looked back across the bay where *Reliance* floated peacefully. "I'll not be staying," Giles informed him, and the overseer looked on the verge of panic.

"Then you'll have to sell your slaves off quickly. Scatter them, maybe one big auction with the neighbors."

Giles's mouth fell open in horror. "Sell them?"

"Aye, tomorrow if you can."

He ran the fingers of both hands through his untidy hair as though he might tear it out by the roots. "I'm not selling anybody. Listen—what is your bloody name?"

The man huffed, clearly insulted. "Cornell. Roger Cornell. Edmund introduced us before the wedding."

"Forgive me. I was—distracted. I'm thinking that I will free them. The sooner the better."

Now it was the overseer's turn to look horrified. "You cannot free them!"

"Watch me."

"Courtney, let me ask you something. It matters naught to me what you think of slavery. Where will these workers go? Nearly a hundred and fifty newly freed slaves? They'll slaughter every planter's family within their reach. And then what? They'll be maroons and have to scrape out a living in the mountains. You'd not be doing them any great kindness."

Giles cast another desperate glance at the ship. Geoff was waiting for him. They were sailors, not farmers, and neither of them had ever owned so much as a single slave. If Grace were there, he would seek her advice, but she wasn't, and the whole situation felt like salt in a wound. Then he realized that he might not have Grace there to help him, but he did have the person to whom *she* would have turned for counsel.

"Where is Matu?" he demanded.

Just the name made Roger jumpy. "She's in the kitchen with Keyah, the two of them stirring up trouble, no doubt."

"Send her to the house, if you please. I'll see what I can do to get to the bottom of all this."

"Have a care."

Giles gave what he hoped was a reassuring smile. "I will."

The overseer, clearly relieved to have gotten through to him, nodded and headed off to the little building behind the big house.

When Giles reached the house and stepped into the keeping room, he took a long moment to look around him. Nothing was out of place. There was no sign of violence. It did not seem the scene of two deaths only a few days before. He walked through the space, opened the back door, and leaned against the frame, waiting for Matu. Roger exited the kitchen and nodded to him in acknowledgment before he returned to the sugar house. A few seconds later, Matu and Keyah followed him as far as the courtyard, then veered off to where Giles stood.

Matu gave him a somber look and tapped her fingertips upon her cheek, a sign that he had seen her use in reference to Grace. His throat tightened. He had anticipated that it would be hard to tell Edmund what had happened. He had not considered the fact that he would have to tell Matu, and he found that it was harder still. Tears threatened.

"I'm sorry, Matu. She—she wasn't in Havana anymore. Someone took her somewhere. But there is a woman with me who saw the man who took her, and she said that he was trying to help her. I think—I hope— that she's safe for a while. I'm going to try to find her again."

Matu nodded, touching her chest and then her head.

"Matu sey she know you try," Keyah supplied. "Me Keyah. Me know her sign pretty good. Not like Miss Grace, but pretty good."

Giles nodded gratefully. "Thank you." Then he addressed Matu. "What happened, Matu?"

Matu walked past him through the door, over to the two upholstered chairs with the tea table between them. She pointed to a cracked crystal dish on the table and then to the floor. As Matu moved around and gestured fluidly, Keyah translated.

"Her come in an' find de dish on de floor by de mistress. Dem almonds was scattered all ova, an' de mistress hands still wrap 'round her troat." She cast an edgy glance at Matu. Her voice faltered periodically, but Matu moved briskly and too calmly, Giles thought, considering the grisly nature of her tale. Keyah took a shaky breath and continued to translate Matu's gestures. "De maas be deh, by de chair, an' deh an empty bottla rum on de table."

Matu opened a drawer in the sideboard and withdrew two little glass vials.

"Dey be in his hands," Keyah explained, looking away from Matu. It seemed that she knew this part of the story without Matu's help. "De bakra—ovaseea—him sey it poison. Him de one dat figure out de mistress choke."

"So," Giles summed up dryly, "Iolanthe choked to death and Edmund, consumed by grief for his beloved wife, swallowed poison."

Matu turned and looked at him, her face inscrutable. Keyah shrugged uneasily. "Dat whey it look like."

Giles's voice was laced with skepticism. "Indeed, that is what it *looks* like." He turned his gaze toward the windows that faced out back, toward the slaves' quarters. "The overseer insists that this is the least of my worries. Tell me, how stand things with your fellow workers? Cornell seems to think them on the verge of insurrection."

This time, both women appeared worried, and Matu nodded emphatically. Giles sank into one of the chairs and drummed his fingers on the arm. "Think you that I should set them free? Cornell says not. He says 'tis a danger to the neighbors and that they would have nowhere to go."

Keyah looked grim. "Me hate a sey it, but de bakra right. Big trouble be brewing in de huts. Matu keepin' dem in line, but none of us don' wanna go bak on de block."

"Can you manage to keep things under control until I can find Grace and return with her?"

Matu shook her head, and Keyah said, "Dey not a-go wait. De slaves touchy, de bakra an' de guards touchy. Sinting a-go happen, an' even Matu not have de way a stop it."

Leaning back in the chair with a sigh, Giles asked, "Have you any ideas?"

Matu nodded enthusiastically. She pointed toward the front of the house, gesturing for a boat on the sea. She rubbed her hand over the skin on her arm and pantomimed mopping and then pulling on a rope. Back to her arm and the boat, finally pointing excitedly to Giles.

Keyah's brows pulled together in a confused frown. "De maas ship? Whey, we all a-go be sailors now?"

"Please, don't call me 'the master'," Giles interjected.

"Whey we a-go call you?" Keyah asked, her voice doubtful.

He puzzled for a moment. "Captain," he said, at last.

Keyah laughed harshly. "Matu right? We all a-go to sea?"

Matu shook her head in frustration. She rubbed her arm, mopped, pulled the rope, pointed to Giles. Then she began another series of gestures. They were meaningless to Giles, but Keyah followed them easily. "Cuttin' cane? De mill? Shugga vats? We a-go be sailors or slaves?"

Matu gestured for a manacle and shook her head. After releasing her wrist from the manacle, she pantomimed the stirring of a sugar vat, following with the boat gesture, the release of a manacle, and pointed again to Giles.

He didn't know why, but suddenly her confusing gesticulations made perfect sense. He jumped from the chair. "It just might work. Can you communicate with them, Matu? Tell them what it is that we want them to do?"

Matu's face split into a wide, happy grin, and she nodded.

Keyah threw up her hands. "Whey dem a-go do?"

But Giles continued speaking to Matu. "We cannot afford to just free them if we're to continue operating this place. They'd be indentured servants. Even though they've already served some time here, they would have to work for their freedom. Seven years is typical. After that, they may stay for wages or leave as they see fit."

"Africans don' live seven year," Keyah interjected.

"*Slaves* don't, but indentured servants do. 'Tis the status that matters, not the color. I can't pay much. By the time we repair the huts and bring the food and clothing up to some reasonable standard, there will be little left of Edmund Welbourne's wealth. But if the Africans are willing to work, this place could be self-sufficient without slaves."

"Deh not be much left for you," Keyah observed.

Giles's smile broadened. "I've made do on less. Matu, will you explain to the workers that we will arrange shorter shifts with plenty of food and water? Can you make them understand that 'tis safe to stay, and that no one will ever again drop dead from heat in the sugar house?"

Matu nodded.

"You a-go need a new bakra," Keyah advised. "Dis one too hated. Me not tink dey a-go trust anotta White."

Another obstacle, but not one he couldn't overcome. It occurred to Giles that he might have just the man for the job. Granted, Jawara knew nothing about sugar production, but he was a fast learner and an exceptional leader.

His voice brimming with hope, Giles proclaimed, "This plantation will succeed, by God, and without a single slave."

Then he sobered. At what cost? Every day that he was forced to spend here, getting Welbourne on track for the safety of its workers and its neighbors, meant that Grace was another day farther away. She had to be here, had to see her home transformed into a place she would be proud of. God, he hoped that Encantadora was right, and that their mystery man was protecting Grace.

Matu seemed to follow the path of his thoughts. She went back to the rear door, gesturing for Giles to follow her. Out past the kitchen, Africans labored at the mill and in the sugar house. Beyond that, they moved throughout the cane fields. She pointed to them, gestured for Grace, and patted her hand over her heart.

Giles understood perfectly. "You are absolutely right, Matu. She loves them. She would want me to see to them first, and I will. But I cannot stay for long. We have to make this work, and we have to do it quickly."

Matu nodded and gestured toward herself and the slaves' quarters, but Giles put out his hand to stop her.

Looking over his shoulder, into the house, he said to Keyah, "Again, thank you for your help. I won't keep you from your work."

Keyah gave Matu a dubious look, but Matu waved her off to the kitchen, and the cook reluctantly took her leave.

Once she was back in the little outbuilding, Giles addressed Matu. "I'm glad I have you on my side."

With a soft smiled and a chuckle, she pointed to him and then herself, patted her heart, and touched her cheek.

"Aye, we both love Grace, that's sure. She is my life. I'm surprised you're still speaking to me, after how I reacted when—"

Matu waved her hand in the air, a gesture of dismissal. It was water under the bridge.

He hesitated, then said, "'Twasn't easy, was it, Matu? As much as Iolanthe and her brother needed to die, 'twasn't easy for either of us to be the one left with the task."

The woman studied him hard in the bright afternoon light before she finally shook her head.

He took both of her tough, little hands in his and squeezed. "One of the first things we are going to do is build you your own little cottage, just over there." He pointed to a space across the yard from the kitchen. "Grace and I are going to need all of the help that we can get with all of the children we're going to fill this place with."

Matu smiled and squeezed back.

Dear God in Heaven, he prayed, *let that be the truth.*

Twenty-two

Standing in the midst of the slaves' huts and sweating in the hot sun, Giles would have been lying if he had said that he wasn't intensely nervous. After all, he was surrounded by a sea of dark faces with expressions ranging from wariness to open hostility. This was a tremendous leap of faith. Upon being informed of the upcoming changes in the nature of Welbourne's work force, the regular overseer and guards had quit and were stubbornly holed up in their cottages. Seven of the guards lent by neighbors had stayed, armed to the teeth and preparing to face the insurrection they believed to be just around the corner. They knew that they were outnumbered, and that the slaves would see any weakness in the unity of the Whites as an opportunity for revolt.

"Our blood and the blood of every planter's family around you will be upon your hands!" one of them had ominously warned. Now, they lurked around the perimeter of the gathering, carrying flintlocks and muskets.

Matu, Keyah, Encantadora, and Jawara stood with Giles. Matu would sign as clearly as she could while Keyah translated into Mande and Jawara into Fula. Both were major West African languages, and they hoped that, among them, the message would get through to the majority of the workers. Those who did understand would be responsible for communicating with others, if at all possible. Encantadora stood with them in a show of solidarity, one more African who could attest to Giles's fairhandedness with Blacks, should such testimony be needed.

"My name is Giles Courtney. I am married to your former master's daughter, a daughter given to him by a slave many years ago." While the three Africans translated, Giles worked hard to maintain an air of confidence and relaxed authority. He continued, pausing periodically for interpretation. "Now that your former master and mistress are dead, Grace and I have inherited the farm. I have never owned a slave in my life, and as I said, my wife is the child of a slave. I can speak for us both when I tell you that we have no wish to own you."

There was no mistaking the palpable dread and anger that swelled around them among the Blacks. Giles hurried on. "Nor would we sell you. We need workers. There is a way that Whites often work for other Whites. They work for seven years, and then they are free to do as they please. We could free you now, but where would you go? We offer you decent food, clothing, and housing, far better than you have ever had under the old master and mistress, in exchange for your labors. We will feed and clothe your children, and they will not work in the fields until they are old enough. Even then, they will work fewer hours. At the end of seven years, you may leave or stay. If you stay, you will receive money for your work."

What Giles had envisioned as a brief speech followed by much relief from his new workers turned into an hour-long ordeal, trying to communicate with everyone and allay their fears and suspicion. Finally Keyah suggested that Giles go back to the house and take the white guards with him.

"We gotta talk a dem witout you. Let Jawara an' Matu tell dem what it like a work for you. Let dis 'ooman," Keyah pointed to Encantadora, "tell dem how you look for Miss Grace. We gotta be open togetta, an' we can't be wit' dese guards here."

"But if they have questions . . ." Giles protested.

"We can ansa," Jawara replied. "Dis a way for slavery in Africa. Dem seen it, but dem not trus' you. Maybe dem not trus' us. Africans gotta bad habit of sellin' each otta."

"We're not leaving these bloody Negroes alone," one of the guards shouted. "'Tis suicide, and murder besides!"

Giles looked hard around him, and finally his eyes lit on Jawara and Keyah. "Is it safe?"

"Maybe, maybe not," Jawara said, "but me tell you dis, me tink dese people a-go kill you all before dem let demselves be sold."

Giles looked to Matu. "Matu, if you tell me that we can leave and be at all safe, I'll take the risk."

Matu nodded with confidence.

"Her right," Keyah said. "Her de oldes' one here. Dem respec' Matu. You be pretty safe."

Giles looked across the crowd at the guard who had spoken. "You said it yourself. If they sense that we are not in agreement, we haven't a chance. If you don't obey me, why should they? Now will you follow me into the house, or will you strike the flint that sets off this powder keg?"

Reluctantly, all seven accompanied Giles. They took

up positions around the keeping room, watching at the windows. The ticking of the clock in the sitting area seemed to echo in the tense silence. Giles moved from guard to guard, offering words of encouragement and bits of advice. Well he remembered the needs of men facing battle, and the air of quiet authority that he'd gained in his years as quartermaster on a privateer ship gradually eased the tension between them.

As the afternoon wore on, they all pulled wooden chairs from around the table and placed them in front of the windows so that they could rest as they kept their vigil. The light had begun to fade and the tree frogs had begun to sing ere Matu, Jawara, Encantadora, and Keyah returned. They seemed neither relieved nor overly worried.

"Well?" Giles prompted as soon as they walked through the rear door.

"Me tink dem listen," Jawara said skeptically.

"Dem listen," Keyah asserted, and Matu nodded her agreement. "Me know dese people. Dem not a-go fight a war ova dis. Dem seen dat dem can' win. What you offa dem, it not all dat different dan what dem seen at home. It be pretty hard for de ones dat was free in Africa, but dem smart enough a know dat dis a betta way."

Encantadora gazed up at Jawara and added, "You mon Jawara tell dem dis how tings be on you ship. Matu sey it her idea a try it on de plantation."

"Me tell you," Keyah added, "dem respec' Matu."

"Dem respec' Jawara, too," Encantadora replied tartly. At her emphatic defense, Jawara gave her a speculative glance, and the young woman blushed underneath her dusky skin.

"Summa dem a-go run away," Jawara added, looking

back at Giles. "Dem be maroon before dem be any kinda slave if dem can help it."

"Aye," said Keyah, "deh no way a stop dat." The life of a maroon, in the mountains of Jamaica, was not much easier or longer than a slave's life, but it was a free existence. For some, it would be preferable. "But Encantadora right. Me tink dem like Jawara. Him a good mon. Him tell dem true wheneva him can, an' him admit when don' know sinting. Him a good choice for de new ovaseea. Him not a bakra, not aways a-go use de lash."

The white guard who had been most outspoken rubbed his eyes wearily. "I suppose we had better get out there. Tell your *white* overseer," he sneered at Jawara, then looked back at Giles, "that until he finds transportation out of here, he still works for you. Your dogs won't obey us."

"No dogs!" Keyah snapped.

"You see!" the man said to Giles, his voice accusatory. "She's black and a female besides, and she thinks she's in charge. This will never work."

"You tink you can stop dese people if dem decide a come afta you an' de res' of de Whites?" Jawara asked. "Dis deh only chance a be free. You can offa dem freedom you way, or dem gonna take it dem way." He turned to Giles. "Keyah know dese people. Her help me pick guards, black ones. We tell dem, dese guards don' keep you in, dem keep Whites out. We tell dem, you all sleep safe tonight or go in de hills. Dem gotta make a choice, you know?"

"They'll murder us in our sleep," one of the guards predicted.

* * *

Given the various sets of circumstances that everyone had been through, it had been days since most of them had slept in more than bits and snatches. Giles retired to Edmund's old room. Keyah and Matu wanted nothing to do with Iolanthe's quarters. They squeezed into Grace's bed with Encantadora, while the girl who had come with them from Havana slept on Matu's old mat. Jawara hadn't known Iolanthe, and he wasn't about to refuse a real bed, so he took that room. The keeping room chairs and floor became the domain of the guards. By the early morning hours, every White in the house was sound asleep, and in varying degrees, each was surprised to wake with the dawn to a calm and quiet island day.

Giles accompanied the others to the slaves' quarters, where the workers had already begun to gather in the clearing. It was the first time at Welbourne Plantation that they had been awakened by the sun rather than the plantation bell signaling a long and brutal workday. Once the huts were empty and the workers accounted for, it was clear that the labor force had gone from one hundred and forty-seven to one hundred and nine.

Giles sighed with relief. "Only thirty-eight gone. Surely not enough to cause our neighbors any worry," he added, for the benefit of the guards.

"For now," came a surly response. But it seemed satisfying enough that the men set out for their respective employers' farms.

The day was declared a holiday from sugar production. The first order of business was to repair the huts and begin work on new structures so that they would no longer be as crowded as they had been. Jawara oversaw this, while Matu and Keyah spoke at length about food. The slaves' steady diet of cassava and corn had not provided adequate nourishment and had been a major contributor to the abhorrent mortality rate of Welbourne's Blacks. They needed meat, and while cattle were expensive, the women thought that pigs might not be out of the question. Fish were plentiful, but sparing workers to catch them would be tricky. Furthermore, they would need chickens for eggs and goats for milk and cheese. And all of this would require more space allotted to the keeping of animals. They and the Captain had much to do.

Encantadora lingered a while with the women, then wandered back out to the slaves' quarters where Jawara supervised repairs on old huts and the framing of new ones. She fetched a dipperful of water and took it to him. There was no trace of prostitute in the shy young woman who handed the big man the refreshment. He smiled at her as he took it, his teeth dazzling white against ebony skin.

"Whey Matu an' Keyah up to?" he asked after finishing the water.

"Dem talkin' 'bout food," she answered. "Me don' know much 'bout farmin'. Me work de fields once, but me tell you, me neva do it again."

"Whey you a-go do, den?"

Her smile was simultaneously sweet and sly. "Me gotta plan."

Jawara handed the dipper back to her, his eyes never leaving her face. "Whey you plan, Encantadora?"

Her face hardened again, just for a moment. "Encantadora a slave name, a whore name. Deh no slaves nor whores here. Me madda call me Ciatta, an' Ciatta a-go be de ovaseea wife."

Jawara's smile faded, and he gave her a doubtful look. "You tink so?"

"You tink dis place a-go work?" she challenged.

"Aye," he replied. "We all a-go work hard an' make it work."

"You don' tink dat jus' a silly dream?"

"Me tink sintime dreams come true."

"Aye? Well, me tink so, too." She gestured around them to the progress being made on the huts. "You work for you dream," she tapped him lightly on his bare chest with the dipper, "an' me work for mine." When she turned her back and strutted back to the water barrel, there was a pronounced swing to her skirts despite her slight limp. Unable to help himself, Jawara watched her go with a little smile on his face.

On board *Reliance*, Giles encouraged Geoff to return to Faith and Jonathan, promising not to leave Jamaica without him. Once he had placed his friend in temporary command, he sent the ship and Welbourne's former white employees back to Port Royal.

The next morning, he and Jawara toured the outbuildings with one of the sugar workers. There were language barriers to overcome, but they got the general gist of how it all worked. Together, the captain and overseer devised work shifts in the sugar house and mill that would occupy morning and night hours, when the weather was cool. The field workers would be away from the huts during the day, so the production workers would have plenty of quiet in which to sleep during that time. At least, until the children grew healthy enough to become normal children. Then Giles expected the desolate clearing to ring with childish voices.

Within a week, routines had begun to establish themselves, some from the way that things had run before, some forming roughly and sluggishly as everyone worked to build an organization unlike any that had ex-

isted before. Where once workers had needed to look
no further than a man's skin to know who fell where in
the plantation's hierarchy, now they needed to work out
a new system, and nearly everyone in it was sick and
tired of being under someone else's control. Women insisted that cooks should be released early from the
fields, while men argued that they had been able to cut
cane all day and then cook before and that things were
no different now.

Giles had taken a few days off to track down oxen to
run the mill. It was then that several of the strongest and
most assertive sugar workers challenged Jawara's authority. He was just an African, like them, and he had
never even worked a sugar mill. Who did he think he
was? These concerns were hardly foreign to him. He
knew the frustration of having to take orders from men
who were only his equals in rank, merely because they
were white. But he had also spent years serving under
his captain. He had seen a true leader at work. He listened to each challenger, showed his willingness to
learn, but held fast to his belief in himself. In the end,
he gained a much better understanding of his new job
and earned the respect of the men he now led.

At each day's end, Giles met with the people he had
come to think of as his first and second mates, Jawara
and Matu. Ciatta, well pleased to have reclaimed her
African name, had found her place in the kitchen,
which was being enlarged so that it could be used to
cook for everyone. The women all agreed that she was
a terrible cook, and not even particularly useful for
chopping and toting since she had an aversion to work,
in general, but her teasing nature and scandalous sense
of humor were enormously entertaining. Her recently
made friends watched with avid interest as the pretty

Mulatto waged an all-out campaign for the heart of the new overseer. For a people deprived of laughter and happiness, she was like the breeze after a rainstorm. To Giles, she was an endless source of information regarding the hopes and fears of his people. Saran, the child he had rescued from Jacques, also worked in the kitchen and blossomed in the nurturing warmth of the women working there.

In bits and pieces, everything was coming together. But one piece was missing, and she had left a hole in Giles's heart. At night, he lay in Edmund's bed and listened to the endless singing of tree frogs, acutely aware of the empty pillow beside him. Every day he was helping to shape something that he could feel proud of, a little corner of the world just as he wished it, but that had been a dream that he had shared, and his partner in that dream was God knew where. He knew beyond all doubt that it would never be enough without her.

Nearly a fortnight after his arrival, Giles stood at the dock and watched the sky turn the sea into a swath of shimmering sapphire satin shot through with silver, then gold as the sun set. A choir of frogs began to warm up for the night's performance, and the evening breeze brought with it the scent of jasmine that tormented Giles with memories.

Jawara walked toward him across the lawn, the last of the day's sweat drying on his bare chest. He studied Giles, who once again looked his fastidious self, his hair tied neatly back, his shirt pristine.

"Me don' know how you do it," Jawara commented.

"Hmm?"

"You work hard like ev'rybody, but you look like de maas dat don' lift a finga."

Giles smiled, but it didn't touch his stormy gray eyes.

"You didn't see me this afternoon. More to the point, you didn't smell me. While you were getting the evening shift started at the mill, I was helping to finish the kitchen. 'Tis done, and the women are thrilled. I had to wash. I couldn't stand myself. If Grace had seen me, she wouldn't have believed it." And there it was again, the vice that closed around his throat every time he said her name. Every time he breathed in the scent of jasmine at dusk.

"Tings be runnin' pretty smooth. Me tinkin' it 'bout time for you a find you 'ooman."

Giles nodded, his eyes fixed on the horizon where sea and sky were one and the same, each melding into the other. "I think so, too."

"How long you a-go look?"

"Until I find her."

"Cap'n." When Giles didn't respond, Jawara put his hand on his shoulder. "Cap'n, look here. You gotta try; me know dat. A mon gotta try a protect what be his. But dis place gotta have a white mon at de helm. It not be long 'fore de rest of de planters a-go make trouble. It be good dat we know we be free, but dat don' mean nutten to de rest of de Whites on dis island. Deh be sum tings we jus' gotta face."

Giles fisted his hands at his sides. He had wanted to do something important with his life, to make his mark upon the world, and he had. It was here, all around him. But what about happiness? What about love? Was it so much to ask for those, too?

"I cannot enforce a time limit on this, Jawara!"

"You got no choice. Dat be de ting about saving sumbody life. Dem don' owe you, you owe dem. Why trouble youself if you jus' a-go let dem down in de end?"

"Why did I marry Grace if I was just going to let her down in the end?"

"Me never say dis be an easy choice, Cap'n. Maybe dis be de price of bein' a good mon."

Twenty-three

It was a perfect day. The wind ripped briskly across the water, and *Destiny* raced with it. They had chosen *Destiny* above *Reliance,* for 'twas her name and that of her captain that brought Spanish sailors to their knees, enabling Giles and Geoff to board and search their ships with little resistance. It had been two years since the ruthless privateer Geoffrey Hampton had stalked Spanish waters, but he had not been forgotten.

The voyage had met with its share of problems. Though all had gone well as they'd skirted Cuba and Florida, they'd run into naught but foul weather amid the Bahamas. To everyone's relief, the rains had fallen behind ere they'd neared Santo Domingo. Then, in the heart of the Caribbean, halfway to the Spanish Main, they had outrun the wind, as well, and sat becalmed, the men slowly growing more and more restless. Three or four fistfights were erupting each day ere the sails rippled and snapped and caught another breeze. After so much, it was good to be sailing again on such a fine day.

Of course, the Spaniards on board the ship Giles had spotted might disagree ere the day was out.

"She's not on board that ship," Geoff protested.

Having been at sea well over a month now, Giles knew that he was running out of time. He gave his friend an impatient scowl. "D'you see that flag?" he demanded, gesturing with the spyglass they'd been sharing.

"Aye," Geoff answered, his voice edged with impatience, as well.

"And?"

"'Tis Spanish. I see that, Giles. She's a tiny merchantman, a waste of valuable time."

"That's the very thing, isn't it? I have so little time, Geoff! We have agreed, we skirt the Serranilla Bank, and then 'tis back to Jamaica. If I've not found her, 'tis done. I have over a hundred people and a bloody farm that depend upon me!" He looked back at the tiny speck of a ship in the distance. "If we do not board, I will wonder the rest of my life if I missed her here today."

Geoff nodded. "As you wish, then. I am, after all, a mere figurehead on this mission, lending my name and fearsome reputation. The command is yours."

"I didn't mean it that way. What you risk here is . . ."

Geoff forced an uneasy grin. "One of us must lead, and this time, 'tis you. As for what I risk, it only fires the blood."

But Giles saw the lie in his friend's face. "I'll have you home to your wife and son soon, Geoff. Safe and sound. I swear it."

Geoff sighed. "She's unmanned me, I fear."

And Giles laughed. "Her belly will be rounding in no time and give the lie to that statement." But the laughter died on his lips. His own wife's absence threatened to drag him back down under the ocean of despair that he fought daily.

It wouldn't do! Self-pity would not help him find Grace. His eyes hardened and he set his jaw. "Hoist the red flag!" he shouted. "The chase is on!"

* * *

"What do you think?" Enrique asked his captain. If the ship following them meant any harm, the captain would know.

Diego squinted against the sun. From this distance, he could tell very little. Still, he refused the spyglass that his first mate offered. There was no more heat or light in the air than the sun cast down upon them, no strange sensation heralding a message from his patron saint. If they were in danger, Magdalena would have alerted him by now.

He shrugged casually. "Nothing to worry about," he replied. "Another merchant, like us."

"English? In these waters? She is far off course."

Diego closed his eyes and took a deep breath. Still, no sense at all of Magdalena's presence. "Blown off course by some ill wind." Then, he had an idea. "Wait! Perhaps we should let them catch up. If they are honest merchants, and their captain seems an honorable man, perhaps he could take our passenger. She works hard not to show her impatience while we make short runs along the coast of the Main, but she wants to go home. We have not been able to approach Jamaica, but perhaps he could."

Enrique gave him a doubtful look, but Diego turned to give the order to heave to, and then the unthinkable happened.

"Captain," his man in the crow's nest shouted, "she has raised a red flag!"

"What?" Diego cried, and his crew stopped in their tracks, stunned into silence. Captain Diego Montoya Fernandez de Madrid y Delgado Cortes was *not* taken off guard by pirates. He had been caught once, but had cleverly talked his way out of it. Since that time, *Magdalena* had been charmed, a fact that everyone on board had come to take for granted.

How could it be that he had been left with no warning? "Fight or flee, Magdalena?" he chanted softly under his breath. "Fight or flee?"

Emptiness. No voice, no strong sense of her guidance. What had he done to offend her? There was no time to ponder this. He had grown soft, lazy, too accustomed to having an unfair advantage. From Enrique's hands, he grabbed the spyglass that he had previously disdained. A brigantine, he saw, much larger than his little carrack and likely with far more crew. The last time that he had run into a brigantine, he had lost. He had been a very new captain then, and only just beginning to forge the bond between himself and Magdalena that had protected him ever since.

Without wasting another second, he bolted to the helm, shoving the helmsman aside and taking the wheel. "Make sure that I have every bit of sail available!" he shouted to Enrique, and the first mate leapt to follow the command.

Apprehension gnawed at Diego's stomach and inside of his head. His ship was small and fast, but a brigantine was built for speed and maneuverability. If it had been merely him and his crew, he would have found it much easier to accept whatever fate dealt them, but he had a woman on board, one who had already been through too much.

Grace! He should have someone inform her of what was happening. He had been teaching his cabin boy some rudimentary English. Just now, the lad was at the rail, staring wide-eyed at their pursuers.

"Galeno," he called, and the boy skipped over nervously. "Go below and give *Señora* Courtney this message." He switched to English and spoke slowly and clearly. "We are avoiding a pirate ship. Stay in your cabin. The captain will come when there is news." He went back to Spanish. "Repeat that."

Once he was assured that Galeno could deliver the message, he focused all of his attention upon evading the ship closing fast behind them.

Galeno pounded on *Señora* Courtney's cabin door with all the force of a tiny hurricane, calling her name over and over. She opened it, and for a moment he froze, staring up at her with dark, excited eyes. What were the words the captain had spoken?

"*¿Sí, Galeno?*" she prompted.

Her voice snapped him from his momentary paralysis. In his thick accent, he said, "We are avoiding a pirate ship."

"A pirate ship?" Grace cried. "What country? If they are French or English, then *Capitán* Montoya will need me to translate." She rushed past him through the door.

"Stay in your cabin," Galeno continued carefully.

She turned back and took his face between her hands. "You poor thing. You must be so frightened. You stay right here." She led him to her bunk and pushed on his shoulders until he sat down.

"The captain will come when there is news," he recited dutifully.

"Aye, that's right. He'll come and get you when 'tis safe," Grace replied, then she patted him on the head and rushed out the door, closing it tightly behind her.

Galeno sat on the bed, blinking in confusion. Obviously the captain's message had something to do with summoning *Señora* Courtney, but if he had wanted Galeno to stay in her cabin, would he not have said so directly? Still, she had clearly indicated that he should stay here. Perhaps that was part of the message as well. He would have to study his English much harder. How else would he become a captain like the great Diego Montoya Fernandez de Madrid y Delgado Cortes, who could defy pirates in their own language?

"She's running!" Geoff called out, and Giles's heart leapt. When Geoff had accepted Spain's terms for his pardon, Giles had been more than happy to leave behind their life of thievery and feuding, but he couldn't deny the pull of excitement when two ships employed the same wind and the same water in fierce competition. It helped to know that, once they caught the other ship, there would be no killing, no theft. They would use one of the crewmen hired for his command of Spanish to interrogate the captain, search the ship, and then be on their way.

Or better still, they would find Grace.

Destiny seemed as caught up in the chase as her commander, swallowing the distance between them in greedy gulps of crystalline water. With a merry grin of his own, Geoff took another look through the spyglass, then let out a string of curses worthy of the most hardened pirate. "Hard to port!" he shouted. "Hard to port!"

It was second nature. Giles's hands spun the wheel, even as the crew scrambled to compensate for the abrupt maneuver. "What is it?" he called.

"'Tis the bloody *Magdalena!*"

Though he continued to turn the ship, Giles countered him. "But that's perfect. Montoya can help us find Grace."

"We are chasing Montoya with a goddamned red flag on our mast!" Geoff snarled.

Giles looked overhead at the banner. What had he been thinking? He had been so intent upon Grace that he had completely forgotten the implications for Geoff. "Oh, Jesus! Somebody pull that bloody flag down!"

Diego Montoya had been moved once to spare Geoff's life, but he had done it for Faith, certainly not Geoff. 'Twas he who had delivered Geoff to the executioner to begin with. Now, Geoff was in direct violation of his pardon from Spain, and Montoya was a man with an ironclad sense of honor. There would not be another pardon.

Giles gave Geoff a worried look. "They'll not give chase," he said, more to assure himself than his friend.

"If he saw who we are, he'll follow me to hell and back," Geoff replied. "Honor and duty and all that rot. Of course, he'll be only too happy to console my wife!"

It seemed to Giles that Geoff ought to be more grateful to the man for saving his life, but gratitude was dangerous at a time like this.

"We'll sink him if we must," Giles assured him. "Prime the cannons!" he called out. Better safe than sorry.

Grace wanted to grab Diego by the collar and shake him. The only thing that stayed her hand was the sure and certain knowledge that she would not be able to budge him and she would only end up making a fool of herself.

"If you do not go back below, I will have one of my men pick you up and carry you there!" he barked.

"You most certainly will not!" she retorted. He had made several similar threats since she had first climbed on deck, but he had yet to make any move toward fulfilling them.

"If that pirate crew sees you up here, your fate will make you regret leaving the brothel. At least there you would entertain only one man at a time!"

Grace gaped in shock. It was entirely unlike the captain to speak so basely to her. "If they board, they will find me sooner or later," she reasoned.

Diego opened his mouth to reply, but excited shouts from the first mate and several crewmen interrupted them, and Diego turned away from her, raising his spyglass. Grace had been working hard on her Spanish, but when it was spoken too quickly, she was at a loss. She craned her neck to see what had caused all of the commotion. The pirate ship seemed to be turning away!

She spun toward Diego with a wide smile. "You've done it! They've given up!"

"*¡Maldito sea! ¡Hijo de puta! ¡Cabrón!*" Diego spat.

A month surrounded by Spanish sailors had left Grace with an interesting vocabulary. Not that she specifically knew what any of those words meant. She only knew that whenever one of the sailors accidentally used any of them in her presence, he would duck his head and mutter, *"Lo siento,"* in apology.

"Is that not good news?" she asked timidly. "We didn't want them to catch us, did we?"

"Destiny!" he snapped at her.

"Destiny?"

"I gave my word of honor that he would repent! It is

not just his honor. He has none! But *my* honor is another matter! I gave him the woman I loved, and what has he done? Does he not understand that when a man marries, his life is no longer his alone? He has *obligations!* Obligations to me, obligations to her!" His tirade dissolved into Spanish again, but by now, Grace was no longer paying attention.

She snatched the spyglass from him and focused it on the ship now sailing away from them. "Merciful heavens, give chase!" she cried. "Why are they running?"

"Because he knows who it is that he faces. We are even, the two of us, each has defeated the other, but now I have Magdalena on my side! I put my honor on the line to save his stinking life, and he has spit upon it. I will not make the same mistake again. You are right, *Señora* Courtney, we must give chase!" His hands spun the wheel as he shouted to his men.

"Nay, Captain, you do not understand! Aye, give chase, but you mustn't hurt Geoff. Do you not see? He is looking for me! He must be! He loves Faith and Jonathan with all his heart. He would never risk his life with them, unless Giles needed him, and Giles has no desire for Spanish wealth! If Geoff is pursuing Spanish ships, he does so in search of me!"

"*Señora* Courtney . . ." he began, shaking his head.

She looked at him with pleading eyes. "Please, Captain. Even if I am wrong, and Geoff has, for some reason, gone back to plundering Spain, he has it in his power to reunite me with my husband."

Diego narrowed his dark eyes in a calculating scowl. "Do you think that friendship means anything to a man without honor?"

She shook her head in incomprehension.

"Will he exchange himself for his best friend's wife?"

Grace gasped. "I cannot ask that!"

Diego's face was set like steel. "I can."

The two ships were sailing to windward now. Under the circumstances, the competition had less to do with the ships themselves than the skill of the men who sailed them. In that, it soon became clear that *Magdalena*, her captain working with men who knew him well, had the advantage. *Destiny's* crew felt their loyalty divided evenly between two commanders, both of whom were shouting orders, and they were unsure to whom they should respond.

"'Tis *my* ship, Giles! *My* life!" Geoff shouted when Giles contradicted yet another of his commands.

He was right, of course, but somewhere along the way, Giles had lost his taste for taking orders, even from his friend. And in truth, he knew himself to be as capable of evading the Spanish vessel as Geoff. Still, one of them had to give; the price of pride was too high. "You want the bloody helm? Take it!"

He stalked away, grinding his teeth. There was a glimmer of contrition in Geoff's eyes, but he took the wheel anyway. Giles ripped the spyglass from Geoff's hand and looked through it. Sure enough, Diego Montoya stood at the helm of his ship, his face a mask of fury. But it was the woman standing behind him and to one side that made his heart jump into his throat.

"Heave to!" he yelled at the top of his lungs. "Heave to!"

Geoff looked over his shoulder at Giles and the Spanish merchantman. "Are you mad?" he called out. Then he took one look at his friend's face, and all discord, all rivalry vanished. "Heave to!" he confirmed. "Heave to!"

Confused and apprehensive, the men obeyed, and *Destiny* gradually slowed until she appeared nearly motionless in the shining surface of the sea. *Magdalena* pulled up beside her, and the two crews eyed one another tensely across the water.

"Captain Hampton," Diego called over in a challenging tone.

"Diego! Cousin!" Geoff shouted with an arrogant grin. "Seems you've a bit of cargo we might relieve you of!"

"You son of a bitch!" Diego shouted back. "If you try to steal one thing off of my ship . . ."

"There now!" Geoff cried in mock indignation. "We were only trying to retrieve a little something that belongs to us. Well, to my friend, actually . . ."

Giles ignored their posturing and banter. He set the men to work, carefully closing the distance between the two ships. There at the rail opposite him, wearing a prim, Spanish-style gown of dove gray, her wild curls flying in the wind, was the most beautiful site e'er to meet his eyes.

I want this man, Grace thought to herself. She watched him direct the crew with his trusty confidence and easy manner, and she wanted him as she'd never wanted anything before. She had only to look at him and she could smell the scents of sandalwood and musk, feel his warmth radiating through the cotton shirt that rippled in the wind and molded itself to his solid chest. She wanted to touch him, breathe him, assure herself that he was not an illusion only.

She heard Diego chuckle behind her. "If you keep

looking at him like that, he is going to go up in flames," the Spaniard warned her.

She turned to him and smiled, not even blushing at having worn her heart so plainly on her sleeve. "I can never thank you enough."

"*No importa,*" he replied. "He is coming. Go to him, *Señora.*"

Giles swung gracefully across the gap between the ships and landed lightly on *Magdalena's* deck, but he came no farther, and Grace was afraid to move. What if he knew? What if things had changed between them? Changed for him, anyway.

Finally he closed his eyes, and she could see his throat contract when he swallowed hard. "God help me, Grace, I thought I had lost you."

"Nay, Giles, I am not lost."

All at once she was in his embrace, and she wrapped her arms around him and buried her face in his shirt. She breathed in the smell of sweat and sandalwood while he sank his face into her hair and drew in the scent of jasmine, clean and sweet.

Giles pulled back and took her face between his hands. "When I found out about your uncle, and then learned where he had taken you . . . and then, in Havana, I thought I'd found you, but you were gone." His voice cracked as he forced words through his tightly constricted throat. "And we didn't know who had taken you or where."

"'Twas Faith's cousin," she answered. "He heard me speak of Geoff, and he helped me."

Suddenly remembering that they had an audience, the two of them looked around. The sailors on board both ships had been watching the exchange with avid interest and more than a few sentimental smiles, but Diego and Geoff still glared at one another.

"You dare to fly that flag when you have given your word?" Diego demanded. "I should blow a hole through your hull here and now. We will see how many ships you plunder with your own at the bottom of the sea!"

"You'll not find one Spaniard on this sea who can claim ill treatment or robbery at my hands," Geoff retorted. "I've done naught but pluck a few feathers from various Spanish peacock's tails! We are not out for gold, Montoya, but something even you would agree far more precious and worth any risk!" He pointed to Giles and Grace.

Giles buried his hands in Grace's hair and rubbed its texture between his fingers. "I think that we are in need of more privacy."

Grace nodded, feeling a curious mix of dread and relief. One way or another, they would be done with the secrets and lies between them, and then they would begin or end their marriage, but the question would be decided.

Twenty-four

It was instantly apparent that Giles had been inhabiting the captain's cabin on board *Destiny*—apparent because there was not one personal item belonging to him anywhere in evidence. Grace smiled softly and ran her hand over the scarred but empty surface of the big desk. And yet, 'twas also clear that the cabin was not his. In the light that poured in through a large window, she saw that the oaken desktop was marred, perhaps by boot heels, and bore rings from the bottoms of a few wet tankards.

"'Tis a mess," Giles commented apologetically.

Grace laughed. "I have missed you so, Giles."

The sound of her laughter was sweet, but the look of uncertainty in her eyes tore at him. He wanted so to ease her fear. "I must tell you something. This whole time that I have thought you were gone forever, been tortured by thoughts of what might have become of you, I realized something. Something I am so grateful to have a chance to tell you." He reached for her, pulled her close. "Grace, I . . ."

She put her hand to his mouth. "Stop!" Her eyes burned and her chest ached, but if she let him say what she knew was coming, she would never be able to tell him what she had to tell him. "Don't say it. Not yet. Not when you may only have to take the words back."

"I love you, Grace."

"Nay!" she cried. "You do not know me, Giles!" She tried to pull out of his arms, but he held her tight.

"Nay, we are beyond that old argument, you and I," he said. "Do you know what I love about you? I love that you are strong. You have been to hell and back again, and yet here you stand, looking just as fit and fine as ever. I love that you know your own worth, for even a purely evil bitch like Iolanthe Welbourne could not touch your spirit. I love that you are smart and shrewd and care not who knows it." He laughed out loud. "Nay, woe betide the man who thinks that he can master you. And you are beautiful."

"Stop, Giles."

He ran his hands through her hair. "I love your hair, and your beautiful nose, and your lush lips." He kissed her upon them, not hard, but not without passion. Then he pulled away and looked deeply into her eyes. "As far as I can tell, all that is best in you came from your mother, for it is not Edmund I see in you."

"I have to tell you about my mother . . ."

"What is there to say but that she must have been no slave? No woman who could give life to someone as brave and passionate as you could ever have truly thought herself anyone's slave."

Grace stared at him, unable to so much as breathe. He knew. He knew, and he loved her. He loved her, not in spite of who her mother had been, but in part, because of it. She didn't think about it, didn't plan it, had hardly even admitted it to herself. Nonetheless, she opened her mouth and the words fell out. "I love you, too, Giles. You are kind and gentle and giving . . ."

He laughed again. "Then I've the makings of a terrible pirate. 'Tis fortunate that farming appears my fate."

The comment made no sense to her, but she didn't care. She pulled him to her and their reunion became a heated melding of lips and matching of breath. The dread that had become a familiar presence to Grace was absent. Between Faith and Encantadora, she knew that she had nothing to fear. It seemed that couplings between strangers were endurable, and couplings between real lovers were truly wondrous. On this glorious afternoon she was but relieved to have been spared the former, and rather eager to experience the latter.

"I'll not hurt you any more than I must, I swear," Giles said to her, his voice low and smooth.

"I know," she answered. Then she smiled. "It only hurt a little dis time an' den it ova," she snapped her fingers, "jus' like dat."

Giles shook his head dubiously. "What?"

"Kiss me."

She didn't have to ask him twice. He wrapped her in his arms and felt a surge of joy when she did the same, pulling him close to her. Her lips were soft, yielding, opening eagerly under his and welcoming his tongue into her mouth. He couldn't explain this change in her, but neither did he care much at the moment. All that mattered was the heat and moisture of her tongue against his, her hands threading through his hair, and the quickening of her breath.

Grace felt as if something deep inside her core was becoming molten. Heat radiated from where their mouths met, coursing through her and inflaming her. Her breasts tightened and tingled in anticipation of his touch. As though he had read her mind, one hand stayed flat against the small of her back while the other caressed her through the stiff bodice of her gown. Grace pressed herself impatiently into his palm.

Giles pulled away. "'Tis a dreadful color on you," he said, and Grace gave him a quizzical look. "Gray. It doesn't suit you."

She blushed self-consciously. Diego had obtained a few things for her, and she had been in no position to dictate color or style. As soon as she could, she would find something more pleasing to Giles. "What color do you prefer?"

"Gold."

She thought for a moment. She didn't have much in that shade.

Giles watched her fret a moment. He loved watching her thoughts play across her face, as legible as any book. "The color God made you to wear, and naught else," he prompted.

"Actually, I think it rather washes me out. With my skin and my hair—oh!" She blushed even more deeply.

"If you'd rather not—"

"Would it please you?"

The mere thought made him ache. "Aye, very much."

"I am to be yours today," she said.

"And I yours."

"Then I think it only fair that, well, all things being equal—" She plucked at the sleeve of his shirt.

Giles grinned. "Mayhap I should wash first. I worked into a sweat between alternately chasing and running from you."

"Nay," she replied. The smell of his sweat was not offensive. Quite the opposite, it stirred something in her.

The bodice of her gown laced up the front, and Giles's deft fingers nearly flew as he unfastened it. His hands brushed softly against her, and she felt her nipples tighten in response. This time she felt no concern over the fact that he was so skilled at this. She was only glad that one of them knew what he was doing. Once the gown was on the floor and she was stepping out of it, Giles reached to pull his shirt over his head.

"Nay!" Grace cried. "If I am your gift to unwrap, then so are you mine."

He took her hands in his and led her to the bed, where he sat so that she could more easily pull his shirt off herself. She ran her hands under the garment, letting the light dusting of hair there tickle the palms of her hands ere she took the fabric in her fingers and pulled the shirt off. He rested his hands lightly on her hips while she ran hers over the firm, hot flesh of his shoulders and chest. Then he reached down and tugged her shift up over her thighs so that he could pull her into his lap, her legs straddling him.

They kissed again, tongues exploring mouths, hands exploring bodies. Giles untied her shift and pulled it down to her waist so that he could feast upon her bare, honey-colored breasts. His face was so deeply tanned that, in the dusky light, it seemed to Grace that there was little difference in the color of their skin. His torso was somewhat lighter, but only somewhat. He must have worked without his shirt from time to time, for his trunk was also tanned. He lifted his head and began nibbling and sucking at the tender flesh of her throat, and with a sigh, she let her head fall back to give him more.

Grace's skin was smooth against Giles's mouth, and between the ardent murmurs of desire that slipped through her lips and the fact that she had begun to press her core against him where she straddled him, he had to fight to take things slowly. Somewhere along the way, she had mastered her fear of him, but he wasn't about to press his luck. He broke away for a moment to gently pull her shift off her. In all his life, he would swear he had never seen anything more exquisite than his wife, naked, there in his lap. He took each of her breasts in his hands, hefting their weight and brushing his thumbs across their dark, rigid crests.

"You are so beautiful," he sighed. "This cannot be real."

Grace slipped from him, kneeling on the floor and untying the waist of his breeches. She was tired of fearing the unknown, of only having half of the story. She wanted to see him. He lifted his hips from the mattress and she slid the breeches from him. Mayhap she should have been embarrassed or shown more modesty, but she studied him openly, and he did not seem to mind. The sight of his turgid sex wasn't frightening. He was large enough that she could see why joining might hurt, but not so large that it would be unbearable. She took him in her hand and he moaned.

"Did I hurt you?" she asked, drawing her hand away.

He shook his head vigorously, and she smiled. This was so different than anything she had ever before experienced. She was not restrained in any way, and now he was leaning back against his arms, his nude, work-hardened body completely open to her. She could do with him as she wished, and stop whenever she chose.

Grace had rather more knowledge than most virgin brides, been told far more about the things that went on between men and women than anyone should have told her. What had seemed an utterly repulsive act when she was told of it now struck her as completely natural, and she leaned forward and brushed her tongue across the tip of him. He gasped, and she looked up at him, worried that she had committed some unpardonable perversion.

"Is this bad?" she asked.

"Nay," he answered, his voice strangled. "'Twas only unexpected. Do not let me stop you." He smiled shakily, and she took him into her mouth, savoring his firm flesh and salty flavor, even as she looked up into his face softened by surrender.

He allowed her to have her way for a moment, but soon, with a groan that was very like pain, he lifted her chin. "Not yet," he whispered. "Mayhap you need a taste of what it is you do to me."

He pulled her back up and then guided her onto the bed where he had sat. Then he took her place kneeling on the floor.

"Nay!" Grace protested, pressing her knees together.

"And why not?"

"Because you will see me!"

Giles laughed heartily. "You saw me!"

"'Tis different!"

"How so?"

"I know not, but it is!" No one had ever told her that a man might do the same to a woman! It had been one thing when he had been at her mercy. This was another.

"As you wish," he conceded. She relaxed, and he eased his hand between her thighs and caressed her. "But you do not find the thought wholly displeasing, I can tell."

She blushed at the moisture she knew was coating his softly stroking fingers. And then it began to happen, that strange and frighteningly intense building of sensation that had made her stop whenever she had tried touching herself. "Giles," she protested, trying to push his hand away.

"Lie back, Grace. Let go."

She tried to say something else, but with one hand he kept stroking while with the other he pressed her back onto the bed. She lay on the soft mattress, moving with the rocking of the ship and the rhythm of Giles's touch, gasping for breath as something inside of her kept tightening and tightening until she was sure that she was going to break somehow. She felt his hands, warm and rugged, part her thighs, and then felt his mouth plunder her sex. At last that inexplicable feeling that had been building inside of her exploded, and her entire body was consumed by wave upon wave of agonizingly exquisite sensation.

There was no terror in his wife's screams this time, Giles knew. For one thing, he could feel the pulse of her pleasure against his lips. For another, she had her fists clenched tightly in his hair and held him fast against her as she raised her hips from the bed and arched her back. Perhaps, some other time, he would pleasure her thus for a long while, but at this moment, he had a burning need of his own. He raised himself from the floor and moved over her.

The ecstasy waned too quickly. For all that had just happened, Grace panicked. The thought of being pinned underneath him filled her with the urge to flee. She squeezed her eyes shut, ashamed of her fear after what he had given her.

Giles watched her face carefully, determined that nothing would mar this first experience. He sat next to her and, with one finger, lightly traced a line over her breast, circling her nipple. It puckered prettily. She wasn't too frightened. When she opened her eyes, he gestured to his lap. "I rather liked having you up here."

She smiled nervously. "As did I."

This time, as she swung her leg over his hips, he positioned himself at her entrance, and she held herself above him, her weight on her knees. Giles put his hands on her hips and looked up into her face.

"We'll go as slowly as you like. If it hurts too much, you may always stop." She nodded, and he gently pulled her toward him, letting her determine the pace and the pressure. It was excruciatingly erotic, being ever so slowly enveloped inside of her. He felt the barrier of her innocence, and she paused, flinching slightly.

"I-I think it would be better to have done with this," she whispered.

"You're certain?"

"Aye."

She closed her eyes, took a deep breath, and nodded. Giles thrust his hips upward as Grace pulled herself hard against him with a little cry of pain. The moment he had entered her entirely, he stopped and watched her. She slowly opened her eyes.

"Was that all?" she asked.

He swallowed. God, he hoped not. "Not quite. Can you . . . ?"

"Aye, if the pain isn't much worse."

He smoothed her hair away from her face. "I think the pain is mostly done."

Grace relaxed as his hands moved gently from her face, down her shoulders, over her breasts, finally coming to rest again upon her hips. He used them to urge her to move up and down upon him, while he moved sensually underneath her. He was right. The pain was mostly done. It was a little uncomfortable, but she began to feel her belly tighten and her nether regions tingle. She knew now where she was going, and began to move faster, hastening to get there.

They wrapped their arms around each other, sweat-slicked torsos sliding over each other, mouths pressed together, tongues lapping at one another's moans, hips grinding until they each cried their release into the other and then their heads fell back and they panted to catch their breath.

The ship must have hit a swell, for Grace felt it lift and then fall, an echo of the surge that had lately risen within her. She languidly lifted her head up to look down upon her husband. His face was soft, blissful, and she smiled at him in wonder.

"Did I do that to you?"

He raised his head, too, and smiled back. "Have you some doubt? We are still joined, though not for long I'm guessing."

"I *know* I did that. I mean, did I do *that*? Make you feel as though you were dying somehow, like you were no longer yourself alone but . . ."

"But somehow a part of you, as well? Aye. You did that."

"This is what I have been so afraid of for so long?"

"You need never fear again."

"Indeed not." She threw her head back and laughed, then cast him a rueful look, for her mirth had cost them their connection. "We shall do this again."

He nuzzled her neck. "Indeed we shall."

"Soon."

He laughed softly and his breath tickled her throat. "How soon?"

"Now?"

"It may take a bit of work."

"Then we should waste no time." She brushed a sweat-dampened strand of hair from his face and tucked it behind his ear. "How sad to think I feared you once.

My uncle had best hope he need never face me again, damn his depraved soul."

Giles face sobered. "There is time enough to speak on that, my love. This is not pillow talk."

She tossed her wild curls. "What is?"

He whispered in her ear and she blushed all the way down to her throat, and later, when he pressed her body into the mattress, she welcomed his weight.

Epilogue

Grace sank down onto the grass beside two graves at the far edge of the rear courtyard. Simple wooden crosses marked them both, but one was carefully tended, while the other was gradually beginning to vanish under the rapidly encroaching ground cover. She ran her fingers across the name carved in one of the crosses, then dropped her hand to her stomach. It was just beginning to expand, and her bodice pulled uncomfortably across her waist.

"Well, Father, you shall have what you always wanted. Welbourne will pass from you to at least two heirs. But I will not be a meaningless splotch somewhere in family history. My mother will not be forgotten. Your grandchildren and their grandchildren will know that they have African blood flowing through their veins. It will not be some terrible secret for which innocents must suffer." She paused and leaned down to lay her cheek against the mound. The fecund soil and green grass were as warm as living flesh. "But I forgive you. I just want you to know that."

She sat up again and studied Iolanthe's grave. She would never understand what had turned Iolanthe and her brother into the cruel and calculating people they had become. She wasn't sure that she ever wanted to.

For her own peace of mind, she wished that she could forgive them, as well, but that would be a long time coming. Faith had once said that she did not believe anyone was beyond redemption, but God help her, Grace hoped that Iolanthe and Jacques had earned their own little space in hell, at least for a few millennia.

Footsteps behind her startled Grace from her brooding thoughts, and she turned to find that Matu had joined her. Matu stared down at the graves for a moment in supreme indifference, then reached down and helped Grace to her feet. She made the sign for Saran, Grace and Giles's adopted daughter, and pantomimed reading a book.

"Saran needs help with her lessons?" Grace asked, and Matu nodded.

One of the first things that Grace had done when she had returned home was to start a school for all the plantation's children so that they could learn basic reading and ciphering. These seemed like vital skills, although she knew that the children would be unlikely to use them in the Caribbean. They were not likely to grow up to be clerks or merchants, but this was, after all, their own little corner of the world. Mayhap they could do little to change what went on around them, but on this patch of earth, anything was possible.

Grace joined Saran, who sat in an upholstered chair in the keeping room. The little girl was learning to speak English very quickly and even to read, with the help of her primer. She was also adapting well to her most unusual new parents, the horrors of Havana well behind her. When Grace lay her hand on Saran's head, the girl looked up and smiled, eager to show off her latest accomplishment.

"Listen, Mama." Her finger carefully followed the

words. "'*T* is for turtle.' I know turtle. De turtle make good soup!"

"Aye, it does," Grace agreed. "Perhaps we should ask Uncle Geoff to bring us a turtle the next time he comes. Then Keyah could make us some soup from it."

Grace's hand fell back to her stomach. Saran was the dark-skinned child of her heart, but the child growing in her body would likely be fairer even than she. In time, it would learn that not every light-skinned, straight-haired youngster had a sister with ebony flesh and midnight hair that curled tightly against her head. But Grace would delay that awakening for as long as possible.

"Dis lesson be hard work," Saran said.

"Her spoiled, you know," Ciatta said to Grace, leaning through a rear window left open to the courtyard.

Grace laughed. "Come in here, silly. 'Tis far too hot out there for a woman in your condition."

Ciatta waved her hand in a dismissive gesture, but she accepted the invitation. She stepped through the back door into the shade of the house and sighed. "You soun' like me husban'. Ev'ryting 'bout me *condition.*" She rubbed her hands over her round belly.

"I'm going to enjoy it while I can," Grace replied. "Giles hardly lets me lift a hand. Once these babes are born, the real work will begin."

Ciatta laughed. "Dat a fact!"

"Of course," Grace amended, pulling Saran from her chair and hugging her tight, "mine shall have a fine big sister and a strong father to help keep him or her out of trouble."

Ciatta rubbed her hands over her stomach again. "Mine not do so bad. We got us a fine, free African wit' big shouldas."

"Not much jingle in Jawara's pockets, I'm afraid."

"Not much jingle in anybody pockets 'roun' dis place, but we all happy. Beside, Jawara got sinting to make up for it." She rolled her eyes and smiled. *"Oh, muy grande, Señor, muy grande!"*

Saran pouted. "Mama, her talkin' Spanish again!"

"Well, you gotta wait maybe two, tree year," Ciatta explained, "den me start talkin' English 'roun' you 'bout dese tings."

"Oh, she'll wait longer than that!" Grace warned.

Matu marched through the door next, carrying two earthenware cups, one in each hand. The good china had long since been sold.

"Me already tell you, Matu, me not drinkin' dat stuff no more!" Ciatta exclaimed. "It taste like—" she glanced over at Saran and wisely held her tongue.

Matu scowled at her and held out one of the cups. Grace let go of Saran and took it. "'Tis no use arguing. All the worker women drink it when they're carrying or when they have any little ailment."

Saran nodded sagely. "Aye, de cerace tea give Mama a strong son."

Grace took a deep breath and downed the bitter contents of her cup. It was a brew made of local herbs, and Matu swore it was good for pregnant women. Once she had choked it down, she asked Saran, "Mightn't you like a little sister?"

Saran shook her head. "A boy."

Giles walked in through the front door. His hair and shirt were damp from washing at the pump in the yard, and he looked handsomely mussed. "No one told me 'twas teatime," he observed.

"You wan' summa dis?" Ciatta asked, offering the still full cup she had finally accepted from Matu.

Giles laughed and shook his head. "The smell makes me ill."

Grace grimaced. "Then you should try drinking it when a baby is already making you queasy."

Beaming, Giles held his arms open to Saran, who scampered right into them. "How's the prettiest little girl in the world?" he asked, leaning down and rubbing his pale nose against her dark one, and Grace smiled. Of course Saran preferred a brother. She was well content being her papa's only princess. 'Twas hard to believe that she had been terrified of Giles at first.

"C'mon, Saran," Ciatta said. "Matu an' me take you a play wit' de otta chil'rens."

Saran nodded happily and skipped out the back door with Ciatta and Matu close behind.

Grace followed Giles up to their room, where he stripped off his dirty work shirt and pulled a clean one from one of two wardrobes—the one whose drawers shut completely.

"I hope Geoff and Faith will be here soon," he said. "We're certainly ready to ship."

"Where would we be without Geoff? No one else will touch Welbourne's goods."

Giles just grinned. "Well, the point is, we do have him. We've no need of anyone else. And at least our neighbors have stopped trying to burn down our outbuildings."

Grace gave him her cynical smirk. "That may have something to do with your mentioning at church that we've well over a hundred free Africans held in check by nothing more than their ties to Welbourne. What was it you said? I think 'twas, 'I'd hate to see what they'd be capable of if anything truly terrible were to happen to this place.'"

"It worked," he reminded her.

"So it did. I see what it was that made you a good pirate."

"Privateer," he corrected.

"Do you miss your boat?" she asked.

"My *ship?* Nay. This is a good life, Grace." He reached for her, rubbing his hand over the nearly imperceptible swell of her stomach. "I never thought to have a legacy that meant much to me, but I'll admit, I hope that Saran and whoever this is," he patted her belly, "will keep Welbourne going this way."

"Careful. You're beginning to sound like my father."

"God forbid! Our children may live their lives as they please. But this place means so much to so many people." He changed his mind and tossed his clean shirt aside. "Saran will be gone an hour or more," he mentioned, a wicked look in his gray eyes.

"Giles Courtney," Grace chided, "'tis the middle of the afternoon. Have you no shame?"

"None," he confessed.

She sighed and shrugged. "Alas, neither have I."

Much happened at Welbourne these days that had never happened when Edmund and Iolanthe had run it. Happy, chatting voices drifted from the kitchen, field and sugar workers took pride in what they wrought, and two people who loved one another made slow, passionate love while a sea breeze blew in through the window over their fevered flesh.

For a preview of Paula Reed's next romance,
NOBODY'S SAINT,
coming from Zebra Books in March 2005,
please turn the page.

Magdalena had entered into the Gulf Stream days ago, and the change in both the weather and the nature of the ocean was always a welcome one. The water had gone from an impenetrable green to a crystalline blue, reflecting the warm sun and clear sky above it. A brisk but pleasant wind kept the sails round and taut, and Diego, at his place at the helm, was enjoying the feel of it through his hair. He could only hope that it was the sun's warmth that made him suddenly dizzy, or its brightness that forced him to close his eyes for a moment, but he knew better.

"*Diego.*"

He tried to open his eyes again, but couldn't do it.

"*Diego!*"

She was back in her modest robes, still beautiful, but no trace of seduction. As always, her Spanish had that foreign, lilting quality.

"*Yes, my lady?*"

"*Send half your men below deck. Have guns and cannon at the ready.*"

"*Maybe we should run. The men will not like this, even if we win.*"

"*IF you win? When have I led you astray? Do you question me, Diego?*"

"No, Magdalena."

"Then order your men below. You will need the element of surprise."

Diego rubbed his eyes and opened them, giving his men a weary look. "I need half of you below deck. Prime the cannon and your firearms."

"But Captain," one protested, "there is not another ship to be seen."

"A ship, Captain!" his man in the crow's nest called. "Just there on the horizon!"

The first crewman looked at Diego in horror. "How?"

Enrique, the first mate, stepped in. "Perhaps it would be better to let this one pass," he suggested.

Diego turned to him, feeling torn. He, too, would prefer to let it pass, but he was too close to his dreams to turn his back upon the woman who made them all possible. In a voice that brooked no argument, he said, "We fight."

"But we do not know yet what kind of ship she is. She may have us outgunned."

"It will be an even match. Let her think she has us out-manned. Hold the crew below until we are boarded and I give you the signal."

As always, Enrique obeyed without further question, but Diego's heart sank to see his second in command glance at him and then cross himself as he ordered the rest below.

"She's Spanish, Cap'n!" The crewman who delivered the report to the pirate captain stood just inside the cabin doorway. "And from what we can see, she's short some crew. Easy pickins."

The captain showed what few teeth he had through a

nasty grin. "She'd better 'ave somethin' good in her 'old. The booty from the last ship weren't bad, but it'll take a damn sight more to make up for 'avin' to put up with 'er." He nodded his head toward Mary Kate, who sat bound in a miserable heap at the foot of the captain's filthy, rumpled bed.

Damned if she would let him see how desperately she hoped that there would be enough men on the Spanish vessel to save her.

"Well, aren't you fine ones?" she snapped. "You haven't the guts to take on anyone your own size! God forbid you give chase to a ship with a full crew."

"We made short enough work of yours."

Mary Kate gave a contemptuous sniff. "They were English."

"*We're* English," the captain rejoined.

"Humph! Maybe you and half a Spanish crew are an even match after all."

The pirate glowered at her from under one enormously long eyebrow. "Shut yer mouth, wench. Fer yer sake, ye'd better 'ope yer man can pay yer ransom. If 'e can't, I'll rip that she-devil's tongue right out of yer mouth."

For all of her bravado, she couldn't shake the fear that she was to be witness to another massacre. She had despised *Fortune's* captain and crew, but they hadn't deserved their fate. She hadn't watched, but she knew that they had gone down with the ship. Sir Calder could never have foreseen this, but somehow, she hated him all the more for it. He had shipped her off across the ocean to be kidnapped by pirates and watch helplessly while innocent men died.

"When the day comes that they hang you in irons,"

she snapped, "I swear, I'll sail all the way from Ireland to see it!"

"If the poor swab 'oo's marryin' ye 'asn't killed ye first," the captain rejoined, then slammed out of the cabin.

Left alone, Mary Kate went back to the task that she had been working on while the captain was sleeping. She had convinced him that the bindings on her wrists were too tight and that, if they infected, the damage would impact her value. It wasn't a lie. Her wrists were truly a mass of lacerated skin. But the pain didn't stop her from slowly loosening the binding, pulling and stretching the strips of cloth, letting her own blood wet them and make them more pliant. When she had started, she had no further plan than to get loose. Now, she had far greater motivation. If she could surprise someone, be of real help to the Spaniards, she might help them to victory, and they would owe her something. Passage to Ireland would be ample compensation.

Magdalena's crew stood in groups, whispering nervously. The white flag had been hoisted, and now they waited for the pirate crew to board. They'd win the day, they had no doubt of that, but none were eager to taste victory if it was delivered in the hands of Satan. How had the captain known about the ship before the lookout had spotted it, and how had he known that they were, in fact, an even match, in terms of size and weapons?

Although he knew what occupied his crew, Diego had to concentrate very hard to keep from smiling. He could not help the sense of elevation, the thrill that came with the anticipation of another sure victory. But he was under the pirate captain's close scrutiny, and he could not afford to let his confidence show. He had enough men to win a hand-to-hand fight, and the element of surprise would make it all the easier.

When the grappling hooks hit the side of the ship, he heard a quick flurry of activity below, but it was abruptly quashed. He had made it very clear that they were to remain absolutely silent until they heard the order to ascend. Although it was tempting to cry out the moment the first of the pirates swung from their ship to his, he waited. None of his crew raised a weapon, but as could be expected, the pirates drew cutlasses and flintlocks. They swaggered on board, pleased to have the Spaniards surrender without a fight, and they brandished their weapons carelessly, obviously not prepared to actually use them.

"Now!" Diego shouted, and the hatch flew open, spewing sailors onto the upper deck. Flintlocks thundered and clashing blades rang out. Diego systematically worked his way past enemy seamen and over bodies of friends and foes to take on the captain of the pirate vessel. That man, seeing the dogged determination in Diego's eyes, fled to the rail, grabbed a rope, and swung back to his own ship. Undeterred, Diego followed.

They were, by no means, the only two to have carried the battle from the decks of *Magdalena* back to the other ship. The scene here was very similar, with Diego's men beating back the pirates, even as the pirates tried to retreat. His quarry, the filthy, bearded leader of the criminals who had attacked them, stepped ever backwards, never taking his eyes from Diego's. It was with satisfaction and pride that Diego read the hint of fear in the other man's eyes.

And then, for a critical, split second, Diego was distracted by a shocking jolt of recognition. In the midst of the battle around him, a vision of beauty and vengeance stole his attention. She wore the clothing of any woman of the day, but the long, dark hair, the sapphire blue eyes, the bold mouth set in a delicate face were unmistakable.

Magdalena stooped down and seized a fallen sailor's cutlass, brandishing it with the gleam of retribution in her eyes. Above the hands that clutched the sword, her wrists were ravaged and bloodied, like a tortured martyr, but she seemed oblivious to the pain they must have surely caused her.

That split second of distraction should have cost Diego his life. The pirate captain saw his moment and seized it, lunging toward the Spaniard, blade held high. As if time had slowed down, Diego watched Magdalena leap forward and sweep her own blade with all her might against the pirate's neck. The force was not enough to sever it, but she hit the crucial artery, and blood pulsed forth in a wide arch, splattering the deck.

"What the hell is the matter with you?" Magdalena berated him. "You can't stand there like a bloomin' idiot in a fight. The bastard would've run you right through your bloody heart!"

His mind was in such a dizzying spin, he could barely spare a thought for the next attacker, whom he ran through with his blade almost without seeing him. *English? Why was she speaking English?*

"Look about you!" she cried.

Diego spun and took on the man behind him. He could not think of her now. He wanted to look over his shoulder, make sure that she was safe, but she was right, he needed to be aware of the men around him. Besides, she was a saint. What harm could befall her?

But why was she speaking English? And what had happened to her wrists? And were saints permitted to use that kind of language?

He was about to dispatch his latest adversary when the man threw down his weapon.

"Mercy!" the man cried.

His sword already poised over his head, it would have been easy for Diego to bring it down. Was not a swift death a form of mercy? From all around him, Diego heard similar pleas. He glanced about to see that the battle had been won. What few pirates remained were on their knees, begging for clemency.

He wiped away the sweat that stung his eyes and sought Magdalena, though he knew that she would be gone, of course.

But she was not. Her skirts stained with blood, she was leaning against the main mast, trying to catch her breath. One of his crew approached her, reaching out to touch her shoulder. She twisted away, eyes on fire, cheeks flushed.

This was no vision, no saint. She was a woman. *The* woman—the one that Magdalena had promised. He was as certain of that as he had been of his victory here.

"Enrique!" Diego shouted across the deck to his first mate, but he kept his eyes on the woman. "You and the men, put the pirates who are still living in the brig. Let their surgeon treat their wounded there. Empty this ship, then set her afire."

"Yes, Captain." He gave Diego a wary look, then followed orders.

Diego walked over to the woman, who watched him approach with a look no more trusting than Enrique's had been. In rapid Spanish, an apology tumbled from his lips. "I am so sorry. I thought you were a vision. Forgive me, forgive me, please. But our saint, she was guarding us both, no? She made sure that we would, at last, find each other."

The woman only stared at him, not the slightest trace of comprehension on her face.

"Forgive me," he said again. "You are in shock, as am I. But you are safe now, and I promise, no harm will ever again come to you."

She took a deep breath. He smiled, and his heart soared at the anticipation of the first words his flesh and blood saint would speak to him.

"I don't suppose you speak any English," she said.

The smile of delight froze on his face. Switching to her language, in a voice of disbelief, he asked, "You are English?"

"You may have saved me from a fate worse than death, but that doesn't give you leave to insult me," she replied.

Hope surged back up. "You are not English?"

"Irish."

It died again. "That is the same thing."

The woman's eyes scanned the deck full of dead and injured men. She seemed about to say something else to him, but then she set her mouth in a grim line. "I don't want to stay here," she said.

Ashamed again at having been so insensitive, Diego quickly stepped in front of her, blocking the carnage from her line of vision. "Of course not. Come with me. I will help you to my ship." His gaze fell back to her wrists. "You were bound?"

"Aye." She glanced down at them. "They'll heal."

"I will have my surgeon look at them."

"Nay, you must look to your men first."

"Soon, then," he promised. He had to admire her for thinking of his men before herself.

Mary Kate nodded and let the Spaniard lead her to the rail just across from his own vessel. She could have swung across on her own, but it felt blissfully secure to wrap her arms around this man's lithe torso and let him hold her with one sinewy arm while they swung together. He smelled of sweat, and his body was still hot from combat, his clothes slightly damp. The fevered rush that had engulfed her when she had swung the cutlass at the pirate captain's neck still churned inside of her. She had actually killed a man.

When her feet found the deck of the Spanish ship, she pressed herself closer to its captain, reluctant to leave his embrace. She could feel his heart beating hard against her cheek, hear its distinct thumping. Finally she peered out around them. It hardly seemed possible, but the scene on the Spanish ship was worse than that on the pirate vessel. The crew was busy tossing pirate bodies overboard and respectfully tending to their own few dead. An older, well-dressed man was stitching a deep gash on one man's arm, and Mary Kate assumed that this must be the ship's doctor. Judging from the number of injured men on board, it would be a while ere he could see to her wounds.

The Spanish captain's arm tightened around her. "Look away," he whispered, and though it felt cowardly, she obeyed. He was whipcord lean and firm, and she suddenly wished that he would stop and kiss her, long and hard. She almost laughed at the bizarre notion. There were stories of old, tales of Celtic warriors and of the lust that came in battle, first for blood, then for women. Was that what was happening to her? She had taken blood, and now she wanted this? Mary Kate wet her parched lips and looked up into his deep brown eyes. He looked back, and his gaze became darker still with answering heat. The passion of the fight seemed to be taking the same turn in her rescuer, and the thought sent her emotions into a heady tumble.

He led her down a ladder, below the main deck, and into a fairly spacious room. Light poured in through a window, illuminating a neatly made bed and a table filled with charts.

"This is my cabin," he said cordially. It was as though he had willed away every trace of whatever she had seen in his face on deck. "As soon as I can, I will see to it that my first mate's cabin is made ready for your use. For now, rest here."

Mary Kate didn't know if fear had at last begun to take hold, or if desire still had her in its grip. She knew only that she didn't want this man to leave her. Not yet. "I—I think I may have some things on board the other ship. If you could look ere you sink it, I would be in your debt." She added a silent prayer that her ledger was still safely tucked inside one of them.

The captain nodded. "We will try to find them."

"My thanks. And Captain—?"

"Montoya. I am *Capitán* Diego Montoya Fernández de Madrid y Delgado Cortés, and I am at your service."

She curtseyed. "Mary Katherine O'Reilly. Captain Montoya, 'tis *not* the same thing."

He looked at her quizzically. "What?"

"Irish and English—they're not the same."

He smiled apologetically, and Mary Kate became acutely aware of her heart beating inside her chest. The expression tugged one corner of his mouth just a bit higher than the other, and his teeth were dazzling against his olive skin. "I meant no offense."

"You're forgiven."

"I will send water so you can wash away your ordeal."

"Again, my thanks." She smiled back and heard the satisfying sound of his own breath catching in his throat.

"Catholic, no? The Irish?" he asked.

"Not officially in Ulster, where I'm from."

"Oh." He seemed disappointed. With a sad shrug, he turned away.

Mary Kate laughed lightly. "Not officially. Nonetheless, d'you think that where you're headed you can find me a priest that speaks English? I'll be doing penance for a year over that pirate, I'm sure."

Captain Montoya turned back with a grin, and Mary Kate thought again of that hard, lean body against hers. "It was self-defense, and the man was surely Protestant. Nothing a few *Hail Marys* and *Our Fathers* will not absolve you of. Trust me, yours is a sin I have confessed to many times."

"I suppose you have duties," she said.

He sighed. "*Sí*, but I will be back as soon as I can."

As soon as he shut the door behind him, Mary Kate sank onto his bed, her thoughts humming in her head like a swarm of bees. She had to regain control of her senses. He was a fine specimen of a man, that was sure, but it wasn't as if she'd never been in the presence of a handsome fellow. She'd even been kissed by a few and kept her wits soundly about her. Still, if the Spanish captain was as drawn to her as she to him, he could be putty in her hands, for it was a well-known fact that women were much better than men at controlling their physical desires. Aye, opportunity was ripe here. She was as good as on her way home.